ABOUT THE AUTHOR

Marion Leigh was born in Birmingham, England. She studied Modern Languages at the University of Oxford and worked as a volunteer in Indonesia before moving to Canada where she enjoyed a successful career as a financial translator. Then she retired to Spain to write.

This is Marion's third adventure thriller featuring Marine Unit Sergeant Petra Minx of the Royal Canadian Mounted Police. *The Politician's Daughter*, set in Spain and Morocco, was published in 2011; *Dead Man's Legacy,* which takes Petra from the Bahamas to the Great Lakes, was published in 2015.

Marion divides her time between Europe and North America. She loves boating and living close to the water. To learn more about Marion, visit www.marionleigh.com.

A HOLIDAY TO DIE FOR

MARION LEIGH

Matador
9 Priory Business Park,
Wistow Road, Kibworth Beauchamp,
Leicestershire, LE8 0RX, UK
Tel: (+44) 0116 279 2299
Email: books@troubador.co.uk
Web: www.troubador.co.uk/matador
Twitter: @matadorbooks

ISBN 978 1789014 198

British Library Cataloguing in Publication Data
A catalogue record for this book is available from the British Library.

Printed and bound in the UK by TJ International, Padstow, Cornwall

Typeset in 11pt Aldine by Troubador Publishing Ltd., Leicester, UK

Matador is an imprint of Troubador Publishing Ltd.

This book is for Peter
who opened my eyes to the beauty of Southern Africa

PROLOGUE

Henny watched the girls from a discreet distance as they approached: giggling, unsuspecting, luscious in their ripe young bodies, just waiting to be picked. This was the part of the game he enjoyed most. In the off-season, when he was back in Port Nolloth with his fishing and diving buddies, he could fantasize about it to his heart's content.

The Master called it fishing with a difference. He'd got it all worked out. *Take your time. Go where the fish are – the airport, the Waterfront, the line-up for the cable car at Table Mountain. Be patient. Wait for the young, fair-skinned, good-looking, unaccompanied ones. Check out their clothing, bags and electronic equipment. No bottom feeders and no princesses. When you've spotted what you want, use a variety of lures. Catch 'em but don't get caught.*

Two more. That's all Henny needed to complete his group. He moved out of the shadows and ran a hand through his blonded hair. The Mohawk fade along with the black rock band T and tight jeans pulled them every time. Holding out his flyers, he smiled in a tough but you-know-I'll-be-good-to-you kind of way, the way he had been taught.

'Welcome to Cape Town. Care to sample the real Africa?'

CHAPTER

1

Marine Unit Sergeant Petra Minx folded the printout she had been studying, slipped it into her bag and pushed the bag under the seat in front of her. In a few minutes, they would be landing in Cape Town. Carlo, her friend from Italy who worked for Interpol, would be waiting at the airport to meet her. In a moment of what she now thought of as madness, she had agreed to accompany him to his cousin's wedding. At the time it had seemed like a good idea – the chance of a lifetime to go to South Africa with someone who knew the country. But weddings were not her favourite thing. They reminded her that she was heading for 30, had no significant other, and while she didn't particularly want one, her mother was beginning to drop hints.

Carlo had warned her that his uncle, Tony Broselli, had remarried some ten years ago, not long after the death of his first wife. The "new" wife was, as he put it, a blonde princess from Johannesburg whose family owned a biscuit factory, among other things. Along with the factory, Sandrine had brought a teenage son named Florian who was almost the same age as his stepsister, Tony's daughter Julia. It was Julia who was getting married in the style Sandrine dictated.

Petra shuddered as she ran through the timetable for the next few days in her head. Everything had been planned down to the last detail. She wouldn't have a minute to herself. As a member of the Royal Canadian Mounted Police, she was used to regimentation and didn't object to it in her professional life. Being told what to do, sent on special missions, shipped out on a moment's notice was fine when she was working. Vacations were a different matter.

Then there was the problem of Carlo. She had known him since her teenage years. He was one of the trio of young men she had hung out with during summer holidays in Italy with her mother's Italian relatives. *Carlo, Romeo and Ben.* Ben had gone to Australia, Romeo had gone … to heaven, her mother had said when she heard about the motorcycle accident that had killed him. Had her mother known what was going on, she might well have come to a different conclusion, Petra thought wryly. She had planned to marry Romeo as soon as she turned eighteen, but his death had shattered those dreams.

Petra shook her head and leaned towards her neighbour to catch a glimpse of Table Mountain. Cloud lay on the top like a clean white cloth. As she watched, it began to roll wispily down the side forming a lacy edge like a bridal veil. It had taken her years to get over the disappointment and a life dedicated to law enforcement to put things into perspective. Now here she was, attending a wedding with Romeo's best mate. Madness indeed!

After the overnight flight from London, passengers were keen to deplane and it wasn't long before Petra found herself wheeling her animal-print weekender towards passport control. Ahead of her she noticed two giggling girls, barely old enough to be out of school, wearing fancy tops, leggings and metallic sneakers. One after the other, they were cleared for entry into South Africa.

Petra was next in line. She approached the desk and waited while the Immigration Officer scrutinized her passport. Unconsciously she felt for the black and silver cross that she normally wore. Tom Gilmore, RCMP Liaison Officer in London, had advised her not to take expensive jewellery to South Africa and cautioned her that despite outward appearances and some improvement the country was still a violent place.

'Don't flaunt it,' he had said more than once during the hours she spent with him.

When she had told him she was breaking her journey in London, he had insisted on meeting her, driving her to her sister's house, and taking her back to the airport next day.

Petra smiled as she remembered the first time they met: how he had surprised her in the bathroom at Dolphin Square, drying herself after a long hot shower. She had turned on him in fury and swept his glasses to the floor with her towel. How long ago had it been? Two years? Three years? Whatever. After that inauspicious start, they had worked well together on the Mortlake case and become firm friends.

The Immigration Officer gave Petra a quizzical look. She realized he was waiting for an answer to his question and felt her usually pale face flush with blood. She realized too that there was nothing round her neck.

'I'm going to a wedding, then on safari,' she managed.

'Very nice,' he said, fixing his dark eyes on her chest. 'Enjoy your stay.'

By some miracle, Petra's soft-sided suitcase had made it to Cape Town without apparent damage. One of the giggling girls had not been so lucky. The zip on her sports bag had broken. The girl shrugged and stuffed a mass of clothing back inside.

Petra followed the signs through Customs to the exit and eagerly scanned the waiting crowd. Despite her misgivings, she was looking forward to seeing Carlo. His smile was catching and his eyes – "bedroom eyes" someone had once called them – sparkled with humour. Where was he? She scanned the crowd again, more slowly. Plenty of good-looking men, but no Carlo. And no one holding up a card with her name on it.

She began to push her trolley towards the main exit, wondering if he was waiting outside. The two girls she had noticed earlier were a little way in front, giggling again. She hoped someone was meeting them. They looked much too young to be on their own in a strange city such a long way from home.

When she reached the main exit doors, Petra stopped. There was still no sign of Carlo. Frowning, she steered her trolley to one side and parked it next to a bench. She pulled out the itinerary the Brosellis had provided and the smart phone Tom had given her. Thank God he had insisted she bring it.

'Just in case,' he had said. 'If you have any problems, use it. It'll work.' No issue there, but his next words had thrown her completely off balance. 'The boss is worried about you – he wouldn't want to lose one of his best investigators.'

Had Tom guessed that she had started to think about leaving the RCMP? Worse, had A.K. guessed? She loved her job but A.K. was a frustrating boss. He withheld information and seemed to take her for granted. When she had asked him for three weeks' holiday in order to make the trip to Africa worthwhile, there had been an initial silence. Then, in his customary gruff voice, he had said 'Fine'. No more, no less.

A feeling that she was being watched made Petra look up. Across the hall, a skinny guy in black jodhpur jeans and a black T-shirt with some sort of image on the front was leaning on a pillar. Even from a distance, she could tell he was assessing her.

She stared back. Mohawk-style fair hair with shaved sides, square chin no doubt covered in stubble, broadish nose. After a minute or two, he turned away and walked off with what appeared to be a slight limp. Petra kept her eyes on him until he disappeared from view then filed his face in her new "Africa" memory folder. She would know him if she saw him again.

She glanced at her watch. 'Bugger Carlo,' she muttered, using the same kind of language her RCMP partner Ed would have used. There was no point hanging about any longer. She fired off two texts, one to Tom to say she had arrived safely and one to Carlo asking where the hell he was.

Twenty minutes later she was racing along the N2 in a licensed taxi whose driver clearly didn't know what a licence was. Dwellings lined the highway on both sides: on the left, acres of miserable shacks thrown together from scraps of wood, metal, cardboard, anything that might offer some protection from the elements; on the right, row after row of concrete cubes. These were a cut above the shacks. They might have electricity and running water.

The shanties had communal taps, shared outside toilets and overhead floodlights. An ominous sign hung above the road: 'High Crime Area. Do not stop at night'. But the most striking thing, apart from the litter, was the sheer number of satellite dishes on the meanest of roofs.

CHAPTER

2

Petra left the Waterside Hotel with a spring in her step and a determination not to worry about Carlo. After a wonderful hot shower and four hours' sleep, she was ready to enjoy whatever the Victoria and Alfred Waterfront had to offer. The map showed a vast area of historic buildings, modern apartments, luxury hotels, shops and restaurants set around Cape Town's working harbour. There was entertainment to suit every taste – museums, markets, an amphitheatre, an aquarium, even a croquet lawn – and most inviting from Petra's point of view, boat basins and docks.

She set off quickly, keen to begin exploring before evening fell. Against the dramatic backdrop of Table Mountain, Capetonians of all hues mingled with tourists from around the world. The hustle and bustle reminded her of the Toronto waterfront on a summer's day, yet she didn't feel quite as comfortable.

Mindful of Tom's warnings, she slung the shoulder strap of her bag over her head and across her chest. She made sure the bag was in front of her where she could see it and checked that the zip was firmly done up. Elementary precautions she told herself, as she battled her way through a tour group. The women were in saris, the men in jeans and the children all over the place. Perfect cover for pickpockets.

It was approaching six o'clock. The sun began to sink slowly towards the horizon, spreading tendrils of orange and purple across the sky. Petra pulled out her camera. Just as she was taking the picture, someone walked in front of her.

'Shit,' she said before she could stop herself.

'Sorree.'

Another voice chimed in. 'We were admiring the sunset.'

Two girls. The same two she had seen at the airport. At close range, they looked very alike, except for their hair colour: one fair, one reddish. Probably natural.

'So was I. Didn't you just arrive from London?'

'Yes. Me and Hilary are travelling together.'

Petra winced.

'I'm Megan,' continued the red-head. 'Isn't it awesome?'

Indeed it is, Petra thought, then relented. They were kids. 'What are you doing in South Africa? Are you staying long in Cape Town?'

'This is our gap year. We left school last July and are going to Uni in September, but for now we're travelling. We made loads of money sorting the Christmas mail in Colchester, then as chalet girls in Switzerland.'

'Chalet girls?'

Hilary took up the baton. 'Yes, cooking and cleaning at a ski chalet. It's fun and the pay's good if you include the tips. The only snag is if you get a bunch of guys who think the all-inclusive includes sex too.'

'Did you have that problem?'

'Nao! Me and Megan know how to deal with that kind of thing, don't we, Megan?'

Petra winced again. 'What are your plans now?' They still looked too young to be out on their own.

'Sightseeing, whale-watching, chilling on the beach … then we're going to volunteer …'

'Yes,' Megan interrupted Hilary. 'You can go to the Kruger Primate Sanctuary or there's a place in Plettenberg Bay where you can learn about Orca Conservation …'

'It sounds as though you'll have a whale of a time!'

Megan and Hilary grinned at Petra's deliberate pun. 'We will,' they chorused.

'Just be careful,' Petra couldn't help adding. 'Not everything's always what it seems. If you need anything, I'm staying at the Waterside Hotel. My name's Petra … Minx, Petra Minx.'

Once the sun set, the sky darkened quickly. Henny watched Megan and Hilary walk away from the older girl, the one with the wing of black hair that fell across her face. Minx, Petra Minx, staying at the Waterside, she had said. Her colouring was wrong, and she was probably too old for his purposes, but cute nevertheless. There might be something they could use her for. He chuckled as a number of possibilities occurred to him. For now, though, his focus had to be on the two teenagers.

They were chatting happily to each other, unaware of his interest. At this point, that didn't phase him at all. In fact, it was how it should be. He upped his pace a little as they turned into a walkway that led to the Victoria Wharf Shopping Centre. He pulled his phone out of his pocket.

'Looks like they're going shopping. Are you ready, Tem?' He held the phone in the crick of his neck and nodded, keeping his eyes on his quarry. 'I'll call you. Be an hour or more, I guess, before they get hungry.'

Megan and Hilary crossed the ornamental bridge over the canal and joined the flow of devotees to the temple of consumerism. Petra forced herself to go in a different direction. The two girls might not look it, but they were adults, weren't they? At their age she had certainly thought of herself as mature. *Mature enough to get married* repeated the voice in her head, reminding her of the wedding she was going to – if ever Carlo showed up.

Petra realized that she had walked away from the centre of the action – the restaurants and the shops – and was now close to the seawall. Here there were far fewer people and the lighting was poor. She glanced around, assessing the risk. No one looked likely to pose a threat.

It was a beautiful evening. Warm, with low humidity and a light breeze. She took a deep breath of sea air and stood listening to the water swishing against the rocks. How different from April in Canada, where the winter hadn't yet said goodbye. In her hometown of Sudbury, the snow would be lingering in dirty piles; it might melt during the day but temperatures still dropped below zero at night, causing it to refreeze and coat the sidewalks in dangerous sheets of ice. Spring would come suddenly, the trees bursting into leaf, to be followed almost immediately by the heat of summer.

In Cape Town it was the beginning of Fall. No, autumn, Petra corrected herself. Somehow the Canadian word seemed inappropriate in a land where the trees were palms and pines and eucalyptus and jacaranda, not maples whose leaves turned a dusky red and fell to the ground in heaps.

A low buzzing interrupted her musings. She rummaged in her bag and pulled out the phone.

'Carlo, what's going on? Where are you?'

Silence.

She was about to end the call when A.K.'s staccato tones reached her from what seemed like a million miles away.

'In Cape Town are you?'

'Yes, Sir.'

'I need you to do something. Before you go to your wedding.'

Petra began to shake her head. No way.

'Daughter of a friend's working at the Cape Sands Hotel. Vicky Dunlin. Check she's OK, will you?'

'Is there a problem?'

'No problem, just check and report back.'

That was it. Petra stared at the phone. The line had gone dead. So much for communication. What was she supposed to do? Go running off to the Cape Sands to find someone she knew nothing about? She didn't even know what this girl was doing at the hotel. Did she really want to keep working for A.K. under these conditions?

Petra shook her head again, wishing that Tom had never given her the damn phone. Wishing too that she hadn't answered it, that she wasn't feeling obligated to do A.K.'s bidding and – almost but not quite – that she had never accepted Carlo's invitation to his cousin's wedding in South Africa.

CHAPTER

3

Night had fallen. Petra turned to retrace her footsteps to her hotel. She walked quickly away from the seawall, keeping as far as possible to lighted areas. The buildings seemed huge and the distances between them much greater than during the day.

After a while she came to a crossroads. It didn't look familiar and there were no signs. No traffic or other pedestrians either. Which way was it to the hotel? She tossed a mental coin and turned right. When the road started to curve away towards the mountain, she made a left. If she was wrong, she would have to go back.

She ended up at a small roundabout. Two of the three exit roads were blocked by concrete barriers. The third was bound on either side by hoardings. It narrowed to almost nothing as it bisected a deserted construction site that was in total darkness. The ideal spot for a mugging.

Hold your course and speed, Petra told herself firmly. Ten minutes later, she came to another junction. This time there was a sign with a cartoon figure on it pointing towards the Alfred Mall and Pierhead. In the distance she saw lights and an open square and heard music reverberating across it. Suddenly, she was in the thick of things again. The uncomfortable feeling of being lost in an urban setting, something that should never have been possible for a trained policewoman like herself, gave way to an irrational excitement. She wiped her damp palms on her jeans and quickened her pace.

As she reached the square, a deep rumble in her stomach reminded her that it was dinner time. There were plenty of restaurants to choose from – seafood, pizza, fusion, Malay – but most of the outdoor tables were taken, so she carried on.

Halfway round the plaza, her phone buzzed again. A.K. calling back.

'Hallo?'

'Bella, bellissima!'

'Carlo! Where the hell are you?'

'Here, *tesoro mio*, right behind you!'

Petra felt the phone sliding out of her hand as an arm went round her waist and pulled her close.

Carlo planted a warm kiss firmly on one cheek then the other. 'My little treasure!' he said, pushing her away again and appraising her from head to toe. 'You look divine, though not as hot as when I last saw you.'

Petra knew she would have to put up with a certain amount of ribbing from Carlo – Mercutio as she still called him because of his temperament. Like quicksilver, that's how he was. It was one of the things she loved and hated about him. And he could be merciless. Three weeks on holiday together might test their friendship.

'Different circumstances, Mercutio. But I do have a little blue and gold number for the wedding.'

'Skimpy, I hope.'

'What about the leather pants you poured yourself into

in Mallorca? All the guys were drooling, not to mention the girls.'

'As you say, Minx: different circumstances. Now, how about something to eat? I'm famished.'

'Me too, me too,' Petra said, quoting one of her favourite movies.

'Shouldn't that be "I am too"?'

'Truce, Mercutio. Let's just get some food.'

'If we're quick, we'll get that table,' he said, pointing to the terrace of a restaurant on the next corner where two girls were getting up to leave.

'I know them,' Petra exclaimed. 'Megan and Hilary. They were on my plane, and I saw them again this afternoon.'

'It's a small world, *carissima*, and we're all tourists in the most touristy part of Cape Town.'

'They've come to do volunteer work.'

'Are they old enough to be let out of the nursery?'

'I'll introduce you and you can judge for yourself. Come on.'

Megan and Hilary were on their feet. They pushed their chairs under the table and moved away into the square. Megan's bag was hanging open on her shoulder. She pulled out her phone and stepped back to take a picture of the restaurant. Hilary did the same. Then they turned to face each other to snap giggling selfies.

'They spend their lives taking photos,' Petra said. 'Oh, no! Trouble!'

Two strapping dark-skinned men had grabbed the girls from behind. Their giggles turned to squeals of anger and fright as they struggled to break free and hang on to their phones. Petra broke into a run and raced towards them.

Before she could reach them, two men jumped up from the terrace and entered the fray. Suddenly the attackers broke away and fled across the square. The two diners took off after them, followed by Megan and Hilary. By the time Petra and Carlo reached the site of the incident, it was over. All those involved had disappeared.

Petra stared after them. 'I can't believe how quickly that happened.'

'You're slowing down in your old age, *cara*.'

'No, Carlo. It was weird.'

'Slam, bam, thank you, Ma'am! Truth is stranger than fiction.'

'Maybe, but I don't buy it. Something wasn't right.'

'Look, it's over. You can't do anything now. Let's grab a table.' Carlo pointed again to the restaurant where several groups of people were leaving, talking animatedly.

Petra sat in silence while Carlo ordered a bottle of Backsberg white wine from the smiling African waitress.

'Chin-chin!' he said, chinking his glass against Petra's. 'You can't win every time.'

'Can't I?' she demanded. 'We'll see about that. Anyway, where the hell were you this morning? You show up nearly twelve hours late with nothing but a twinkle in your eye, no apology, no explanation …'

'Something came up.'

'What something?'

'I can't tell you now, *tesoro mio*. Maybe later.'

4

'Carlo, I have to go to the Cape Sands.'

'The schedule says we're catching the 10 a.m. boat to Robben Island. Our tickets are waiting for us at the front desk.'

'Fuck the schedule!'

'Tut, tut! I don't remember such a foul-mouthed person.'

'Sorry, blame it on jet-lag. I was awake half the night. I guess I can go later.'

Petra and Carlo walked out of the hotel breakfast room into the lobby. Megan and Hilary were standing at the reception desk. On the floor beside them were their travel bags.

'Surprise, surprise!' Petra said as she came up behind them. 'Need any help, girls?'

Megan and Hilary turned in unison. They looked more subdued than the previous day.

'Why would we need help?' Hilary said truculently.

'I saw you having dinner in the square last night. Then you were taking photos and two guys strong-armed you and ran off with your phones. Are you sure you're OK? You must have been terrified.'

'We're fine, just fine.'

'Are you checking out?'

Hilary shrugged. She was holding something back.

Petra tugged at Carlo's sleeve. 'Meet my friend, Carlo. We're going to his cousin's wedding at a winery in Stellenbosch.'

'Awesome,' Megan gasped, twinkling at Carlo. 'I'd love to get married at a winery. I was looking on line before we came. Loads of them do it.'

'Do you have a man in mind?' Carlo twinkled back. 'My step-aunt is an event planner. She specializes in weddings.'

That explains the schedules Petra thought, watching the effect Carlo was having on the two girls.

'Nao, but we'll have a good look round while we're here, won't we, Hilary?' Megan gave a coy smile. 'We've decided to go on a discovery tour for young people, leaving today …'

'So soon?' Petra interjected. 'I thought you were spending some time in Cape Town.'

'We changed our minds after what happened last night. The guys who helped us get our phones back were awesome. They said we shouldn't be on our own, it would be safer with a group, and they run these all-inclusive programmes that include sightseeing and a safari. And once we've familiarized ourselves with the country, we get to do volunteer work in an African village.'

Megan poked around in her shoulder bag and pulled out a shocking pink phone, then a tour brochure. 'Here's their pamphlet. It tells you all about it. They're small groups and not expensive. And they gave us an extra discount because two people had just cancelled at the last minute.'

Petra's antennae began to quiver. 'Have you checked them out? It sounds a bit too good to be true.'

Carlo was busy rolling his eyes. Then he tapped his watch.

'Forget the schedule, Mercutio! This is more important. Are you sure you're not rushing into this?'

Hilary dragged her canvas holdall to the side of the lobby. 'Look, leave us alone. We came out here to see the country and have some fun before we go to Uni. We worked and saved hard for this trip, and we can spend our money how we like.'

Petra couldn't have been more stunned if she'd been the parent of a teenager who had suddenly turned and flung a glass of cold water in her face. 'Of course, that's your prerogative. Let's go, Carlo.'

Petra let herself into her hotel room and went straight to the chair by the window. She flopped down and took off her shoes. Tours and tour guides could be most annoying. Sure, Nelson Mandela had been held captive for eighteen years in deplorable conditions on Robben Island – Seal Island, Carlo said it meant – and he was a remarkable man, but their guide had glossed over the fact that for a long time he had been considered a terrorist. Another member of their group, a visiting professor of political history, had challenged him several times.

Thinking about the tour reminded Petra of the pamphlet Megan had given her that morning. At first she ignored the feeling that she should get up and find it. Then she gave in.

Splashed across the front page was the name of the company and a rousing call to action:

Higher Ground Tours
Explore the hidden Africa with us!

Enjoy Africa in a completely new way with our small group tours for 18 to 25-year-olds. We offer a variety of itineraries that will take you from the delights of the city through our scenic countryside into the wilds of our game parks. Each unique journey will bring you closer to understanding our true culture and ideals.

Your trip will culminate in a traditional African village where you can experience a way of life that has stood the test of millennia. Your skills will be put to good use to help build the community and foster our efforts to make Africa a better place. You may stay as long as you have a contribution to make to the village way of life.

Discover the real Africa with us!

Pretty abstract stuff, designed to appeal to the young and the idealistic like Megan and Hilary, Petra decided. Higher Ground seemed to offer everything they were looking for. They were keen to volunteer and fit right into the age profile. No wonder they'd been seduced. She turned the page and continued reading.

The ultimate eco-adventure with Higher Ground

19 days from Cape Town, South Africa, to Katima Mulilo, Namibia

Week 1	*Cape Town, Springbok, Fish River Canyon, Lüderitz*
Week 2	*Sossusvlei, Swakopmund, Cape Cross, Damaraland*

Week 3   Etosha National Park, Zambezi Region,
              Katima Mulilo
Week 4 +   opportunity to do volunteer work
              in a local village

Our camper vans are custom-built to accommodate eight passengers plus the crew (your tour leader and your driver). They carry everything we need for our adventure with enough space for a small amount of personal luggage.

During the expedition, your crew will share their in-depth knowledge and passion for the continent with you and attend to all your needs. Part of the joy of participating in our tours is the opportunity to help with day-to-day matters such as meal preparation and setting up for the night. If you have a special skill, let your leader know!

How funny, Petra thought. If this was the "eco-adventure" Megan and Hilary had signed up for, they'd be spending most of their time in Namibia. Until a few weeks ago she had had only the vaguest idea where Namibia was. Then Carlo had emailed her, suggesting that they go there after the wedding and she had done a quick Google search. It was a long, fairly skinny country northwest of South Africa, bordered by Angola to the north and Botswana to the east. With no time to do more research, she had told him to go ahead and make the arrangements. Unlike his step-aunt, he had not sent her an itinerary. He had talked about going on safari in Etosha National Park and some of the other place names sounded familiar, but their trip would be nothing like nineteen days long.

Page three of the Higher Ground brochure contained

fulsome references from delighted campers and volunteers. Petra read a couple of them and wondered whether they could possibly be genuine.

'Amazing journey! Our crew took care of every last detail. The community spirit infused us all right from the beginning. I can truly say I will never feel the same thrill again.' **Christina D., Frankfurt**

'Awesome sights, brilliant leaders, super everything! The climax of the trip was most definitely the chance to work with other like-minded young people for the greater good of mankind.' **Penny S., Exeter**

The last page was devoted to price and insurance information, terms and conditions. It gave an address and a phone number for the company and looked frightfully professional. But the way the brochure was put together bothered Petra. The verbiage was slick, too slick, and almost hypnotic in its power. She could feel herself being drawn in even though she hadn't the faintest intention of signing up for a tour.

5

Petra threaded through the crowds and made her way past the fishing harbour to the west side of the Waterfront. As she approached the Cape Sands Hotel, she asked herself why she felt duty-bound to try and find Vicky Dunlin. She had made no promises and A.K. had given her precious little information. He was still her boss, though. In his own way, he looked out for his people. Perhaps that was the answer: she could do no less.

After the hurly-burly of the Waterfront, the reception area was cool and quiet. Subdued tones of sepia, grey and silver combined with sparkling glass doors and chandeliers to create an atmosphere of cloud-like calm. A painting of Cape Town in the 16th century caught Petra's eye: schooners riding at anchor in Table Bay in the lee of the famous mountain. She paused to admire it then went to the reception desk.

The receptionist greeted her with a smile. 'How can I help, Miss? Are you checking in with us today?'

'Unfortunately not, I'm staying at the Waterside. I'm trying to contact the daughter of a Canadian friend of mine, Vicky Dunlin.'

'Is she a guest?'

'No. I understand she's working here but I have no idea where.'

'I'll have a look at our staff directory if you give me a minute.'

'Thank you so much.'

Petra glanced round the lobby and through the picture windows. Behind the hotel was a marina full of magnificent yachts, both power and sail. Her pulse quickened. If the Broselli forced-march wedding included outings on some of those dreamboats it wouldn't be half so bad. She turned back to the receptionist.

'Vicky Dunlin is a massage therapist in our wellness centre, Miss?'

'Minx, Petra Minx.'

'Yes, Miss Minx. The centre is open, but I don't know if Miss Dunlin is in. I can direct you there and you can speak to the Manager if you like.'

'Thank you, I will.'

When Petra reached the wellness centre, a.k.a. the spa, overlooking the harbour, there was nobody at the desk. For a while she waited not too impatiently, enjoying the view through the softly veiled windows. Then she spent several minutes trying to figure out the meaning of the red and yellow motif on the wall – if it had any meaning.

She picked up a booklet outlining the spa's treatments. The Rolling Sands massage and the Body Cocoon body mask sounded intriguing, but spas weren't her thing. Glumly, she drummed her fingers on the desk. Finally, the ants in her pants got to be too much and she set out to find a human being.

She pushed through a door next to the desk and entered a lounging space furnished with soft white recliners and bamboo side-tables. Still nobody. Passing behind a carved screen, she continued into a corridor where a row of closed doors greeted her. Each bore a plaque engraved with the name of an exotic plant – Gardenia, Hibiscus, Frangipani, Bougainvillea … Just reading them made her want to sniff. Red lights glowed above them. Then she spotted a green light over a plaque that read *Omumbiri*. She turned the knob and went in.

She was met by an unfamiliar citrusy smell and the sound of waves unfurling softly on a beach. In front of her lay a large mummy-like figure covered from head to toe in white powder. Eyes as large and as green as cucumber slices stared back at her.

'Sorry,' she whispered, and backed out hastily.

A young woman was hurrying down the corridor carrying a tall glass containing a colourless fizzy liquid, a slice of lime and a pink paper parasol. She gaped when she saw Petra.

'What are you doing here? We're not ready for you yet. Please wait in Reception. Your therapist will be available soon.'

Petra blocked her passage. 'I'm looking for Vicky Dunlin.'

'Yes, I know you were booked for the Rolling Sands massage with Miss Dunlin. But I'm afraid she isn't here.'

'I haven't come for treatment. I came to see Miss Dunlin, to bring her a message from her family in Canada.'

The young woman sighed. 'Come back to the desk with me. I thought you were our five o'clock …'

'Sorry to disappoint you,' Petra added sarcastically. She had already spent far too long at the desk. 'Will Miss Dunlin be in tomorrow morning? I really need to see her.'

'I have no idea if she'll be in tomorrow.'

'Is there someone else I can speak to who would know?'

'Look, to put it plainly, Miss Dunlin has left the Cape Sands.'

'What? When? Why?'

'I have no idea.'

'OK, let's take this step by step. You have a number of staff here. Who else worked with Vicky Dunlin? Someone must know something.'

The young woman looked down into the glass she was holding as if she were consulting a crystal ball. 'There's only one therapist here right now – our new temp. She's treating Mrs. Pinderally.'

'The woman with the cucumber eyes?'

'That's right. Mrs. Pinderally will be in the relaxation room in a few minutes' time. I could ask her if she'll speak to you.'

'Thank you. Do that.'

After a further ten-minute wait, Petra was admitted to the relaxation room. Mrs. Pinderally was sprawled by the window in one of the recliners. On the table next to her was the tall glass of lime and soda. She had emerged from her cocoon and was wearing a turban on her head and a short white robe that was having trouble containing her ample chest. Vestiges of white powder clung to her shiny mahogany skin. Without the green discs, her eyes were sharp, brown and accusing.

'You're the young lady who disturbed my meditation.'

'I apologize for that.'

'And you pose many questions about Vicky Dunlin. Why?'

'To find out where she is. Her parents asked me to see how she was doing. You know Vicky?'

'Of course. She was my regular cocoonist: every Monday, Wednesday and Friday.'

Three times a week! Small wonder the alien aroma had accompanied Mrs. Pinderally to the relaxation room.

'Was?'

'Yes, dear girl. Miss Vicky bade me farewell at five o'clock on Friday and Bob's your uncle!'

'Bob's your uncle?'

'Gone, vanished. Now I must break someone else in. And they charge the same price.'

'Where did Vicky go?'

'That information I am not privy to.' Mrs. Pinderally blew some powder off the top of her bosom. 'I do know she was lonely.'

'Homesick, you mean?'

'That is possibly what I mean.'

'Was she friendly with the other therapists?'

'Is anyone friendly with an interloper? In my opinion they were jealous. She was fair-skinned like you, pale-pretty and svelte, I think one could say.'

'Was she good at her job?'

'Under my tutelage, she became an excellent masseuse and cocoonist. I rewarded her well for her ministrations.'

'Did you discuss anything in particular with her, Mrs. Pinderally? Anything that might give me a clue as to where she's gone?'

'We talked a little during our Rolling Sands sessions. Not a lot. I don't like chatter during therapy. Capable hands are so soothing. Now, if you don't mind, it is time for my third degree meditation, Miss?'

'Minx, Petra Minx.'

'Very well. Goodbye, Miss Minx.' Mrs. Pinderally blew more powder off her chest and closed her eyes.

As Petra closed the door behind her, she sneezed three times.

CHAPTER

6

Petra left the Cape Sands feeling frustrated and unsettled. She walked towards the marina barely noticing how the sun was setting to the west, bathing the white hulls, superstructures and sails in reddish gold. Why had Vicky Dunlin left her job at the hotel and where had she gone? Was the information Mrs. Pinderally had given her any use at all? She suspected that the frequently massaged and cocooned Mrs. P. was prone to exaggeration and would never be a reliable witness. The truth was that Vicky Dunlin's disappearance had come as a shock and Petra wondered whether to call A.K.

While she was debating the pros and cons, she felt her phone vibrate. She pulled it out of her pocket and looked at the uninformative screen.

'Hello?'

There was nothing but a prolonged silence. Petra pressed the OFF button and rammed the instrument back into her pocket. She didn't need to spend her vacation answering phones, and if Carlo was calling, she'd be back at the Waterside by six o'clock.

The beauty of the sky finally caught her attention. She searched for her camera to take a photo of the marina.

The two English girls, Megan and Hilary, had spoiled last night's sunset picture. Just as she found the best angle, the damn phone rang again.

'Hello?'

There was a short pause before A.K.'s gravelly voice reached her.

'Have you been to the Cape Sands?'

'I'm there now – at the marina, actually. But I was going to call you, Sir. Vicky Dunlin has left, disappeared you might say. It seems rather strange and I wanted to speak to you. What should we do?'

'Nothing. She's gone for a week's working holiday with the Tabernacle Youth Collective.'

'Are you sure?'

'She cleared it with her father, and the hotel. It's a religious group.'

The random piece of information didn't make Petra feel any better. Neither did A.K.'s parting shot.

'Go and see her next week after your wedding …'

The satellite connection broke and his last words were lost.

Petra just managed to stop herself from throwing Tom's phone into the water.

When she got back to the Waterside Hotel, Carlo was waiting outside, looking up and down the street.

'Where on earth have you been?'

'To the Cape Sands to find Vicky Dunlin. You knew I was going.'

Petra told him about her lack of success and A.K.'s call, then about Mrs. Pinderally and the strange aroma that accompanied her.

'*Omumbiri*, you say? It's a resin used by the Himba

30

women of Namibia to perfume their skin, a type of myrrh I think. But enough of that, Sandrine is sending a helicopter to take us to Camps Bay.'

'What for?'

'That's where other members of the wedding party are staying and where we should have stayed last night. She insists we stay there tonight and have dinner together, so get your luggage.'

'But I've paid already for tonight. So have you!'

'I'm sure Sandrine will refund our money if we ask her.'

'It's principle, not money, Mercutio.'

'Sandrine has plenty of the latter but little of the former I fear.'

'Not your favourite aunt then?'

'Step-aunt. No blood connection there, thank goodness. Uncle Tony's first wife was a much sounder apple though I have to confess, not as hot.'

'Lusting after someone we don't respect, Mercutio?'

'Is that so unusual? Think Don León, *tesoro mio*!'

Petra felt herself blush at the reference to her quest to find Emily Mortlake who had vanished after taking a summer job on board Don León's megayacht in the Mediterranean.

'How quickly can you be ready?' Carlo added.

'Give me five. I hardly unpacked. I'll change when we get there.'

The liveried flying machine carried them over Table Mountain and Signal Hill, past Sea Point and Clifton, and deposited them at their new digs in under half an hour. The boutique hotel offered a completely different experience from the bustling Waterfront. Petra's Italianate suite, decorated in aqua and white, was stylish and comfortable.

She caught her reflection in the sunburst mirror and noted that her cheeks and nose had acquired a little colour on the tour to Robben Island. She made a mental note to protect her skin well.

The last streaks of pink were lighting up the sky as Petra and Carlo seated themselves on the hotel's terrace overlooking the Atlantic Ocean. The waiter hurried over with flutes of South African sparkling wine. Petra took a sip and pulled out her camera with an apologetic glance at Carlo. This time neither Megan and Hilary nor A.K. spoiled her composition.

'Don't I recognize that gold silk chemise?' A sly grin that reminded Petra of Inspector Clouseau in the Pink Panther films contorted Carlo's face. 'Let me take a picture for posterity.' He reached into a black camera bag and drew out what looked like a new Nikon.

'And talking of posterity, I'll take one of that too.' He had swivelled round in his chair and was facing the double glass doors where a woman of about Petra's age was making her entry, accompanied by a bearded man some years her senior.

The cheetah-print mini-dress was less than a metre long from bandeau top to tight bottom, Petra calculated. Her skin was dusky, her hair blonded and pinned up in a loose coil on the back of her head. Easy to shake out and toss, Petra thought, summing her up. Her beau could only be described as hairy: head, chin, chest, arms and legs, as revealed by his open-necked short-sleeved shirt and Bermuda shorts.

Carlo stood up as they approached. 'Gina and Diego,' he hissed. 'Long-time friends of the family according to Sandrine. From Rome.'

As the evening wore on, Petra found it difficult to maintain an interest in the conversation. Carlo and Gina discovered mutual friends and lapsed into Italian which she understood but spoke less well than she had done as a teenager. Diego was keen to practise his English but dripped sweat each time he leaned towards her, coming on strong. His arms between the elbow and shoulder were covered with complicated geometrical patterns in black and coloured inks. When Carlo began to count the spots on Gina's dress, Petra could contain her annoyance no longer.

'Basta, Carlo. That's enough. I think it's time we called it a day.'

If that was how the week was going to be, she'd rather go home now.

CHAPTER

7

Sandrine Broselli hated anyone to call her Sandy. If they did, she would raise her perfectly arched eyebrows and walk away. Her servants and staff called her Miz' Broselli. Tony, her husband, called her 'darling'. She called him Anton.

This Petra discovered next day, soon after the limousine dispatched by Sandrine deposited her, Carlo, Gina and Diego in front of the Cape Dutch homestead in the heart of the Stellenbosch Winelands. She quickly began to suspect that Sandrine Broselli hated other things too.

The woman was poured into flesh-coloured jeggings worn without underwear. A fuschia-pink shirt was buttoned tightly across a pair of uplifted boobs and tied underneath them. The diamond flashing in her navel reminded Petra of the one that had decorated Don León's hapless assistant, Monica. In Carlo's words, Sandrine was hot and clearly thought so herself. She came gliding down the steps of the homestead in high heels as if she were a model on a Paris catwalk.

Tony Broselli followed her out of the house. Petra was expecting a dark, handsome, Mediterranean type, a foil for Mrs. Broselli's blonde Afrikaner looks. Instead, she saw an older man with a crew cut and a pleasant oval face. Medium colouring, not quite as tall as Sandrine in her heels, soft spoken. There was genuine warmth in his voice when he greeted them.

'Welcome to Vredehof, our peaceful farm. The estate has been associated with wine production for nearly two hundred and fifty years,' he said. 'The house dates back to 1789, the year of the French Revolution. In fact, the row of camphor trees at the back was planted at that time to commemorate the storming of the Bastille. I'll show you where …' The large diamond in the signet ring on his right hand caught the sun as he made an expansive gesture.

His wife threw him a warning look. 'Not now, Anton. Wellington will show them to their rooms and we'll all meet for pre-lunch drinks on the terrace at noon. Lunch will be served at twelve-thirty. Dress is casual until six this evening.'

'Of course, darling. I'll wait for my appointed time slot.'

Petra and Carlo exchanged glances.

'The schedule for the next five days, one copy for each of you, has been placed in your rooms,' Sandrine announced, her voice as chilled and dry as a Martini. 'Please study it and address any questions to me.'

Carlo drew himself upright and saluted. 'Yes, Ma'am.' He lowered his voice. 'This is much worse than the last time I was here three years ago,' he said to Petra.

Wellington, a grizzled African with impossibly white teeth, took them to a long two-storey building constructed in the same style as the gabled main house. Petra and Carlo were given a twin-bedded room next door to Gina and Diego's.

'A good job I brought my PJs,' Petra said.

'What? A girl of mine wearing clothes in bed?'

'Yes, Mercutio, and I'm not a girl of yours.'

He made a moue that caused her to burst out laughing.

'I wonder whether Sandrine ever laughs,' she said.

'What a challenge! Now you've set me thinking.'

Petra picked up the schedule that lay on the night table and groaned: ten pages of instructions. Three meals a day, fixed times and locations, dress specified. Four formal evenings, plus the wedding on Saturday. She hadn't anticipated such formality and doubted she had enough clothes. Between now and the wedding, there was only half a day at leisure. She felt exhausted already and wondered whether she could skip lunch. But Sandrine's 'we'll all meet for pre-lunch drinks' had been an order. The only way out would be to plead illness.

'Do you know how many guests are expected, Carlo?'

'Ninety I heard, but only thirty are staying here. The rest are being bused in on Saturday for the wedding.'

'That's still a lot of people to accommodate.'

'Not on an estate as extensive as this.'

Petra nodded at the first page of the schedule. 'We get the grand tour after lunch.'

At noon, the guests, who now numbered sixteen, mustered on the terrace behind the manor house for drinks. The twelve newcomers had arrived in two white limousines just in time. They included a family from Florence, another from Venice, two English girls not unlike Megan and Hilary, and two fair-skinned Spanish girls from Galicia. Carlo stuck as close as he could to Gina and Diego, while Petra befriended the Spaniards, Ana and Raquel, enjoying the opportunity to speak Spanish again.

After a delicious meal served by three Xhosa women overseen by Wellington, Tony Broselli led them into the house. It had been in his wife's family for over eight generations, he said. As soon as Petra stepped into the cool high-ceilinged interior, she felt history envelop her. She hardly dared walk on the rich patina of the wooden floors.

Beginning his dissertation in the main hall, Tony described how the Delapore family had come from France via Holland in the seventeen hundreds, bringing wine-making skills from the Rhône valley.

'We hold our special invitational evenings with wine and food pairings in here,' he intoned, ushering them into a dining room with a massive oak table and an antique beige and blue Persian rug. Petra's eye was drawn immediately to the blue and white Delftware pieces displayed on a Dutch dresser at the far end of the room.

On the other side of the hall was a flagstoned great room with tall, mullioned windows. Straight-backed chairs and sofas upholstered in tapestry fringed with gold braid stood round the walls. An enormous highboy with a bulbous bottom and ball and claw feet resembled a fat waddling duck.

Tony shepherded them back to the main hall. He pointed out portraits of Delapore bigwigs that hung in the stairwell and drew their attention to the hand-carved balustrade and newel posts but did not take them upstairs to the family's private quarters. Instead, Sandrine appeared on the stairs as if on cue and divided them into groups of four.

For the next two hours, Tony led four golf carts driven by white-uniformed staff around the vast estate. At pre-arranged stations, they alighted from the carts and listened as he taught them everything they could possibly want to know about growing vines and turning the various grape varieties into red and white wines. They visited stables and outbuildings housing everything from tools to new and old barrels. Spying trapdoors in the floors of a number of outbuildings, Petra asked Tony what was below. Cellars, came the answer, unused nowadays except for occasional storage.

By the end of the afternoon, Petra was close to breaking point after too much sun, lunchtime drinking and a surfeit of indigestible information. Anton was showing them the family cemetery and reeling off the names of illustrious forbears that meant nothing to his captives. When she heard him say, 'Our last stop will be at the sunken garden, our outdoor functions area,' she clasped her hands together as if in prayer.

But the flow of information continued unabated. 'We are a working wine farm, open to the public on Tuesdays, Wednesdays and Thursdays. Tastings are conducted in our new purpose-built tasting centre which also houses the family museum. We'll be meeting there this evening for drinks before dinner.'

'Where does he get his energy?' Petra ground out.

'The Broselli genes, of course. We Brosellis never give up.'

Despite her weariness, Petra whistled with delight when they came to the sunken garden. It was surrounded by low white walls that doubled as flower boxes. They were bursting with blue and white agapanthus, also called the flower of love or African lily, Tony told them.

Rows of chairs draped in white were already set out under an open-sided marquee ready for Saturday's wedding. Facing the first row of chairs was a tented wrought-iron gazebo around which grew rosebushes thick with white flowers.

'This is where the wedding of my daughter, Julia, and Max De Witt will take place,' Tony Broselli said with a touch of pride that caused Petra to half-forgive him for tutoring them so rigorously throughout the afternoon. 'By Saturday, the chairs, the pillars and the gazebo will be covered in blossoms and vines symbolizing love, happiness and intimacy.'

'I don't know how much your poor uncle gets of that,' she murmured.

'Yet he's in his element and never complains.'

'I'm looking forward to meeting Julia and Max,' Petra said while she was changing for dinner in the scant hour that Sandrine's schedule allowed them. She and Carlo had worked out a system for using the bathroom and giving each other a bit of privacy.

'What was that?' he called.

Petra repeated what she had said more or less to herself. Carlo came out of the bathroom drying his face and hands.

'Julia is Tony's daughter, as you know. A lovely girl, though not blessed with much in the looks department.'

'Not hot then, like her stepmother?'

'No. Homely, you might say. She'll probably make a very good wife.'

'Your sexist comments drive me bananas, Mercutio!'

'That little number you're wearing could drive me bananas too, *tesoro mio!*'

Petra smoothed her purple Lycra and rayon dress with the silver flecks in it over her hips. 'Sandrine, Gina, watch out! Here I come! What about Max, Julia's intended?'

'Don't know him. Last time I visited South Africa they weren't an item.'

'Sandrine has a son, isn't that what you told me?'

'Right. A beautiful blue-eyed boy, literally and figuratively. He's the apple of her eye, to use another cliché.'

'I get the picture. And do I sense that Sandrine's not so enamoured with the bride-to-be?'

'Right again. Julia doesn't meet her exacting standards.'

'And how is Julia's relationship with her stepbrother, what's his name?'

'Florian, if you can believe it,' Carlo said. 'They'll be at the "Meet the bride and best man" dinner tonight. You can tell me what you think after you've had time to observe them for a while.'

Petra knew who she was looking at as soon as she walked into the tasting centre a little later that evening. Florian was at the door, monitoring everyone who entered. Switching his big blue eyes to full beam, he clasped Petra's hand and assessed her through long, thick, bovine lashes. He didn't smile because there was no need: the force of his personality was in those vivid eyes and the sweet mobile mouth. And his assessment was anything but bovine.

Tagged and tallied, Petra thought, as Florian dropped his eyes to read the nametag she had attached to her evening purse. He let them glide upwards to where the black and silver crucifix she had retrieved from her suitcase nestled in its usual place.

'Catholic?' he queried.

'Half,' she replied, thinking *None of your business*.

'You'll like Father John then.'

'Will I?'

'You will.'

He turned his attention to Carlo, and Petra moved forward to where a young woman was standing next to Tony Broselli. She had his wide build and oval face and because she wasn't very tall, appeared dumpy. Tony put a protective hand on her shoulder.

'Petra, this is my daughter, Julia.'

'Julia, how nice to meet you! You're the bride-to-be. Congratulations, and thank you so much for inviting me. You must be looking forward to the big day.'

Julia gave a small nod and mumbled something Petra couldn't quite catch. Nerves, Petra thought, then looked more closely at the young woman. Her eyes were veiled. They didn't sparkle like Carlo's or reveal intelligence like her father's. There was a droop to her shoulders, and none of the enthusiasm Petra would have expected in someone who was only four days away from a spectacular wedding.

'Is your fiancé here?' Petra continued. 'I hope you'll introduce me.'

At that moment, Sandrine breezed over to them and took control. 'Max and his family are arriving tomorrow, as you can see if you consult your schedule. Thursday Father John joins us, Friday will be the rehearsal, and Saturday, of course, the main event.'

The way Sandrine referred to the wedding celebration as "the main event", as if she were just the organizer and not a member of the family, struck Petra as unnatural. Julia dropped her eyes and ducked from under her father's hand.

Petra caught up with Carlo at the long marble-topped counter where samples of various wines were being served. He was chatting to Gina. She interrupted them with a curt 'Hi!'

Ignoring Gina, she carried on, 'Have you had a chance to talk to Julia since we arrived, Carlo? She doesn't seem the most excited bride-to-be I've ever met.'

'Not like you when you thought Romeo was going to marry you, eh?'

Carlo's comment landed like a double punch in Petra's stomach. She closed her eyes for a split second then opened them with such a look of fury on her face that he took a step back.

'That was beyond the pale, Mercutio! Don't ever do that again! I was devastated by Romeo's death, and I dealt with it as best I could. Your wit is so sharp you'll cut yourself one of these days. Then you'll know how it hurts.'

'I'm sorry, *carissima*, truly I am.' His expression and his tone told her he meant it.

Immediately, Petra regretted her outburst. It was unbefitting not only a cop and a seasoned professional, but also someone who had been kindly invited to a friend's cousin's wedding. When she accepted, she had known the risk she was running: known that her old feelings for Romeo might surface and that Mercutio was apt to make jokes about those far-off days. She thought she had her emotions under control. *Wrong*, she said under her breath, tapping herself on the nose. 'I'm sorry too,' she murmured.

Carlo took her arm and drew her to one side. The clutch of people who had witnessed the scene turned back to their drinks.

'Back to your question. No, I haven't had a chance to talk to Julia. I agree she seems dispirited, but from what I recall she's never very outgoing. I put it down to living with Sandrine.'

'You're probably right. Maybe once the wedding's over, she'll be able to make her own life away from her stepmother's influence.'

CHAPTER

8

Wednesday morning's schedule prescribed a tour of the Simonsberg area. Petra was mildly surprised when Florian joined Tony Broselli as the second guide for the two minibuses.

'Make sure we get on Florian's bus,' she hissed to Carlo. 'It'll be interesting to see him in action.'

'Righty-ho, unless our dear Sandrine has shuffled us already like a pack of cards.'

'Shuffled or dealt?'

'Whichever.'

Florian was a rare creature: a truly beautiful boy. Each time Petra looked out of the window at the passing scenery her eyes were drawn back to his face. From her seat near the back, she saw that the bus was full of singles. The two families had boarded Tony's bus. And all the girls were having the same problem.

Like a professional tour guide, Florian was balancing at the front of the bus, facing his flock and holding a microphone. Just in case we miss his words of wisdom, Petra thought with a tiny smile. His gaze flitted from one face to another, pausing occasionally then moving on. She noted that he spent more time on the women but didn't ignore the men.

'What does Florian do?' she asked Carlo in a soft voice.

'Do?'

'Yes, as in work. Does he live on the estate? Help with the vineyards?'

'Florian often keeps his mother company, but they also seem to go their separate ways. The Broselli/Delapores have a lot of business interests. The Delapores made money originally from wine, then Sandrine's father set up a biscuit factory. When he died five years ago, she took over. Tony Broselli's main business is fishing. He owns a fleet of trawlers that operate out of Port Nolloth. That's on the West Coast, up towards the Namibian border. He also has a fish-packing plant, and a hunting and safari lodge on the Orange River.'

'That's more than enough to keep everyone gainfully employed.'

'Yes. Julia is the only one who doesn't seem to take an interest in fish, animals, biscuits or wine. When I was here three years ago, she was talking about going to South America to work with some charity or other.'

'Isn't there more need here in Africa?'

'Of course, and the family sponsors various projects, including township tours where the fees charged to tourists fund amenities for the townships. Julia could easily get involved in those good works, but she chooses not to. Probably the Sandrine factor again.'

'And now she's getting married, perhaps as a means of escape.'

Carlo gave Petra a nudge.

Florian had noticed them talking quietly and was looking at them stony-faced. 'As I was saying, we will explore the Kayamandi township on foot. You were all instructed to wear sensible footwear.' He pointed out of the window to his right without taking his eyes off Petra and Carlo. 'We're arriving at the township now.'

Mesmerized by his gaze, Petra hardly took in what he was saying. His voice was as mellifluous as his beauty was compelling, yet there was a harsher undertone which disturbed her.

The four younger women – Ana and Raquel, Pam and Joanna – clustered round him as he led his group into the township. Their blonde heads were easy to spot among the adults and children who surged forward and threatened to envelope them. To clear a path and keep his troops moving in the right direction, Florian brandished an ironwood walking stick to which he had tied a white flag. He began to explain some of the plans for the township.

'This is the kind of thing we need to eradicate,' he announced, pointing his stick at a shanty area that was grafting itself onto the side of the established township. 'We need to move people out into areas with basic amenities. If we don't and they continue to flood our country, they will swamp our traditional culture and destroy our values. That is why we have to work together to make it happen. Especially those of us in the upper socio-economic bracket.'

Petra raised her eyebrows at Carlo.

The response from Florian's acolytes was instantaneous.

'What can we do to help?' Pam asked. 'Please tell us.'

'There's so much to be done,' Joanna chirruped. 'We'll do whatever you want.'

Petra watched Florian caress them with his blue-blue eyes. 'You will have the opportunity to make your contribution as soon as the wedding is over. We need you, I can assure you of that.'

46

The four girls were putty in his hands. If he had wanted to bed them there and then in full view of everyone, Petra knew there would be no resistance. Even she – not to mention Gina and the men too, judging by the looks on their faces – was impressed by the strength of his vision. Its substance, though, gave her pause. As he swung his stick around, his lips curled in a slightly sardonic way that didn't quite jibe with the noble sentiments he appeared to be expressing.

'What do you think?' Petra asked Carlo.

'Interesting. Did I hear echoes of Nazi Germany? Or did my ears deceive me?'

Florian shook his stick as if in triumph, threw Petra and Carlo a gloating look, and led his group back to the bus.

CHAPTER

9

Henny tried to ignore the feeling deep in his gut that this trip wasn't going to go to plan. The six girls in the group were beginning to drive him mad. The troublemakers were the two young English girls, barely out of school. Megan and Hilary. When he had spotted them at Cape Town airport, they appeared to have all the characteristics he had been instructed to look for. He had had no idea they could be so annoying.

They had crossed the border into Namibia and the girls were bitching about the lack of mobile phone coverage. To make matters worse, their batteries were nearly flat and they wanted to charge their phones so that they could take pictures and more pictures. They must have taken hundreds, and for all he knew, shared them on Facebook with family and friends. Just what the Master didn't want.

Last night on their arrival in Springbok, he had delivered the company's standard spiel regarding electronic equipment and social media. In his first year with Higher Ground, he had had difficulty with some of the wording, but he had worked at it. Now it was engraved on his memory.

'At Higher Ground Tours, our prime objective is to give participants the most authentic African experience possible. Nature is our constant companion, the bush our natural habitat. Our camper vans are self-sufficient and if you need anything, you have only to ask me. In return, we ask for your complete commitment to our values: community, serenity, the pastoral life.

One of our primary goals is to help you re-engage with your inner selves so that you can appreciate the true beauty of the world without relying on electronic gadgetry. To prevent the intrusion of secondary concerns into the lives of our guests for the duration of the tour, we will therefore collect all mobile phones and other electronic devices and store them for you until we reach our destination. You will have the added advantage of knowing that they are locked away safely. This will ensure that each and every one of you enjoys the tour to the full.'

At the end, he swept his gaze over his audience: three of the four girls in the last two rows of seats gave a nod, the fourth, a shrug. But there was a different response from Megan and Hilary.

'That's bullshit! My phone is my camera and I'm keeping a travel log.' He could still hear Megan shouting it out.

'I agree. I promised to send pictures home.' Hilary, milder but stubborn.

It had happened once or twice in the past and Henny knew what he had to do: act as though it was no big deal, wait a day or two, then arrange an incident.

Fish River Canyon was the place to do it. Next day they would begin a three-day hike to a mystical place of hot springs and lava rocks. The going would be rough. He would suggest that Megan and Hilary leave their devices at the camp. If that didn't work, he would make sure they didn't come back with them.

10

The fair-haired De Witts were from solid Flemish stock. Jacob De Witt and his son, Max, had thick necks and big beefy arms. Marina and her daughter, Betta, who was a few years younger than Max, had pleasant round faces and sturdy child-bearing hips. Sandrine greeted them all with a formal handshake. Tony clasped the men's hands warmly and kissed both the women. Betta's eyes flew to Florian and she propelled herself towards him. Julia had not yet appeared.

Petra wiped a bead of perspiration from her brow. It was a sultry evening. The humidity was up and swarms of gnats had invaded the terrace where Wellington was serving MCC, *Méthode Cap Classique,* the South African equivalent of French champagne, to the assembled guests. She wished she had stuck to her original plan and worn the long-sleeved sheer gold tunic and navy blue leggings she had inherited from Don León's megayacht *Titania*. Then again, some people said mosquitoes were attracted to the colour blue so perhaps she had been wise to put on an off-white lacy dress.

Florian passed close to her. 'Virginal as well as Catholic? I had no idea Carlo was squiring such a hot cookie.'

Did she dream it or did he really bat his silky lashes when he spoke? She shivered in spite of the temperature.

Max De Witt approached her carrying two glasses. 'We haven't met yet, though I've heard about you. You're a cop, aren't you?'

'Yes, but on leave and not thinking about police work. I intend to enjoy my vacation.'

'So we're not being investigated then?' he said with what appeared to be complete seriousness.

'Not by me, and not unless you've done something wrong.'

'A speeding ticket or two … that's about it.'

'Then you've nothing to worry about.'

Max nodded and moved off.

Petra took a sip of her bubbly and looked around her. What she had said to Max was true. She had no intention of spending her vacation on police work, yet her years in the Royal Canadian Mounted Police had trained her to stay alert and observe. That she could never change.

Marina De Witt was talking intently to Tony Broselli, lecturing him almost. What about, Petra couldn't hear. Betta De Witt was standing goggle-eyed with the other young women who swarmed round Florian. Diego, Gina and Carlo formed their own little group. Jacob De Witt was monopolizing Sandrine who looked bored.

Abruptly, Sandrine broke away and strode across to Florian. She seized his arm and pulled him to the side of the terrace not far from where Petra was standing at the back. Petra stayed where she was, making herself as unobtrusive as possible.

'Why did you stop at the township? It wasn't on my schedule.'

'No, but it was on mine. Look at them, Mama, they're converts.'

'To your sordid plans?'

Florian shook off his mother's hand. 'You don't own me now.'

'I told you to go easy, darling. Father John arrives tomorrow. His involvement is crucial in making this a success.'

'A washed-up pervert in a black robe? You think that's what will sway them?'

'You used not to be rude about him like that. He taught you everything you know.'

'Some things I didn't want to know, and I had lessons from you too, Mama, remember? Though I agree he's persuasive.'

'Especially at the confessional. That's on Friday.'

Florian shrugged. He moved away from Sandrine, glancing over his shoulder as he did so. Petra averted her eyes as quickly as she could, but he must have realized she had been observing them. Luckily, Wellington was bearing down on her with a plate of mixed hors d'oeuvres and she made a show of asking him what each one contained.

When the gong sounded for dinner, Carlo sought her out. The meal in honour of the groom and his family was being served in the manor house where there was room for twenty around the dining table. It was laid with blue and white china and half a dozen crystal glasses of different shapes and sizes stood at each place.

'Have you seen the table plan?' he asked.

Petra shook her head.

'My dear step-aunt has honoured you by seating you

next to the bride-to-be. Perhaps because you're the senior single, the equivalent of the matron-of-honour.'

'What about Gina? Surely she's older than I am?'

'More used, perhaps, but a year younger I'm told.'

'Women lie about their age all the time.'

'What's wrong with being the matron-of-honour?'

'First, I'm not a matron; second, I don't want to draw attention to myself.'

'Therein lies a problem. Your striking black hair, blue-green eyes and china-doll complexion make it impossible to do otherwise.'

'Give me a break, Mercutio!'

'Ah, there's Julia – finally! Coming through the garden.'

Sandrine pounced on her stepdaughter as soon as she climbed the steps to the terrace.

'Where the hell have you been? Your guests are waiting, the De Witts are waiting, we're all waiting.'

'I'm in time for dinner,' Julia said flatly.

'That's not good enough. You were supposed to be here to greet Max. And you're not wearing the green dress and the diamonds. Not even your engagement ring.'

'Green's unlucky, and I don't like bling.'

'Diamonds are not bling. They pay for a lot of what we have.'

'I prefer tanzanite: it restores my spiritual balance.'

'What a load of rubbish! I don't know what to do with you, Julia. I've gone to great lengths to secure this marriage. Go and do your duty.'

The De Witts and most of the guests had taken their seats in the dining room, but a few, including Petra and Carlo, had heard the exchange. Petra couldn't understand it. Julia seemed to be working very hard to antagonize her stepmother. Surely during this important week it would have been sensible to do exactly the opposite. Then, once the ceremony was over, she could fly the coop with Max. So far, Petra hadn't seen the two of them together. Did they love each other, or was the marriage an arranged one, as Sandrine had implied? Maybe that was one of the wedding planning services Sandrine offered – selection of a suitable groom.

'What are you chuckling about?' Carlo asked Petra.

'My imagination working overtime, as usual,' she replied. 'Who are you sitting next to?'

'I've been relegated to the far end of the room as a sandwich-filler between Marina De Witt and Signora Botticelli from Florence.'

'Good luck!'

Petra slipped into her seat between Julia and Diego. Max was on the other side of Julia, talking to Gina on his right.

She smiled at Julia. 'Those are nice colours you're wearing,' she said, looking at Julia's blue and yellow dress and trying to engage the girl. 'They suit you.'

'Not according to my stepmother.'

'Mothers aren't always right, even if they think they are.'

'Stepmother.'

'It must have been tough, losing your real mother when you were how old?'

'Thirteen. Unlucky number.'

'Not at all. But a difficult age when you're already trying to deal with so many changes. You have to learn to cope with the shock and the anger, and then with new people in your life. Bereavement counselling can help. Did you have that?'

'Dad made me go and see a woman who had no idea how to talk to me.'

As I don't.

'She looked like a witch with black eyebrows and a beaky nose. I only went to one session. Then Dad looked after me – until *she* came along.' Julia gestured in Sandrine's direction.

'Is that your engagement ring?' Petra asked.

'No, if it were, I'd be wearing it on the other hand.'

'Well, it's very attractive, and unusual.'

Petra was about to give up on Julia and turn to Diego who was crowding her when the girl showed a spark of life.

'It's my mother's ring: a blue tanzanite. She inherited it from her mother.' Julia moved her hand to show off the colour.

'Incredible how it changes when you do that. Now it's more violet and burgundy.'

'That's part of the magic of tanzanite, the mood changer. It can restore balance and good fortune.'

'I hope it works for you,' Petra said.

'So do I. The sooner I get out of here, the better off I'll be.'

CHAPTER

11

At half past nine on Thursday morning, Petra and Carlo boarded Florian's minibus, eager to visit the town of Stellenbosch.

Florian blended well with the students who thronged the streets of the historic university town. The majority were Afrikaners, typically bronzed and blonde with the energy unique to young, bright, beautiful people. Petra noticed the gleam in Carlo's eyes and knew it was reflected in her own.

Although Florian was no blood relation to Tony Broselli, some of Tony's enthusiasm for the past had rubbed off on him. He walked them through the tree-lined streets and lanes, pointed out the earliest buildings in what he said was the second-oldest town in South Africa, and waxed lyrical about the range of cultural activities on offer.

By the end of the morning, Petra was smitten. As she liked to tell her friends, she was at heart a small town girl. The mountain backdrop and the village atmosphere reminded her of summer days spent in the Alps with Carlo, Ben and Romeo. To her surprise, she found that the memory was sweet, not bitter, and put it down to the magic of Stellenbosch. There was only one thing missing: water.

She preferred to be close to a lake or the sea. South Africa's dry river beds didn't cut it.

Florian's looks could easily lead people to underestimate him, Petra thought as she noticed how he kept his flock under surveillance. Today he had chosen not to bring his stick. Instead he was relying on his sharp eyes and natural magnetism to keep them together. Certainly none of the girls was going to stray far.

Petra took her seat in the minibus and kicked off her boat shoes. They were the most comfortable type of shoe to wear for sightseeing she found, yet her feet were sticky.

'I'm ready for an afternoon at leisure,' she remarked to Carlo as they began the drive back to Vredehof for lunch. 'A swim then a lounge by the pool.'

'Ah,' he said. 'I forgot to tell you. I've arranged for us to visit the biscuit factory this afternoon.'

'What? Are you crazy? We've been running on eight cylinders since we got here and now you want to visit a biscuit factory!'

'Cakes, too, I'm told.'

'Forget it, Carlo. I'm resting up. There's another dinner tonight, and I'm about socialized out.'

'This isn't socializing, I can assure you. It took me a while to convince Sandrine to take us. Please, you must come with me. I need your eagle eyes,' he added quietly.

'Now that sounds intriguing. What have you got up your sleeve?'

Carlo put his index finger to his lips. 'Our gorgeous guide is ever watchful. I am as you know supremely interested in baked goods.'

Petra nodded with understanding. 'Of course.'

He racheted his voice up a notch or two. 'Look at those mountains ...'

Petra turned to the window and looked out. They were south of Stellenbosch heading back to the wine farm. The jagged hills were purple in the distance.

Why was Carlo so keen to visit the biscuit factory? How far was it from the estate? How were they going to get there? Was Sandrine going to show them around? Were other guests going too? As she was pondering these questions and naturally getting no answers, the minibus drew up at what South Africans called a "robot", in other words a traffic light. Drumming her fingers idly on the window frame, she suddenly sat up and took notice.

Parked on the verge was a white van with a curtained window in the back. Stencilled on the side in large letters were the words Tabernacle Youth Collective. She tugged at Carlo's sleeve and pointed.

'Carlo, look!'

'What's so interesting about a white van?'

'It belongs to the Tabernacle Youth Collective.'

'Who are they?'

'Remember I told you about Vicky Dunlin, the daughter of a friend of A.K.'s? She was working at the Cape Sands and A.K. asked me to check on her.'

'Right. So?'

'Vicky Dunlin went off on holiday with that group.'

Petra stared at the van. She could see a man sitting in the driver's seat, but not his face. There was no door in the back of the van or on the side facing the road. Most likely there was a sliding door on the far side. She wondered why they were stopped.

'What a coincidence!' she said as the lights changed and

the minibus pulled away. 'A.K. asked me to go and visit her after the wedding.' She craned her neck to see if she could see anyone inside or in the passenger seat of the van. 'Now I'm curious. I must find out more about the group. They might be doing a project near here.'

'How will you find out? There was no address or phone number on the van.'

'I'm sure I'll be able to find a number and call them. And if Vicky's in the area, I could go and see her this week instead of after the wedding.'

'Work it into Sandrine's schedule you mean?'

'I'll find a way. I can always pretend I'm sick.'

'Not this afternoon, we're going to the biscuit factory, remember?'

'All right, but you must promise to tell me what's going on.'

CHAPTER

12

Sandrine had left a new set of instructions for Petra and Carlo. Instead of "leisure", they were to meet Florian and herself immediately after lunch, at half past one. They would return to base at half past four.

'I didn't expect two minders,' Carlo remarked. 'I was hoping you'd have the opportunity to do what you're good at: wander round and snoop a bit.'

'Why, Carlo? What's all this about?'

'Probably nothing, but a colleague of mine who works for Interpol in France called me last week. His area of expertise is trafficking in illicit goods. He knew I was coming to South Africa and asked if I could visit a company called Dragées d'Aix, S.A.'

'Dragées are sugared almonds, aren't they? The French often give them to guests at weddings and christenings to take home as gifts or favours.'

'Right, the Italians too. In this case, the South African company has taken the name of one of the most famous almonds in France. Not only that, but the French manufacturer alleges that the South African company has ordered identical keepsake tins from China, is filling them with inferior product and exporting them to Europe –

essentially passing them off as the real thing and stealing their business.'

Petra gave a Gallic shrug complete with hands. 'It sounds unlikely to me. I'd have thought that the cost of importing the tins, filling them with locally made product, and re-exporting them back to Europe would be too expensive to make it worthwhile. In any case, why bother? Sooner or later, the French manufacturer would get an injunction or something against the company.'

'That was my thinking too. And South Africa doesn't produce anything like enough almonds to meet demand, so the nuts would have to be imported as well as the tins. Anyway, I said I'd take a look if I could. My colleague gave me a Post Office Box mailing address for the company in the Western Cape and an email address.'

'That's all?'

'Yes, but after a lot of searching, I found a page that seemed to link Dragées to Delapore Biscuits.'

'You think Delapore makes them?'

'That's what we're going to try and find out.'

Sandrine was waiting in her silver BMW at the bottom of the manor house steps when Petra and Carlo arrived just as the clock in the stable tower struck half past one. She had traded jeggings for a micro-skirt that left the whole of her slim tanned legs in full view. Not a lot of imagination was required to visualize what she had on under the skirt. Silver heels completed her outfit. She pointed to Carlo and patted the seat beside her. Florian was in the back seat. He leaned across and opened the door for Petra.

The sprawling complex that belonged to Delapore Biscuits was on the outskirts of Durbanville. Petra counted at least four structures in the front row and there were more behind.

Sandrine led them inside the first building, where biscuits were made, and attached herself to Carlo. Clearly he didn't mind. From time to time, Petra caught him taking a peek at Sandrine's impressive chest. Florian steered Petra along behind them.

Over the clatter of machinery, Sandrine began to explain the biscuit-making process. She showed them the industrial mixing machines that handled the dough, the cutters that made the shapes, and the ovens where the biscuits, or cookies as Petra called them, were baked.

Petra noticed that all the staff were female, wearing pale blue dresses, white aprons, and white mob caps to cover their black hair. When she asked Florian why there were no men, he gave a curious reply:

'If the women are working, they're off the streets and don't have time to make babies.'

Stunned, she couldn't think of anything to say.

Once the biscuits were baked, they were left to cool; then the trays were slotted into tall trolleys and wheeled to the packaging area. Petra looked for tins, but the women were putting the biscuits into boxes. 'Where are your tins of fancy mixed biscuits?' she asked Florian.

'That's a limited market. We prefer to go for volume, and boxes are cheaper and easier to store.'

She couldn't fault him on that response.

Sandrine moved them swiftly out of the packaging area, through a door that led outside and across a courtyard. Petra fell into step with Carlo.

'Fascinating, isn't it, Carlo? I had no idea how complicated a process it was. What's in the other buildings at the back?' she asked Sandrine, waving a hand in their general direction.

'Offices and the order department. Nothing of interest to visitors. The next part of our tour is the cake division.'

Petra glanced around the courtyard. She noted a small white-washed hut that had a water tank and a solar panel on its roof. The door was slightly open and there was a faint aroma that had nothing to do with cakes or biscuits. Florian was watching her, so she made an effort to catch up.

There was an element of pride in Sandrine's voice as she conducted them into the cake section of the factory. 'Diversifying into cakes was my idea, after my father died.'

'Brilliant!' Carlo said. 'You must tell me exactly how you did it.'

While Florian closed the door behind them, Petra managed to whisper 'That's it, Carlo, keep her busy. Florian too if you can.'

The cake division was set up in a similar way to the biscuits. Industrial quantities of flour, sugar, fat, powdered egg, milk and other ingredients were poured into giant mixing vats. The women lifted the huge bags as though they were feather pillows and seemed impervious to the high-pitched whine of the mixers that grated on Petra's ears.

Sandrine was responding nicely to Carlo's ministrations. He had his hand on her elbow, and it struck Petra that their roles were reversed: now he was the one in charge. She hid a smile. She had seen Carlo use flattery before to great effect. One of the machines stopped and she caught the words 'scrumptious fruit cake'.

Petra had left the phone Tom had given her back at the wine farm. Carlo had brought his, in case of emergency he said. Now Petra heard a loud ring from the phone holster on his belt.

'I'm so sorry, *carissima*! Let me turn it off,' he said to Sandrine.

Petra felt a stab of jealousy at the endearment and frowned. What was Carlo playing at?

He took the phone from its holster, looked at the screen and fiddled with a few buttons. 'There, I've put it on silent,' he said, winking at Petra.

The next moment an ear-splitting alarm began to sound. The din came from somewhere outside. Sandrine spun round and shouted at Florian:

'That's my car! Go and see what's happening, Florian. I'll kill anyone who's been tampering with it!'

'I'm sure there's nothing to worry about,' Carlo said, patting Sandrine's arm. 'Those alarms can be triggered by the slightest thing: heat, wind ... I should know, I have the same car.'

Petra couldn't believe her ears but didn't waste any time. Carlo was making soothing noises and leading Sandrine away from the mixing section towards the ovens and beyond to where a group of women were decorating cakes.

As soon as Florian disappeared in the direction of the noise, Petra seized her chance. Before he came back, she wanted to take a look at the office and administration buildings – the ones Sandrine had said were of no interest.

She moved swiftly across the courtyard and went into the first of the low buildings. Inside, a ceiling fan turned lazily. Two employees sat at desks in front of computers. A large bookcase on the wall behind them contained shelves full of green-bound ledgers.

The woman nearest the door hastily minimized the game she was playing as Petra spoke.

'Hi! A friend of mine is getting married. She wants to order some dragées, sugared almonds, as favours. I believe you make them here.'

The woman shook her head. 'We only do biscuits and cakes.'

'Are you sure? I was told they were a specialty of yours.'

The second woman abandoned her screen. 'She told you: biscuits and cakes, that's all. Here, take one of our catalogues or have a look at our website.'

Petra took the proffered catalogue. 'Thanks, I will. Do you know who does make them?'

Both women shook their heads.

'Oh well, I guess I'm out of luck.' *No point flogging a dead horse.*

The car alarm was still wailing like a banshee. Once it stopped, Petra judged she would have only a few minutes before Florian came looking for her. Behind the main buildings, there were several more she wanted to have a look at. Quickly she said, 'Do you have a bathroom I can use?'

'Go out of here and you'll see it in the courtyard. It's a small white building. You can't miss it.'

'Thank you so much.'

Instead of heading for the bathroom, Petra turned left and hurried to a long low building similar to the first one. The windows were closed and the door locked. Then there was an even longer building, shut up tight and no noise of machinery. Beyond that was an air-conditioned warehouse with a white van parked outside. 'Delapore Biscuits and Cakes, the best you've ever tasted' it proclaimed.

The roll-down door to the warehouse was open. Petra darted inside and looked around the dim interior. A forklift was parked in one of the aisles, but no one was about. She did a quick recce. The left-hand section housed bags of ingredients: flour, sugar, dried fruit, but nothing labelled as almonds. The right-hand side was reserved for the finished products: boxes of biscuits and cakes. No tins that she could see.

The car alarm stopped as she was about to leave. In the ensuing silence that was welcome to her ears but not to her fast-beating heart, she heard whistling. A young man in a white coat entered the warehouse through a side door. He looked startled to see Petra.

'What are you doing here?'

'I'm trying to find my way back to the cake section. I must have taken a wrong turn. If you're the manager, you keep the warehouse very nicely,' she added. 'Do you ever have problems with rodents?'

'Rodents?'

'Yes, rats and mice for example. I'm sure they love all this stuff. Squirrels too probably. They love nuts.'

The young man gave her a bewildered look. 'I keep the place free of rats and mice, and I've never seen a squirrel here. Anyway, there are no nuts. We at Delapore Biscuits don't use them. Our products are allergen-free,' he said as if he were a commercial.

'What about gluten? That's an allergen,' Petra said before she could stop herself. 'Never mind. I must get back to my party.'

'You should never have left your party,' Florian said, coming up behind her. 'I've been looking for you.'

'I must have turned left instead of right when I came out of the bathroom. It's easy to get confused.'

Florian's blue eyes stared frostily at her through his lashes. 'Come with me.'

Despite the car alarm and Petra's unsanctioned deviation from the official programme they arrived back at the estate at exactly half past four. Carlo had persuaded Sandrine to let him sample some of the cakes.

'I can confirm that there are no nuts,' he said when Petra told him what the warehouseman had said. 'Sandrine's grandfather had a peanut allergy, hence the company policy.'

'So we wasted our time!'

'Not exactly,' Carlo said smugly. 'I think I'm making progress with Sandrine. She's hot to trot, and I'm game!' He gave a wicked wink.

'Mercutio! Isn't that incestuous?'

'Not in my book – or in any book, for that matter. She's no relation. Just a good-looking woman with needs, and I will definitely find a way to make her laugh.'

CHAPTER

13

Carlo and his dubious morality. Petra closed the door loudly in protest as she left the room. Sandrine was probably old enough to be his mother. Still, he had done a good job of keeping her occupied so that Petra could look around while Florian was busy with the car.

Petra wondered about the alarm as she walked round the rose garden Tony Broselli had shown them two days earlier. Was it coincidence that it had gone off just after Carlo's phone had rung, or had he managed to set it off with some cleverly programmed gadget? She suspected it wasn't just a fluke.

Opposite the rose garden was a large herb garden. After examining the plants, Petra made her way to the stable block. Inside were boxes for a dozen horses, but only four were occupied. She rubbed the nose of a chestnut mare whose soft brown eyes were trusting and warm. Although she had never wanted to audition for the Mounties' Musical Ride, she was a competent horsewoman. Sandrine had the toned buttocks and legs of someone who rode regularly, Florian too.

In the next stall was a black stallion with a white blaze and socks. He whinnied when Petra approached and backed up temperamentally when she extended her hand cautiously towards him.

'I wouldn't touch him if I were you. He likes to bite strangers.'

At the sound of Florian's voice, Petra took a step away from the box and whirled round. He was wearing riding gear and carrying a crop. And he was eyeing her up and down.

Two can play at that game, she said to herself. She met his gaze then let her eyes move slowly down to his boots. His beige breeches were moulded to his frame.

Florian smacked the crop against the palm of his gloved hand. 'Do you want to ride?' He threw the question at her like a medieval knight throwing down his gauntlet.

'If you lend me a helmet and let me ride in these jeans.'

'That's fine with me.'

'OK then.'

A groom entered and hurried over.

'We'll take my horse and the chestnut. Saddle them up.'

Fifteen minutes later, Petra mounted the chestnut mare and they set off. Florian led her away from the concentration of outbuildings, down a long track through the vineyards and through a wooded area. Soon the trees thinned out and they came to an area of rolling grassland. She knew for sure that he would challenge her. As they came to the top of a rise, he reined in his horse.

'See that folly in the distance? It's exactly four furlongs away. I'll race you there.'

It was clear from the way the mare took off after the stallion that they had done this before. Petra had no need to guide her mount, just hang on and enjoy the wild gallop. When they reached the folly, the stallion a nose ahead of the gallant mare, the horses' sides were heaving.

Florian swung down from his horse and tied the reins to a post. Then he held Petra's mare while she dismounted.

'Your mother's mare I presume?'

'Yes, her favourite out of all the horses she's had over the years.' The way he said it made them sound like lovers.

'I hope she's not as possessive about her as she is about her car.'

'Oh, she'd tan my hide if she knew,' he said, striking his palm with the riding crop. 'Maybe you can do it for her.'

His tone was semi-serious, the blue eyes daring her to respond.

Suddenly Petra wondered if it had been sensible to leave the farm with Florian. She fingered the crucifix that was hidden under her T-shirt.

'Come into the folly,' he commanded. 'Leave your helmet here with mine.'

He led her through a narrow archway onto a covered ramp. At the bottom was another arch leading to a high-walled area that was open to the sky and the sun. Farther back, the stone walls rose to form an elaborate grotto above and behind a long pool. Fountains splashed into the pool, the water spurting from between the legs of nymphs and satyrs.

Petra stood silently taking it all in. Whoever had built the folly had gone to a great deal of trouble, not to mention expense. Florian was testing her, watching her reactions.

He crooked his finger. 'Come and see what an old devil my great-grandfather was.'

After a moment's hesitation, she followed him to the grotto at the far end of the pool. In the shadows stood statues of mythical creatures – half-man, half-beast – cavorting with an assortment of women with long trailing hair. On the very edge of the pool stood the figure of a dwarf endowed with not one but a trio of tiny penises.

'According to family lore, he was a small man with an immense lust for life. The only time he stopped carousing was when he had to take a piss. He didn't do it often but when he did, it was full flow.' Florian glanced at her face and let out a roar of laughter.

The next moment he was on her. He pushed her against the wall of the grotto with the grace and strength of a ballet dancer, vaguely effeminate yet all male. She could feel and smell his arousal. She struggled to throw him off but he had her pinned to the wall with his groin and his hands on her shoulders. His lips pressed down on hers and a hot current ran like wildfire through her body. His tongue began its exploration, slow at first, then harder and more insistent. She had no breath left with which to battle. Her legs began to buckle.

Without warning, he released her.

'Mmm. Not so virginal. But I'd rather not have virgins, they cling too much.'

Petra was taking deep breaths to regain control of her body.

'You're my partner at the wedding. Now I know what kind of couple we'll make: best man and senior bridesmaid, but not too senior.'

Petra bit back a sharp retort. *Use your head. Think.* That's what Tom Gilmore would tell her.

'Come, follow me.'

CHAPTER

14

Carlo never missed a trick.

'You look hot and bothered,' he said as soon as Petra stepped into the room. 'What's up?'

She tried not to let her embarrassment show as she said, 'I went for a ride with Florian.' Fortunately Carlo chose to joke about it.

'Of course! I should have guessed, you're a Mountie. Never separate a Mountie from his, I mean, her horse.'

'Right on, Mercutio. Now I must change for dinner.'

After as long a shower as she could – to wash away the taste of Florian – Petra donned the gold silk shirt and skinny navy leggings she had salvaged from her trip to the Mediterranean. She made her way with Carlo to the tasting centre for another perfectly choreographed evening of drinks and dinner. The main players were all there, including the happy couple who looked happier than the previous night.

As usual, Sandrine made herself the centre of attention. Dressed in a cling-fit dress made out of some shiny material that appeared to be closely related to aluminium foil, she looked almost as young as the bride-to-be and many times slimmer and sexier. Julia was wearing the green brocade and diamonds that didn't help her rather sallow complexion.

Sandrine swept her eyes round the tasting centre and tapped her glass with a spoon to call the assembly to order. The main purpose of the evening, she announced, was to introduce Father John who would be conducting the ceremony on Saturday. Petra was eager to meet the man whom Florian had called "a washed-up pervert", but still he did not appear.

Finally, after they had all taken their allotted places at smaller tables facing a long head table, Sandrine escorted into the room a tall, black-robed figure with unruly hair and a chin covered in stubble. Petra noted that he was not wearing a dog collar. His robe was a loose-sleeved kaftan with a round neck slit in typical North African fashion. Age-wise she estimated he was in his fifties, somewhere between Sandrine and Tony Broselli. Robustly built, not fat.

Petra found it hard to put Florian's derogatory comments out of her mind as she sized him up and listened to Sandrine's introduction.

'Ladies and Gentlemen, I would like to introduce a very close friend who has magnanimously agreed to officiate this Saturday at the marriage between Julia Broselli and Max De Witt. Father John is one of our most trusted counsellors. He has advised us on religious and secular matters since I was a child.'

'She's giving him a good build-up,' Carlo whispered.

'Marketing doublespeak if you ask me,' Petra replied.

Sandrine continued. 'He has graciously offered to spend time with us tomorrow and give us the benefit of his wisdom. I hope you will all take the opportunity to talk to him. You will find details in the schedule you have been given. Now I will ask Father John to bless the food we are about to receive.'

Father John stood up and made the sign of the cross. He bowed his head and began to intone something in Latin. Petra recognized the first few words then lost the thread.

'Is he a Catholic priest? Do you understand what he's saying?' she asked Carlo.

'It's not one of the standard graces or blessings, but he does look as though he's seen a lot of medieval portraits of Jesus Christ.'

Petra nodded. 'I noticed he was wearing sandals.'

Father John finished with the sign of the cross, raised his eyes to the assembly and took his seat at the head table between Sandrine and Julia. He exchanged a few words with the bride-to-be then turned to speak to her stepmother.

While the priest was occupied, Petra saw Julia slide her chair away from him. She kept them under observation while she tucked into the food. The ride had sharpened her appetite – Florian's too. Her cheeks flushed as she watched him devour the rack of lamb with scalloped potatoes and French-cut green beans.

Julia seemed to be eating very little and set down her knife and fork before Petra was halfway through her meal. Again Petra put it down to nerves. It wasn't uncommon for brides to lose weight in the run-up to the wedding, sometimes to the point where the wedding dress had to be taken in at the last minute.

Suddenly Julia pushed back her chair. She stood up quickly and walked out. Max, who was chatting with his mother, simply nodded when she left. Carlo was engrossed in a long tale about killer whales. No one seemed concerned about Julia. Petra had a strong feeling something was not right. She got up to follow her.

Most likely Julia was heading for the ladies' cloakroom, but when Petra checked, she wasn't there. Outside on the terrace where the pre-dinner drinks had been served, Wellington was filling a tray with short crystal glasses. He looked up, his dazzling smile absent.

'Have you seen Julia, Wellington? She wanted to speak to me about the toasts.'

'It's not my business to watch who goes where. Nor should it be yours, Miss.'

'This is important, Wellington. I won't tell anyone I spoke to you.'

'I don't know where Miss Julia is,' he said firmly. At the same time he waved his white-gloved hand in the direction of the manor house.

Petra nodded. 'Very well. I'm sorry to have bothered you.'

In houses with serving staff, the old retainers always knew what was going on far better than anyone else. If she could win his confidence, Wellington would be a good source of information, but she would have to determine where his allegiance lay. First though, she had to find Julia.

What would she do if Julia had gone to her room in the private quarters of the manor house? Would she follow her upstairs? Petra hesitated. She was hardly on intimate terms with the bride-to-be, even if she had been sitting next to her the night before.

Petra cut through the area Tony Broselli had described as the octagonal garden and began to cross the lawn to the manor house. In the centre of the lawn stood one of the oldest trees on the estate, a giant oak planted before 1800.

An owl hooted a warning as she approached. She stopped, not wanting to disturb the bird, but it was too late. She caught a glimpse of its yellow eyes before it flew off in the direction of a sister tree planted by one of Sandrine's ancestors a hundred and twenty years later.

Petra watched the bird land and detected faint movement under the tree as someone sitting on the bench below reacted to the noise. It was Julia, with her head between her knees.

'Julia? Are you all right?'

Julia didn't lift her head. 'I'm fine,' she muttered.

Petra sat down beside her. 'Are you sure?'

'No, but leave me alone.'

'If you tell me what's bothering you, I may be able to help.'

'I doubt it.'

'Try me. Is it pre-wedding jitters? That's normal you know.'

'Why does everyone think I'm a nervous wreck?' Julia said irritably.

'Are you having second thoughts about Max? You didn't look happy last night.'

'Max is OK.'

'You don't sound very enthusiastic.'

'Look,' Julia said, finally raising her head. 'Max is fine, I'm fine, we'll get married and get out of here. End of story.'

Petra sat quietly for a few moments. 'OK, if that's the way you want it, that's fine by me. We're all fine. But I don't believe you. There's something more. Come on, Julia, I can help you.'

Julia exhaled heavily and opened her mouth to speak. The next moment her demeanour changed. She stood up and straightened her dress and moved away from Petra. 'I was feeling faint and I needed some air. I'm perfectly all right now. Thank you for your concern. Let's get back to the party.' She began to walk quickly across the lawn.

A shadow moved and Florian stepped out from behind the tree. He caught hold of Petra's left arm before she had time to escape.

'The bride and the chief bridesmaid, eh? A pretty pair. But don't forget you're paired with me. I showed you earlier how nice it will be. Like this.' Florian grabbed Petra's other arm and pulled her hard towards him.

She did her best to break free, but he forced his lips onto hers and his tongue began to probe deeper and deeper into her mouth. He seemed to know exactly how far to go to inflame her. He eased off, thrust again and explored until she began to gag. Finally, he withdrew and stepped back, laughing.

Petra sucked air into her lungs. Her pulse was racing and she knew her cheeks would be scarlet. Damn it, what was he doing to her? Playing her like a fiddle, working her to arouse the response he wanted then dropping her like some mischievous sprite.

Abruptly Florian's mood changed. 'Don't believe anything my stepsister tells you. She loves to denigrate me and my mother.' He stared into Petra's eyes as if to cow her into submission then took off across the lawn after Julia.

CHAPTER

15

Halfway through the night Petra woke up drenched in sweat. Surely it had been a dream, a product of the mind: his attack, her capitulation, the spasms that had rocked her, and the release her body had demanded? She calmed her breathing and lay quiet, not wanting to disturb Carlo. He had an uncanny knack of sensing what was going on.

With a supreme effort of will, Petra cast Florian out of her mind. She didn't want to think about him, she wanted to think about Julia who had seemed unhappy from the moment Petra had met her on Tuesday evening. Wednesday she had been late for the "meet the in-laws" dinner. Last night she had hardly eaten anything and said little to her fiancé, Max. She didn't seem excited about the wedding and had indicated at least once that it was purely a means of escape. The question was from what?

In families where there were second marriages and stepchildren, tensions often ran high. Petra pinned a mental picture of Julia to the centre of the fact board she was creating in her head. She ran through the facts and added questions where necessary, as if she were investigating a serious crime: Julia Broselli, mousy brown hair, mid-twenties, only daughter of Tony Broselli, not interested in the family businesses, getting married – against her will? – and leaving the country. Relationship with her father? Outwardly good.

Petra moved on to Tony, placing him in the top left and joining him to Julia by a diagonal line: a man in his fifties, hospitable and mild-mannered, protective and affectionate towards his daughter, obedient to his wife's wishes but not subservient, self-styled lord of the manor and historian of his wife's family estate, owner – wealthy? – of a fishing fleet, processing factory and a hunting and safari lodge. What makes him tick?

She drew a horizontal line from Tony to his second wife, Sandrine Delapore, and pictured Sandrine in skin-tight clothing and high heels. Confident, cold, controlling, callous, cunning … What else? Petra added another diagonal from Sandrine to Julia to complete the triangle, an upside-down prism. Relationship between them: strained – to breaking point?

Which brings us back to Florian. Sandrine's blue-eyed boy, the only other major player: charismatic, charming when he wanted to be, imperious when he didn't. Petra linked him to Sandrine with a vertical then to Julia with a horizontal line. His relationship with his mother was close, intense, and troubled. The relationship between him and his stepsister was harder to define. There was disdain, distrust, malice, hatred, fear …

Petra was certain Julia had been going to tell her something, however reluctantly. As soon as she had seen Florian, her whole attitude had changed. Petra guessed she was afraid of her stepbrother, and in some ways Petra didn't blame her. The way he lived by his looks and used them to manipulate people was scary. And why had he suggested Julia was dishonest and out to discredit him and his mother? Petra had no idea as yet, but the fact board should help.

'What are you so pensive about?' Carlo suddenly asked.

'I didn't know you were awake.'

'How could I sleep with the noises you were making?'

'Noises? What noises?'

'Shrieks … mewlings … growls … animal noises.'

'Mercutio, I wasn't, and if I was, I was dreaming.'

'So you say, and who am I to doubt a lady's word?' Carlo propped himself up on one elbow and looked at Petra. 'But I bet you're blushing.'

'Aaargh!' Petra pulled one of the pillows from under her head and lobbed it at Carlo. 'Now can we have a serious discussion?'

'In the middle of the night? Well, I suppose we could if it'll take your mind off sex.'

Petra ignored the comment. 'This is my first visit to South Africa, but you've been here before. What do you think of the way things are going in this country?'

'What do you mean?'

'Well, Florian was ranting on about values and ideals during our visit to that township. He said we needed to eradicate the shanties and move people into areas with basic amenities.'

'Ah, I knew Florian was involved.'

'Cut it out, Mercutio.'

'OK, OK. Here's my take. Nelson Mandela did a good job of smoothing the changeover to democracy for all South Africans in the post-apartheid era. His successor, Mbeki, continued more or less successfully on the same path …'

'But?'

'Mandela's open borders policy has caused and continues to cause immense problems. The black population has grown exponentially through immigration as well as reproduction, while the white population – the primary wealth-generating segment of the population – continues to shrink.'

'Was that what Florian was referring to when he said that if people continue to flood the country, they will swamp the traditional culture and values?'

'Yes, but my guess is that he wasn't talking about traditional African culture. Some whites can't stomach the government's black empowerment policies that award huge projects to companies who haven't the faintest idea how to carry them out.'

'I'm sure that happened in reverse during the apartheid era.'

'Yes, but not on anything like the same scale. The level of corruption is unbelievable, the judiciary is being overridden, and then there's talk of land redistribution.'

'So people like the Broselli/Delapores might be very worried.'

'Yes, *cara*, very worried indeed. Now, I need my beauty sleep and, as the senior bridesmaid, you do too. I'll continue Introduction to South African Politics 007 some other time. And please, no more noise!'

CHAPTER

16

Breakfast was the most casual meal of the day and the one Petra looked forward to the most. There was no dress code and guests could serve themselves from the continental buffet and order hot dishes from Wellington and his staff. Wellington acknowledged Petra's greeting with a genuinely friendly smile.

'I hope you found what you were looking for last night, Miss,' he said.

'I did, thank you. And today looks like being a good day.'

Petra had hardly finished her second cup of coffee when Sandrine summoned her to try on her bridesmaid's dress. Petra considered making her wait a while then decided she might as well get it over with. Why she had been chosen to lead the group of five bridesmaids was a mystery.

Besides herself, there were the bridegroom's sister Betta De Witt, a friend of Julia's from her schooldays named Roz, and two diminutive flower girls. Usually, all the bridesmaids were relatives or friends of the happy couple. Petra couldn't help wondering how long ago the decision to make her a bridesmaid had been taken. Certainly no one had mentioned it until after she arrived. Had Julia made the request? Or was it Florian so that he could sit next to her at the wedding?

The dressmaker was waiting for her in the great room of the manor house, next to a rack full of dresses. Petra's was pink brocade with a lace midriff. She held it up in front of her and looked in the mirror: hip-hugging, knee-length, no sleeves, and a high rounded neck with a long slit in it like Father John's kaftan. It could be worse.

She took off her shorts and T-shirt and put them on the nearest chair. When she put the dress on, she found that the fit was surprisingly good. Whoever it had been intended for originally – Gina probably – was fractionally taller and broader than she was.

While the dressmaker, holding a mouthful of pins, fussed with a couple of small adjustments to the darts, Father John entered the room. He made the sign of the cross and walked straight over to Petra.

'Our chief bridesmaid! What a pleasure. Petra, isn't it?'

'Yes, Petra Minx.'

'Delighted to meet you. I won't shake hands because Sandrine has already warned me not to disturb the dressmaker.'

Then why did you come in?

Father John hovered round her as the dressmaker completed her task and told Petra she could get changed again. Petra looked pointedly at the bogus priest. He had been sensitive to the dressmaker's needs but didn't seem at all concerned that Petra might have to take off her clothes in front of him.

She coughed politely then shook her head in disgust. 'Do you mind?'

'Of course,' he said, 'I wasn't thinking.'

'Thank you,' she said with a touch of sarcasm.

With help from the dressmaker, she unzipped the bridesmaid's dress and stepped out of it. Father John had turned away, but she didn't trust him not to watch what was going on. Not that it mattered; she was no shrinking violet and couldn't actually care less what he saw. She had been in far more embarrassing situations in the line of duty and had only said something because she was trying to figure him out. He was a strange bird with his beady eyes and wild hair.

As quickly as she could, she pulled on her own clothes. The deep V of her T-shirt was far more revealing than the bridesmaid's dress, and the crucifix that hung between her breasts was now in full view. If Father John spotted it, he might want to examine the 18th century heirloom that had belonged to her mother's Italian family. She was lifting the chain over her head to put it away in her pocket when he beat her to it.

'That's a wonderful piece,' he said. 'May I see?'

Chagrined, Petra let the chain fall back round her neck and held the silver cross out for him to have a look. She kept her hand near the top, covering the first two inlaid black stones. She waited impatiently while Father John studied it.

'It's as lovely as its owner.' He inclined his head as he made the sign of the cross over her then added, 'May it keep you safe. Are you Catholic?'

'Long ago, on my mother's side. What about you?'

'I could say the same thing,' he said, attempting a smile. 'I left the established church some years ago to found a Christian outreach group.'

'Does that mean you're a missionary?'

'That's part of what we do. We also pride ourselves on our ability to reach out to various segments of the community through charity work. I run a number of major projects in South Africa and Namibia.'

'But you're still able to perform marriages?'

'Of course. There are many ways of solemnizing marriage in the eyes of God.'

And many ways of pulling the wool over the eyes of God and Sandrine's friends, Petra thought.

'I understand you're hearing confession today,' she continued. 'Isn't that a Catholic rite?'

'Yes, but not exclusively. In my opinion, it is best to confess your sins and receive absolution before entering into sacred vows or taking part in a ceremony where such vows are exchanged.'

Petra studied Father John's face as he spoke in a rich deep timbre. His tone and his words were designed to be convincing, but the savage gleam in his eyes gave her goose bumps. He returned her gaze with supreme confidence.

'Sandrine has allowed me to set up my tabernacle in the first of the old slave lodges,' he said.

Petra put on a surprised look. 'Tabernacle? What's that?' She knew the word had several meanings in English, and in Montreal, Quebec, where she had grown up, *tabarnak* was used as a swear word in French.

At the same time, her mind was racing. Vicky Dunlin had joined the Tabernacle Youth Collective for a week's working holiday. Could there be a connection between that group and Father John?

'For me it signifies two things,' he said. 'A place of meeting and worship, and the casket I carry with me always, containing the tools of my trade. The way we do confession is a little different. If you come along this afternoon at three o'clock, you'll see. I'm sure you'll find it very useful.'

Father John didn't wait for Petra to reply. He turned on his heel and left her staring after him, her head full of questions.

Some years ago, her partner in the RCMP's Marine Unit had been a young man from Montreal – a good cop with a great sense of humour, as well as a fiery temper. She had memorized some of his more colourful strings of curses and was tempted to use them now.

Instead she walked deliberately away from the house in the opposite direction from Father John. She passed the row of ancient camphor trees whose thick foliage prevented grass from growing underneath and carried on. Half an hour later, after following various paths through the vineyards, she found she was near the outbuildings Tony Broselli had shown them during their tour of the estate.

He had told her that the cellars beneath the buildings were used for occasional storage. For what, she wondered. The first building was full of gardening equipment and the only trapdoor she could see was partially covered by a pallet containing bags of fertilizer. If she recalled correctly, the next building was also a repository for garden stuff.

Then there had been two storerooms with very little in them. A quick look confirmed that there was nothing of interest in the first one, and the trapdoor appeared not to have been used for a long time. She was about to move on to the adjacent building when she heard voices.

Florian backed out of the building that had been her next target, carrying one end of what appeared to be a heavy machine. Tony held the other end. They turned in Petra's direction. She pulled back inside and moved away from the door. She hoped they weren't planning to deposit the machine in the storeroom where she was. If they did, she would say she was exploring the estate, which was true.

She let out her breath as the two men passed the door to her building. Then she heard them grunt and put down the machine. Conveniently they had stopped in front of the glassless window set high in the wall. It was covered with a wire mesh screen.

'How far do we have to carry this brute? I've got better things to do.'

'Than help your mother?'

'She's got a worm in her brain.'

'And you don't, Florian?'

'This is the wrong time to take Julia out of the business.'

'Julia won't be out of the business, she'll just be at the other end. The De Witts are what we need. Jacob has the skills and can easily spend six months a year here.'

'Until the rules change, as they will. Visas are already harder to get.'

'All the more reason to do this now. A thirty percent uptick on rough, and no questions asked as to provenance,' Tony said mildly.

'You think your hare-brained scheme will work?' Florian sneered.

'A darn sight better than your feeble attempts to restore a balance in this country. If you did some proper work instead of messing around with that priest and indulging your appetites, you might have some success.'

'You don't get it do you, old man? People with vision are the only ones that count. I have no time for you and your kind. Get one of the bloody slaves to help you with this thing!'

Florian stomped off and for a minute there was silence. Then Petra heard Tony's footsteps moving away. She waited another few minutes before checking that the coast was clear and leaving the storeroom. As she walked back to her bedroom in the lodge, she replayed the conversation in her head. What the hell were the Brosellis involved in?

CHAPTER

17

The slave lodge was well removed from the manor house, the guest accommodation, and the estate's frequently used buildings like the tasting centre and the stables. Father John parked his golf-mobile outside, unlocked the door and went in. The air was cool but stuffy. Reaching up, he opened two small windows and looked around.

At one end of the room stood a rough-hewn table. At the other end, a brown curtain hung wall to wall from brass rings on a wooden rod. In between, he counted six rows of benches and nodded to himself. A few minutes' preparation and everything would be ready.

He checked his watch and went to the door. Florian pulled up in another of the estate's golf carts.

'Where's Julia? You were supposed to bring her.'

'I can't find the bitch. Someone said she felt sick during lunch, but she isn't in her room. She'll show up.'

'She'd better.'

'You can't conduct your charade without her, is that it?' he said with a mocking smile.

'Don't be so antagonistic, my boy. The routine works, you know that. Of course we can do it without her, but she inspires confidence in the others.'

Florian shook off Father John's hand. 'And now she's leaving. Where's the logic in that?'

'It's better than having her turn on us. Go and fetch the group.'

'Don't forget to close the windows.'

Petra brushed her teeth to get rid of the taste of garlic and checked her face in the mirror. She hadn't caught the sun during her morning wander round the estate. A pity Carlo had skipped lunch and gone off on a mission somewhere. She would have to tell him about Tony and Florian later.

She decided to walk to the slave lodge instead of using the transport arranged by Sandrine. On an impulse she took off her cross and put it in the safe. Father John would have no excuse to get too close.

As she approached the lodge, a figure emerged from behind a row of trees. She recognized Julia and waved, but Julia ignored her and went in. Petra followed.

Father John, wearing his standard black robe, was standing in front of a table covered in a red cloth, facing Julia. 'There'll be no way out for you if you refuse. This is your last chance to prove yourself. I guarantee you'll regret it …' His mouth fell open as he spotted Petra standing in the doorway.

He recovered himself quickly. 'Miss Minx, welcome. Miss Broselli, our beautiful bride-to-be, is filled with panic at the thought of what lies ahead. I have been telling her she need not worry. With my help and the help of you all this afternoon, she will do her penance and prove herself worthy to make her marriage vows tomorrow.'

Before Petra could process Father John's words, the door opened and Florian came in leading seven women:

Gina, Betta, Julia's school friend Roz, Ana and Raquel, Pam and Joanna. They broke into smiles when they saw Julia.

'Welcome, ladies, to my humble tabernacle. Please take a seat,' Father John said. 'Julia, our chief penitent, will sit here at the front.'

Petra debated whether to sit near the front where she would be close to the action or at the back which would give her a good overview of the proceedings. She decided on the latter.

Father John positioned himself behind the table in the middle of which stood a carved casket with a domed lid. He opened his arms wide as if to embrace all the women at once and began to speak.

'This is an important afternoon: the prelude to tomorrow's ceremony in which I will unite this young lady, Julia Broselli, and Max De Witt in holy matrimony.' He pointed at Julia's bowed head.

'Julia has come here today to cleanse herself in preparation for tomorrow's sacred rite. To do this she needs you to accompany her on the path of righteousness. I call on you all to give her your complete support and to obey her commands.'

Petra noted that Gina was the only one besides herself who was paying any attention to Father John's carefully scripted words. The others were watching Florian who was letting his eyes move slowly from one girl to the next. He deliberately made eye contact for a few seconds, making each member of the group feel special.

Father John opened the casket, took out what appeared to be an incense burner and began to swing it in a wide arc. The rather sickly smell reminded Petra of her childhood.

Then, as the scent filled the air, she began to detect more complex layers beneath the incense. She closed her eyes and drew a few deep breaths, trying to distinguish the various aromas in the heady mix.

After a few more swings, he handed the incense burner to Florian. He drew himself up to his full height and began to rant like a fire and brimstone priest. 'Who is ready to support Julia? Who is ready to confess? Who is ready to join the true penitents? Are you? What about you? And you?'

With each question, he pointed his finger at one of the girls.

'Many of you, I can see, are ready and willing to take the next step towards enlightenment. Some are still hesitant,' Father John continued with a blazing look at Petra.

Annoyingly, she felt herself blush. *What the hell?*

Gina jumped to her feet. 'I'm ready, Father John.'

'And me, take me!' Betta shrieked, imploring Florian.

Ana and Raquel were next, then Roz. Finally Pam and Joanna stood up. To avoid drawing attention to herself, Petra got to her feet as well. Julia was still sitting with her head bent low.

Father John began to chant in cadence. Florian continued to watch the women and swing the incense burner. The chanting coupled with the repetitive motion of the incense burner and the heavy perfume was becoming hypnotic.

Then Father John started to holler: 'Children of sin, the time has come to cleanse your minds. Look at me. Watch my eyes. You know what guilty pleasures you enjoy. Think of them now, every one of them, food, love, sex … The more you can visualize the objects of your desires and explore in detail the feelings they arouse, the easier it will be to achieve absolution.'

His tone was so melodramatic that Petra found it hard not to laugh. At the same time, the picture of a large box of dark mint chocolates imprinted itself on her brain and she turned the laugh into a cough.

Then unbidden came a series of images like hallucinations as she remembered Romeo and other boyfriends over the years. Yet more thoughts followed – sensual, erotic even – thoughts of swimming naked with Don León in Spain, of responding to James Freedy's advances the previous summer, then of Florian who looked like an angel and could kiss like the devil arousing just the kind of feelings and desires Father John was asking them to evoke. *What the fuck was happening?*

Petra shook her head and sneezed twice. She could have sworn there was a charge in the air that hadn't been there before. Gina appeared to be in a trance; Betta and the rest of the girls were swooning over Florian like groupies at a rock concert. Just as she expected them to storm the stage, Father John took a leather-tipped gavel from his box and turned to strike a heavy brass gong that hung on the wall behind him. The sound reverberated around the room for several minutes.

He swung round with a face like an avenging Fury. 'God has expressed his anger at the nature of your thoughts. Yet he is willing to forgive you through me.' Once again he pointed at Julia. 'Child of sin, arise. Bring these your handmaidens robes of purity that they may enter the fold.'

Petra stared at Father John in disbelief. How much longer was he going to keep up this pantomime? And why was Julia going along with it?

Julia got up and walked down the aisle between the benches. She vanished behind the curtain and reappeared carrying a pile of pale blue robes. As she returned to the front, she handed a robe to each girl. The last one she kept for herself.

When she reached the altar, she put her robe on the bench, crossed her arms and stripped off her T-shirt in one rapid movement. Underneath she was naked. Quickly, she pulled the robe over her head. Then she addressed the group for the first time.

'So that we may receive absolution, take off your sullied garments as I have done.' She spoke in a monotone and kept her eyes fixed on the ground.

Despite the lack of enthusiasm in Julia's voice, the girls shed their tops almost as one. Reluctantly, Petra followed suit. She was wearing her bikini under her clothes, thus denying Father John and Florian even a glimpse of lacy underwear or naked flesh. In any case, she knew that wasn't their game. Power and domination, yes; voyeurism, no.

It wasn't over yet. Father John placed a hand on Julia's shoulder and said, 'Bring your handmaidens to me.'

Like an automaton, Julia reached for the two girls closest to her and pushed them towards the altar. She beckoned to the remaining five who shuffled forward. When all the girls were lined up, she indicated that they should kneel.

To avoid being singled out for special treatment by Father John, Petra hurried to join them. In any case, she wanted to see what the self-styled priest was going to do.

First, he waved his hands over the line of girls and intoned a few words in Latin that he might have borrowed from a traditional Catholic service. Then he approached each one in turn, lifted her up and hugged her to his chest.

Petra was last in line. He picked her up and held her close. A frisson went through her as Florian caught her eye over Father John's shoulder and puckered his lips.

Suddenly Petra had the urge to hoot with laughter. The whole afternoon was a farce.

CHAPTER

18

The Higher Ground tour was into its fourth day. Henny knew because he was counting the hours until he could unload the English girls, Megan and Hilary. Fucking menaces. He wished he'd never set eyes on them at Cape Town Airport. Never had he had so much trouble with a Higher Ground group. *It's not my fault*, he assured himself. He had applied exactly the same principles as on previous tours.

For the first couple of days, he let the girls help him and the South African driver with the chores if they wanted to but didn't insist. He dished out smiles and praise, and kept as calm as he knew how. Then he stepped up the pressure. As soon as he did, it was clear that Megan and Hilary weren't going to play ball.

'We haven't paid good money to work our butts off,' Megan snapped.

'You're the roadie. We'll offer our help if and when we feel like it,' Hilary added.

When they reached the Namibian border, Henny sent the driver back to Cape Town by bus, on the pretext of a family emergency. With no one else to help, they'd have to muck in.

The establishment of a daily routine that would keep tour participants fully occupied was the first step in a carefully orchestrated plan to reduce their independence until they reached a sublime state of subservience to the cause. Henny believed as fervently as the Master that this was the only way to restore hope for the future.

After checking them into the Fish River Canyon campsite, he had called a meeting and spoken to them about teamwork. His plan was to create two teams of three, with Megan and Hilary on different teams. Each team would be given specific tasks.

But Megan and Hilary refused to be separated. He had almost concluded that their bitching and moaning was not worth the advantage to be gained when suddenly they saw the light. Now he realized he had been outsmarted. Instead of two manageable teams, he had two pig-headed team leaders who wouldn't comply, and he couldn't watch both of them at the same time.

As he led the six girls along a narrow trail at the bottom of the canyon, Henny scratched his head. The fifteen days to go before they reached the village where the girls would begin their induction into African tribal life stretched ahead of him like a river flowing endlessly to the sea. For the first time since he had joined Higher Ground, he felt like throwing in the towel.

CHAPTER

19

Carlo was lying on his bed, his arms behind his head.

'Ah, the confessee returns! All sins washed away, I hope,' he said as Petra walked in.

He wrinkled his nose and sniffed like a bloodhound. 'Do I detect cloves, cinnamon, spice? A perfumed candle shop perhaps? No, something more like marijuana with a hint of incense. Am I right?'

'Sometimes, annoyingly, you are.'

'Not always?'

'No, I'd say about fifty percent of the time, but today you've hit the nail on the head. Father John and Florian had an incense burner that definitely contained something much headier than incense. I've just been to one of the weirdest ceremonies ever. You won't believe it.'

'Try me.'

Petra sat on the edge of her bed and launched into a description of Father John's afternoon-long charade. She was conscious how far-fetched it sounded and waited for Carlo to interrupt her with facetious remarks. Instead, he listened intently until she came to the part about Father John lifting up all the girls and embracing them.

'You're blushing, *cara*! Is there something else I should know?'

She had no intention of telling Carlo how Florian had kissed her down at the folly, nor how catching his eye that afternoon had made her feel. Instead she said, 'I'm sure Father John had nothing on under his robe.'

'The old so-and-so!'

'Gina likes him.'

'Does she now? Well, there's no accounting for taste. What happened after that?'

'Florian kept swinging the censer. Father John delivered a few prayers for our well-being, blessed us fervently, proclaimed that our minds were now clean and pure, and that we were ready to take the next step, whatever that means. Julia indicated that we should pick up our clothes. Then she led us behind the curtain to change. At the end it was all very decorous.'

'How did the girls seem?'

'Somewhat subdued and lethargic, maybe embarrassed. There was no excited chatter or discussion of what had happened. I'm feeling tired too. It was a crazily intense experience.'

'What about Julia?'

'As soon as she had changed, she walked straight out the door. Neither Florian nor Father John tried to stop her. Florian drove us all back in the buggy and reminded us not to be late for the rehearsal dinner.'

'So how would you describe the afternoon?'

'Witchcraft and group therapy mixed with sexual suggestion.'

'A bit like my afternoon.'

Something in the way Carlo said the words rang a warning bell in Petra's head.

'Oh?'

'Sandrine hauled you off for your dress fitting this morning then had me help her with a few errands. While we worked, she told me something of her family's history. After that it was nearly lunchtime. I went looking for you at the manor house and found Uncle Tony preparing a speech for tomorrow. I suggested a few improvements, shared a sandwich with him, and tackled him about Julia.'

'Good. What does he think?'

'He agrees that she's been out of sorts for the last few weeks but feels that once she gets away on honeymoon with Max, everything will be OK.'

'Just what I've been saying. Where are they going?'

'To Europe, starting with Italy of course. Sandrine has arranged everything.'

'Why doesn't that surprise me?'

'Right. Now comes the witchcraft part of my story.'

'I'm not sure I want to hear this. I presume Sandrine is the witch.'

'Witch, wizard, and everything in between. She told me one of her forebears built a folly and used to hold candlelit séances there. I was curious and you weren't around, so I borrowed a golf cart and went to see it. It's a strange structure …' Carlo's voice tailed off.

'And?'

'Sandrine said she was going to swim there this afternoon and I figured it might be an opportunity to make her laugh as I promised I would.'

Petra groaned. 'I thought it would be something like that. Carlo, sometimes you're despicable!'

'Not me, *cara*. Somebody beat me to it, although he wasn't making her laugh – at least not until I showed up.'

'What do you mean? Who?'

'Diego.'

'Ugh!'

'My sentiments exactly. A beautiful body like Sandrine's exposed to the ministrations of a Neanderthal. I could hear him grunting as I walked down the ramp.'

'Enough! I don't want to know.'

'You haven't heard the best yet! There she was gloriously naked, lying on her stomach on a stone bench that was covered in a white towel. Diego was concentrating on her buttocks …'

Petra covered her ears.

'No, not like that. I admit he was naked too, but he wasn't doing anything with it. In fact, it seemed rather insignificant. He was busy drawing circles and weird symbols on her backside with a black pen.'

Petra took her hands away from her ears.

'He turned her over and drew circles round her breasts …'

'With his pen?'

'No, with his fingers. Then he clasped his hands together and ran them down to her navel. It was like some sort of ritual. He massaged her stomach and moved on down. That's when Sandrine saw me watching from the archway and shouted at me to join them. In her book, two is better than one.'

Carlo paused. 'I must confess that the whole scene was having an unwanted effect …'

'Wanted, you mean,' Petra muttered.

'No, *cara*. I love sex but not that kind of stuff. I beat a hasty retreat and left them both laughing their heads off at me. So I did succeed in making her laugh, though not in the way I'd anticipated.'

'How will you face them both tonight?'

'Forwards, *cara*, facing forwards, as always.'

CHAPTER

20

On the day of the wedding, Petra woke with a slight headache when a member of Wellington's staff knocked on the door at 7 a.m. She accepted her breakfast tray and set it aside. Carlo twitched and groaned, rolled onto his back and began to snore. *Too much booze at the rehearsal dinner and afterwards.* She tapped his shoulder to shut him up.

Her hair appointment was at 8.30 so she had time for a swim to clear her head. She pulled on her bikini and left Carlo to sleep it off.

The sky was clear with no clouds on the horizon. This early in the morning, the air was cool; so was the pool. Both would warm up quickly once the sun strengthened.

Petra took a deep breath and executed a shallow racing dive which kept the shock to her system to a minimum as she entered the water. She decided on a medley: ten lengths of breaststroke to warm up, twenty lengths of front crawl, thirty of back crawl, twenty of butterfly, and finally ten of sidestroke to cool down. Three-quarters of an hour later, she swam to the shallow end of the pool and climbed the steps to get out. She peeled off her goggles and pushed back her hair.

'Dear, dear! Chlorine in the chief bridesmaid's hair!

Mother's hairdressers will have a fit.' Florian was lying on the sunbed next to where she had placed her towel, wearing a pair of blue and black Speedo briefs.

Petra hadn't realized quite how slim and well-proportioned he was. A Greek god with a wicked tongue.

'I thought you might like a ride,' he continued in a way that brought out the innuendo and made Petra cross.

Carlo's banter she could cope with, Florian was too unsettling. She wondered how long he had been watching her.

'That would be too much,' she said primly, grabbing her towel and wrapping it round her body.

'Too much as in awesome, I agree,' he replied, deliberately batting his eyelashes. 'I'm looking forward to partnering you this afternoon.' In one supple movement he jumped up and nuzzled Petra's ear before she could pull away. 'See you later.'

His touch was enough to set her heart beating rapidly, which made her all the more annoyed. With Florian, with herself – and then with Carlo who, she discovered, had eaten most of her breakfast.

'What is wrong with you guys?'

'Ach, an angry woman is a lovely sight. Watch you don't lose your towel!'

Petra found refuge and fresh coffee at the manor house. Outside, the driveway was full of delivery vans. Sandrine and Tony were both there, directing traffic. Sandrine was like a well-programmed robot: calm, efficient, emotionless. Petra wondered whether sex could ever be more than a mechanical release for her. Or was someone like Diego able to unleash deeply buried desires?

For the bride's father it was a big day. Tony was businesslike but tense, "keyed up" Petra's father would have said. For a moment, she felt sad that he hadn't lived long enough to give her away. Not that that was likely to happen any time soon, if at all.

Sipping her coffee, Petra walked away from the house. Halfway down the drive was a white unmarked van parked the wrong way to everyone else. Whoever was driving it had disappeared and left the back doors open. Inside were stacks of cardboard boxes. Stencilled on the side of the ones Petra could see was a heart-shaped symbol containing the words "Dragées d'Aix". Her eyes lit up. After their fruitless visit to the biscuit factory, she hadn't considered that some might be delivered for the wedding.

If all the boxes contained sugared almonds, there would be more than enough for the number of guests, whatever type of container they were in. If she took one or two, Carlo could look at them while she was being groomed by Sandrine's minions.

Petra glanced up and down the drive. *Damn! Too late.* A lanky young man was walking back towards the van, zipping up his fly. As he drew closer, she recognized him as the warehouseman from the biscuit factory.

She gave him a beaming smile. 'More goodies for the wedding? How was the traffic this morning from Durbanville?'

'Not too bad. It's early.' At first he didn't recognize her. Then his eyes clouded over with suspicion. 'I didn't come from Durbanville.'

'Where did you come from?'

'Miz' Broselli asked me to do a pick-up.'

'From one of her factories?'

'A special order.'

The young man hadn't answered her questions. He slammed the rear doors of the van, climbed into the driving seat and switched on the engine. Petra tapped on the window and leaned on the windowsill when he opened it. A bit of cleavage never hurt.

'Could you take a special order for me? I'll pay you well.'

'No chance. Get out of my way. I've got to turn round.'

'OK, then at least tell me where I can place the order for my friend's wedding in Cape Town.'

He stared back at her. *Time for a new approach.*

'You'd better tell me where these come from, or I'll tell Miz' Broselli what you were doing just now along the side of her driveway. I'm sure she'll approve of that.'

Fear flared in his eyes.

'I don't know.'

'Yes, you do. And look, here she comes! You have about twenty seconds before she gets close.'

'Alaix Imports. In Montagu.' He gunned the engine and Petra stepped quickly away from the van.

Petra burst into the bedroom where Carlo was playing with his phone.

'Guess what!'

'What? You beat the Olympic record for the number of lengths' swim without drowning after a night of revelry. Am I right?'

Petra rolled her eyes. 'No, Carlo, I left the hen-do early – much earlier than you left the stag by the look of you.'

'You missed a really good party!'

'But I found out where Sandrine makes the dragées!'

'Seriously?'

'Yes, unless her warehouseman is leading me up the garden path. But I don't think so. He's afraid of her, and he knows I saw him peeing in her best flowers, so he's eager to help.'

Carlo jumped up and gave Petra a hug. 'Fantastic! Where then?'

'Alaix Imports in Montagu, wherever that is.'

'It's about a hundred kilometres from here. We won't be able to do anything until after tomorrow.'

'What's tomorrow?'

'The post-wedding luncheon, and preparation for our hunting and fishing trip.'

'Yours, maybe, Carlo, not mine. I'm going back to Cape Town.'

'It's all arranged. We're going with Tony to his hunting and fishing lodge on the Orange River. Then we're going to Etosha on safari.'

'Well, unarrange it, at least the first part. As I said, I'm going to Cape Town for a couple of days, to see Vicky. If you pretend you're coming with me, you can go and snoop round Montagu. Then we can meet up later. How's that for a plan?'

Carlo wrinkled his nose. 'It's a plan.'

CHAPTER
21

The spa next to the pool was where Sandrine's personal hairdresser and beautician came to pamper her on a regular basis. For the wedding they had brought reinforcements. By two o'clock, the bridesmaids, the bride, the mother of the groom and Sandrine had to be ready, and everything tidied up and cleared away.

Petra looked resentfully in the mirror at the hairdresser who was teasing her hair into ringlets. When she was on duty or on her beloved boat *Petrushka*, she tied her hair back in a ponytail. At other times, she preferred to wear it loose and down. Occasionally for a function, or if it was really messy, she would wind it up into a chignon. Was it really necessary to be made into something one wasn't for an occasion lasting only a few hours?

Roz and Betta looked equally disgruntled. Roz's short dark hair had been augmented by a hair piece, Betta's blonde locks had been crimped and curled, and her mother was sitting with rollers in her hair under a hood dryer.

Gina came waltzing in with the flower girls. Her eyes widenend when she saw Petra. 'Ringlets?'

'Sandrine's decision.'

'I'm glad I'm not in the wedding party.'

Ouch! Petra wondered if she knew about Diego's involvement with Sandrine while Father John had been staging his irreligious extravaganza. Probably not. And if she did, she might not care.

'Can you tell Julia we're ready for her?' Sandrine's hairdresser asked.

'Sorry, I'm on my way to meet Father John,' Gina replied as if she had read Petra's mind. 'Isn't he a great guy?'

Clearly whatever spell he had cast over Gina the previous afternoon hadn't worn off yet. Usually Petra had a weakness for older men, but Father John made her cringe. He was slick, devious and twisted. Florian at least didn't dissemble.

Petra flinched as the beautician who was doing her pedicure bent her big toe too far forward. A dribble of Scarlet Blaze, the official colour, fell on the towel. The smell of nail varnish permeated the room.

Sandrine poked her head through the door. 'Where's Julia?'

'Not here,' Petra said.

'That girl is never where she's wanted.'

'You mean never where you want her to be,' Petra murmured.

Half an hour later, Petra pleaded to be let outside. The smell was making her head ache again and she'd had enough of female chit-chat: Betta had had an argument with her brother, Roz was sure Florian liked her better than he liked Betta, the flower girls talked incessantly in their high-pitched voices.

'Make sure you stay on the stoep. You'll ruin your nails if you don't.'

Petra was sitting quietly in a chair on the verandah with her eyes closed when a gruff voice interrupted her reverie.

'You're a cop. Go and find her, and find out what the hell's the matter.'

She opened her eyes and looked into Max De Witt's tortured face. He was upset, clearly, but that didn't excuse his peremptory tone.

'You're ordering me to do what exactly?'

'To find Julia, and ask her why she wants to call the wedding off.'

Petra sat up straight. 'How do you know that's what she wants to do?'

'She said so this morning and now nobody can find her.' The groom's face crumpled. 'I'm sorry, I didn't mean to be rude, but …'

Max De Witt had not made much of an impression on Petra over the preceding few days. He had been present without being a player. If anything, she had judged him to be somewhat simple and little more than a convenient match for Julia. In the face of his emotion now, she wondered if he loved the girl.

'All right,' she said, jumping up and ignoring her still tacky toenails. 'I'll do my best. I presume you've checked her bedroom and the rest of the manor house.'

'Several times, and the tasting centre. Nobody's seen her.'

'Where were you this morning when she told you she wanted to call the wedding off?'

Max stared at the ground. 'On the couch in her bedroom.' He reddened and added: 'After the rehearsal dinner last night, we had our stag and hen parties. You were with Julia then, weren't you?'

'For a while. Gina and Roz got us drinking tequila. I figured if I had too much, I'd never be able to get up early this morning. You guys were drinking beer and shots by the pool.'

'Ja, but then Florian and Father John said they'd fetch the girls and we went to the folly. It was all decked out in mini-lights with music and … you know …'

'I can imagine: frolicking, skinny-dipping, more drinking … no wonder Carlo didn't come in till 3 a.m. and couldn't wake up this morning!'

The red on Max's neck deepened and spread. Petra took his arm and led him off the stoep.

'Look, I know how these things go, and how out of hand they can get. But I think there's something you're not telling me. Something that might have a bearing on Julia's state of mind. What is it?'

Max looked as if he was going to die of embarrassment.

'I'm a cop. You said so yourself. There's not much I haven't seen.'

'It was all that stuff, like you said … Thank God the parents weren't there …'

'But Father John was there?'

'Ja, with Gina, then Diego started on Ana, and …'

'Carlo?'

'Paired off with Raquel …'

'What about Florian? Come on, Max, you've got to come clean.'

'The English girls were all over him. He was going from one to the other, fondling, kissing, rubbing against them … Betta too!'

Petra felt a surge of anger as Max described Florian's behaviour.

'He's a wolf in lamb's clothing. I dragged Betta away and told her to be careful, he was using them all, but she started to argue with me. Then …' Max's voice broke. ' … he went after Julia. He grabbed her by the shoulders and pressed his mouth on hers and kept kissing her … he made sure I saw. It was horrible … the best man … oh, God!'

Max was shaking like a jelly. 'I was furious, I couldn't stop myself. I ran across to them and tore them apart and punched him in the stomach.' Light dawned in his eyes. 'Is that why Julia wants to call the wedding off?'

'Maybe. It could be she thinks you have an aggressive streak that she doesn't like.'

'Doesn't she know I love her?'

'You said you were in her room. So you took her to bed?'

'Not like that. We haven't slept together – she wouldn't until after we were married.' A mournful note crept into his voice. 'Now we might not.'

Petra felt a twinge of exasperation. The big ones were often the spineless ones: no stamina except in the wrong circumstances. 'What happened this morning then? What did she say?'

'She woke up and saw me on the couch and yelled at me to get out. She kept repeating, 'It's over, get out, it's over!' She was like a madwoman, so I left.'

'Have you seen Florian this morning? Have you asked him where Julia is?'

Max shook his head.

When Petra had encountered Florian at the pool, he had been his usual cavalier and irritating self. No signs of any malaise as a result of too much alcohol or being punched by Max.

'Go and find Carlo. Tell him what's happening and

start searching the outbuildings and the rest of the estate. Do Sandrine and Tony know?'

'No.' Max's hangdog expression said it all.

'OK. Well, don't say anything yet. I'll do what I can.'

22

Petra kicked off the thin flip-flops the beautician had slipped onto her feet and ran through the gardens to the stables. Julia could be anywhere on or off the estate, but Petra had a hunch that she would have gone back to the scene of last night's fracas. It depended how she felt about Florian. If Julia, the victim, had feelings for her "captor", she would definitely have gone back there.

One of the estate's golf carts was parked outside the stables. Florian's black stallion was in his stall, Sandrine's mare had gone. The stallion whinnied when he saw Petra. After tossing his head a few times, he let her rub his nose. Like his master, he was a beautiful beast with power and grace and a big mean streak. In Florian's case, that mean streak might prevent his stepsister's marriage.

Petra released the brake on the golf cart. She wished she had been at the after-party; then she might have understood better what had happened. It seemed that Max – the protective brother – had removed Betta from Florian's clutches and Florian had retaliated, deliberately and nastily. The effect on Max had been predictable. Yet however scandalous Florian's behaviour had been, it wasn't incestuous. Julia wasn't Florian's sister or even half-sister.

Something else had crept into the equation. Did Max think Julia was responding to Florian's advances?

Stag and hen parties seemed to bring out the worst in everyone. Sandrine would be furious if she knew how her carefully planned event was being sabotaged. The best outcome would be if Petra could find Julia and talk sense into her before Sandrine and Tony found out.

Sandrine's mare was tied up outside the folly. She laid her ears back when Petra drew up in the golf cart but calmed down when Petra whispered endearments. In spite of her efforts to block them, memories of the mad gallop with Florian and his assault on her mouth came flooding back. She could well imagine Julia being unable to resist yet she had given no hint that she liked Florian the way most girls did.

Petra walked down the covered passageway to the folly, thinking quickly. A party such as Max had described would leave plenty of evidence: empty bottles and glasses, pieces of lost or discarded clothing, other detritus. She ducked as she went through the archway, as if she were entering an evil place with dark secrets.

She emerged into bright sunlight. As her eyes adjusted, she saw that the folly was exactly the same as it had been on her first visit. There was no indication that it had been used for a party. Even the mini-lights had been taken down. According to Max, Sandrine had not been present, but her staff must have known about it and come early to clean up.

Petra sat down on one of the stone benches in a patch of sunlight. The folly was just what its name suggested: an ornamental building, whimsical and costly with no practical purpose. But the word was also used to denote foolishness or a lack of good sense. Last night, in that place, the two had come together to cause who knew what mischief.

Petra stood up and looked around carefully. There was no sign of Julia. She began to walk towards the shadowy recesses behind the pool. If someone was trying to hide from the bright light of day, they would almost certainly be in the grotto. The water looked cool and curiously inviting with a silvery sheen. It was about a metre deep, maybe a bit more, and uniformly so: deep enough for playing around, and plenty deep enough to drown in as Petra well knew from her years in the Royal Canadian Mounted Police's Marine Unit.

She shook off grim memories and studied the pool area again. The mini-lights would have been wound round the pillars and statues, the music seeping from hidden speakers and echoing round the chamber. The curved steps at either end of the pool would make it easy to enter and exit the water gracefully.

Suddenly she had a vision of a parade of naked women entering the water at one end, sinking down and keeping the water swirling around them, then rising up in the middle to display their bare breasts as an invitation for men to join them. Is that what Julia and her friends had been doing last night under the influence of alcohol … drugs … who knew what?

'*Tabarnak*! What's the matter with me?' Petra cried. 'I must be going mad! There's nobody here.'

She cast her eyes over the statues. Water gushed from the dwarf's trio of penises. Did Tony Broselli know the story about Florian's great-grandfather? As he was the family historian, he must do.

A shaft of sunlight hit the streams of water and

something broke into rainbow colours. Julia's diamond engagement ring had been placed on the centre penis. The ring was wet and Petra nearly dropped it, but finally she held it up like a trophy.

'You have been here but where are you now?' she whispered, slipping the ring onto the middle finger of her right hand.

'Long gone, I fear.'

Petra spun round. Father John stepped into view, clad in a black robe, his hair a tousled mane about his face. He spread his hands and adopted a humble look. 'Our Lord works in mysterious ways.'

What about you? Petra said to herself. And who exactly is your lord? What are you doing for him?

She wanted to challenge Father John there and then, force him to admit that there was a deeper purpose behind everything that was happening, but a glance into his eyes told her that now was not the time. She had classed him as a suspect in a crime that had no substance, no motive, and no means of discovery – not yet. Interrogating suspects too early gave them the opportunity to cover their tracks.

So instead of a targeted attack, all she said was: 'Gone where?'

'To have her hair and nails done.' The answer came from behind her.

'What?' Petra stared at Florian. Father John threw him a surprised glance.

'I'm not joking. I found the stupid cow mooning about in here so I took her back where she belongs. Let's go, Sandrine's waiting. I'll take the mare.'

CHAPTER

23

'Thanks to you, we're running late,' Sandrine said accusingly as Petra re-entered the spa. 'And you've ruined your pedicure. It'll have to be done again.' She waved one of the beautician's over. 'Sit here. I can't imagine what got into you.'

'If only you knew,' Petra muttered.

Instead of sitting, she walked over to Julia. Her mousy brown hair had been shampooed and trimmed and was being blow-dried in a simple bob. In the mirror, her face was an inscrutable white mask.

'I found your ring.'

Julia's eyelids fluttered. After a second's pause, she said: 'Was it in the tasting centre? I thought I'd left it there. I spent a lot of time looking for it this morning.'

Petra nodded. *And we for you*. 'Here you are.'

The big diamond glittered as Julia slid it onto the fourth finger of her left hand where it fitted perfectly. She looked at it for a moment then turned away. 'Cinderella will be ready for the ball,' she murmured.

Carlo led Max into the tasting centre where pre-wedding drinks and snacks were being served to the guests who had been bused in from Cape Town. Wellington had tipped them that Julia had been found, but the groom was still acting like a baby.

Carlo escorted him over to the bar and asked for two beers.

'Shape up, man. You're marrying my cousin, don't forget. Tough stock the Brosellis. You never met Julia's mother, but she was a good egg.'

'A good egg?'

'Indeed. Never floated to the top to become flotsam or jetsam as a bad egg would.'

Max looked bemused.

'We Brosellis have an unusual sense of humour. You'll get used to it. How about your family? You're Belgian, aren't you?'

'Yes, although my mother's family is from Amsterdam.'

'How did you meet Julia?'

Max looked surprised at the question. 'Through a friend of my father's.'

'I gather you're taking Julia to Europe. Will you live in Belgium?'

'No, Amsterdam. That's where I work.'

'What do you do?'

'I'm a customs broker and freight forwarder.'

'That must be good business – Schiphol's a very busy airport.'

Max shrugged. 'I make a living.'

Carlo glanced at the nondescript watch he had brought to South Africa with him, then at the diamond-studded Rolex on Max's left wrist. 'I'm sure you do. Come on, it's time to be thrown to the lions. Oops, what am I saying? A good job you're not going on honeymoon to a game park.'

Tony Broselli looked as nervous as a teenage boy on his first date despite the fact that by Sandrine's standards, it was a small wedding. He exhaled deeply as Carlo arrived with Max.

'Cheer up, Uncle! Where's the second-best man? I'm the first, of course.'

'Florian's gone to check on the bridesmaids.'

'Why didn't I think of that?'

'Here he comes,' Max said, with a grimace. He ran a finger under his collar to detach it from his skin. 'With Father John.'

Father John was wearing a white robe and a black scarf embroidered with gold motifs draped over his shoulders. He clapped Tony on the back and made the sign of the cross. Then he went to stand under the rose arbour next to a small table covered with a white cloth on which lay a black leather-bound book.

A ripple went through the assembled guests as Florian, dazzling in his white jacket and black trousers, joined Max and Carlo in the arbour.

'I presume you've got the ring, buddy,' Carlo said.

'Naturally.' Florian dipped a hand into his top pocket and brought out a simple gold band which he immediately put to his lips.

Max's face turned a deeper shade of red.

'Cut the crap, Florian,' Carlo snarled. 'Or I'll beat the shit out of you!'

'My, my, tempers are high. Julia has my blessing. I'm sure Max here will take care of her once she's left the fold, won't you, Max?'

Max's face was purple. Carlo grabbed his arm.

'You'll soon be shot of him. Here she comes.'

The horse-drawn carriage conveying the bride and bridesmaids drew up as the first bars of Mendelssohn's Wedding March drifted across the rose garden. Wearing a short magenta dress that clung in all the right places and a white wide-brimmed hat, Sandrine was waiting at the entrance to the garden with Tony and a footman to help them out of the carriage. She fussed around Julia, straightening her headdress and rearranging the veil that obscured her face. Tony dropped a kiss on top of his daughter's head and held out his arm.

Petra had been instructed to keep two paces behind Julia to leave room for her train. The two flower girls would follow; Betta and Roz would bring up the rear. The little girls were by turns giggly then solemn, reminding Petra of Megan and Hilary. She wondered how they were getting on and how far into their Higher Ground tour they were.

Julia should not have been wearing what she was Petra realized, as she walked behind her up the aisle between the rows of wedding guests. Unlike Sandrine's magenta number, Julia's cream lace concoction clung in all the wrong places. The bow neck emphasized her broad shoulders and the cap sleeves did nothing to hide the thickness of her upper arms. The train springing from the centre back of the dress added weight round her middle where she didn't need it. Sandrine was not such a good wedding planner if she had allowed the bride to choose that dress, unless she deliberately wanted Julia to look dumpy and unattractive. And if that were the case, what was her motive? Something to do with Florian?

Petra added these questions to the long list she had already compiled in her mind, stubbing her toe as she bumped against the first step up to the arbour. Sandrine waved her back. The bridesmaids didn't climb the steps but waited at the bottom while Father John conducted the ceremony. There was room in the arbour only for the bride's father, the bride, the groom and the best man. Florian had his back to the audience yet still managed to turn his head, causing another ripple to run through the crowd.

'Too gorgeous to be true,' Petra murmured crossly with an annoying twinge of something she was reluctant to identify.

Mercifully Father John kept the ceremony brief. He made no reference to the kind of things he had eulogized the previous afternoon: purity, ritual cleansing, sacred vows. Instead, he gave a five-minute pep talk on the importance of procreation then asked if anyone objected to the marriage. Nobody did, though Florian rolled his eyes for the crowd.

Following the exchange of vows, Florian produced the ring, and Max and Julia were pronounced man and wife. Julia lifted her veil just enough for Max to brush her cheek with his lips. By four o'clock, the ceremony was over and Petra was ravenous.

She smiled into the video camera wielded by the photographer's assistant and half-hoped the clouds that had moved in would encourage the photographer to cut the posing for formal pictures short. He was agonizing over background and camera angles, shouting and bullying the bridal party as he pulled them into position, trying to impress Sandrine. She gave him free rein until he made a fatal mistake that delighted Petra. He called her Sandy. The effect was instantaneous.

Sandrine clapped her hands. 'Right, everybody. We

have enough pictures. Drinks are being served on the pool terrace. Wellington will show you the way.'

With a sigh of relief, Petra moved away from the bridal party to look for Carlo. She felt a hand on her waist and spun round.

'Love the ringlets and the flowers,' Florian said, twisting his other hand into her long dark hair where the hairdresser had sown a few white daisies.

Petra's stomach lurched. Beneath her dress, between her breasts in the underwired bra, hung her black and silver cross. It would be so tempting to pull it out, reveal its secret, and use it to repel his advances – if she could. She knew better than to underestimate Florian's strength and determination. His beauty bordered on the effeminate, but his body was lithe and muscular. And part of her that she couldn't always control was responding in a most irresponsible and unladylike way.

Not for the first time, Florian seemed to change his mind. He withdrew his hands and walked across to where Roz and Betta were holding on to the two flower girls. He squatted down in front of the group.

'Tinkerbell and Sweet Pea, my Fairy Princesses!' He lifted the hand of the four-year-old to his lips and kissed it, then the hand of her five-year-old cousin. 'Prince Florian, at your service.'

The little girls giggled uncontrollably, adoration lighting up their faces.

CHAPTER

24

Petra walked into the marquee and grudgingly admitted to herself that Sandrine had staged a fine wedding. The food looked scrumptious, and whether by accident or design, she had devised an innovative table plan that should prevent any bad scenes between the bridal couple and Florian.

Instead of the usual long head table seating the bridal party, she had placed two round tables for eight in the centre of the marquee. The first was reserved for herself, Father John, Tony, Julia, Max, and three of the De Witts: Marina, Jacob and Betta. Florian had been assigned to the second table with Petra, Roz, Gina, Diego, Raquel, Carlo and Ana.

Although she was sitting on Florian's left, Petra hoped he would pay more attention to Roz and Gina on his right. Carlo was lolling back in his chair, keeping an arm round the shoulders of Raquel and Ana.

Petra looked across to Sandrine's table. Betta had her eyes fixed on Florian. Julia had taken off her veil and appeared serene but not smiling. Father John was laughing at a private joke with Sandrine.

Petra had been to several Italian weddings in Canada so it was no surprise when Carlo stood up and banged his spoon against his wine glass, shouting 'The bride and groom, the bride and groom!' Other guests joined in until the glasses rang. The din would only end when Julia and Max kissed. Eventually they did. After the third or fourth time, Julia seemed to relax and even enjoy the attention.

During a quiet interlude, Petra put down her spoon and patted her stomach. The last mouthful of guava cheesecake had been a stretch. Coffee would be next, then the speeches. That would give her time to digest before the dancing.

Florian caught her off guard. Standing up, he banged his spoon against his glass and yelled 'The bride and groom – and the best man and the bridesmaids!'

Petra shied away but he was too quick. He grabbed her and kissed her with such an exquisite combination of strength, passion and expertise that she was unable to put up a fight. Betta ran across the floor and dragged at Florian's arm. Then it was Roz's turn. Petra could see by the demonic gleam in his eyes that he loved every minute of it … the adulation, the spectacle, the power. If Sandrine was jealous of her blue-eyed boy's success with women, she wasn't showing it. She was watching with a smile on her face, but Petra would have wagered that it didn't reach her eyes.

Florian rose to his feet again, his glass ringing. Petra pushed back her chair, ready to flee. She breathed a sigh of relief when he focussed his attention on the centre table. Carlo caught her eye and winked.

'Ladies and Gentlemen, friends, relatives and guests, as the best man here and the de facto master of ceremonies, I have the honour of saying a few words about my good friend Max who has today plighted his troth to the lovely

Julia. I know I should make you laugh by telling you stories about Max's adolescent escapades and Julia as a chubby teen or by letting out some of the secrets all families have, but I'm going to break from tradition. I have too much respect for Max and Julia to embarrass them in front of you all. However, I do want to say something about my dear stepsister Julia and apprise you of ways in which, like her, you can help this beautiful country of ours to fulfill its destiny.'

What a nerve. Julia had gone chalk white and Petra was afraid she might faint.

'First of all, I want to thank Julia for the work she has done in spreading the word about Father John's outreach programmes which are bringing change to African villages. Over the past few years, she has devoted herself to the cause and allowed us to introduce many more people to our schemes. Of course we rely heavily on donations and volunteers, and I want to thank too my dear mother, Sandrine, and my stepfather, Tony, for their contributions.

At Italian weddings, it is customary not only to make a lot of noise,' he continued, banging his spoon against his glass again, 'but also to dance with abandon. During the dancing, it is also customary to stuff money into the pockets, cleavages, etc. of the bridal couple or to pin bank notes to their clothing. Those who prefer the more decorous approach will find a dish of pins in the centre of each table. In any event, Julia has decreed that all the money collected tonight will be donated to the African villages that we and Father John support. So be generous, my friends, and have fun! To the bride and groom!'

After the toast, there was a round of applause. Florian took a 5,000 Rand note out of his jacket pocket. He held it up for everyone to see then marched across to give it to Julia. For a moment, Petra feared he was going to stuff it down the front of her dress and cause a scene. Instead he presented it to Max with a flourish, as if he were repaying a debt.

Petra leaned across the table to speak to Carlo. 'Isn't it amazing how he can say so much so convincingly without giving any real information? I'd like to know exactly how the money is going to be spent. Have you any idea?'

'I know Tony and Sandrine support charity work in the north of the country as well as in Namibia, but that's it. If you want details, you'll have to ask the man himself.'

Raquel nudged Carlo's arm. 'Ana and I have decided to go and work in one of the villages.'

'To do what?'

'Anything we can to help. But first, we're going to travel around. Florian has a friend who runs tours that combine sightseeing and volunteer work.'

Petra leaned closer. 'Do you know who he is or the name of the company?'

'Not yet. Florian's bringing us more information tomorrow.'

Petra made a mental note to talk to Ana and Raquel again in the morning. It could be just a coincidence, but it sounded suspiciously like what Megan and Hilary were doing.

'Thank you,' she said as Wellington placed a plate of petits fours on the table then disappeared. When he returned, he was carrying a pile of heart-shaped silver tins. He gave one to each person at the table. Petra studied hers then looked questioningly at him.

'What's this, Wellington?'

'A special gift from the bride's mother – pardon me, I mean stepmother – to say thank you to all our guests, especially our visitors from overseas. I believe the tin contains sugared almonds.'

'The elusive dragées!' The top of Petra's tin was decorated with sparkling stones set in a random pattern. The centre stone was bright red. Carlo's tin was similar, except that the centre stone was blue. He turned the tin over and read the paper label pasted on the bottom:

'Dragées d'Aix, S.A. Alaix Imports, Montagu, Cape.'

'It looks as though my informant was telling the truth,' Petra said. 'Are you still going to go to Montagu?'

'Yes, to find out who is behind Alaix. It could be Delapore. Either way, I need to know.'

'Are you going travelling too?' Raquel asked. 'Why not come with us?'

Carlo patted her arm. 'I have some business to attend to then I'm going fishing with Uncle Tony. But Petra and I might see you in Etosha, if you're going that far.'

'We don't know where we're going yet – we're in the hands of the Gods.'

The harpist who had played throughout the meal was replaced by a band. Max and Julia were first on the dance floor. Sandrine and Tony joined them, then Tony danced with Julia and Sandrine with Max. With a quickening pulse, Petra knew what would happen next: Florian would claim his dance with the chief bridesmaid. She refused to let him catch her unawares again and was determined not to be seen as another of his conquests.

Years ago, waiting outside an art gallery, she had noticed a group of at least twenty young women all holding toddlers by the hand and nearly all pregnant. With the group were three men. She had sworn then that she would never stand in line to receive a man's favours.

Right now though, she was first on Florian's list. He advanced on her like a duellist claiming his prize. She steeled herself to show no response to his touch. The band, in what seemed like the far distance, was playing another waltz.

When he took her hand and put an arm round her waist, she locked her elbows and kept her muscles rigid. Then she looked up into his face and batted her eyelashes. 'You stay in your space and I'll stay in mine.'

Florian the demi-god wasn't sure what to do. Petra chuckled to herself. He tried again to close the gap between them. Then he tried to bend down to place his lips on hers.

'Uh uh, don't even think about it!'

He cocked his head and regarded her coolly.

'And I thought you were a hot one.'

'Let's just say you were wrong.'

'Never. I'll prove it to you.'

There was no point continuing the dialogue. Petra pirouetted out of reach and was immediately replaced by Joanna.

An hour later, Sandrine interrupted the band and addressed the guests who were on the dance floor and at the tables.

'Ladies and Gentlemen, I'd just like to say a final few words. First of all, thank you for coming to share Julia and Max's special day. We are very grateful to you for having made the effort, especially our visitors from overseas, and hope you will take away many happy memories as well as the keepsake tins of dragées. Thank you too for your generous donations to our charitable activities. Julia and Max will be leaving shortly, so I'd like all the bridesmaids to come forward for the throwing of the bride's bouquet.'

Oh crikey, she'd forgotten that. Petra grimaced as Carlo crossed his index fingers and said, 'Make sure you catch it. Then you'll be next!'

'I don't want to be next.'

Petra hung back as much as she dared. At the last minute she decided that was the worst place to stand and moved closer.

Sandrine tied a gauze scarf over Julia's eyes and spun her round two and a half times until she was facing away from the bridesmaids. Julia threw her bouquet over her shoulder, straight into Petra's face. In a reflex action, Petra caught the damn thing and stood looking at it in horror. Julia pulled the scarf from her eyes.

'If you're lucky, you'll be able to escape too,' she said.

25

Petra was suffocating. There was a hand over her mouth and a weight on top of her. She struggled to break free.

'Shh, shh,' Carlo said. 'You're all right. I'm going to let go, but I want you to stop making noises and writhing.'

'What are you doing to me?' Petra shouted.

'I'm not doing anything. Someone else must have been doing something in your dreams.'

'What do you mean?'

'I don't know, *cara*, but I have my suspicions. The gallant Florian, perhaps? Like the other night?'

'No way, Mercutio.' Petra hesitated. 'What kind of noises?'

'If I tell you, you'll blush.'

Petra closed her eyes.

'Don't pretend you're falling asleep. Florian's on the lookout for a mate, and you caught Julia's bouquet, remember?'

A vision of pink carnations, white roses and blue forget-me-nots entered Petra's head. 'I can't believe I did that!'

'It obviously gave you ideas. And Florian looked delighted.'

'Stop it, Mercutio. I made it clear to Florian last night that I'm not in the least bit interested.'

'Nature will have her way.'

'In any case, I'm sure Florian isn't looking for a mate. At least, not just one. He has so many good-looking women in love with him that he can have as many as he wants.'

'Except you.'

'Exactly. Except me.'

Petra watched Sandrine directing the staff who were clearing the last tables away from the pool deck. She was like a driver whipping his horses to get the last ounce of effort out of them. The only concession to her guests' general exhaustion after the week's round of excursions and parties was that breakfast was an hour later.

Petra filled a mug with black coffee, picked up a cranberry muffin and walked across the lawn to sit under the old oak tree. This was where she had found Julia on Thursday night and where Julia had been going to confide in her until Florian suddenly stepped out of the shadows. Since then, she had had no opportunity to speak quietly to Julia again. Now the newly weds were safely on their honeymoon, no doubt on their way to Europe after a night in Cape Town – at the Mount Nelson Roz had said.

Petra realized she had always thought of Julia's wedding as a destination wedding, but it wasn't – not in the way youngsters used the term to denote a wedding in an exotic location not home to either the bride or the groom. In this case Max was Belgian and Julia was South African, even if her parents had come from Italy, so it was logical that the wedding should be held here.

For Petra, though, it was a destination, and a chance in a lifetime to visit a country about which she knew little. She had learned something about the politics from Carlo, and her experiences during the week had shown that a lot of people, from inside and outside the country, were willing to donate time, money and effort to help make South Africa a better place. But somehow it all sounded rather futile – and rather fishy. Exactly how the Brosellis, Delapores and Father John intended to turn their noble ideals into reality, she didn't know.

Out of the corner of her eye she saw Florian making his way from the stables towards the terrace, carrying some papers. She shrank back under the tree, not yet ready to face him and deal with the barbed comments he would doubtless make. Carlo could be infuriating – especially when he teased her mercilessly as he had over the bouquet – but that was easier to cope with than Florian's conceit.

Petra drained the last of her coffee. A couple of days on her own in Cape Town would give her time to regroup. Carlo was going to leave her at the Waterfront, go to Montagu and come back on Monday or Tuesday to pick her up. They planned to rent a camper van and head first to Tony Broselli's hunting and fishing lodge, then to Namibia.

Tony had been surprised when Petra told him she enjoyed fishing as well as boating. Many women didn't, he said.

Thinking of fishing, Petra remembered her last fishing trip. It had been in the Bahamas, aboard the yacht belonging to Betty Graceby, the legendary Canadian singer and ex-Vegas dancer. Betty had invited Petra and her friend Martin to accompany her on a pilgrimage to Santiago de Compostela in Spain. Martin had accepted, but Petra had already made a commitment to Carlo to attend Julia's wedding. Right now, Martin would be with Betty's group in Spain.

For a moment, Petra wished Martin were with her in South Africa instead of Carlo. The week had been so filled with tension that his calm approach and journalist's nose might help her make sense of it all. And she could do with a little TLC. She'd had enough of whiz-kids like Florian and Carlo. Martin would look after her, pamper her, bring her coffee or wine depending on the time of day, make her feel whole again …

She woke to find Carlo easing the coffee mug out of her hand and replacing it with a rolled-up brochure.

'Everyone says goodbye.'

Petra blinked. 'What? Why?'

'The wedding celebrations are officially over.' Carlo looked at his watch. '12 noon. Sandrine and Tony are leaving for the north. The contingents from Rome and Florence are on their way to the airport. Father John has taken Gina to visit his inner-city projects. The others have departed,' he said, counting off on his fingers.

'But I wanted to speak to Ana and Raquel!'

'Too late. Your boyfriend has loaded them into a mini-van, along with Pam, Joanna and Diego. They're off to see the Wizard.'

'What wizard?'

'Didn't you ever watch The Wizard of Oz?'

Petra nodded. 'It scared me.'

'This is from your boyfriend. It'll scare you too,' Carlo said, tapping the brochure.

Petra unrolled it slowly. The exhortations jumped off the page:

The dark continent needs you to create light!
Dedicate your life to restoring balance!
Make your contribution now before it is too late!

She turned the brochure over. At the bottom of the page in the centre were the words Higher Ground Community Interchange, followed by a Post Office Box number in Stellenbosch and an email address.

'Dare I look inside?'

'I suggest you leave it for later. Our transport awaits.'

26

The white limousine pulled up in front of the Vredehof Manor House. The driver loaded their luggage and Petra climbed gratefully into the back seat beside Carlo. The leather was soft and inviting and she fancied she would be fast asleep within seconds.

At the last minute, Wellington came down the steps holding two carrier bags.

'These are for you, Miss Petra, Mr. Carlo. Miz' Broselli sent them in case she doesn't see you again before you leave South Africa. She said to please pack them in your luggage and take them home to give to your families. You're flying to Geneva, I understand, before you go on home.'

Petra nodded. 'Yes, Carlo lives in Milan and I live in Sudbury, Ontario. That's not too far from Toronto, in Canada,' she added when she saw the look of incomprehension in Wellington's eyes. 'We have a good friend in Geneva.'

'You can give him one too,' Wellington said with a twinkle. 'Miz' Broselli is spoilin' you.'

The bags were full of keepsake tins of dragées.

'We've got enough to sell and make a small fortune,

I reckon,' Petra joked as she counted the tins after saying goodbye to Wellington.

'I'll certainly be able to take a close look at one, and pass one on to the guy who asked me to investigate,' Carlo said.

'I'm surprised there's no engraved date and names, nothing to relate them to Julia and Max's wedding. But that's lucky in a way. It means I can give one to Vicky Dunlin, and maybe Mrs. Pinderally.'

'At that rate, the tins will be gone before we know it.'

'How long before we get to Cape Town?' Petra asked.

'An hour maybe, but it depends on traffic. It is Sunday afternoon.'

Once they left the wine-tasting areas and reached the N2, the limousine sped along. Both Petra and Carlo closed their eyes. Petra opened hers with a jerk when the driver braked hard to avoid a young man who was dodging the cars to cross the road. 'He'll be lucky to make it! Why doesn't he use the footbridge?'

'He must be late for his plane,' Carlo said, waving his hand at the airport entrance sign.

'Hah, hah! Which reminds me ...'

'Oh, no!'

'Yes. You've never explained why you weren't at the airport to meet me last week. You said you'd tell me later. Now is later.'

Petra never forgot anything completely, that Carlo knew. He drew in a long breath.

'Right. Are you sitting comfortably? Then I'll begin. As you know, a few days before I was supposed to meet you here, I flew to Dubai for an International Police Conference. The morning I was due to pick you up at the airport, I was still in Dubai.'

'I thought your conference finished the day before.'

'So did I. There was a last-minute extension. A Dutchman – a gemologist and specialist in the diamond trade – flew in to give a talk on international diamond smuggling. There's a lot of concern that the Kimberley Process isn't working as well as it was.'

'I thought all diamond trading was done through De Beers.'

'It used to be. Then countries started objecting to the monopoly and De Beers lost a very big lawsuit. But of course, they didn't want to lose the control they'd had over the industry. Somebody came up with a new idea and in 2003, the Kimberley Process Certification Scheme was implemented.'

'What's that?'

'It's a voluntary scheme whereby member states agree to put in place national legislation and institutions, as well as export, import and internal controls.'

'The object being?'

'To prevent the trafficking of rough diamonds to finance terrorist activities, so-called "blood diamonds". All international shipments of rough diamonds must be accompanied by a Kimberley Process certificate guaranteeing that the diamonds are "conflict free". And Kimberley Process member states can only legally trade with other protocol participants.'

'So essentially those participants control the diamond trade.'

'Yes. Kimberley Process members account for something like 99.8% of the global production of rough diamonds.'

'I'd say it works then!'

'Most of the time it does. But there's been an increase

in illicit diamonds with no certificate of origin appearing on the market. That's what this guy came to talk about. And that's why I wasn't at the airport to meet you. I flew in later that afternoon.'

'Hmm.'

Suddenly she sat bolt upright. 'Talking of diamonds, there's something you need to know. I forgot all about it until now.' She threw him a warning look. 'No banter, Mercutio. Let me finish. This might be important.

The morning before the wedding, that slimy bastard Father John inveigled his way into my fitting for my bridesmaid's dress. To get away from him afterwards, I walked to the outbuildings we visited with Tony on the day we arrived. While I was exploring, I saw Tony and Florian carrying a heavy machine. They didn't see me – I managed to hide in an empty storeroom – but I did overhear a very interesting conversation.'

'Go on.'

'Florian said it was the wrong time to take Julia out of the business. Tony replied that she would just be at the other end, whatever that means. Then he said Jacob De Witt has the skills they need and could spend six months a year here. But here's the real nugget,' she said triumphantly. 'A thirty percent uptick on rough, and no questions asked as to provenance. Those were Tony's words. Given what you just told me, it sounds as though he could have been talking about diamonds.'

Carlo gave a long whistle. 'It sure does. Cut diamonds are about thirty percent more valuable than rough stones, and they don't need a certificate of origin. The De Witts come from Antwerp and Amsterdam, prime diamond cutting and trading centres.'

'And Julia's going to live in Amsterdam which puts her at the other end of the business!' Petra reflected for a few moments. 'I have a feeling there's more than one business involved though. Florian called it a hare-brained scheme, and Tony was quite volatile in his reply. 'A darn sight better than your feeble attempts to restore a balance in this country,' he said. Then he ranted on about Florian indulging his appetites. What do you make of that?'

'Let me turn that around. What do you make of it? You've had more dealings with Florian than I have.'

Petra felt the tell-tale blush rise in her cheeks. However hard she tried to control her emotions, the Polish-Italian gene pool had left her with a fatal flaw. 'Florian can charm a snail out of its shell. If he started a youth movement and insisted that everyone shave their heads and wear blue robes, the girls – and boys – would be flocking to join.'

'Boys too? You think Florian likes boys?'

'It's possible, but I would guess that if there's a sexual element, it's more likely to be latent – like when you're a teenager and you have a crush on someone who is a magnificent specimen of your own kind. Florian's magnetism is so powerful that he can attract anybody he wants. He has the ability to make you feel as though you're the only one he's talking to even if he's addressing a crowd.'

'What about the ones he doesn't want to attract?' Carlo asked.

'I suspect that behind the alluring façade lies a ruthless dictator. He will eliminate anybody he doesn't want in his entourage unless they can be useful to him. Like Julia. He used her to manipulate Max.'

'What about Father John? The things you've said about Florian could apply equally well to him, couldn't they?'

'Not really. First of all, he doesn't have the charisma Florian does. He relies on his position and his rhetoric, plus a few underhand tricks of the trade, to exert influence. During his confessional the other afternoon, the only person lusting after the dear Father and not Florian was Gina. God knows why! In my book, he's sneaky, creepy, physically repulsive …'

'So how does he fit into the picture? Sandrine seems to think he walks on water.'

'There must be something in the past we don't know about …' Petra said.

'There are lots of things we don't know about. We need to investigate the almond factory, Jacob De Witt, your friend Father John, and the rest. The list is getting longer by the minute.'

CHAPTER

27

Petra hurried to the Cape Sands Hotel. A lengthy delay
caused by an accident on the N2 meant that it was now
nearly four o'clock. The spa reception area was deserted.
The desk was tidy and the glossy magazines arranged in
neat rows on a table near the window. Petra tried the door
in the wall that led to the treatment and relaxation rooms.
Damn! It was locked.

If it hadn't been for the accident, she'd have arrived
in time to find out whether Vicky Dunlin was back after
her working holiday or, if she wasn't in, to determine
her schedule. Not that the staff had been particularly
helpful on her last visit. The only person who seemed
to know anything about the girl was the expansive Mrs.
Pinderally … who just might be a hotel guest.

Crossing her fingers, Petra made her way to the main
lobby. The junior clerk on duty at Reception clearly had
not heard the name before. She checked her computer and
threw Petra a look of regret.

'I'm so sorry. We have no guests by the name of
Pinderally. Could she be with someone else?'

*Of course she could. Or she could be anywhere in Cape Town
or not in the city at all. And why were people always sorry?*

Petra sighed and decided to spare the receptionist, who was trying her best. She turned away from the desk with a curt 'Thank you', walked across the hall and stood looking at the schooners lying at anchor in Table Bay in the massive painting on the wall.

Frustration was part of every investigation. '*You'd better get used to it,*' the RCMP instructor had told his class of raw recruits. '*And ignore the temptation to give up. The more you think laterally about a problem, the quicker the solution will present itself.*'

Petra stared through the finely drawn rigging and began to think. Mrs. Pinderally was a creature of habit: three massages a week plus the body cocoons. She didn't look as though she travelled far. So if she wasn't a hotel guest, perhaps she lived in one of the apartment buildings surrounding the marina.

'Mrs. Pinderally lives on her boat.'

The low whisper came from a white-gloved steward wearing a white turban who pressed an orange-coloured drink into Petra's hand as she spun round to face him.

'On her boat? You know Mrs. Pinderally?'

'Yes, Miss. I'm sorry, Miss, I heard you asking at Reception about her.'

'I'm glad you did! How can I get in touch with her? Where is her boat?'

'It's here in the marina. *Scheherazade*. Follow me. We take Mrs. Pinderally the tea every Sunday at 4.15.'

Petra fell in behind the turbaned steward and a couple of lackeys carrying trays laden with finger sandwiches, scones, strawberry jam and cream, a silver teapot and a small dish of lemon slices. The cucumber slices were probably in the sandwiches.

Scheherazade, a sleek tri-deck motor yacht, was moored along the dock wall conveniently close to the hotel. A wide boarding ladder with double handrails led at a shallow angle from the dock to the yacht's main deck. The steward and his lackeys carried their loads effortlessly up the ladder and onto the boat.

'Come!' bade the steward, stepping onto the aft deck and turning to face the tinted aft doors. They opened as if he had said a magic word.

Petra followed him into the vast salon. The décor was minimalistic and monochrome – a far cry from the gaudy Eastern draperies, gold-braided cushions and Persian carpets she had expected in a yacht dedicated to an Arabian princess. Two long white sofas faced each other on the port and starboard sides of the boat. Four black tub chairs, two forward, two aft, completed the square. In the centre stood a black lacquered coffee table. Forward of this seating area was dining space for ten: white leather chairs and a black marble table. Two white rugs with a widely-spaced wave pattern demarcated the areas on a dark cherrywood floor.

Mrs. Pinderally was sitting in the middle of the white sofa on the port side, wearing a lounging robe of white muslin. She had slipped her feet with their pink-painted toenails into jewelled flip-flops. 'Teatime,' she announced greedily. 'Thank you, Ali.'

Ali bowed as his lackeys set down their burdens on the coffee table. As he righted himself, Petra caught sight of a woven insignia on the pocket of his tunic and realized that he was not an employee of the Cape Sands but a member of Mrs. Pinderally's crew. Embroidered in black on a flying pink carpet was the name *Scheherazade*.

'This lady is seeking you, Madam,' Ali said. 'I judge her AOK so I bring her with me.'

Petra waited for Mrs. Pinderally to respond with anger and was pleasantly surprised when she gestured for her to come forward.

'My dear girl. Now you are not interrupting my meditation. You may share my tea. Sit.'

Petra sat down on the sofa opposite her hostess.

Mrs. Pinderally's sharp brown eyes scoured Petra's face. 'In one week you have aged. And you are too thin. This is not good. What have you done?'

Petra frowned. *She* hadn't done anything. If she had aged, it was Sandrine's fault for scheduling so many activities and not enough down time.

'Tsk, tsk, tsk,' Mrs. Pinderally said, making a series of clicking noises. 'The creasing of the brow is a very bad thing indeed. It is the mark of a distressed mind. You must endeavour to be as free of trouble as I am.' She ran a finger across the middle of her forehead, leaving a sticky trail. 'Now tell me why you have aged.'

'I went to a wedding. Every day we were kept busy. There was no time to relax.' The words spilled out. 'And there was a lot of drama.'

'Drama? What drama?'

Petra found herself describing the events of the past few days while Mrs. Pinderally started on the mountain of sandwiches.

'This Florian,' Mrs. Pinderally said, waving her hand about and dropping a cucumber slice onto the table, 'Methinks he is very sexy, no? And you like him, yes?'

The air in the salon suddenly seemed unbearably stuffy.

'Then you will see him again.' Mrs. Pinderally moved her bulk slightly forward to gaze sternly at Petra. 'But I do not like this Father John. He is a sleazy ball.'

'You know him? How?'

'I have listened carefully to what you have been saying, and I know many things.' Another cucumber slice fell out of Mrs. Pinderally's sandwich, this time onto the carpet. Ali rushed forward to pick it up.

'Your wedding was in Stellenbosch, at the Vredehof Manor. The same place where I arrange my daughter's wedding one year ago.'

Petra could hardly believe what she was hearing.

'This Father John marries many brides, but not my daughter. A Marriage Officer must be congenial to the bride and groom and to the parents. Especially to the parents. Father John is not congenial, his fee is not congenial, so I change him. And Bob's your uncle!'

That would have thrown a spanner into Sandrine-the-event-planner's works. Sandrine did not like to be overruled.

At that moment, Petra remembered the tin of sugared almonds she had brought with her to give to Vicky Dunlin. She dipped into her shoulder bag and fished it out. The lid was decorated with yellow, blue and white stones set in a random pattern round a large red central stone.

'This is for you: it's one of the favours we were given at Julia's wedding.'

Mrs. Pinderally wiped her fingers on her muslin robe and took the heart-shaped tin. After examining the top and the bottom carefully, she said, 'The tin is the same. The maker is the same. The jewels in the lid are different. We choose orange sapphire, green tourmaline and colourless zircon like diamond to represent India and the origins of my daughter.'

'I didn't know you could choose your colours.'

'With money, you can arrange everything. Except honesty.' Mrs. Pinderally wiped a tiny tear from the corner of her eye. 'Sadly the tins I send to Geneva to my beloved relatives did not arrive.'

'What happened?'

'Stolen from the luggage. Iniquitous bandits!'

Idly, Petra wondered whether the tins she and Carlo were taking home via Geneva would suffer the same fate. Then she shook her head and tut-tutted for Mrs. Pinderally's benefit. The muscle at the base of her neck where it joined her right shoulder was tight and she rubbed it absent-mindedly.

With the keen eyes of a fox, Mrs. Pinderally didn't miss a thing. 'Did the organizers of this wedding provide a massage therapist?'

Petra shook her head again.

'I thought not! That is the problem,' Mrs. Pinderally pronounced. 'You need a Rolling Sands massage given by an expert. I will lend you Miss Vicky. Ten o'clock tomorrow morning, here.'

'Here?'

'Indeed. Miss Vicky is becoming my personal masseuse and cocoonist. Now eat.'

She gestured at the pile of scones and began her attack.

28

It was the middle of April, not the first of January. Nevertheless, as she strolled back to her hotel after eating far too much, Petra made a resolution never to get as big as Mrs. Pinderally. Vicky Dunlin must be a very courageous young woman to have accepted an offer of employment to be her personal masseuse and cocoonist. No doubt she had decided that the opportunity to live aboard *Scheherazade* would outweigh the disadvantages.

The live-aboards Petra had encountered in the course of her duties as a Police Sergeant in the Marine Unit tended to be sailors who took their boats to the Caribbean during the winter. It was a long haul but preferable to the ice and snow in Northern Ontario. Living in luxury aboard *Scheherazade* in South Africa would be something else.

In the hotel's business lounge, Petra ran through the specs and photos of the British-built Princess 30 M on the company's website. The boat hadn't hit the headlines in North America yet but she deserved to. There were some great features: a powered folding balcony entered through sliding double doors from the salon, a spa bath on the flybridge, a hardtop with integrated sunroof, a hydraulic swim platform with stern garage for a decent-sized dinghy, and more. The master stateroom, set forward on the main deck, offered frameless picture windows, handcrafted cabinetry and fabric wall panels. Mrs. Pinderally must have very lucrative business interests to afford such a sensational boat.

As she prepared to turn in for an early night, Petra scrutinized her face in the bathroom mirror. No new lines that she could see. Faint circles under her eyes caused by a week of dinners and parties. She hadn't aged and she hadn't lost weight. If anything, she had put on a kilo or two. Mrs. Pinderally was way off base. But she had been shrewd in her analysis of the movers and shakers at the Vredehof Manor House. What a coincidence that she had chosen to host her daughter's wedding there. And how strange that she should have developed such antipathy towards Father John. Carlo would be amazed at the turn things were taking.

Her phone was charging on the night table. She grabbed it and dialled his number. 'Carlo?'

'Shh. I can't talk now.'

'OK. I'll be busy until two o'clock tomorrow. Pick me up here at the Waterside any time after that.'

'That's fine. Ciao.'

He was probably doing something he shouldn't be.

'Mrs. Pinderally begs you to make haste,' Ali said. 'She is in her suite.'

Petra looked at her watch. It was just before ten o'clock. She wasn't late.

'I hope Mrs. Pinderally is all right.'

'Very all right, but befuddled.'

Petra had a vision of Mrs. Pinderally like an elephant

drunk on Amarula Cream liqueur. She followed Ali through *Scheherazade*'s rather clinical-looking salon. The master suite was on the main deck, forward of the galley. She peeked into the galley as they passed: grey counter tops, stainless steel appliances, white tile floor. More like an operating theatre than a place for preparing sumptuous meals. Perhaps Mrs. Pinderally ordered all of hers from the Cape Sands.

Ali rapped on the door of the master suite.

'Enter!'

He pushed open the door and, inclining his head, stood aside to allow Petra access. Her mouth dropped open.

It was like walking into Aladdin's Cave. Directly in front of her, on a U-shaped bed covered in red velvet, Mrs. Pinderally lay sprawled against a pile of garish embroidered cushions. She sported a bejewelled turban and a technicolour dressing-gown that gaped to reveal knobbly brown knees.

Hurriedly Petra averted her eyes. To the right and left of the enormous bed, windows partially covered in red velvet curtains allowed glimpses of the world outside. Between the windows, gilded pilasters ornamented the walls. Below each window a built-in dresser in cream lacquer with gold pulls provided plenty of storage.

But it was what stood on each of the dressers that made Petra stare in wonder. Everywhere she looked were mannequin jewellery holders festooned with rings, necklaces and earrings: voluptuous female figures in evening gowns with wire arms and headdresses. Dozens and dozens of them, wearing strapless sweetheart gowns, off-the-shoulder mermaid gowns, Victorian crinolines, princess dresses, in all the colours of the rainbow.

'I am most befuddled,' Mrs. Pinderally said.

'Me too,' Petra murmured.

'You like my ladies?'

Petra nodded. She had seen similar figures in shops in Venice but never such a variety and so many in one place. Nor so much jewellery.

'Mr. Pinderally, my husband, God rest his soul, was a very generous man. And a very shrewd diamantaire.'

'Diamantaire?'

'A specialist in diamonds and precious stones. He did not believe in banks. See, over there, in that frame. Our wedding picture.'

Petra studied the photograph. A much younger slimmer version of Mrs. Pinderally stood with her arm round a small dapper man. Both of them wore traditional Hindu dress and happy smiles.

'Very nice.'

'Nice indeed, but I am still most befuddled.'

Petra waited for Mrs. Pinderally to elaborate.

'You have given me a most expensive gift. I do not understand.'

Petra wrinkled her forehead. 'The dragées were given to me at the wedding. They're not expensive.'

'No, no. The dragées were good. It is the stone!'

'The stone?'

'Yes. Almost I break my teeth. Look there!' Mrs. Pinderally waved in the direction of a tray full of rings.

Tentatively Petra sorted through the gold and platinum rings set with what appeared to be very precious stones. 'Do you mean this?' she said, holding up a round brownish stone the size of a small coin.

'Eureka! That is a diamond.'

'A diamond?'

'Alluvial, in the rough. That is why I ask why you gave me such an expensive gift.'

'I didn't know it was there. Sandrine Broselli gave me the tin to take back to Canada.'

'Canada?'

'Yes, via Europe.'

'Europe?'

'Geneva.'

'Ah, Geneva is suspect! That is where the tins I lose were going.'

'This is incredible,' Petra said. 'Why would the Brosellis put diamonds in tins of almonds?'

'To get them to market without the certificate!'

Petra nodded slowly. 'Are you sure it's a diamond?'

Mrs. Pinderally gave Petra a look full of pity. 'You think I could be married to Mr. Pinderally, God rest his soul, for forty years and not learn about stones?' She raised herself up on the embroidered cushions. 'An expert gemologist can tell where a stone comes from. I am better than expert. That stone is from Namaqualand.'

As far as Petra was concerned, it could have come from Fairyland and Mrs. Pinderally could be making the whole thing up.

'Where's that?'

'Namaqualand is an arid region stretching over one thousand kilometres along the West Coast of South Africa and Namibia. The Orange River divides it into two.'

Mrs. Pinderally sounded as though she was quoting from a textbook memorized many years ago.

'It is an area rich in alluvial diamonds carried there by ancient water courses as kimberlite pipes eroded. Some ninety percent of these diamonds are gem quality. They can be found in old river beds, on terraces, beaches, and in shallow and deep ocean waters,' she continued.

'Golly! Can you just pick them up on a beach?'

'Once upon a time, indeed. Now the best places are governed by concessions.'

'I don't think the Brosellis have diamond mining concessions. Apart from wine, they produce biscuits and cakes, maybe sugared almonds; they have a hunting and safari lodge, and fishing trawlers.'

'There you have it! Where are these trawlers?'

'I don't remember. I'll have to ask my friend Carlo. He's picking me up after my massage.'

'Ah, massage!' Mrs. Pinderally wagged a finger. She reached inside her dressing-gown and pulled out a gem-encrusted watch on a gold chain. 'There can be no massage without Miss Vicky. Ten o'clock has come and gone. Where is she?'

CHAPTER

29

Henny's leg was giving him hell. The drive to Lüderitz was usually a welcome relief after the hike through the Fish River Canyon. Most of the way the road was tarred and in good shape, but today it was blowing a gale. The wind whipped the desert sand onto the road where it formed dangerous slicks and drifts. Visibility was poor. Getting rid of the driver had been a bad mistake. Twice his vehicle skidded and he narrowly avoided losing control.

As they came into town, the old German-style houses provided some shelter. Not so out at the campsite on the Shark Peninsula, where the Southwester scoured the already barren earth.

'What kind of hellhole is this?' Megan groused. 'We'll never get the tents up in this wind.'

Henny gave her a tight-lipped smile. 'This is your eco-adventure, remember? I'm sure you'll do it. If you really can't manage, I'll give you a hand later.' *Keep them working, keep them dependent.*

He walked away from the campsite to the edge of the rocky promontory, trying not to limp. Down in the harbour, the diamond boats tugged at their lines. Like the ones in Port Nolloth, his old hunting ground, the larger boats used robots to dig trenches in the seabed at depths of up to a hundred and fifty metres and heavy duty pumps to suck up the diamond-bearing gravel. Then the diamonds were automatically sorted and sealed in what they called Neptune cans. For the independent divers operating small boats under licence to the big mining corporations it was a different proposition. Mates of his worked long hours in the icy waters but still dreamed of hitting it big.

He had too. Then, on a foul day like this, on board a trawler out of Port Nolloth, a line had snapped and whipped across the deck, slicing into his shin bone. It had mended badly, leaving him with a permanent reminder of why it was so important to keep the upper hand.

A year later, he had spotted the Master and begun a new life. The girly-looking guy with the blue eyes and blonde hair was sitting at the bar, chatting up the barmaid. He could have been a spy or a new breed of informant for the diamond police. Like the rest of the regulars, Henny kept his distance.

The next night was a repeat, the only difference being that the barmaid's tits were almost falling out of her top. Finally, on the third night, curiosity and craftiness drove him to ask the stranger to buy him a drink. At least, that's what Henny told himself it was at the time. But he knew it was the guy's sheer animal magnetism that had lured him. Or put more crudely, it was the goddamn light shining out of his arse.

In the Port, if the talk wasn't about women, fish or diamonds, it was about the state of the country. And the man had vision. A vision for the future that would restore things in some measure to the way they had been.

After a few beery evenings that ended how and where

Henny couldn't remember, he was hooked. The Master had a plan that surpassed anything he'd ever dreamed about. Yeah, it was far out and Henny struggled at first with some of the concepts and the big words, but the bottom line was that it fit with his own vision of how things should be. And it was based on attracting more and more women to the cause. Henny had no beef about that.

Next thing he knew, from March to October he was a scout: dressed like a roadie, pulling the chicks, all expenses paid and decent money to boot, kowtowing to no one but the Master. Even having a little fun – until now.

But with this bloody group Henny had started to question the wisdom of recruiting only white girls. In his fantasies, he re-wrote the Higher Ground policy to include women of different ages and colours, all of whom would do exactly as he instructed.

CHAPTER

30

There was a rap on the door of the master suite.

'Enter!'

Ali opened the door and waved in a lackey carrying a gold tray with all the fixings for coffee along with a plate of chocolate biscuits. The lackey deposited the tray and left. Ali advanced with a silver salver on which lay a white envelope marked with the Cape Sands logo.

'This missive just arrived from the hotel, Madam,' he said with a bow.

'Goody, an invitation. A gala dinner this Saturday. Open it, Ali, and read it to me.'

Petra thought she saw him shake his head before he lifted the flap of the envelope and extracted a folded piece of paper.

'Not an invitation, Madam,' he said as he smoothed out the paper. 'A message from Miss Vicky.'

'Miss Vicky is late. It is not reliable to be late, especially on the first day of a new job. Go on, Ali.'

Petra edged a little closer to Ali. The message was typewritten and quite long.

Ali read as if reciting from memory:

Dear Mrs. Pinderally,

I know you will be waiting for me and have offered me a wonderful opportunity to be your private masseuse and live aboard your fabulous yacht. My experience last week working with the Tabernacle Youth Collective in the Winelands was the most illuminating thing I have ever done. There are so many unfortunate young women who need help and love to find their way along the path to enlightenment.

I have given this much thought and I am sorry to disappoint you, but I have decided to stay with the Collective. I have been chosen to work within one of their outreach programmes at a community village near Langebaan. This is not too far from Cape Town. Whenever I visit, I will come and give you a massage. I hope you will understand. This is my destiny.

Sincerely,
Vicky Dunlin

For what seemed like an eternity, there was silence. Then came an eruption from the bed. With surprising speed, Mrs. Pinderally hoisted herself upright and swung her legs over the side.

'Stuff and nonsense!' she exclaimed. 'Again, Ali!'

As Ali reread the letter, Petra had a strange feeling. Some of the phraseology was startlingly familiar. It was almost as if somebody she knew had helped to write it.

'Does that sound like Vicky?' she asked Mrs. Pinderally.

'Most dubious, yet possible.'

'In what way?'

'Massage is for calming the mind and the body. Miss Vicky talked too much. So I instruct her in meditation.

First degree only, of course. She was far from reaching enlightenment.'

'She mentions enlightenment. Was she religious?'

'This is not the same. Certainly she was searching for something.'

'It would seem she's found it.'

'The pretty-pale side has overcome the practical side.'

'What do you mean?'

'Ali, show Petra Miss Vicky.'

Ali went to one of the top drawers in the dresser on the right and pulled out a pink file folder stamped with the *Scheherazade* logo. He extracted a colour photograph and handed it to Petra.

Mrs. Pinderally was sitting by the window in the relaxation room at the Cape Sands' wellness centre. Next to her stood a sturdily built young lady with a face that was pale and pretty but somewhat too narrow given the width of her shoulders and hips.

'I see,' Petra said. 'When was this taken?'

'Saturday.'

'You saw her two days ago, on Saturday?'

'Indeed. After the very best cocoon, I realize I cannot do without her. I made the photograph and the offer of employment.'

'Did she say anything about wanting to rejoin the Tabernacle Youth Collective?'

'She did not, but she was too quiet.'

'I thought you didn't like to talk during your massages.'

'Correct, but Miss Vicky had been gone one week. Like you with your drama. She should have told me about her experiences. Romance, a pinch of spice … '

Petra's eyes fell on a paperback that was lying on

Mrs. Pinderally's night table. The cover showed a half-naked couple in a close embrace, the girl's long black hair flowing over the tattooed back of a stud with a buzz cut. Suddenly Petra understood. Gossiping and reading romantic novels brought Mrs. Pinderally vicarious pleasure. But she also had a talent for getting right to the heart of a matter.

Although she didn't say so, Petra would have liked to hear about Vicky's experiences too. She settled for commiserating with Mrs. Pinderally.

'It's a shame she's not here. I was looking forward to a massage. I brought a tin of dragées for her as a small thank-you.'

'Ah, the diamonds!' Mrs. Pinderally yelped. 'And Miss Vicky is in breach of contract. Ali, make haste. Prepare the boat.'

'What are you going to do?'

'Go to Langebaan. To find them both. You and me.'

'I can't. Carlo is picking me up from my hotel this afternoon. We're going hunting and fishing.'

'Exactly!'

'Carlo!'

'Soon on my way, *cara*, soon on my way. Just a few more questions I need to answer.'

'Don't bother to come to Cape Town.'

'Why on earth not?'

'I won't be here. I'm going with Mrs. Pinderally to Langebaan – on her boat. You can meet me there instead.'

'You can't just change people's plans because you want to go on a cruise, Petra. The camper van is booked for pick-up at the airport. What the hell's going on?'

'Carlo, Mrs. Pinderally is a gemologist. She found a diamond in the rough in the tin of dragées I gave her.'

There was a strangled gasp at the other end of the phone.

'I know, it's crazy.' Quickly Petra explained. 'Now she wants to show me a place near Langebaan ...'

'Why Langebaan?' Carlo cut in. 'They don't mine diamonds there as far as I know.'

'Two reasons. She says it'll teach me what to look for, and Vicky Dunlin has gone to Langebaan.'

'I don't believe this. Why are you chasing halfway across the country after Vicky Dunlin?'

'Gross exaggeration, Carlo. It's not halfway across the country at all. Langebaan is north of Cape Town, virtually on the route we would be taking anyway. Vicky has reneged on her contract with Mrs. Pinderally and I have a horrible suspicion she's getting into some kind of trouble.'

She spent a few minutes giving Carlo the gist of Vicky's letter.

'I want to investigate this Tabernacle Youth Collective. Father John is involved in community outreach and it seems to me more likely than ever that there's a connection.'

'What if there is?'

'He's a very sleazy ball, as Mrs. Pinderally calls him.'

'She knows him?'

'Yes. Look, Carlo, I've got to go. I have to pick up my luggage from the hotel before the boat leaves. We'll be in Langebaan by this evening. I'll call you later.'

After she rang off, Petra realized she hadn't asked Carlo anything about the success of his mission. Oh well, there wasn't time.

CHAPTER

31

Mrs. Pinderally had a larger crew than Petra had anticipated. Besides Ali, the steward, and his two lackeys, she counted a captain and two deckhands. Ali showed her to a guest stateroom on the lower deck decorated in pastel tones that bridged the gap between the extravagance of Mrs. Pinderally's cave and the austerity of the salon.

'Madam is snoozing until tiffin,' Ali informed her. 'You have the freedom of the yacht. If you wish swimming, the pool is on the top deck.'

That might be nice once they had left Cape Town and passed Robben Island, Petra thought. The map she had brought with her showed that the coast was fairly straight and low-lying. Unless they travelled close inshore, she wouldn't be able to see much anyway.

Petra watched from the aft deck as Table Mountain receded into the distance. Being on the water again was a treat, and *Scheherazade* rode well. If the wind stayed as it was, blowing at ten knots out of the southwest, they should be able to cover the sixty nautical miles north to Saldanha Bay in about four hours. From there, it was a short run east to Langebaan and its lagoon.

Carlo had no right to make a fuss. Langebaan was not

a huge distance off the route they had planned to take – the N7 which ran all the way to the Namibian border. On the other hand, rushing off with Mrs. Pinderally to try and find Vicky Dunlin when they had no information to pinpoint her whereabouts was, she admitted, like looking for a needle in a haystack.

The swimming pool on the top deck was more like a plunge pool with Jacuzzi-style jets. Still, it was refreshing and Petra spent half an hour doing aquafit exercises. Feeling pleased with the workout, she wrapped herself in a fluffy white towel embroidered with pink magic carpets, stretched out on a sunbed and closed her eyes. Even if she couldn't have the promised massage with Vicky Dunlin, a little relaxation would do her good after the rigours of the wedding. The guests had gone their various ways: Max and Julia were honeymooning in Italy as Mr. and Mrs. De Witt, Sandrine and Tony Broselli would be at their property near the Orange River, Florian … she preferred not to think about Florian. What was it Carlo had said about the others yesterday?

A few seconds later, Petra opened her eyes wide and stared at the sky. Gina had gone with Father John to visit some of his community projects. Florian had taken the two Spanish girls, the two English girls and Diego on a Higher Ground tour. Carlo had given her the brochure and, if she remembered correctly, there was an email address and maybe a website. If she could find a computer, she could check it out and perhaps find out more about Father John's outreach activities as well.

Petra jumped up and went to her cabin. Without bothering to change, she searched for the brochure. There it was: Higher Ground Community Interchange. She began to read.

The first thing that struck her was how similar yet how different it was to the Higher Ground Tours brochure Megan and Hilary had given her. The emphasis then had been on discovering the delights of Africa through a scenic tour, though if you analyzed it closely the main thrust was still to attract young people as volunteers. Higher Ground Interchange was a charity; it was all about service and doing good. Plenty of exclamation marks and wording designed to entreat and persuade, beginning with the ringing appeal on the front page:

The dark continent needs you to create light!
Dedicate your life to restoring balance!
Make your contribution now before it is too late!

Page two began on a more serious note:

Higher Ground Mission Statement
Our mission is twofold:
- to raise awareness of the needs of the community and improve standards through programmes designed to foster progress and promote the joy of living
- to offer young people the opportunity to find balance, peace of mind and comfort in service by living in harmony with nature and each other

Ways You Can Help
There are two ways in which you can help:
- Monetary Contributions
Higher Ground welcomes monetary contributions, great and small. Money allows us to provide food, shelter and other basic necessities to ensure the success of our programmes.

- *Voluntary Service*

We welcome with open arms and hearts young volunteers aged between 18 and 28. In the prime of life, you have the vigour, the energy, the desire and the ability to help us meet our goals.

Page three continued in the same vein.

Our Watchwords

Nurture, nature, simplicity, economy, devotion to one another

Outreach Programmes

Our outreach programmes are carefully designed to allow you to experience Africa as it was meant to be while contributing to the development of the local community. Over the years, we have found that complete immersion in the local way of life is the best way to guarantee success.

We begin by assessing your skills and determining how and where your contribution can be of most benefit. This usually takes place during a short working holiday at one of our small outreach projects in the South African countryside. After demonstrating that you possess the right attitude and skills, you will be assigned to a long-stay village where your capabilities will be put to good use.

Petra took a deep breath and turned to the back page.

Seize the day!

With villages in South Africa and Namibia, Higher Ground offers plenty of scope for you to experience the real Africa while working to benefit others. Volunteers should be physically fit and ready to sublimate their own desires for the greater good. We recommend a minimum stay of one year.

By dedicating yourself to the service of others in our community villages, you will ensure your place in a freer purer world.

**Join with us to create light in place of darkness!
Email us now if you are ready to fulfill your
destiny!**

Petra put down the brochure and rubbed the sore muscle in her right shoulder. There was plenty to take in. The abstract jargon of the last section reminded her of Father John's afternoon confessional in the slave lodge at Vredehof. Lots of fluff, no real substance, and no indication of what volunteers would actually be doing.

Twenty or so photographs edged the centre pages of the brochure: pictures of village compounds, rondavels with thatched roofs, groups of huts surrounded by wooden stave fences, white-washed barrack-style buildings, long and low. They were little more than thumbnails so detail was difficult to see, and there were no place names or captions that might identify them. But one thing was clear: all the pictures featured young white women.

White women with fair hair. Like Vicky Dunlin. Who had said in her letter that she had been chosen to work with one of Tabernacle Youth Collective's outreach programmes. Questions swamped Petra's brain. How had she been chosen? Why had she been chosen? Was the working holiday Vicky had just been on linked to the "short working holiday at one of our small outreach projects in the South African countryside" mentioned in the Higher

Ground Interchange brochure? And if Vicky had indeed gone to work on a project near Langebaan, how the hell were they going to find her?

Petra was tempted to do what she had done so many times in the past – go undercover, join a group and see what she could find out. Carlo wouldn't like it, though, because they'd made commitments to the Brosellis. Best to start by expressing interest then take it from there.

She got up swiftly and went to look for Ali. He was in the galley supervising the creation of what looked like much more than a snack.

'Ali, does Mrs. Pinderally have a computer?'

'Mrs. Pinderally is not literate.'

'She loves to read romances,' Petra said, surprise showing in her face.

'Naturally. But literate with computers she is not. However, the captain is very literate. We have all mod cons for him. A computer with charts for navigating on the bridge and a second computer for plotting in the office.'

Petra nodded. The second computer would be for plotting *Scheherazade*'s course using navigational software. With any luck, the yacht would be equipped with internet too. She had seen two enormous domes on top of the flybridge.

'May I use the computer in the office, Ali? I need to check something very urgently.'

'Come with me.'

He didn't seem at all bothered that Petra was wearing a towel. He led the way down a steep companionway forward to a small office area. 'There, Miss,' he said, proudly indicating a large screen next to a printer and a mouse. 'When tiffin is ready, I will get you.'

'Thank you, Ali. Is there a password?'

'It is arabiannights, small letters with no spaces.'

Petra sat down and entered the password. It worked like a charm. She went into Google and accessed an email account she had set up under the name *boatgirl* for use when she didn't want to reveal her real identity. Thinking quickly, she typed in the email address given in the brochure followed by a short message:

I am very interested in the opportunities you offer to do volunteer work in African villages. Please let me know how I can join your outreach programme.

She paused. Everything would be fine if they responded before she left the yacht; after that she would be on the road and wouldn't always have access to email. In the end, she added her phone number and signed off using the name of her best friend Alice in Canada. She pressed send and wondered how long it would take to receive a reply.

32

Mrs. Pinderally brushed pastry crumbs off her ample bosom onto the wave-patterned rug. 'Now something sweet would tickle my fancy.'

Petra reached into her bag and took out the second tin of dragées she had planned to give to Vicky Dunlin. 'I think you finished yours last night, but we could eat some of these.'

She held the tin out to Mrs. Pinderally who grabbed it with a greedy sigh.

'Red, blue, white and yellow. The stone in the centre is white,' she said, stating what Petra had already noted. 'The label on the bottom is the same. We will take a look.'

The tin was sealed shut with clear tape, as the other one had been. With surprising dexterity, Mrs. Pinderally found the end of the tape and unwound it. 'Your gift, you open it!'

Petra held her breath as she prized off the lid, not wanting to scatter dragées and diamonds all over the floor. She handed the open tin back to Mrs. Pinderally. 'You are better than expert.'

Mrs. Pinderally studied the dragées. She poked around in the tin with a bejewelled index finger then emptied the contents onto an empty plate.

'No diamonds,' she said. 'No danger to teeth. Try one.'

Petra took a dragée and tried to hide her disappointment.

'Like you, there is no wind in my sails.'

If ever she wanted to hide anything from Mrs. Pinderally, Petra realized she would have to be very clever. In a snap decision, she determined not to reveal that she had more tins in her luggage. She would examine them later with Carlo. He was the one investigating breaches of the Kimberley Process.

To avert questions that might put her on the spot, she asked about rough diamonds versus cut diamonds. 'Cut diamonds are more valuable than rough diamonds, aren't they?'

Mrs. Pinderally nodded her head like a marionette on a string. 'The better the cut, the more valuable the diamond.'

Textbook English again.

'A good cutter can make even a mediocre stone look fantastic,' she continued. 'It is a question of faceting. You must learn the 4 Cs: Colour, Clarity, Cut and Carats. And you must learn how to use the loupe for seeing flaws. The best place to do this is in my suite. Thanks to Mr. Pinderally, God rest his soul, I have magnificent specimens.'

Mrs. Pinderally's suite was so full of jewellery that Petra wondered how she would find the pieces to illustrate her lecture. But she knew exactly which lady held which ring or necklace. After the first half hour, Petra realized there was a subtle hierarchy among them.

Taking a splendiferous ring from the centre of the headdress worn by the first lady next to her bed on the right – at least three carats Petra estimated based on what she had learned – Mrs. Pinderally waved it in her face.

'What colour and clarity is this? What is the most valuable colour of diamond? Use the loupe!'

To Petra, squinting through the jeweller's magnifying glass, it looked flawless and so white as to be nearly ice blue. 'It can't be a blue diamond, can it? FL?'

'Bob's your uncle!'

Petra felt an inordinate sense of pride.

'Now I teach you about tanzanite, the essence of Africa.' Mrs. Pinderally selected a heart-shaped pendant from the arm of a lady dressed in a blue off-the-shoulder evening gown. 'What colour is this?'

Petra looked carefully at the gem. 'Sapphire blue.'

'And now?'

'Violet.'

Mrs. Pinderally moved the pendant so that it caught the light differently. As she did so, Petra remembered the first dinner at Vredehof when she had been sitting next to Julia. Sandrine had rebuked Julia for not wearing her diamonds. Julia had shown Petra her mother's tanzanite ring.

'Burgundy!' Petra almost shouted out. 'The mood changer. And it can restore spiritual balance and good fortune.'

'Eureka!'

Julia had talked about spiritual balance. Was that what Florian too had meant by restoring a balance? If so, it might explain the involvement of Father John. Petra turned the idea over in her mind. She had the feeling she was missing something important.

Mrs. Pinderally was flipping open the cover of a watch that was part of the gold bracelet on her left wrist. 'Only one hour more to Saldanha Bay. Teaching is most tiring, even if the student is attentive. I will take refreshment and see you later.'

Petra knew when she was being dismissed. 'Thank you, Mrs. Pinderally. I know much more about diamonds now than I ever thought I would.'

She made her way to the aft deck and sat in one of the teak chairs. The yacht's wake unfurled evenly behind them creating a smooth path through the waves. How she wished there was a clear path going forwards. Here she was, supposed to be on vacation, worrying about girls she didn't even know. She could phone A.K. – in fact, should she phone him? – and tell him that Vicky Dunlin hadn't returned to Cape Town and that she, Petra, was now going to spend the rest of her valuable time off enjoying her holiday, exploring South Africa and Namibia, seeing the exotic animals she had come to see.

But once a cop, always a cop. The instincts and suspicions never went away. Having sent her email, she could only wait. If she received a reply in the next day or so while she was in the Langebaan area, she would do her best to check up on Vicky Dunlin. Otherwise Carlo would insist on their heading north to the Broselli's lodge.

The waiting was the worst part of any operation. Like the deadly calm that preceded a major tropical storm, it weighed you down. There was nothing to be done except prepare and sit tight.

Petra pulled out the phone Tom Gilmore had given her and checked the signal. He had assured her it would work, but she didn't hold out much hope miles off shore on board a boat heading for a sparsely populated area. The screen was blank.

She looked up to see Ali who was bringing her a glass filled with pink juice.

'Guava,' he said.

Petra took a sip. It was thick and delicious, unlike anything she had tasted before.

'We approach Saldanha Bay, Miss. You should watch for dolphins.'

'Are there whales too?'

'No, Miss, wrong time of year. Sorry. But there are many birds – gannets, cormorants, oyster catchers, penguins, pelicans … on the granite islands, you will see.'

Petra drained the glass of juice and jumped up. Time to move to the bow. Penguins and pelicans were among the birds she loved best.

Ali had come to find her at exactly the right moment. They were coming closer to land and beginning to turn to starboard to enter Saldanha Bay. An ore carrier passed in front of them. As she watched it make its way to the harbour entrance, she felt a faint vibration in her pocket. Her heart in her mouth, she pulled out the phone.

'Yes?'

A.K.'s raspy voice was faint. 'Good wedding?'

'Oh, yes, Sir.' Petra guessed it was a good one as weddings go. A.K. didn't want details, he was merely being polite because she was doing him a favour.

His next question hit her before she had time to prepare.

'How's Vicky Dunlin?'

Petra hesitated. 'I don't know. She …'

'Isn't back at work?'

'No. Apparently she signed on for a longer stint with the Tabernacle Youth Collective.'

Petra thought she heard something like a groan.

'Doing what?'

'Working at one of their community villages.'

'It's imperative that you find her.'

'I'm trying my best. Why …?'

'Do whatever you have to do. Just keep me informed.'

'Of course.'

And that was that. End of conversation. She didn't have a clue why Miss Vicky was so important to A.K. that she had to upset all her plans.

33

'Carlo!'

'*Carissima*! I've been waiting for your call. Where are you?'

'We're coming in to Langebaan. We'll be anchoring near the Club Santorini Resort. Where are you?'

'Not far from there, at Calypso Beach.'

'Go to the yacht club at the resort. Mrs. Pinderally will send her tender for you at seven o'clock. You can't miss it. It's a pink and white custom limousine named *Sheri-baby*. I didn't realize it at the time but it followed us from Cape Town. Dinner's on board *Scheherazade* at eight. Greek, I'm told. And you can stay overnight.'

'That's very kind of Mrs. P. I'm looking forward to meeting her. Should I bring flowers?'

'Something edible would be better. By the way, I haven't told her we have more tins of dragées. I think we need to keep that secret and check them out ourselves.'

'Fine, I'll see what I can find.'

'See you later.'

Petra went with one of the deckhands and one of the lackeys to pick up Carlo and food from the resort's Greek restaurant. Ali had set the table on the aft deck. When they returned, Mrs. Pinderally was ensconced in a large chair awaiting their arrival.

'This is your cousin Carlo.'

'No, my friend. It was Carlo's cousin who got married.'

'Just so. Welcome, young man!'

Carlo twinkled at Mrs. Pinderally and handed her a rectangular package beautifully wrapped in gold paper and tied with a red ribbon. She tilted her head sideways. 'A charmer. Be careful the snake doesn't turn on you.'

Petra hid a smile at the expression on Carlo's face.

Throughout dinner, Carlo picked Mrs. Pinderally's brains about diamonds. 'I can see that your husband had a great eye for fine jewels. How did he get them?'

'Ah, Mr. Pinderally, a lovely man, God rest his soul. Boarding school men! Always they maintain excellent relationships. He could buy the best stones.'

'Did he cut them here in South Africa?'

'Yes and no. There are many diamond centres: Antwerp, Amsterdam, Geneva. Now India.'

'What does a diamond cutting machine look like, Mrs. Pinderally?' Petra asked suddenly.

'In equipment I am not expert. In design, yes. Now I think we have laser machines. Not so big and heavy as once upon a time.'

Petra remembered the photograph showing a diminutive Mr. Pinderally and had visions of him trying to carry a large machine like the one Florian and Tony had been moving. As soon as the two of them had gone, she had inspected it quickly before making her escape from the area.

'Do you still cut diamonds and make jewellery?' she asked.

'The next generation family business is in the pink. In Europe and India. I have everything I need. Excepting Miss Vicky to sort my pains.'

During the meal of succulent lamb kleftico and the lively conversation about diamonds, Petra had stopped thinking about Vicky Dunlin and the lack of response to her email. Now her worries came flooding back.

'Dessert, Ali, if you please. Then I will retire. Tomorrow is a busy day.'

'How so, Mrs. P.?'

Mrs. Pinderally didn't seem to mind that Carlo had begun calling her Mrs. P. to her face, shortening her name in his usual roguish way.

'Ali, explain what is arranged,' she said as Ali placed a plate full of sticky baklava on the table in front of her.

'At ten o'clock, the water limousine will take you to the yacht club. Madam's driver will meet you. You will go to the West Coast Fossil Park. There you will learn much. At teatime Madam will answer questions.'

'Aren't you coming with us, Mrs. Pinderally?' Carlo asked.

'I am busy taking the waters. Saltwater is good for the body and soul.'

Petra and Carlo lingered on the aft deck after Mrs. Pinderally had gone to bed. The air was warm and still.

'Wonderful, isn't it?' Petra said. 'Aren't you glad to be here?'

Carlo shrugged. 'I still think it's a waste of time.'

'What about the diamond in the tin of dragées I gave Mrs. Pinderally? You can't tell me it was accidental.'

'The only way to know is to examine the other tins.'

'We should each keep a couple to take home. Mrs. Pinderally told me that most of the ones she sent back to her relatives in Geneva were stolen out of the luggage.'

'I must say I thought it odd that Sandrine gave us so many to take home with us.'

'Did you find any tins at the factory in Montagu? What happened there?'

'I was waiting for you to ask.' Carlo swirled the Cape brandy in his glass. 'It was a dark and stormy night, the cats were on the prowl ...'

'Mercutio! You're as bad as Mrs. Pinderally with her "Once upon a time".'

'The factory is quite a place. Three buildings in a compound surrounded by a high wall, controlled access gates.'

'How did you get in?'

'Don't ask and you'll hear no lies. But I was able to disable – temporarily of course – the night watchman and complete his rounds for him. It's definitely the place where the dragées are made. All the ingredients are there.'

'And the tins?'

'Yes, but they appear to be brought in from China undecorated. There's a workshop full of equipment for cutting, welding, engraving, and so on.'

'Diamond cutting?'

'I'd have to bring in the experts to answer that, and to test the stocks of stones I found.'

'Were there any diamonds?'

'There were some clear stones, but I don't think the Brosellis would leave diamonds lying around, and I didn't spot anything that could have been rough.'

'Did you find anything to connect the factory to the Brosellis?'

'Nothing specific. I didn't have time to go through all the records. Some of the files were locked and there was a large safe in the manager's office.'

'Still, you confirmed that the tins are decorated and filled here in South Africa, and we know that at least one contained a good-size diamond. It seems like an awful lot of trouble to go to, not to mention risk, to smuggle a diamond out of the country.'

'Remember I told you about the Kimberley Process that controls the supply of diamonds throughout the world, ostensibly to prevent war and terrorism from being financed by the trading of rough diamonds? It also makes it difficult for people who find caches of rough to sell the diamonds for what they're really worth – and there are independent prospectors who search promising areas and sometimes hit the jackpot. If they're forced to take them to the big mining houses to get a certificate, they'll inevitably get a lower price.'

'So what you're suggesting is that the Brosellis may have found a source of rough diamonds and are trying to maximize their profits from them.'

'Something like that.'

CHAPTER

34

The Langebaan lagoon was an incredible turquoise blue. Like the shallow waters around the Bahamas Petra thought, as she studied her surroundings next morning. Carlo was still in his cabin, sleeping no doubt. Petra's early shifts as a Marine Unit Sergeant jibed well with her natural body rhythms. As a result, she loved the quiet period between sunrise and the rush of people going about their business. Carlo was a night owl and his work at Interpol kept him close to his desk.

For the umpteenth time, Petra looked at her phone. She didn't need to, she told herself. If a call or a text was coming in, she would feel the vibration. Then a thought struck her. What if the phone rang and she answered it and it was Father John or Florian? Voices were the hardest thing to disguise. Wouldn't they think it odd that she was enquiring about volunteering with Higher Ground? Then again, they would probably have staff – or volunteers – to handle simple requests for information. If it got to the interview and assessment stage, she would have to be more careful. They might enjoy conducting those themselves.

Mrs. Pinderally's water limousine was flat with a glassed-in top and three rows of seats. It reminded Petra of the *bateaux mouches* on the Seine in Paris. The regular limousine was pink and large enough to accommodate Mrs. Pinderally and several friends easily. Petra could see that the chauffeur was none too pleased when they had to leave the main road and jolt along the gravel road to the fossil park.

At the small café and visitors centre, they transferred to an open jeep for the bumpy ride with their guide across what once had been the site of a phosphate mine. In place of the dusty glass cases Petra was expecting was a large enclosure housing an on-going archeological dig. Narrow walkways led around and through the site, enabling viewers to see the fossilized bones of long extinct animals in situ.

'I give it ten on the Wow-scale,' Petra said. 'I've never seen anything like this. Can you imagine what this land was like five million years ago – not arid desert but green and watered, full of four-tusked elephants, three-toed horses, short-necked giraffes, sabre-toothed cats …'

'Not to mention big African bears!' Carlo added.

The guide had described the huge diversity of animals that had been found there. Now he was asking them questions. 'How do you think these bones got here?'

Carlo shook sand out of his hair.

Petra recalled something Mrs. Pinderally had said about ancient waterways and erosion.

'Was there a river here?'

'Yes, the Berg River.'

'Did the bones get washed up on its banks?'

'Yes, but why here in particular?'

'Topography? Floods?'

'Right. The Berg River was a mighty watercourse that swept everything before it. During catastrophic rains, hundreds of animals would get caught and drown. Their bones would pile up in the estuary among the islands and weirs formed by the river.'

'Quite an eye opener,' Carlo commented as they got back into the limousine for the return journey to Langebaan. 'It makes me think about the Brosellis and their property on the Orange River.'

'That's the border between South Africa and Namibia, isn't it?'

'It is, but its course used to run farther south. The mouth was likely in the vicinity of Lambert's Bay.'

'So there'd be alluvial diamonds there too,' Petra said happily.

Mrs. Pinderally was waiting on the aft deck to greet them as they climbed out of the water limousine onto the swim platform.

'I should have bought her something in the gift shop. I saw some crystallized fruit,' Petra murmured.

'We didn't all shirk our responsibilities.' Carlo delved in his pocket and grinned. 'A sabre-toothed tiger bone!'

To Petra, it looked like a chunk of rock.

Mrs. Pinderally examined it closely. 'Wonderful,' she exclaimed. 'I shall treasure this!'

Carlo smirked at Petra.

'You see how the water carried bones to that site,' she continued. 'So it is with alluvial diamonds. All along the coast of Namaqualand. The first one was found in Port Nolloth.'

'Port Nolloth?' Carlo scratched his nose.

'Indeed. Now the diamond fishing is very big there.'

'My uncle has a fleet of fishing trawlers,' Carlo said slowly. 'I've been fishing with him and seen what he catches. I never thought about diamonds.'

Mrs. Pinderally leaned forward and became very serious.

'I have been with my yacht in Port Nolloth. Many fishing trawlers search for diamonds under the sea.'

'Are they legitimate? I mean do they have permits?' Petra asked.

'I'm sure some do,' Carlo answered in place of Mrs. Pinderally, 'but Port Nolloth is the Wild West, full of rogues and rascals. If we have time, we'll go there and take a look.'

'I've still got to find Vicky Dunlin.'

Carlo groaned. 'This is a vacation …'

'Yes, not a mission to uncover a diamond-smuggling ring!'

'OK, OK. You do your thing, I'll do mine.'

Ali appeared carrying his silver salver. 'Someone is messaging Miss Petra. Come with me, Miss.'

Petra leaped up, her grumpiness vanishing. 'Thank you, Ali.'

Her inbox was up on the screen. There was one new message, the subject highlighted in bold type: **Volunteering with Higher Ground**. Petra shrugged. Ali, like all good retainers, knew everything that was going on. Quickly she read the response to her enquiry:

Dear Alice,

Thank you very much for your interest in Higher Ground. We have numerous programmes. To find the most suitable one for you, please tell us which area you are in, how old you are, your interests and any special expertise you may have. We would also like to know how you heard of our organization. Your Outreach Officer will be in touch as soon as we have had the opportunity to match you with one of our programmes.

Sincerely,

Marcus Zen

Outreach Programme Coordinator

By the time Petra finished reading, she had begun to draft her answer in her head: *Saldanha Bay, 28, adventure tours, aquafit, aromatherapy*. She cheated a bit on her age and added that she had seen a brochure, not wanting to mention any names. Keep it simple. Innocuous. Sincere. Perhaps then they'd hire her.

During the evening, Petra's spirits rose every time Ali appeared on the aft deck where they were enjoying another al fresco meal. But he never delivered another message.

35

Henny was glad to be back on the road. Two blustery nights in Lüderitz was enough. The wind had sand-blasted them throughout their visit to Kolmanskop, the ghost town that had once been the hub of the local diamond industry. Finally it had abated. Now every kilometre they covered brought him closer to the moment when he would hand over his group to the Master.

He checked his rearview mirror. Megan and Hilary were suspiciously quiet.

'There it is!' Hilary had spotted the "feral horses" sign.

'We saw them already.'

'Well, we want to see them again. We love horses.'

Henny gritted his teeth and drove down the track to the observation deck. This wasn't the way it was supposed to be. He was the tough guy, the one in charge.

There wasn't a single wild desert horse in sight.

'We'll wait.' Megan selected a few of the brochures and pamphlets she and Hilary had been accumulating since they arrived in Namibia. Their collection had grown in inverse proportion to their ability to download information onto their mobile phones. Most of it ended up on the floor next to their seats.

'This says the owner of Duwisib Castle – that's where we're going this afternoon – was a fanatical horseman. Some of the horses came from there,' Hilary announced.

An hour later, after repeated cajoling, Henny got them back in the van. He decided to skip the visit to the castle.

'Isn't this where we should be turning left?' Hilary leaned forward and tapped him on the shoulder. 'The map says that's the scenic route to the castle.'

'We're behind schedule,' he ground out.

'Who cares?' Megan said. 'We've paid for this trip and we want to make the most of it, don't we, girls?'

A chorus of voices from behind her confirmed her thinking.

Megan found the pamphlet she was looking for and began reading loudly enough for the whole bus to hear.

'Duwisib Castle has a fascinating though rather sad history. Hansheinrich von Wolf and his wife Jayta commissioned the building of the castle in 1908. They lived there from 1909 to 1914, breeding horses and cattle. In 1914, they left for England to buy another stallion. While at sea, they learned of the outbreak of the Great War. The German liner they were sailing on had to find sanctuary in Rio de Janeiro, where they were interned by …'

Henny tried to tune out Megan's shrill voice and focus on the rough gravel road along which he was driving. If it went on like this, he'd rather go back to Port Nolloth. He'd soon find employment maintaining the vacuum hoses and on-shore suction pumps for independent divers. And if he kept a few stones for himself, he'd be set for life. Then he could retire to a shack in the hills with a few women to assuage his appetites and do his bidding.

'You don't have to read the whole thing, do you?' he screeched.

'Why not? It's really interesting. Von Wolf found passage to Europe aboard a neutral ship and joined the German forces. He was killed just fourteen days later during the Battle of the Somme.'

'OK, your starter question for ten points, girls,' Hilary squawked. 'When was the Battle of the Somme?'

Man oh man! The pay and the perks were just not worth it. Maybe he could lose the troublemakers somewhere. He began to plot where and how.

Too late he saw the pothole in the road. The rear left tire blew and they lurched to a standstill.

CHAPTER

36

Petra woke early after a patchy night's sleep. Ali was in the galley making coffee and preparing breakfast. Still no messages. He must have seen the disappointment in her face because he handed her a mug of coffee and promised to check the computer again after breakfast. At his suggestion, she took the kayak and spent an hour exploring the lagoon.

When she returned, Mrs. Pinderally was already fuelling up for the busy day ahead. She had given Carlo a map of the West Coast National Park and, between mouthfuls, was instructing him on what to see and do. Except in the Postberg section, the roads were tarred so they could take the camper van. Postberg was only open in August and September for viewing the carpets of wild flowers.

'Wrong season for whales, wrong season for flowers,' Petra murmured.

'You have hiking boots?' Mrs. Pinderally asked.

'Hiking boots? Couldn't fit them in with my wedding clothes. How about sneakers?'

'Bingo! You can walk Eve's trail. Thirty kilometres through the wilderness. You follow the footsteps of Eve, a young woman who lived one hundred and seventeen thousand years ago. Her prints were discovered in the rock, formerly sea sand. Now in the museum at Cape Town.'

'It sounds fascinating, but I don't think I could manage thirty kilometres in a day.'

'No, no. Two and a half days; I arrange it, fully portered and catered. You will have a good look for Miss Vicky. And see animals.'

Somehow Petra didn't think a hike through the local vegetation Carlo called *fynbos* would shed much light on Vicky's whereabouts. And she certainly didn't want to run into any potentially dangerous wildlife.

'What kind of animals?'

'Many antelope, mountain zebra, dung beetles.'

'Have you done the hike, Mrs. Pinderally?'

'My information is from Mr. Pinderally, God rest his soul. I prefer massage.'

Petra could see Carlo was trying to attract her attention. Finally he burst out, 'Don't even think about it. We have to get going, Petra. The Brosellis are expecting us, and don't forget we've booked to go to Etosha National Park. We'll see loads of animals there – lions, maybe rhino, and plenty of dung beetles. There's a lot to fit into this holiday!'

'Indeed. Biscuit factories, counterfeit tins of sugared almonds …'

'When you find Miss Vicky, send her back to me,' Mrs. Pinderally said as she blew them a kiss from the sofa in the salon. 'And you both return soon. Toodle-oo!'

'Why don't we spend half a day driving round the park, then head up to Springbok tonight?' Petra urged as they returned to shore in the water limousine. 'It does sound interesting.'

'And you're taking us on a wild goose chase.' Carlo blew out through his teeth. 'OK, half a day it is.'

He was jiggling keys in his pocket as they walked across the car park towards two camper vans. The white one looked like a small version of the campers in the Higher Ground tour brochure. The other one must have been spray-painted by a hippie on LSD.

Petra squeezed between the two and tried the door handle on the passenger side of the white van. 'Open it, Carlo, please.'

'I have, *cara*,' he said meekly. 'Ours is the other one.'

'This? No way, Mercutio! Stop having me on. We've only got half a day so let's get started.'

'I tell you, this is ours.'

The van was like a Dormobile with two front seats, tinted windows and a badass paint job that would guarantee them the freedom of the road.

Petra stood there open-mouthed. After a few seconds, she dropped her luggage to the ground and clapped her hands on her head. 'I just don't believe this. We agreed on the 2ST Mercedes camper. You had it reserved.'

'I figured I'd change it, since you'd gone off with Mrs. Pinderally.'

'I see. Tit for tat is it? So while I was helping you with your search for illicit goods, you did a number on me. We're not going to get any undercover work done in that thing.'

'It's less likely to be stolen.'

'Agreed. Nobody in their right mind would steal it!'

'Wicked, isn't it? Come on, admit it!' Carlo said with a big grin on his face. 'Sometimes it's best to stand out in the crowd.'

Petra had to acknowledge that the animals they

encountered didn't seem to be phased by the psychedelic artwork. Some of them looked up and stared at them curiously but most carried on browsing.

She was good at spotting and for the first hour was keen for Carlo to stop so that she could photograph the bucks as he called them.

'Ooh, hartebeest, Carlo, stop!'

'That's a bontebok, *tesoro mio*.'

'They all look the same. It's impossible to tell the difference.'

'I guarantee you'll soon be an expert like your friend Mrs. P.'

By the time they reached the restaurant near the southern end of the lagoon, their stomachs were rumbling. The waitress, a young pregnant Afrikaner girl, brightened considerably when she saw Carlo.

The impact he had on women was extraordinary Petra thought, as she watched him in action. His eyes sparkled, his step was jaunty, and his smile lit up his whole face in a way that appeared both sincere and roguish. Her old flame Romeo had called it "twinkling". Carlo used it to get what he wanted from almost every woman he came into contact with. Their food arrived in double-quick time.

What was it women found most attractive about Carlo? Petra pondered. His irrepressible wit? His vibrancy? His tight butt? A picture of Florian flashed into her head. With him, it was something else. He had the butt, but not the wit. Women fell in love with his angelic looks, with his intensity, with the way he focussed his attention on them and made them feel special, and, she finally admitted, with his sensuality … She blinked to erase the image, but it was etched in her brain.

'You haven't finished your *bobotie*, Petra.'

'It's a bit much for lunchtime and the curry's quite strong.'

'Is that the problem? You looked as though you were seeing a ghost.'

They left the park through the east gate and turned onto the R315 towards Malmesbury. There they would pick up the N7 and head north to the Orange River. Traffic was light. After a couple of kilometres, a vehicle coming the other way passed them. Petra watched it whiz by, then shouted, 'Stop, stop!'

Carlo groaned. 'No, *cara*. You can stop spotting. Start again when we get to Etosha at the end of this week.'

'Carlo, that was a Higher Ground van. Quick, turn round! We can follow them.'

'Of course we can follow them, but what's the point?'

'The point is we're not far from Langebaan and Vicky was going to work on a project in this area.'

'You're clutching at straws, Petra. Anyway, I thought she went with Tabernacle.'

'She did, but I'm sure there's a connection between the two groups. It would be too much of a coincidence if not.' Petra put her hand on the steering wheel and tried to push it round. 'Come on, Carlo, or it'll be too late.'

Carlo gave another groan, deeper and more strangled. 'Fine, we'll turn around and chase the van to God knows where.'

The van had quite a head start. Dust from the side of the road blew up behind it, marking its progress. Carlo stepped on the gas and sped along the paved road. He slowed as the gap narrowed in order to keep a reasonable distance between them.

They were not far from the park gate when the white van turned without indicating onto what looked like a farm track. Deliberately Carlo drove on before doubling back and coming to a stop just before the track.

'This could be difficult. If we follow them now, they're almost sure to see us. What do you want to do, Petra?' He looked at his watch. 'It's almost three o'clock.'

Petra adjusted her sunglasses on her nose. 'I don't know. It's just a hunch, Carlo, but we might learn something. It would be a shame to turn back now. Does it really matter if we don't get to the Brosellis until later tomorrow?'

'I guess not.'

'Isn't the beauty of this vehicle that we're self-sufficient? We can camp anywhere, go anywhere.'

'Just one problem, *cara*. I didn't do any shopping.'

CHAPTER

37

The track stretched into the distance like a ruler bisecting the sandy plain. The vegetation at first was sparse then, as they neared a dry river bed, stunted bushes appeared where the roots had burrowed their way to a little water.

'This isn't a 4 x 4,' Carlo said. 'We can't cross that river bed.'

Petra studied the terrain. 'The track goes to the left, over there.'

For a while the track continued more or less along the course of the river then it began to bear away and climb. Rocky outcrops, *kopjes* according to Carlo, appeared.

'If you keep your eyes peeled, you might see a *klipspringer* – rock jumper in Afrikaans – but I'm not going to stop. I don't want to get stuck. These tracks are tricky.'

The track twisted between two *kopjes*. Petra didn't detect any movement among the smooth grey rocks. As they came down the hill, she spied a cloud of dust in the distance.

'Looks like something's coming towards us!'

'So I see. Hold on!' He turned sharply onto a smaller track leading back in the direction of the river. An illegible sign hung obliquely on one nail from a weathered wooden post.

The vehicle on the other track slowed to a crawl.

Carlo crept along for another fifty metres then stopped. 'We can't risk going any further. Let's brazen this out.'

The driver of the other vehicle, a white Higher Ground van, pulled up where the two tracks converged. He got out and came jogging towards them.

As he approached, Petra saw that he was spindly and light-skinned. He had a buzz cut and was wearing black jeans with a black T-shirt emblazoned with the name of a rock group she had never heard of. He reminded her of someone, but she couldn't think who.

'What are you doing? This is private property.' He looked them up and down with pale unfriendly eyes.

'There's supposed to be a campsite down by the river. I thought that might be its sign,' Carlo said.

'Well it isn't. There's no campsite here. And you can't just set up anywhere you like.'

Petra looked pointedly at Carlo. 'We must have taken a wrong turn. Bad navigation on my part,' she said. 'I'm sorry. We'll turn round and follow you out.'

The skinny guy appraised her. 'All right, but mind what I say. This is private property. Stay off it or there'll be trouble.'

After a bit of manoeuvring, they were facing the other way. The Higher Ground driver jogged back to his van and they lurched along behind him.

'OK, so we follow him back to the road. Then what?' Carlo asked.

'How about doing a little food shopping so that we're self-sufficient?' Petra said sweetly. 'Then we can come back later.'

'You're determined to do this, aren't you?'

'You bet. That guy really didn't want us on the property. There has to be a reason.'

'Other than trespassing you mean?'

They followed the van onto the paved road and drove for several kilometres until they reached a small town. At the main intersection in the centre of town stood a white church. The van turned into the parking lot in front of the church and the driver got out. He locked the van and went inside.

'Not someone I'd have thought went to confession,' Petra commented.

A short way past the intersection they found a small shopping precinct with a grocery store and a liquor store. In just over half an hour they had enough basics for the next forty-eight hours, including a couple of bottles of red wine and some ice for the ice box.

'I'm going to walk back to the church,' Petra said.

Carlo waved his hand in a Mediterranean gesture abdicating responsibility. 'Just be careful. This isn't Rome.'

'I'm a tourist, remember,' Petra answered, putting on her sunhat and waving her camera. 'Anyway, I might be safer here than in Rome. If the van's still there, I want to take a picture.'

Petra walked along the road in the direction of the church. Before she reached the parking lot, the white van drove out and passed her on the other side of the road. It continued past the shopping precinct for a short way then turned left into a forecourt where there appeared to be a number of other shops and businesses. She walked rapidly back to Carlo who was waiting in the camper.

Carlo set off across the road on foot and entered the

forecourt. The van was at the far end. He squeezed between two parked cars and made his way towards it, staying on the covered walkway close to the shop frontages. Ten minutes later he was back with Petra.

'Our young man is sitting on a bar stool, drinking and smoking with a bunch of buddies. The barmaid is showing him a good deal of cleavage and warmth.'

'So he's there for the duration?'

'I'd say so. An hour or two certainly.'

'Come on then. Let's take a peek in the church on our way.'

'Why do you want to do that?'

'Gut, Carlo.'

According to the notice board outside, it was a Dutch Reformed Church founded in 1840. The door was unlocked. Petra and Carlo stepped in expecting to find a priest or pastor, but no one was inside. The interior was plain with dark wooden pews and an altar covered in a white cloth with minimal embroidery. A cross stood on the altar but no silverware. For the size of the community, it was a large church. Carlo inspected the lectern and disappeared into a side chapel.

Petra wandered back towards the door. In an alcove nearby was an impressive font. She caressed the cool green and white marble, recalling some of the Catholic churches she had visited in Italy in the days when she used to holiday there. She jumped as the latch on the door squeaked and began to turn.

The woman who entered was as startled as Petra. She was wearing overalls and carrying a bucket and a mop.

'My God! Are you one of them that's having a baby baptized on Saturday?'

'No way,' Petra said, aghast.

'Shame!' The cleaner chattered on. 'Four this Saturday and a new batch every three months, scrawny squawking little things. I wonder if they're treated properly up there.'

'Up where?' Petra asked.

'That community farm place, out along the old river. Never any men there, except the father of course.'

'The father?'

'Father Joe. He was pastor here then went off to Namibia.' She sniffed. 'All different when he came back with his wild hair and beard. Thinks he's Jesus Christ, trying to save the world.'

'Who thinks he's Jesus Christ?' Carlo asked as he sauntered up to them.

'Father Joe,' Petra said.

Carlo raised his eyebrows. 'Wears a black robe and sandals, I expect, and has a rope tied round his waist.'

'You know him?'

Carlo shook his head emphatically. 'No, I've just seen lots of pictures.'

Petra tugged at his sleeve. 'Come on, Carlo. This lady needs to get on with her work, and we have a long way to go before we get to Springbok. Good luck with the baptisms!'

CHAPTER

38

Petra filled Carlo in on what the cleaner had said.

'Sounds like a sausage factory to me.' He drove fast but by the time they reached the farm track the shadows were lengthening. 'It'll be dark soon.'

'I presume this pop-art creation has headlights.'

'Yes, but this isn't the kind of terrain you want to drive on at night.'

'At least we'll be able to see vehicles coming towards us.'

'God help us if we do. We were warned off pretty strongly.'

'Sometimes you're chicken, Mercutio.'

'Think up your excuses in advance, *tesoro mio*.'

'Well if Father Joe turns out to be Father John, I can tell him how fascinated by his community outreach programmes I am.'

Not long after passing the track where they had turned off earlier to avoid the Higher Ground van, they came to another junction. This time a narrow track led off to the left. It was deeply rutted and, in Carlo's opinion, unsuitable for either the van or their camper.

'Straight ahead or straight back? Your choice, Petra.'

'You know the answer. I think I can see a gate. Give me a minute to find my binoculars.'

Although the sun was low, Petra had a good view down the track. 'Yes, there's a gate in a tall fence. Then I can see trees and what looks like cultivation – could be vines or some type of vegetable. Definitely a farm.'

'Any buildings?'

'No. They must be farther away.' She lowered the binoculars. 'We can't turn up in this contraption. We'll have to hide it somehow and walk the rest of the way.'

Carlo eyed the rutted track to the left. There was a stand of camelthorn at the bottom of a shallow slope. 'If we get down there, we may never get back up, especially in the dark.'

'We can camp there overnight and leave at first light.'

'As I said …'

'We're wasting time. Let's try it.'

The slope wasn't as hard to negotiate as Carlo had feared. Once they reached the bottom, he pulled in as far under the trees as he could.

Petra opened the glove box and found an instruction sheet with a list of equipment. 'There's supposed to be a tarpaulin that can be rigged as an awning. We can throw that over the roof if it's not colour-coordinated with the van.'

They camouflaged the van as best they could and set off. There was a cattle grid at the gate and the fence was electric. Signs on the gate warned that it too was electrified. To temporarily turn off the power and open it, you needed a key to insert into a button.

'OK,' Petra said. 'Why don't we walk along the fence and find another way in, or at least get close enough to see the buildings?'

'I knew this would be a mission.'

In short order Petra began to wish she had hiking boots with her. The veldt was uneven and she was worried about snakes. The fence seemed to go on for miles. Then it took a turn and after a while joined a white wall. They followed the wall until it abutted a building. Over the wall they could see the grey slate roofs of several other white buildings.

Dusk had already fallen. The compound was quiet. No crying babies. No barking dogs coming to investigate.

'Give me a leg up, Carlo. I'll take a look.'

'Better if you give me a boost.'

'You don't know what Vicky Dunlin looks like. I do. Mrs. P. showed me a photo. Come on!'

'You'll hardly be able to see her in this light.'

With Carlo's less than enthusiastic help, Petra scrambled onto the top of the wall. She sat on it as best she could and supported herself against the side of the building, which looked like an old stable block.

For a long while there was nothing. Then in the distance she heard voices. A light came on in a building on the far side of the compound. She tucked herself back into the corner between the wall and the building.

In the centre of the courtyard was a well with a bucket hanging from a rope. Across the way a door opened. A young fair-haired woman in a short blue robe emerged and began to lower the bucket into the well. She turned the handle strongly but was heavily pregnant.

'Next quarter's batch,' Petra murmured.

Another girl came out of the building. Also heavily pregnant, she went to help the girl at the well. Together they carried the bucket full of water back into the building.

Petra waited and watched. Carlo was becoming more

and more impatient. Finally she realized they would have to go. If Vicky Dunlin was there, she wasn't showing herself.

'Are you satisfied?' Carlo asked when they got back to the camper van after laboriously retracing their footsteps with the aid of the penlight on Petra's key ring.

'No, because I'm certain Vicky's there, and I haven't had a reply to the second email I sent Higher Ground from *Scheherazade*. Now we have to move on.' Petra shot a sideways glance at Carlo, wondering whether to risk his wrath. 'I suppose you wouldn't consider going back there at dawn to take another look before we leave?'

'Absolutely not. What would you do if you saw her? Go in with guns blazing and drag her out by the hair? From what you told me of her letter to Mrs. P., she joined the outreach programme because she wanted to help. It's voluntary, Petra. So forget Miss Dunlin and concentrate on enjoying yourself. Have a glass of vino. That'll help you relax.'

Petra knew she was being unreasonable but couldn't shake off the feeling that something was deeply wrong. The stable block at the compound was similar to the one pictured in the Higher Ground brochure. The two girls she had seen were white and pregnant. What the hell was going on? And while it was true Vicky had volunteered, she had also spouted platitudes like it being her destiny. Who could have influenced her that much?

Carlo went to open the back of the van which housed the ice box, water tank, camping stove, kitchen gear, a small sink, and below it a storage area for groceries. For the first time, Petra took a good look at the interior of the camper. She knew that the benches and table inside folded down at night to make one large bed. All the 2-berth campers were similar, so she had accepted that as the price to pay for a self-drive safari holiday in Namibia.

She peered in. Two lightweight sleeping bags brought by Carlo were rolled up on one of the benches. By day the Namib Desert could be scorching hot; at night the temperature plunged.

'Where's the toilet and the shower, Carlo?'

There was a pregnant silence.

'Don't tell me ... the 2ST had one ...'

This was more than she had bargained for.

CHAPTER

39

Outside the window of the Higher Ground camper van, the Namib Desert rolled past. Henny had no eyes for the stony plains with the jutting mountains that formed one of the oldest deserts on earth, part of the ancient Gondwana continent. Yesterday's blowout followed by the puncture in the spare tire had taught him a lesson that he swore he would never forget again. Driving the gravel roads required constant vigilance. He adjusted the visor to block out the fierce rays of the setting sun and slowed to stay clear of the cloud of dust that hid the car in front.

The tire repairs had cost him time and money. They put the van out of commission and forced him to pay for overnight accommodation at the only lodge in the vicinity. The girls had been overjoyed. Egged on by Megan and Hilary, they got talking to a bunch of South African guys. Before he could re-exert any kind of control, they were having their photographs taken, sending messages home, and doing who knew what else.

When they finally set off again, the group had insisted on visiting the fucking castle. Which meant that instead of being at the campsite in Sesriem where the six young women would be preparing dinner and taking care of laundry and other chores that needed doing, they were still on the road. A day and a half behind schedule.

Thank God they would be meeting up with another group led by the Master as soon as they reached Etosha.

Henny swerved to avoid a deep rut that he saw at the last minute. Bloody hell. Concentration was impossible with the incessant noise from the back. Six piercing voices, two more strident than the rest.

CHAPTER

40

Sandrine Broselli ran down the steps in front of Halfman's Drift Lodge wearing black leggings and a khaki shirt. The look on her face was priceless: first incredulity, then distrust and disdain. It mirrored the looks on the faces of many of the motorists they had passed during the long drive. She waved her arms and shouted at them to move on, the campsite was five kilometres away in the Transfrontier National Park. Carlo saved the day by sticking his head out of the window and giving his best wolf whistle. Sandrine pulled herself up short and placed her hands on her hips. Petra collapsed with laughter. The wicked camper had its perks.

The Brosellis' lodge was built along the Orange River just west of the National Park. The décor was rustic chic: rough-hewn stone, thatched roofs, wooden beams, flagstone floors, whirring ceiling fans that reminded Petra of the huge mixers at the biscuit factory. As at the wine farm they accepted paying guests who came, Tony said, to take advantage of the opportunities for canoeing, rafting, fishing and hunting. In recent years, he had encouraged photographic visitors rather than the trophy hunters that liked to shoot the oryx and other antelope. Even so, there were plenty of animal heads on the walls. And Petra suspected Sandrine would not say no to organizing the occasional wedding at the lodge. Anything to keep the coffers full.

As soon as Petra and Carlo had had a chance to clean up, Tony offered to take them on a tour of the property. He seemed more relaxed than he had been at Vredehof.

'Yes, please,' Petra said, 'but why is it called Halfman's Drift?'

'Uncle Tony will show us later,' Carlo answered. 'Trust me, you'll be amazed.'

First they toured the side of the property that bordered the river. They stopped at an overlook where brilliant blue kingfishers darted from the cliffs.

'This is the longest river in South Africa. It rises in the Highlands about a hundred and fifty kilometres from the Indian Ocean and runs more or less westward to the Atlantic, bringing all manner of things with it,' Tony lectured. 'Never underestimate the power of those waters. They've carved this land and will continue to do so.' Below them, the river was a brown torrent.

'Does it ever dry up?'

'Not completely, but in very dry years it might not reach the sea. Because it flows along the southern edge of the Namib Desert, evaporation is huge. The delta is a mass of sandbars. You'll see how quickly the terrain changes between here and the ocean,' he added.

They drove in a southwesterly direction for over half an hour. When they picked up the river again, the winding steep-sided canyons had flattened out. The river was broader and there were numerous rapids. Tony turned away from the river and Petra noticed how the vegetation had all but disappeared. Then they were driving over a sandy plain towards a steep rocky slope which, she saw when they got there, was covered in scrub.

Tony pulled up at the bottom of the slope and pointed out a couple of trees with strong trunks topped by numerous small upward-pointing branches. At the top of each branch was a bunch of green pointed leaves.

'That's the quivertree, a member of the aloe family. It survives well in arid conditions because the branches and trunk store water. Bushmen used to hollow out dead branches to make quivers for their arrows, hence its name.'

There was no doubt about Tony's love for the land and its flora. Petra just hoped they would be back in time for a spot of relaxation before dinner. Then she could ask to use a computer and check her email. Since they had left their hidey-hole near the compound full of pregnant young women at first light that morning, Vicky Dunlin had not been far from her thoughts. Higher Ground hadn't phoned or texted, and now she was a long way north of Saldanha Bay. If they offered her employment, she would have some difficult decisions to make.

Suddenly Carlo, who had been unusually quiet, sat up straight and pointed to something in the distance. 'There's one.'

'You're right, my boy.'

All Petra could see over another ridge was what looked like a person with a mop of wild hair coming towards them. Surely not Father John, she prayed, out here in the wilderness.

'There's your halfman,' Carlo said proudly.

'It's not a real man?'

'No, *cara*, it's a very rare and protected succulent. The head always faces north.'

When they drew nearer, Petra saw that the tree was about the height of a man with a cylindrical stem and a tuft of branches at the top. Drifting sand had piled up round its base.

'Look for the halfman and you'll find one of the beauties of nature,' Tony said.

On the way back to the lodge, Tony seemed to retreat into himself and Carlo slouched down in his seat. Behind him, Petra studied the wild but beautiful landscape and remembered something Mrs. Pinderally had mentioned during her teaching about diamonds.

'Wasn't the first diamond in South Africa discovered along the Orange River?' she asked whoever might be listening in the front of the jeep.

'It was,' Tony replied. 'The Eureka Diamond in 1867, then the Star of Africa two years later. But those finds were much farther east.'

Eureka! Thank you, Mrs. P.

'Isn't there a border crossing near here into the Sperrgebiet, the forbidden diamond mining zone, of Namibia?' she continued.

'You certainly do your homework.'

'I'm a cop, don't forget!' Petra kept her tone light and delivered her line with a smile, but she was sure a shadow passed across Tony's face when he glanced at her through the rearview mirror. 'Having a wonderful vacation,' she added.

'The old forbidden zone has been made into a national park, although security is still tight.' He half-turned to observe Petra. 'You don't look like a cop,' he said almost to himself.

'Is the diamond mining over then?'

'Not over, but nowadays it's mostly alluvial.'

Now we're getting there, she thought, but with his next words he passed the buck.

'If you want to know about diamonds, ask Sandrine. She's more up to speed than I am. I look after the fishing and hunting. You both like fishing, you said.'

Carlo roused himself. 'We do, and we'd love to visit Port Nolloth and go out on one of your trawlers.'

'We'd have to stay on board – the boats go out very early and fish overnight. I'll have to check with my wife to see what she has planned.'

Back to Sandrine.

She met them on the steps and told them they had half an hour before dinner. Petra asked if there was a computer she could use to check her email.

'I thought you were on vacation,' Tony said mildly but nevertheless showed her into his study, opened up the computer for her and left her there.

As soon as he had gone, she went into *boatgirl*. There was one email waiting for her. From Higher Ground. Eagerly she opened it.

Dear Alice,

I am very sorry to have to tell you that we have no openings for volunteers in the Saldanha Bay area, and no need for anyone with your skills anywhere else.

Thank you for contacting us. We wish you well in your future endeavours.

Sincerely,

Marcus Zen

Outreach Programme Coordinator

Petra sat back in Tony's office chair and stared at the

screen in disbelief. She read the email again in case she had missed something, but it was quite clear. They didn't want her. Normally volunteer organizations welcomed new prospects and even if she hadn't made the final cut, she would have expected them to ask for further information or suggest she reapply in a few months' time. Instead they had broken off all communication. She leaned back and put her hands behind her head to think it through.

When the dinner gong rang, she was still smarting from the rejection. She had five minutes to return to the chalet she was sharing with Carlo, put on mosquito repellent and a long-sleeved shirt. Carlo met her on the way.

'So did they hire you as an aromatherapist or an aquafit instructor?'

'Neither. I'm persona non grata.'

'Well I didn't think your skills were quite the right thing for a community outreach programme.'

'On this occasion, you were right, Mercutio. I blew it.'

'Knowing what we do now, you could try telling them you forgot to mention your midwifery skills.'

'Oh yeah, they're extremely likely to believe that. I'll have to find another way.'

'Why not just drop it and enjoy our vacation?'

'I don't think I can, Carlo.'

Dinner was on the verandah – just the four of them, as there were no outside guests that week. Setting aside her disappointment at Higher Ground's response, Petra tried to engage Sandrine in conversation since she hadn't had much chance during the week of the wedding. Maddeningly, Sandrine preferred to interact with Carlo, who seemed to have forgotten the incident at the folly. Any opportunity to get close to a beautiful woman, and Sandrine, Petra had to concede, was beautiful despite her haughty manner. How unattractive and inadequate she would have made Julia feel, especially compared to Florian, her golden boy.

Petra was forced to talk to Tony. 'Have you heard from Julia?' she asked him.

'No and I don't expect to. She and Max should enjoy their honeymoon without worrying about us here at home.'

'What about Florian? Isn't he leading a tour of some kind?'

'I believe he agreed to show some of the wedding guests the highlights of Namibia. He's very knowledgeable and enjoys being a tour guide from time to time.'

'Like father like stepson!'

'Not quite. Our priorities are somewhat different. I have a historical focus; his is more on the future.'

'And your wife's is more on diamonds – oh, and on biscuits and weddings,' Petra added as Sandrine broke eye contact with Carlo and turned to glare at her.

'What are you talking about?' Sandrine snapped.

'I heard you telling Julia last week that diamonds pay for a lot of what you have.'

'Of course. Diamonds are a girl's best friend. Anyone with money buys diamonds.'

'Does your wedding planning service include advising prospective bridegrooms on the purchase of a suitable ring?' Petra asked in her best honeyed tone.

'Naturally, if I'm asked.'

'I'm sure you have excellent connections in the diamond business.'

Petra caught Carlo's eye. He gave a tiny shake of his head as if to say, don't push it.

'Those sugared almonds you gave me were absolutely

delicious. I shared a tin with a friend in Cape Town,' she continued.

Sandrine's face turned white then red with anger. 'Those were gifts for you to put in your luggage and take home to your family, not to waste here in South Africa!'

'They weren't wasted, believe me. And I love the colour patterns in the stones you decorate the tins with. Red in the middle. That's my favourite!'

Petra waited for Sandrine to deny any involvement with the tins, but she didn't.

CHAPTER

41

Henny was at his wit's end. The itinerary was getting away from him. They were supposed to be on their way to Swakopmund, and the Master would be expecting him to report in that evening. Because of the breakdown, they had only one full day to spend at Sossusvlei and Megan and Hilary refused to omit a single activity. To make matters worse, his leg was playing up. Stress, it was the fucking stress. And the driving.

He'd switched things around so that they'd explored the Sesriem Canyon and the watercourse of the Tsauchab River in the morning. The sunset tour of the dunes was happening later that afternoon. Tomorrow morning they'd head for the dunes at sunrise, then break camp and take off for Swakopmund.

He could hear the strident tones of the young women as they discussed the South Africans they'd met at the guesthouse the night the van had been out of service. Squeals of delight drowned out the normal sounds of the campground.

Henny was seriously thinking of dumping the whole lot of them once they reached Swakopmund. He'd call the Master and leave them at the rest camp, and even pay for a couple of nights out of his own pocket. Then he'd make a beeline for Port Nolloth.

After a few beers, he'd find himself a local beauty and get his rocks off. Somebody with a bit of flesh on her who knew how to pleasure him, not one of these spoiled brats that were off limits for him even if others could do as they pleased with them. Just thinking about it gave him a hard-on.

Henny laced the door of his pup tent shut and limped across to the camper van. He switched on the engine and checked the fuel gauge. There was enough fuel for the afternoon's excursion but not enough to do next day's sunrise trip and the drive to Swakopmund. The pumps would be closed by sunset, so he would have to fill up now. No point waiting in line with dozens of other vehicles at 6 a.m.

After filling up, Henny went into the campsite shop and bought himself a pack of Camels and a root beer. As he came out, a mini-van pulled up and disgorged the four young men who had been at the guesthouse. Dammit man, there could be trouble if they were coming to stay the night.

The inside of the camper van was a pigsty. Megan and Hilary had left maps, leaflets and tour brochures all over their seats and on the floor. So far they had ignored his orders to tidy up. He'd have to speak to them again and deliver the Higher Ground cleanliness-next-to-godliness lecture. That was bound to go over well.

He opened the side door of the van and began to clear the floor. Hilary's seat was behind the driver's seat, Megan's to her left, except when one of them insisted on riding up front next to him.

He stuffed a bunch of brochures into the pocket on

the back of the front passenger seat. Two of them fell out and he cursed. Something else was in there, filling up the bottom of the pocket. He pulled it out. It was a small book covered in pink suede. A piece of heavy elastic sewn into the spine held it closed.

Gleefully he opened it. If it was what he thought it was, he'd find out what Megan was thinking! He'd read what she'd written to date and put it back where he found it. If he read her new entries every day or two, he'd be able to stay one step ahead of her. That's how he'd re-exert control.

The name inside the flyleaf was Megan Jones. Running his finger down the page, he began to read.

What fun to be doing this tour then going to volunteer in an African village …

Long drive to Springbok with lots of slowdowns for roadworks. Mobile phone coverage is the pits …

Crossed into Namibia yesterday. Lots of golden oryx, so beautiful, black faces, long straight horns …

Boring stuff. There must be more interesting bits. He turned the page and spotted his own name.

Our guide Henny's a bit of a weirdo. Tried to take our phones away, stupid sod! Wears black and lectures us all the time. But he is kinda cute even if he does limp.
I wonder what he'd be like in bed.

She'd underlined the last sentence several times. Henny felt a stirring in his pants. Once last year, one of the girls on a tour had come on to him and they'd had a thing just before he joined up with the Master's group at Etosha. He still had a few days to make it with Megan. He'd show her how cute he was, and boy did he know a way of stopping her talking.

CHAPTER

42

The diabolical screeching penetrated Petra's brain at six o'clock in the morning.

'That's one thing I won't miss when I leave South Africa,' she said aloud.

'What's that, *cara*?'

'Those horrible birds. Always making a racket early in the morning.'

'Ha-de-dahs? They're just socializing. And you'll be pleased to know that they're a very un-endangered species.'

'Mmm. Carlo, I've been thinking.'

'Oh no!'

'Does South Africa have exchange controls?'

'Indeed it does. The Reserve Bank controls all inflows and outflows of capital.'

'So let's say you had a lot of money you wanted to get out of the country. How difficult would it be to move it?'

'That's a very good question. Right, South African Finance 101. I don't know the finer details but it's really quite simple. All movements of capital – in and out – are controlled by the Reserve Bank.'

'We're not concerned with inflows.'

'True. In the case of outflows, no resident individual

or company may make a transfer without prior approval. Outward payments can only be made for permissible reasons, and all payments to foreign parties must be reported to the Reserve Bank.'

'So it's pretty strictly controlled.'

'There may be ways to sidestep the requirements.'

'Which is what I guess your dear step-aunt is looking for – a means of getting undeclared wealth out of the country.'

Carlo nodded. 'Wealth in the form of undocumented diamonds.'

'If Sandrine does amass money outside South Africa, do you think she's going to follow? She seems so keen on her businesses here, and the Delapore family goes way back. I'd have thought it would be hard for her to leave. For Tony too, although Julia's already gone. And then there's Florian. What's he going to do?'

'One thing at a time,' Carlo said slowly. 'Businesses. That's it! You're wasted in the Royal Canadian Mounted Police, Petra. If anything used in the manufacture of Delapore biscuits or the sugared almonds is imported, Sandrine will need approval to pay her suppliers. There'll be documents on file.'

'We know the tins are imported from China and decorated here, so there'll be a record of that.'

'But the documents won't be enough to establish the link between Delapore and Dragées d'Aix unless Sandrine signed them herself,' Carlo said.

'Customers like Mrs. Pinderally order stones in specific colours for the decoration, and Sandrine prides herself on quote "fulfilling all our customers' wishes". I bet she'll have signed some estimates and proposals.'

'I should have spent more time in Montagu sifting through the paperwork.'

'Sandrine's more likely to keep important or incriminating documents in the safe. If we carry on though, we're bound to find something.' Petra paused. 'Isn't it strange how the two things you were on the lookout for – illicit diamonds and illicit dragées – seem to be coming together?'

'I repeat, truth is stranger than fiction. But this isn't my investigation. I'll report back to my colleague and see how he wants to proceed. Meanwhile, we'll continue our vacation as planned.'

'I'm going to pump Sandrine for more information. She can't keep snubbing me.'

'Be careful. I don't think it'll pay to make an enemy of her.'

Petra found her hostess not far from the lodge, practising yoga on a mat near the swimming pool. Clad in a skin-tight pale pink finely woven bodysuit, she appeared to be stark naked. Her movements were fluid and she made even the most intricate positions look easy.

When Sandrine uncurled herself and sat quietly in the lotus position with her hands palm-up on her knees, Petra approached. She sat down far enough away not to crowd her but close enough to have an intimate conversation. She adopted the lotus position too, then, taking a leaf out of Carlo's book, said, 'You're in amazing shape, I really envy you. Last year I took beginners' yoga but I'm not a contortionist. I prefer Pilates.'

Sandrine didn't answer and Petra wondered whether she was going to ignore her. Finally she said, 'It's all about control.'

'That's why you're such a good event planner. You control and organize every detail so that the final product is flawless – like the best kind of diamond.'

A muscle twitched above Sandrine's left eye.

Petra continued. 'Julia's wedding was perfect.'

'I'd hardly say that. On her wedding morning she was late and threw off all the timing, and you went running off somewhere and had to have your pedicure redone.'

'I'm sorry,' Petra said in her meekest voice.

'Why the sudden interest in the event business? You're a cop like Carlo.'

'Yes, but I have a friend who's inherited a manor house in England and has to find ways to make it pay. She's thinking of doing weddings and special events. How did you get into the business?'

Sandrine stared into the distance as if she was looking back into the past. She crossed her hands protectively over her stomach.

'When my father died, I took over the family businesses. There was no one else. I expanded the range of products at the biscuit factory to include cakes. I added new grape varieties at Vredehof and I built the tasting centre.'

She recited her achievements in clipped tones without a hint of emotion, as taut as a tightrope wire. Then came a blunt admission of failure.

'I underestimated the amount of time and money it would take to sort out the estate and the lag between investing and obtaining a decent return. Not to mention the changes taking place across the country,' she added in an undertone. 'Event planning was a logical way of monetizing the assets.'

'You've built a great team around you: Wellington and

the staff at Vredehof, Father John to conduct ceremonies, Florian to keep the young ladies happy.'

'Florian's much more than good looks,' Sandrine said sharply. 'He has talents and ideals.'

I can vouch for the former, Petra thought. His ideals were equally worrisome.

'What about Julia? Will you miss her now that she's gone to Europe?'

'Julia will work with the De Witt family to promote our interests.'

'They're freight forwarders, aren't they? Do you export to Europe?'

'We're looking at our options.'

Sandrine fell silent and Petra wondered if that was her signal to leave, but suddenly she abandoned her pose and stood up. 'Lemonade with a touch of honey,' she said, pointing to a tray that a member of staff was placing on a table under a sunshade. 'Try it. It's a good cleanser.'

Petra blinked. At last, the breakthrough she had been hoping for. 'You're right, it is. My mother swears by lemon juice in warm water to cure everything from colds to stomach upsets – she's Italian.'

'Carlo told me you used to spend your summers in Italy.'

'He was a good friend during my teenage years. When he asked me to come here with him, I couldn't believe it. Do you get many wedding parties from overseas? Destination weddings are all the rage.'

'There are more during the spring and summer.'

'You mean October to March?'

'Yes, but I have a big one the weekend after next. A group from Frankfurt, guests from London and Paris too.'

'It must be fun working with lots of different nationalities.'

'Fun?' Sandrine shrugged. 'I'd call it challenging, but it keeps the money flowing.'

Petra had a hunch that finding creative ways to get money out of South Africa wasn't Sandrine's only talent. She might well arrange to get paid outside the country by foreign guests, building up a nice Swiss bank account so that if things went bad she could get out.

To keep the conversation going, Petra continued to act as though she was a complete airhead.

'Giving dragées as a parting gift is a really good idea. My friend might be able to do something similar. Maybe she could import them through you. And if you want to expand your export operations, you could use the same tins for wedding cake …'

'You're really into this, aren't you?' Sandrine looked at her sideways. 'And you certainly have imagination.'

'She does, doesn't she?'

Both women turned as Carlo appeared in the briefest of shiny black swimming trunks. He whipped off his sunglasses. 'I fancy a dip,' he said, focussing on Sandrine.

'You don't need me then,' Petra said.

'No *cara*, not for now.'

CHAPTER

43

Petra left Carlo and Sandrine by the pool. She wasn't interested in Carlo as a mate she assured herself as she walked away, but she had a proprietary interest in him as a very close friend. They had weathered the highs and lows of teenage summer vacations together as well as the trauma of Romeo's death. All that translated into a motherly concern for his well-being and a desire to keep him safe from predatory women. Sometimes it manifested itself as jealousy.

She kicked angrily at a stone. Her discussion with Sandrine had been less than satisfactory. She had played the airhead to the best of her ability and succeeded in softening her up, yet Sandrine had let nothing slip that would help them get a real handle on what was going on. Petra began to wish she had stayed with Mrs. Pinderally and carried on hunting for Vicky Dunlin. Right now a Rolling Sands massage would go down well. She must have unconsciously tensed her muscles while talking to Sandrine. Especially once Florian had come into the conversation.

A wave of heat washed over her. It left her feeling agitated and even more bad-tempered. Carlo was behaving like a gigolo. Florian – where was Florian? What was he doing leading a group of girls on a tour through Namibia? Girls who would end up doing volunteer work in one of the villages he and Father John supported. What would he do after that? Would he stay there with them? Or would she and Carlo see him again before they left South Africa? Did she want to see him again?

She began to jog towards the river's edge in a bid to conquer the thoughts and feelings that were invading her mind and body. She sat down on a bench and stared across the river to the other side of the frontier. Florian was somewhere over there. So what? But there was a wetness between her thighs and her nipples were begging to be caressed and it was all she could do to refrain from touching them. This is ridiculous, she told herself. Put a lid on it. It must be something to do with the anti-malarial tablets she had started taking that morning.

Carlo burst into their chalet. 'There you are!'

Petra was curled up on her bed.

'I've walked all over the place looking for you. I even thought you might have taken a mountain bike and gone for a ride.'

Carlo's aggrieved voice broke into Petra's fantasy and she sat up groggily.

'You've been with Sandrine a long time.'

'Not long enough.'

'Poor Mercutio! Did she throw you out?'

'Why would you think that? No, we were getting along very well. I helped her take off that leotard thing she was wearing. Then we went for a dip and I rubbed her down and I was massaging oil into her lustrous skin ...'

'Spare me the details, Mercutio. I'm not in the mood.'

'Are you sure?' Carlo looked penetratingly at her until Petra began to feel the blood rising to her cheeks. 'You know you'd be no good with a lie detector, don't you?'

'You're hopeless!'

'Not so, *cara*. I'm your best friend. We make a fantastic team. So tell Father Carlo what's the matter.'

Petra sighed. Some things she could never tell. 'My approaches to Sandrine didn't work. I tried flattery, humility, admiration, female conspiracy … I blew a magnificent opportunity, just like I blew the application to Higher Ground. I don't know what's wrong.'

'This is Africa, *tesoro mio*. That's what's wrong. You're out of your natural element; I am too. Africa is different. The way people behave here, the way their minds work, their motivations aren't what you're used to. You can't judge Sandrine or Tony, nor Florian or Julia, by your norms.'

Petra gritted her teeth. 'I hope you're not telling me they can break the law with impunity.'

'Not at all. But first we have to prove they're breaking the law.'

'That's what I was trying to do, Mercutio! Get more information …'

'You won't do it by talking to Sandrine, or any of them for that matter. They'll lead you exactly where they want you to go.'

'Even Julia?'

'She may be straighter than the rest of them, but she's out of the picture for now.'

'I did find out there's a big international wedding – not this weekend, but the following one. Guests are coming from Germany, France and the UK. You saw how angrily Sandrine reacted when I told her I'd shared a tin of dragées with a friend in Cape Town. My guess is that she'll try to smuggle some diamonds out by giving them tins to take home, just as she did with us. Unless she gets spooked.'

'I don't think that's likely,' Carlo said. 'People like Sandrine are supremely arrogant. They don't think anything can upset their plans. We need to see the guest list and their itineraries.'

'Sandrine will have recorded everything at Vredehof. We'll be back there at the end of next week.'

'That'll be too late.'

'Do you think she'll have a copy on the computer here?'

'It's a possibility.'

'If Tony and Sandrine go out, I can take a look.'

Carlo raised his eyebrows.

'I watched Tony type in his password.'

'That deserves a kiss!' He picked up Petra's hand and gave it a resounding smack with his lips.

'Mercutio!' She pulled her hand away.

'If we weren't just good friends, I'd do better than that. Now if you can get that information …'

Carlo froze as someone knocked on the door. 'Who is it?'

'Tony. I hope I'm not disturbing anything.'

There was strain in his voice. Carlo opened the door. 'Come in. Is it time to go to Port Nolloth?'

'I'm afraid Sandrine has other plans. She has to take delivery of something for the factory. We're leaving straightaway and won't be back before you go to Namibia.'

'No worries, mate,' Carlo said, putting on an Aussie drawl. 'We can amuse ourselves for the rest of the day.'

'I've asked Kirk to set you up with a 4 x 4 buggy and show you one of the trails. I'm sorry we can't go to "the Port", but you might enjoy this more.'

'We'll see you before we leave South Africa, won't we?' Petra asked. 'You've been so hospitable. I can't tell you how much I appreciate your letting me come to the wedding.'

'Thank Carlo for that, my dear,' Tony said, kissing her on both cheeks. 'It's been a delight to have you both.'

Sandrine was waiting impatiently for her husband in the lodge's Range Rover. As soon as he got into the seat beside her, she laid into him.

'You're too nice to them, Anton. The quicker they get out of our hair, the better. That Mountie is always fishing for information. I don't trust her and you shouldn't either.'

'She has an enquiring mind, my darling, that's all.'

'She pretends to be naïve, but she isn't. We've come so far, I'm not going to let her ruin our plans for the future.'

'I hope you're not going to do anything unnecessary.'

'On the contrary, I'll do only what is absolutely necessary.'

44

The trail followed the curves of the Orange River, testing Carlo's driving skills and Petra's nerve. She hung onto the handhold above the door as they hit an S-bend at the bottom of a steep incline. They were going too fast and the wheels spun on the combination of loose gravel and sand. For a horrible moment, Petra thought they were going to lose it.

'One day I want to do the Dakar to Paris rally,' Carlo said as he pulled out of another bend and they began to climb. 'What say you come along as my navigator?'

Petra shuddered. 'I'm fine on water, Carlo, you know that. On bad roads there are still times when I panic – like back there.'

'These buggies are built for this.'

As they came closer to the coast, the trail wound through arid desert. There was little or no vegetation, and where the wind had blown the loose sand away, the surface was corrugated. They lurched along until they came to a dry creek that hived off to the left. Ruts indicated that vehicles had driven through it.

Carlo swung the wheel. 'Hold tight!' He followed first one branch then another as the creek splintered into crevasses. Like a maze, most of the branches that had once held flood water came to a dead end.

'I hope we can find our way back,' Petra said.

'No worries. We have a compass, my nose and your sharp eyes. I want to go a bit farther and take a walk before we turn round.'

He drove on over terrain that became more and more rugged. A while later he stopped at the entrance to a steep-sided gully. He got out and beckoned for Petra to follow. 'You remember the fossil park and what our guide said about animals and stuff getting trapped by weirs. This is just the sort of place where you might find diamonds … Mmm, I could resign my job and buy a chalet in the mountains. You could …'

'You're so easy to seduce, Mercutio! We could ask Sandrine to help us smuggle them out, is that what you're thinking?'

Carlo led the way into the gully. It twisted and turned and the buggy was soon out of sight. Petra shivered as the temperature dropped. 'I'll wait here.'

Carlo walked on. 'The water must once have flowed furiously through here,' he shouted.

She saw him pause and kick at something on the ground. He bent down and examined it carefully before moving on. Then he rounded a corner and was lost to view. She waited for what seemed like ages as the shadows lengthened. By the time he reappeared in the distance, she felt chilled to the bone.

'What took you so long?'

'Nothing.'

They arrived back at the lodge just before sunset. Kirk met

them on the front stoep in his khakis and bushranger hat. 'How was the ride?'

'Great!' Carlo enthused. 'I wish we had time to do the whole trail.'

'Come and have a drink in the bar. I'll show you some photos of last year's championship rally.'

Petra nudged Carlo. 'I want to go and shower before I do anything else. I'll join you in half an hour or so.'

She could hear the staff's lilting voices floating through from the kitchen as she made her way to the back of the main building. Instead of crossing the verandah and picking up the path to their chalet, she turned into the narrow corridor that led to Tony's office. She tried the door and was pleased to find that it wasn't locked. Perhaps Tony had left in too much haste to lock up properly, or perhaps Kirk as manager had access to the computer. Whatever the situation, she had to be quick.

Stepping inside, she closed the door as quietly as possible then stopped to listen. There were no footfalls on the flagstones of the corridor. Outside, the light was fading fast.

Tony's computer was on the desk in front of the window. She sat down and entered the password she had seen him use.

'Incorrect password,' said the computer.

Shit! Had he changed it before leaving, or had she made a mistake? She didn't think so. Petra closed her eyes, reviewing in her mind the keys he had touched. She had to get it right. Three failed tries and the computer would block access and who knew what on-screen messages Tony would find when he returned.

She took a deep breath, her fingers poised over the

keyboard. Could she have memorized the password wrongly? No, she was sure of the sequence. Tony was not a trained typist. He had picked out each of the eight letters carefully so as not to make a mistake and she hadn't seen him use the shift key for a capital letter. She looked down at the rows of keys.

OK, crunch time. If she hesitated much longer she would have to switch on a light, which wouldn't be a good idea. She typed in the letters picking them out as Tony had done.

Bob's your uncle! The screensaver appeared. She was in.

Without hesitation Petra opened up his data files. She had already decided on the way back along the 4 x 4 trail that she didn't feel the slightest bit guilty. There was a lot going on that shouldn't be, and if she and Carlo could put a stop to it, they would.

Sandrine was a compulsive organizer. She wouldn't want to be at the lodge without access to her documents, and she didn't strike Petra as a paper person. She probably used Excel for spreadsheets and schedules.

Petra began to search. The minutes ticked by. Finally, she hit pay dirt. There was no time to read the file. She copied it onto the flash drive she kept on her key ring, turned off the computer and headed for the door.

When she got to the bar after a three-minute shower, her wet hair was coiled in the nape of her neck. She had put on an orange and black kaftan she'd bought in the Robben Island gift shop, leather thong sandals and a touch of lipstick and powder. No need to stand on ceremony in the bush.

Kirk and Carlo were laughing like old buddies.

'You won't believe what Kirk has been telling me about the diamonds people used to pick up in this area not that long ago. Other precious stones too – garnet, tiger's eye …'

'Mrs. Pinderally said the same thing. But of course what people want most are diamonds.'

'Like I was telling Carlo here, I still do some prospecting,' Kirk said. 'You have to know where to look, and when. We don't often get rain here, but when we do, man it can be heavy. Floods old river courses like Halfman's Drift and washes away the sand. You should see some of the trenches and sinkholes. You can put your hand in and pull up a fistful of gravel and like as not you'll find rough.'

'Do you dive for diamonds too?' Petra asked him.

'Na man, that's dangerous work. That ocean can be brutal. You know how many days a year those guys can dive? Go on, guess.'

Petra thought of the cold Atlantic Ocean and her experiences in the Marine Unit over the years. With cold water, fog was almost always an issue. This was the south Atlantic, far from what she was used to, but no less treacherous. 'Say a third – about a hundred and twenty.'

'They wish. Every year it's less. Say a third of that, maybe forty days a year.'

'But it's still rewarding.'

'Can be. I heard tell of pump sites that have yielded more'n a thousand carats from less than ten cubic metres of gravel.'

'Cool! Is it true that rough diamonds can only be sold to licensed diamond buyers?'

Kirk nodded. 'That's just it, man. You have no choice. You have your concession, you put in what sea-time you can, and your bags of gravel get off-loaded and sent away to be processed. You have no idea how many gems are in there. If you're lucky, you get a cheque every two months.'

'That's the kind of system that leads people to flout the law. I'd want to see the diamonds for myself,' Petra exclaimed.

'It ain't so bad. Most of those guys spend it all on booze and women.'

'What if you hit the jackpot and found a stash of rough on one of your prospecting trips? What would you do?' Carlo asked.

Kirk drained his bottle of Castle. 'Man oh man! I'd say the Lord just placed those beauties there for me to dig out of the ground.'

'Me too,' Carlo enthused. 'But you'd have to know how to sell them on to make real money out of them.'

Kirk dug deep into the side pocket of his shorts. 'I know you're family. See here.'

He pulled out a roundish grey stone with striations.

'Wow! Is that a diamond?' Petra asked. 'Where did you find that?'

'I'm afraid I can't tell you. But there's plenty more.'

CHAPTER

45

Driving along the road that afternoon towards the huge red sand dunes, Henny began to see Megan in a new light. The pain in his leg wasn't so bad and the shrillness of her voice had diminished somewhat. He looked in the rearview mirror and scanned her face.

Not a bad little thing. A few freckles, sun-tinged skin, reddish hair cut short. He hadn't paid much attention to her eyes, but in the mirror they looked greyish-green. Sweet. Her tits were on the small side but well-shaped, like little round apples. He had reappraised her legs as she was climbing into the camper. Strong, a bit heavy round the knees but he could overlook that. That wasn't what mattered.

A horn blared. He was too close to the centre of the narrow road. He swung the wheel a little too aggressively and felt the back begin to slide on the sandy surface. Shit! An accident now would land him in a heap of trouble. And blow his chances with Megan.

'You nearly hit that car! You could have killed us all! Don't you know how to drive? I saw you ogling my friend. Keep your eyes on the road!'

Hilary's voice …

Grunting, he turned onto the side track leading to Dune 45. The east side of the dune was in shadow, the west side glowed a searing orange-red in the late afternoon sun. He pulled into the parking lot.

'OK, this is it for today. Tomorrow at sunrise we'll be going to the pans at Sossusvlei. If you want to climb, follow the crowd. I'll wait for you here.' He pointed to a string of black stick figures toiling like human ants to the top of the dune. Others were running and tumbling their way down.

'Come on! Let's do it!' Hilary shouted, getting out of the van. 'Gimp here's going to have a snooze. He can't make it with that gammy leg of his!'

Henny ground his teeth. 'Don't forget to take your damn water!' he reminded them as the group went off laughing. The sand could be unbearably hot late in the day and the climb was tough. He watched them start up the lower slope. By the time they reached the crest they'd be bushed, but the views were worth it. At least there'd be no arguments about going to bed early.

He reclined his seat and closed his eyes. Being a tour guide for this lot was a total pain in the ass. Why didn't he just drive away and leave them? They treated him like shit. Especially Hilary. She never did what she was told. Maybe she'd die of dehydration on the way up, or fall and break a limb on the way down … or choke to death in the sand. Or maybe they'd all keep on walking along the crest of the dune and never come back. Then he thought of Megan … sweet but fiery … not a bad combination … Megan he could handle …

They got back to the camper van over an hour later, sandy and subdued. The climb had taken its toll. Maybe that was the answer. Tire 'em out. Use 'em until they had no energy left to whine or complain. Was that how the Master did it? Henny had never stopped to think about how or even why, never questioned anybody's motivations. He did what he did because that's how things were.

Back at the campsite, he instructed one of the teams to prepare dinner and picnic packs for the morning. The other he directed to do the laundry.

'We're not going to put your stuff in with ours. It can wait until there's enough to do separately,' Hilary announced. 'In fact,' she added, 'I don't see why we should do it at all. You do it.' She folded her arms and faced him down.

Henny made a fist. He was itching to wipe the supercilious look off her face, to make her do what he said. The Higher Ground Manual was clear. Before they reached the village, tour participants were to be taught to obey orders without question.

'In the true spirit of Africa, our volunteers are required to carry out all household duties for the whole group. Laundry included,' he added.

'Rubbish! This is a sightseeing holiday, not a prison camp. Though sometimes I wonder,' Hilary said.

Megan joined the fray. 'You want to offload your work onto us so that you can slouch around all day and leer at us. Those South African guys we met think you're pretty freaky. They said we don't need to do anything we don't want to.'

'And if this tour doesn't turn out to be what we expected, you can be sure we'll post plenty of reviews on line.'

46

Henny woke with a start in the middle of a bad dream where he was working in a steaming laundry wearing orange prison overalls. He wiped the sweat from his forehead and listened. Someone was moving around outside.

He opened the flap of his tent enough to see what was happening.

Megan was standing outside her tent in a T-shirt that stopped at the top of her thighs. She had sandshoes on her feet and a flashlight in her hand. Sleep had mussed up her hair so that it bristled like a brush, reminding him of the last camper he had bedded: a Swedish girl with blonde spiked hair, long slim legs and shaved pubes. Megan's thighs were on the chunky side, but so what, man? The parts in between would taste just as sweet.

Megan set off across the hard-packed sand surrounding their pitch. The ablutions block was a few minutes' walk away. That's where she'd be going.

Henny watched and waited until she reached the gravel road. None of the other girls had made a sound. He slipped out of his tent and followed her, keeping her in sight but staying well back, savouring the movement of her buttocks as she walked. He felt a welcome surge of blood in his shorts. She'd soon find out that his injury hadn't affected his little head. If anything, it had given him a greater appetite than before when he had nothing to prove.

A light came on as Megan disappeared into the ladies' end of the toilet block. Henny tucked himself back against the wall, round the corner from the door. Absently, he scratched his crotch and thought about his encounter three weeks ago with a Zulu girl. She'd had amazing hands and mouth and given him a good run for his money.

Christ, how much longer would he have to wait? What did women do? His father used to roust his mother out of the bathroom, calling her every name under the sun. And he got results. None of this persuasion through love of Africa and the community crap that Higher Ground spouted.

Inside the block he heard a toilet flush. At last. He moved closer to the corner of the building. Water at the hand basin.

As she got to the door, Henny moved in to block it. He pushed her back into the room and closed the door with one hand.

'You've been a long time, sweetheart. I was worried about you. I came to see if you were all right.' He stroked the bulge in his shorts. 'Look what I've got for you.'

Megan shrieked. He squeezed her shoulders hard with both hands. 'Don't do that, I'm not going to hurt you. I know you like me, you said so yourself. And you like it hot. I'll give you what you want.'

He pulled her close so that he could feel her against him. Her squirming inflamed him further. 'Ja, baby, ja. Keep doing that, that's nice.' He felt the sudden rush of release and groaned. 'Don't stop, I've got lots more where that came from.'

Megan shrieked again and began to cudgel him with her fists. She was a fiery one all right. He grabbed her forearms and held them in a tight lock. She was kicking wildly and he felt a sharp blow as she hit his ankle, then a searing pain as she aimed higher and her foot connected with his shin right where the wire rope had cut into the bone. He dropped her as if she were a burning branch.

She was screaming at him like a fishwife. 'There's nothing I want from you. Stay away from me. Get out!' She picked up the flashlight that was sitting next to the washbasin and brandished it in the air. 'Get out of here or you'll be sorry.'

Henny took a step backwards and flinched as the doorknob hit him in the spine.

Hilary pushed her way in, followed by two of the South Africans. 'Hey, what's going on?' she demanded. 'We heard you screaming, Megan. Has this creep been doing something he shouldn't?'

'Nao, I don't think he could. He caught me off guard is all, but I got him in the shin.' She gave a malicious grin. 'There's more than one place that hurts like hell if you kick it.'

'I hope you won't try anything like that with me,' said one of the guys.

'People get what they deserve.'

Henny made a move towards the door. The little bitch was busy with her friends. If he could slip away quietly, that might be the end of it. If not, he thought with a moment's panic, who knew what complaints she might lodge? Even though he had done nothing, she was already exaggerating her account of what had happened.

'He's been watching me for a while. I'm sure last night

wasn't the first time he's stalked me. Luckily I was ready for him,' she was saying.

He inched closer to the door.

'Hey man, you're not going anywhere,' said the other South African, grabbing Henny's arm. 'At least not yet. What do you want to do with him, Megan?'

Megan cocked her head to one side. 'Kick him in the balls?'

Hilary snorted. 'Good idea! We'll hold him for you.'

Henny blanched.

'Go for it, Megan! Sock it to him!'

Megan cocked her head to the other side and looked Henny up and down. 'I don't know. It might be more fun to teach him a few lessons while we're on the road.'

'You want to continue the tour?' asked the first South African.

'Why not? We've paid our money. We'll be joining up with another group soon and getting rid of this shit.'

'We're all going to Swakopmund, we can hang out together,' Hilary added. 'And as soon as we get there, I'm going to find an internet café and warn people about these Higher Ground tours.'

Henny went even whiter. The last thing he wanted was for the Master to get wind of what had happened.

47

Henny cast a wary glance in his rearview mirror. Not to look at Megan, although she was still sitting next to Hilary in the first row of seats behind him, but to see if they had lost the South Africans. No such luck. There they were, sitting on his tail in their white 4 x 4 camper.

He slammed his fist against the steering wheel. They had followed him to the dunes that morning, accompanied the girls on their walk to the pans, picnicked at the same spot, and generally been a right royal pain.

'Keep your eyes on the road!' Hilary squawked for the umpteenth time.

'And your hand out of your shorts!' piped a voice from the back row.

They all knew what had happened during the night. At least from Megan's perspective. The stupid bitch had delivered a blow-by-blow account of how she had incapacitated her stalker, as she now called him. Each time she mentioned it, the throb in his leg got worse. It wasn't his fault if things hadn't gone the way he expected. She was the one who had led him on and was now accusing him of assault.

As they approached Solitaire, Henny threw another

glance in his mirror. It was a lonely outpost comprising a fuel station, a general store, a bakery and a café. Normally, he would stop for fifteen minutes to let his campers taste the legendary apple pie and check out the local handicrafts. But this wasn't a normal day. Megan and Hilary had refused to break camp and he had had to do most of the work himself.

He put his foot on the accelerator as soon as he saw the sign. Without missing a beat Hilary leaned over the back of his seat and said loudly in his ear, 'Shouldn't you be slowing down? This is where we stop, per the itinerary. Turn here.'

The South African driving the camper behind them sat on his horn until Henny made the turn. He cursed under his breath. 'Ten minutes, no more. We're late already.'

'What's the big deal?' Megan asked.

'The big deal is that we need to re-provision in Swakopmund for our trip up the Skeleton Coast and through Damaraland to Etosha.'

'So? You can do that while we go to the beach.'

Why not? Henny thought. Get rid of them for the afternoon. At least he wouldn't have to put up tents. The way Higher Ground planned it, staying at a rest camp in Swakopmund provided a change of pace after a week of campgrounds and sightseeing. It was the only – and last – town of any size the camper-volunteers would see for a long time. It was also, although they didn't know it yet, their last taste of freedom for a long time.

As they walked back to the Higher Ground van, Megan and Hilary dealt him another blow.

'We're riding with Glenn and Pete,' Hilary announced. 'Luke and Steve will come with you.'

Henny opened his mouth to protest.

'Hey!' Megan interjected. 'There's no issue here, we're

all staying at the same rest camp. So let's get this show on the road. You lead the way.'

Luke and Steve clambered into the van to the evident delight of Henny's four remaining passengers. He spun his wheels in protest as they turned onto the main gravel road that would take them through Kuiseb Pass to Walvis Bay and finally Swakopmund. The Kuiseb Canyon was in sunlight but as they negotiated the steep descents and hairpin bends, the fog that regularly swept in from the Atlantic covered them in grey dankness.

The temperature in the van dropped. The chatter died down and the two girls behind him reached for pullovers. Further back, the other two girls cuddled up to Luke and Steve. How had it come to this? What would the Master say if he knew Henny had completely lost control of his group?

CHAPTER

48

Petra was getting used to the camper. She was even beginning to enjoy the reactions of the few other drivers they passed. At the Sendelingsdrift border crossing, the Namibian guard put his hands on his hips and let out a roar of laughter. Carlo, putting on his Mercutio act, performed a few steps of the hornpipe then bowed from side to side to an imaginary crowd.

'Welcome to Namibia. Which way you go?' the guard asked.

'First to the Fish River Canyon. Tomorrow, the wild horses at Aus then Sossusvlei.'

'Drive carefully. We don' want that fancy van in a million pieces.'

'We will. Thank you, kind Sir.'

Petra was so excited that she overlooked Carlo's antics and forgot about everything except the spectacular mountain scenery around them. The road snaked along the Orange River, twisting and turning sharply. For the first half an hour she handled it well, her enthusiasm overcoming her nerves. Then they pulled out of a tight bend and found themselves at the top of a steep hill.

'Mamma mia! Hold on.'

Petra tightened her grip on the handhold and closed her eyes. 'Right now I'd give anything to be on the river gently paddling my canoe.'

'Be careful what you wish for. We might just end up down there.'

Once they picked up the C37 heading north to the Fish River Canyon, the going was easier. Petra grinned and waved at a group of young people travelling together who had rented more traditional white camper vans.

Carlo smiled at her. 'Happier now?'

'Yes. The wedding was a marathon. I knew it would be, but I didn't realize just how intense it'd be. In fact, if I had to choose one word to describe the Broselli/Delapore family, that would be it: intense. Even Julia, in her rather poker-faced way. I hope she and Max have resolved their issues. Anyway, I'm glad that part of the trip's over. Now we're free to enjoy ourselves in the way we want.'

'It's not all play. I have to follow up on that stuff you sent me from Tony's computer last night. If there's a big wedding the weekend after this one, I need to set wheels in motion for the foreign guests' luggage to be marked and checked. Ideally it should be done at both ends: in Cape Town and Frankfurt, for example. Then we'd have solid evidence as to where the tins originated.'

'What about having a plant at the wedding to photograph the tins Sandrine gives guests to take home, assuming she does?' Petra suggested.

'Not a bad idea. We could do it ourselves if we got back a day or so earlier.'

'You mean cut a couple of days off our trip?'

'Let's see how we go. In the meantime, I'll put my Harry Potter hat on.'

245

When they reached Hobas, they paid the park entrance fee and drove to the main viewpoint. Five hundred metres below them, the Fish River snaked its way through the arid plateau. Carlo brought out the Nikon he had acquired for the trip.

'Hold this, *cara*,' he said, handing her an enormous lens the paparazzi would be proud of so that he could switch to an even bigger one. 'Careful you don't drop it.'

'Mercutio, I'm not your slave. You want all this paraphernalia, deal with it yourself. I've got my binoculars and my own camera to contend with.'

'Tsk, tsk. Touchy all of a sudden, aren't we?'

'Sorry. Blame it on the heat.'

By the end of the afternoon, they had reached the last viewpoint that was accessible without a 4 x 4. Here the river's course made a tight switchback. Petra approached the edge of the canyon and looked down. Pools of water allowed bright green patches of vegetation to flourish. To the left, around the fast-flowing Sulphur Springs, palm trees grew. She turned to ask Carlo a question.

On the far side of the parking area, a dark green jeep stood next to a laced-up camouflage tent. Carlo was sniffing around it in a way that reminded her of Ed Spinone, her partner in the Royal Canadian Mounted Police.

'Pretty impressive,' he said as he finished looking through each of the jeep's windows. 'A lot of equipment in there. I'd say the owner's completely self-sufficient.'

'He or she's not worried about theft then?'

'Not likely, there's hardly a mortal soul here. I wonder why he's got the tent. The park closes at sundown.'

Petra walked to the canyon edge to take a final picture from a different angle with her point-and-shoot camera. A rugged track led down then disappeared behind a group of boulders that looked as though they might fall at any time. She beckoned to Carlo. 'There's your camper.'

A man as wiry as any sailor Petra had ever met was labouring up the track wearing a bulging backpack out of which stuck a tripod. He was wearing army-style fatigues and crossed bandolier straps attached to which were various gadgets. He scrambled the last few metres to the top and swung his backpack onto the ground.

His tanned face was leathery and his light blue eyes held that faraway look Petra also associated with sailors. He didn't seem the least bit startled to see them or their painted vehicle.

Without responding to Carlo's 'Howdy', he got out his tripod and set it up on a rock facing south. He clipped the camera in place on top and busied himself with his light meter. Below them the kinks and coils of the Fish River receded into the distance. The pinks and reds of the sunset blended with a special kind of haziness that was neither cloud nor mist. He clicked and made adjustments for dozens of images while Carlo watched in admiration. Finally he stood upright and drew back his shoulders.

'Just in time. When I went down, I didn't think conditions were right. I've been trying to capture this for over a week.'

'Camping here?' Carlo asked.

'Special permission. I've been commissioned to take unusual photos, to attract more tourists. It's the second largest canyon after the Grand Canyon, but so few people come here.'

He bent over his backpack and took something out of one of the pockets. 'Sometimes I wonder if I'm doing the right thing. One of the hikers must have dropped this eyesore.' He waved a shocking pink phone in the air. 'Are you guys staying in the area tonight?'

'Yes,' Carlo said. 'At the Roadhouse.'

'Will you leave this at Reception? Most of the up-market groups start and end their hikes there. This looks up-market to me.'

'Can I see it?' Petra asked suddenly.

'Sure. I'm Rob by the way. Tell them I found it near Ai-Ais a few days ago. I'd forgotten all about it.'

Petra took the phone and stared at it.

'It won't work here,' Rob said flatly.

She turned it over. 'It's Megan's. I'll take it.'

'Who's Megan?' Carlo asked as they jolted back in the van towards the park exit.

'Remember the two girls on their gap year we met in Cape Town? They were checking out of the hotel the morning we went to Robben Island.'

'Of course! Two nubile young ladies, one with fair hair, one reddish.'

'They were joining a Higher Ground Tour to Namibia. Megan gave me the brochure. Fish River Canyon was on their itinerary.'

'That figures.'

'If they left Cape Town straightaway, Carlo, when do you think they'd have been here?'

'I don't know, a week or so ago? Anyway, how do you know it's Megan's phone?'

'I saw her taking pictures with it. There's a fancy M sticker on the back.'

'Proof enough. So what are you thinking of doing? I can see your mind working.'

'I'll check the itinerary and see where they're supposed to be now.'

'And?'

'If they're anywhere near us, I'll be able to give it back to her, won't I?'

'As long as it doesn't involve extra driving.'

'She must be mad at losing it,' Petra said a few minutes later.

'You're not fretting about someone's phone, are you?'

'Not really. Ever since I read that Higher Ground tour brochure, I've had a peculiar feeling, one that won't go away. And the brochure Ana gave you the day we left Vredehof was just as disturbing.'

Carlo pulled into the forecourt of the Roadhouse. It was full of rusty old vehicles that made Petra wonder if they had come to the right place. They checked in and found their campsite at the back beyond the pool.

'Let's get a drink in the bar,' Carlo said. 'If they have internet, I can put Hubert in the picture.'

Petra found a seat next to a vintage truck and began to study the Higher Ground tour brochure Megan had given her.

The ultimate eco-adventure with Higher Ground

19 days from Cape Town, South Africa, to Katima Mulilo, Namibia

Week 1	*Cape Town, Springbok, Fish River Canyon, Lüderitz*
Week 2	*Sossusvlei, Swakopmund, Cape Cross, Damaraland*

Week 3	*Etosha National Park, Zambezi Region,*
	Katima Mulilo
Week 4 +	*opportunity to do volunteer work*
	in a local village

It was a much longer trip than hers and Carlo's and the girls were visiting far more places. Petra made some quick calculations. By now they would most likely be in Swakopmund. As far as she could tell, the only place where they might have a chance of catching up with them would be in Etosha.

Carlo joined her, bringing two frothing glasses of beer. 'Any luck?'

His face said the contrary.

'No internet, and the phone line's down today. We probably won't have decent communications until we get to Swakopmund. So there's nothing I can do. How do you fancy oryx or kudu steak for dinner?'

'Couldn't we eat something less beautiful?'

'What about eland?'

'I'll go with that. They're more ox-like.'

'You see! I told you you'd learn the difference.'

49

The wild horses at Aus were black specks in the distance – three of them trudging in a line across the sand. The waterhole in front of the observation shelter was half-full but bereft of animals. Then Petra spied movement. She grabbed her binoculars.

'Something's there, Carlo!'

'Well it's nothing very big.'

'It's a jackal, a black-backed jackal! That's strange, they're most often seen at dawn and dusk.'

'Cheat! You've been reading the guidebook you bought at the Roadhouse.'

'I like to be well-informed, Mercutio.'

'Goes with the territory, I guess.'

'Actually, there are two of them if you look carefully.'

Back on the road, Petra fell silent. Carlo let her be for a while then threw her a quizzical look.

'What's up, *cara*? Are you feeling OK?'

'When will we get to Etosha?'

'In about four days' time.'

'What about Swakopmund?'

'The day after tomorrow.'

'But that's no good, Carlo. Megan will have moved on.'

'Look, she's managed without her phone so far, and as Rob said, it's unlikely to work here. Have you tried yours?'

'No.'

'So what's all the fuss about?'

'I have to make sure the girls are all right.'

'Why shouldn't they be?'

'There is definitely something weird about this Higher Ground organization. I don't know what it is, but …'

'You can feel it in your bones.'

'Exactly. Plus I feel responsible for them. They're so young and vulnerable. There are so many predators out there …'

'Exactly. Lions and leopards and cheetahs and caracals …'

'Can't you take anything seriously, Carlo? Megan and Hilary don't realize how exposed they are in a strange land without family or friends to help them if they need it.'

'Stop tormenting yourself. Enjoy the trip.'

A car, the first one they'd seen for half an hour, was coming the other way. Carlo pulled over to the left to give them more room. The driver tooted as they passed and the woman in the passenger seat pointed a finger at them.

'Can't we get there sooner?'

'Only if you want to miss some of the best sights in Namibia. And I must say I don't.'

'What are we seeing today?'

'Duwisib Castle then on to Sesriem.'

'Why do we want to see a castle?'

'It has turrets and battlements and is a hundred years old. Is this a new inquisition?'

Petra poked around in the bag by her feet and found her guidebook. 'Right, page 200.'

Carlo began to whistle.

'We'll skip the castle.' She buried her head in the book again. 'OK, the dunes at Sossusvlei are not to be missed.'

'Not for Megan or Hilary or Julia or Vicky Dunlin or anyone else you've taken under your wing and are agonizing over?'

'Don't exaggerate, Mercutio.'

'Well what is it you're doing apart from spoiling our holiday?'

'I know I should just relax and enjoy it – it's wonderful and I'll never have the opportunity to do this again – but I can't. As you said, it goes with the territory.'

'I do understand, *cara*. I'm a cop too and if I smell a rat, I have to track it down. But I don't know how you expect to find Megan and Hilary in Etosha. It's a huge area with five camps inside the park and numerous lodges near the entrance gates.'

Petra looked crestfallen. 'I'll find a way.'

After a few moments' silence, she added, 'Talking of tracking down, I promised to keep A.K. informed. He'll be furious that I haven't been in touch. Especially when I tell him I haven't found Vicky Dunlin.'

Petra and Carlo pulled up in front of the campsite office at Sesriem. Their van drew a number of curious stares. Petra got out and adjusted her tie-dye top. A couple of wolf whistles acknowledged her success in embracing the hippie look. In answer she twirled the strings of coloured beads she had bought at the Roadhouse curio shop and followed Carlo into the office.

While he checked them in for two nights, Petra wandered about. On the far end of the counter, she found a guest book. Idly, she leafed through it. The campsite had a steady flow of visitors, most of them staying a day or two to visit the dunes at Sossusvlei. Lots of South Africans and Germans and other individuals on holiday she noted. But some were tour groups.

The circuits in her brain fired up. Sossusvlei was on Higher Ground's itinerary. She tried to remember whether there was anything in the tour brochure to indicate where they would camp overnight. The campsite at Sesriem wasn't the only one in the area but it did offer easy access to the park. For a lot of groups this would be a big plus.

She turned back to the beginning of the book. The first entry was dated just over a month ago. She ran her finger down each page fixing the name Higher Ground in her mind so that it would jump out at her. Safari Adventures … GoCamp Travel … Wilds of Namibia Tours … they were regular visitors. No Higher Ground. Of course, not everybody wrote in guest books but most tour operators had standing arrangements with the same places. The staff should know.

Carlo was still at the desk, discussing the merits of two different pitches with a female ranger. Petra approached and nudged him in the ribs.

'Hi,' she said to the ranger. 'I'm hoping to meet up with a friend of mine. She's on a camping trip with Higher Ground Tours. You wouldn't know if they were here earlier this week, would you? I can't see anything in the guest book.'

'The tours are usually in too much of a rush to give us feedback. Anyway, I don't think I've heard of – what was it you said – Higher Ground?'

'Why are you bothering this lovely young lady with that, Petra?' Carlo said. 'Even if she had booked in a Higher Ground group, what would that prove? You already know we're basically following in their footsteps.'

'It would confirm how far ahead of us they are. Idiotic as it may sound, I'm getting more and more anxious about the girls. They went off in a huge rush on that Higher Ground tour.' Petra chewed her lip. 'And it's not just Megan and Hilary. Florian's somewhere in Namibia with his group.'

Then she had an idea. She delved into her shoulder bag and brought out her camera. One thing about digital cameras, you could take hundreds if not thousands of shots before you had to download them. She scrolled back while the ranger leaned forward to talk to Carlo again.

'There! You might recognize this guy. He's one of the Higher Ground tour leaders. Has he been here?' She held out her camera so that the ranger could see the picture of Florian at the wedding.

'Oh yes, I remember him.'

'Blonde hair, blue eyes?'

'Yes, and the most amazing eyelashes I've ever seen on a guy.'

Petra smiled triumphantly. Women never forgot Florian. 'When was he here?'

'A couple of months ago. He said he'd see me again.'

'Was anyone else with him?' Petra asked, thinking of Father John.

The ranger nodded. 'Six girls and a guy.'

'Was he tall, rather wild hair, dressed in a black robe like a priest?'

'He didn't look like a priest, that's for sure.'

Carlo cut in. 'OK, we'll take that pitch you recommended on the edge of the campground.'

The ranger turned back to her computer to finish the registration process.

Petra was curious. If it wasn't Father John with Florian, who was it? A driver? A guide? A friend? How big was the Higher Ground organization? Diego had gone off with Florian, the two Spanish girls and the two English girls after the wedding. Clearly he hadn't been with Florian two months ago, but a question about him might jog the ranger's memory.

'Did he have a beard?'

'Who?'

'The guy who came here with golden boy.'

'No, but he had a bit of a limp. And a Mohawk.'

A shadowy picture formed in the back of Petra's mind. She went to the door of the office and stared into the distance. Suddenly the picture came into focus.

Cape Town airport. The day of her arrival nearly two weeks ago. A skinny guy with a Mohawk-style haircut. Wearing a black T-shirt and black jeans. Watching her. Then limping away.

At the time, she had felt his interest in her to be odd enough to commit his face to memory. Why had he been watching her and what was his connection with Florian?

CHAPTER

50

'What's the matter, Petra? You've been fiddling with your camera ever since we got into the car. Concentrate on the scenery.'

'Yessir!' Petra laid the camera in her lap and covered it with her hands. In the early morning light, the flat plains on either side of the car were a pale grey-green. Strange circular patterns surrounded occasional tufts of weeds in the same greenish tones. She caught sight of a jackal but couldn't be bothered to point it out to Carlo.

What she didn't want him to know was how angry with herself she was. Florian had crept back into her psyche. He had peppered her dreams during the night and she hadn't been able to banish him this morning. Worse, while Carlo had gone to do his ablutions, she had started scrolling back through pictures of the wedding. There were more of Florian than she had realized. Florian with Tony Broselli and the golf carts, Florian as tour leader, Florian with Sandrine … She wasn't a keen photographer but on a trip such as this she had taken plenty.

She stared at the distant dunes. The sun was just beginning to bathe them in a golden glow. It didn't help. The kaleidoscope in her mind kept flashing from image to image, the ones she hadn't taken – Florian swinging the incense burner, Florian dismounting from his horse, Florian watching her swim, Florian bending close to kiss her … Her body shivered in remembrance.

How many other girls had he kissed that week? Betta and Julia for sure, probably all of them, at least with his eyes as he always did. And how many had he slept with? Petra felt anger rise within her. He couldn't help himself, that was it! Not that that was any excuse. Women threw themselves at him, fell over themselves to get close to him, just like the way the ranger had reacted to his photo. He could do anything he wanted with those women.

And what about me? she whispered to herself. She couldn't pretend to be completely impervious to his charms. She closed her eyes and pursed her lips.

Abruptly, Carlo checked his rearview mirror, slapped his indicator on and pulled over to the side of the tarred road. 'Look, *cara*, I know something's bothering you and I sense that you don't want to tell me what it is, so why don't you drive for a while? This road is OK. All the traffic's going the same way and there's no loose sand to make it slippery. You need a break from your demons.'

'What demons?'

'You tell me!'

'You know me too well, Mercutio.'

'Come on, put that little machine away. The dunes await.'

Five hours later, Carlo stopped in front of the campsite office at Sesriem. Petra jumped out.

'I just want to write a comment in the guest book.'

'I thought you didn't like guest books. You said they're usually full of inane comments.'

'Sossusvlei and the dunes are awesome.'

'I'll come and say goodbye to my ranger.'

'You don't have to.'

'I want to.'

'It'd be better if you stay and look after our things. I'll give her your love. I shan't be long.'

Behind the desk stood a guy with a smile as broad as his shoulders. Petra smiled in return and pulled her camera out of her pocket. Quickly she showed him the picture of Florian in his white suit at the wedding.

'I'm trying to get in touch with this guy. Do you know him?'

'Sure. We see him every few months. He's with a company called Higher Ground. Usually has a bunch of women in tow.'

Petra suppressed what she hoped wasn't a pang of jealousy. 'Do you know where he is now?'

'No idea.'

'What about this guy?' Petra brought up a picture of Father John.

'Father Joe? He's with another outfit: Tabernacle Youth Collective or something. Due here next week, I believe.' The ranger turned to the computer and pulled up a file. 'Yep, Tuesday for a night or two. Are you looking for him too?'

'A friend of mine's travelling with him, and I was hoping we'd meet up somewhere.'

The burly ranger tapped a few more keys. 'He's moving on to Etosha. You going there?'

Petra nodded. 'Yes, after a night in Swakopmund.'

'Well you might see him at Halali.'

'That'd be great. Thanks for the info.'

'Make sure you stop at Solitaire. It's just down the road. Their apple pie's the best thing since they invented biltong.'

Petra ran back to the van that she had now christened Lucy.

'Guess what?'

'Florian's asked you to marry him.'

'Mercutio, that's crap.'

'OK. Let me have another try. Mrs. P. has signed in as a guest.'

'No,' Petra groaned. 'Father John, a.k.a. Father Joe, is arriving here on Tuesday then going on to Halali. That means we'll catch up with him in Etosha.'

'So?'

'Gina's with him,' Petra said slyly.

'Mmm. So?'

'We can find out from her where they've been and what they've been doing.'

'So?'

'Mercutio, stop that.'

'But you're going round in circles, *cara*. I can guarantee you won't learn anything of interest from either Gina or Father John. Particularly if his outreach programmes are a bit dicey.'

'That's the other thing! As I suspected, he is with the Tabernacle Youth Collective. Now can we speed up?'

'Yes, if you really want to slow us down. An accident could put us out of commission for several days – and that's if we're lucky.'

CHAPTER

51

The rest camp consisted of a couple of hundred tightly packed cabins, chalets and bungalows inside a high electric fence. For Henny it was a welcome break from the established routine. The camp served dinner, and just a stroll away there was a bar serving German beer that became quite lively at night.

He stopped in front of an A-frame chalet.

'You expect us all to sleep in this?' Hilary screeched.

'There are six of you and six single beds. Two on the ground floor and four upstairs.'

What did the bitches expect? This was luxury if only they knew it.

'Two keys,' he added, placing them in Megan's outstretched hand. 'Don't lose them. If you do, you pay.'

'I don't think so. You'll pay.'

Henny took a deep breath. 'Group briefing at six-thirty. Dinner in the restaurant at seven. Lights out at ten so we can get a good start tomorrow.'

'Says who?' Hilary snapped.

'The itinerary,' he shot back. 'First the Welwitschia Drive, then the seals at Cape Cross. Check it out.'

'And this afternoon?'

'All yours. Go to the beach with your buddies, do what you want.'

'What about the guided walking tour of town? Too far for you to manage, I suppose?'

Henny gritted his teeth. 'It's too late to do the tour and I'm letting you off the provisioning. It's an easy walk to town and the beach from here. You don't need me.'

'We sure don't,' Megan said.

'And I sure don't need you,' he muttered under his breath.

He drove angrily into town to stock up for the next segment of the trip. His eyes were smarting from driving through the fog and the crude swastika on his left forearm was itching. By the time he reached the plaza, his overpowering thirst drove him to the nearest brewpub. He ordered a stein of beer and took it to a table in the corner.

Swakopmund was a solid enclave of burghers proud of their heritage and nostalgic for the time when Namibia, then South West Africa, was under German control. Henny loved their beer and their women and felt more at home in Swakop than anywhere else except Port Nolloth. He had a couple of regulars and looked forward to his visits. If only he'd waited.

This time he was fucking it up big. Higher Ground policy stated clearly that the girls were to be monitored throughout the tour. The lecture given at each overnight stop was designed to draw them further into the fold. He had skipped the Sesriem lecture because of their late arrival and because of what had happened during the night. Now he was giving them free time. The Master would go berserk if he knew.

Henny drained his glass and threw some cash on the

table. Time to regain the upper hand. He couldn't have Megan writing stuff about him that wasn't true. He had to find her diary and destroy it.

The van was the usual mess where she and Hilary sat. He dumped two loads of trash in a metal dustbin then hunted around in the seat pockets and under the seats but couldn't find the little pink book. He'd have to go through her personal things. Cursing loudly, he locked the van and made for the supermarket.

Henny made it back to the rest camp before the girls. He had kept the third key to the A-frame chalet as he usually did: in case of emergency. This definitely fell into that category.

He parked the camper van as close as he could and unloaded a six-pack of water. Bottled water for the night. That'd be his excuse if the girls returned before he had finished. He locked the door to the chalet on the inside and left the key in the lock. That way he'd have a few extra minutes before he had to let them in.

His luck was in! Megan and Hilary, hot little bitches, had chosen the downstairs bedroom. Easier to sneak out from there or let blokes in. Megan's bag was open on one of the beds, clothes spilling out. He started with the side and end pockets. That's where he'd put a diary if he had one.

The dive watch on his wrist beeped. At five-thirty, he had to report in to the Master. He had set the alarm for five-twenty to give himself time to prepare. If he didn't find the diary in a couple of minutes, he'd have to leave it for now. Irritably he turned the bag upside down and shook it. Stuff came tumbling out but no pink book.

Henny crammed everything back into Megan's bag and turned his attention to Hilary's on the other bed. The same untidy mess and no diary. Dammit, Megan must have kept it with her. In a fit of pique he tossed both bags onto the floor.

A church clock struck the half hour. Sweat began to break out under his arms. What was he going to say to the Master? Did he really need to talk to him about his problem, or could he stick it out with these six up the Skeleton Coast and through Damaraland to Etosha? In a few days' time, the Master would take over and he'd be done with them. Then it'd be a spell of R & R, and back to Cape Town to look for the next batch.

Noise outside. The girls were back. Henny unlocked the door and whipped out the key. Opening the door wide he held up the six-pack of water. 'You beat me to it.' He began ripping apart the tough plastic wrap.

Megan and Hilary led the group in.

'I've got wine in the van,' Henny added. 'How about a pre-briefing drink?'

'Sure,' said Hilary.

When he came back with the cheap wine in screw-capped bottles, Megan was standing in the doorway to their bedroom. 'You been snooping through our stuff? Or did it just fall on the floor by itself? Pick it up, jerk.'

'No way.' The afternoon's German beer had given him a little Dutch courage.

'Learning to keep a good house, whether it's a tent, a hut or a mansion, is an important part of the Higher Ground philosophy,' Henny recited. 'During the tour, all volunteers will have the opportunity to hone their skills so that they are ready to educate and serve others once they reach one of our villages. You guys leave a goddamn mess wherever you go.'

'You don't get it, do you? We're on holiday,' Megan shrilled. 'We did enough picking up after people when we were chalet girls. This tour is the pits. It looked good on paper, that's all.'

'The volunteer thing would have been a give-back,' Hilary continued. 'It's a shame to miss that part, but I've posted my review and we're leaving.' She looked to Megan for confirmation.

'Yeah. Glenn and Pete'll take us sand-boarding tomorrow then to Etosha. We can set our own schedule and we'll stay at decent rest camps where we don't have to act like dumb servant girls.'

Hilary picked up the two bottles of red wine. 'Hey, we might as well enjoy these. Courtesy of our tour guide.' She lifted them high in the air and chinked them together while Megan went into the kitchen for glasses.

The phone in Henny's pocket began to play a loud tune.

'Funny, our guide still has his phone. Who's calling, I wonder?' Hilary said. 'One of your whores? That's right, go and make your arrangements.'

Henny hurried out of the chalet and ducked between the buildings until he was as far away as he could get before the phone stopped ringing. Fifteen times was the rule. On the last but one ring, he answered it.

The Master's voice was calm but stern. 'Why haven't you called? You're more than a day and a half late.'

'Back tire blew outside Helmeringhausen. We had to wait for a replacement. I paid for the overnight accommodation myself.'

'Don't whine, Henny. What have you got?'

'Six beauties hot to trot. You'll love 'em.'

'That will be my pleasure. As soon as we get them corralled. How long to Etosha?'

Henny took a deep breath.

'What's up, Henny? You can't fool me.'

It was as though the Master's piercing blue eyes could drill into his soul from afar.

'I have two who want to fly the coop.'

'What are you doing to stop them?'

'What can I do?'

'Use the stuff I gave you, man. That's what it's for. And get here as soon as you can.'

C H A P T E R

52

Fog descended on them as they exited the Kuiseb Pass. It took Petra by surprise, and it was just as much of a surprise when it lifted an hour later and she saw the ocean ahead of them.

'I'd almost forgotten what water looks like since Langebaan,' she exclaimed.

'That's Walvis Bay,' Carlo said. 'The largest deepwater port on this coast and one of the most important birding areas in Africa – over a hundred and fifty thousand migrants, the feathered variety that is, spend the summer here.'

'Look, flamingos! And pelicans!'

'I knew you'd like that. I've booked us into the Dolphin Bay Hotel. You'll be able to watch the birds from the terrace.'

'We're not going to Swakopmund?'

'This is right next door. Quieter – not so many adventure freaks looking for an adrenalin rush.'

'But Megan and Hilary's tour was going to Swakopmund.'

'Yes, and they'll be long gone. Don't push it, Petra. We've got more serious stuff to deal with.'

Lucy's arrival at the Dolphin Bay Hotel drew more than a few raised eyebrows. Carlo ran up the steps and returned a short while later, laughing.

'Is there a joke I should share?' Petra asked.

'They tried to direct me to the municipal rest camp in Swakopmund, but I told them we were special agents on an undercover mission. Now we have a dinner voucher for the restaurant and a large room on the upper floor overlooking the lagoon,' Carlo said, handing her a key.

'With a bathroom?'

'Yes, and two double beds. Telephone, and internet in the lobby so we can do what we have to do. Then it's back to camping.'

Petra put down her bag and slipped her feet out of her boat shoes. 'First thing I need is a shower. I feel as though I have half the Namib Desert on my body.'

'While you do that, I'll get in touch with Hubert.'

Without her thin coating of fine red sand, Petra felt like a new person. She fired up her phone and was pleased to see that there was some sort of signal. Now she could call A.K. The problem was she had no information to give him. On the other hand, if Vicky had contacted her father and told him of her revised plans, A.K. might have information to share. And she really wanted to find out why Vicky was so important to everyone. So should she call, or shouldn't she?

'Sleep on it' she heard her father's voice say in her head. Good advice as always. 'I miss you, Papa,' she whispered.

She took out Megan's bright pink phone and pressed the power button. The screen lit up. 'Searching for network' it said. Petra watched it eagerly. Hilary's phone number would almost certainly be in Megan's list of contacts. Assuming they had a signal where they were, she'd be able to call and find out how they were doing, and arrange to return Megan's phone.

'No signal' said the screen.

'Shit!'

'Tut, tut,' Carlo said. 'I thought you were ageing gracefully, *tesoro mio*. Now I see I was mistaken.'

'I'm not ageing any more or less gracefully than you, Mercutio, although I'm getting grey hairs trying to figure out what's going on with all these young women.'

Petra switched Megan's phone off and tried it again. This time it didn't even fire up. She threw the phone on the bed and picked up her room key. 'I'm going out for some air.'

'Ciao, bella,' Carlo said, picking up the phone by his bed.

Petra followed a walkway through the gardens until she came to a place where she could sit at the water's edge. The birdlife was extraordinary and in the distance dolphins played round the bow of a boat that was coming in. She wondered whether Mrs. Pinderally ever came to Walvis Bay. *Scheherazade* would look stunning riding the swell.

Watching the water and the teeming life it supported buoyed Petra's spirits. After a while, she was ready to move on and explore the rest of the property. Near the lobby she found a small business centre with a computer. On enquiry, she determined that it was free to use. She sat down and activated the screen.

During the drive through the fog, she had been wondering about the Higher Ground organization and trying to make sense of what she knew about it. How large was it? Was it the umbrella for the Broselli/Delapore charitable endeavours? How did the two sides – Tours and Community Interchange – fit together? If Florian was involved in Interchange, who ran the tours? The guy with the limp? There must be something on-line that would answer at least some of her questions.

Petra flexed her fingers and began to search. Plenty of groups used the name Higher Ground: churches, restaurants, bands, not to mention a film and a TV series. When she added the word "Tours", Google dredged up something in Tibet but nothing in Southern Africa. "Community Interchange" threw up a pot-pourri of quasi governmental and religious sites along with a lot about highways. After fifteen minutes' digging, she couldn't find any references or websites for Higher Ground Tours or Community Interchange in Southern Africa.

Petra leaned back on the rather wobbly chair. To attract the young and the idealistic in this day and age Higher Ground would surely not rely solely on print materials, however persuasive. And what about the Tabernacle Youth Collective, the group Vicky Dunlin had gone with in the beginning? Now she had joined one of their outreach programmes in a community village.

Instinctively Petra had associated Tabernacle with Higher Ground because of the outreach programme details in the Interchange brochure Ana had given Carlo. There were too many similarities for them not to be related. She had proof too that Father John/Joe was involved with Tabernacle.

Petra noticed a pimply youth in shorts and a T-shirt hovering nearby. He was glancing over her shoulder at the computer screen. 'Can I help you?' she asked.

'How long you gonna be?'

'Not long, especially if you don't crowd me.'

She waited for him to leave the room before typing in Tabernacle Youth Collective South Africa. Nothing. On a whim she added Vicky Dunlin, not expecting to turn up anything useful. But Google's search engine obligingly revealed that a Vicky Dunlin was on Facebook.

'Bob's your uncle,' Petra murmured. She compared the Facebook picture to the photograph she remembered, taken by Mrs. Pinderally. It looked like the same girl, and there was no doubt that she was a masseuse: all her public posts referred to massage techniques. The most recent one had been posted a week ago, on Sunday, the day after her interview with Mrs. Pinderally.

'The Tabernacle Youth Collective has some wonderful outreach projects. My prenatal massage skills will be put to good use.'

There was a grainy photo of a cluster of white buildings that could have been anywhere – including the community farm near Langebaan, Petra thought excitedly. She scrolled down further. The chair wobbled alarmingly as she sat up straight.

'Working with Father Joe's group has opened my eyes to a whole new world.'

This was accompanied by another low-resolution photo of white-washed buildings in a country setting.

'Bingo!' Petra shouted.

'Found what you were looking for?' The pimply youth came hurrying through the doorway into the small room. 'Care to vacate?'

'Not quite yet,' Petra said. She ran her eye down Vicky's earlier posts. One stood out.

'Working at the Cape Sands is OK, but I want to experience the real Africa.'

With a mental sigh, Petra sent Vicky a friends request, signed out and ceded the rickety chair to the impatient young man.

53

Carlo was lying on his bed talking earnestly on the hotel phone. He acknowledged Petra's return with a motion of his right hand that seemed a trifle dismissive. She frowned. How long was he going to be?

Her head was spinning. Vicky Dunlin's posts implied that she had gone with the Tabernacle Youth Collective to work with pregnant women – quite possibly at the farm they had cased. How she wished Carlo would get off the phone so that she could tell him. She raised her hands in a questioning gesture. All he did was wave her away again.

Frustrated, Petra sat on the edge of her bed and tried to set her thoughts straight. She jumped up as soon as she heard Carlo ending his conversation. Quickly she filled him in on her internet searches.

' … I couldn't find any websites relating to Higher Ground Tours or Interchange, nor Tabernacle Youth Collective. So whatever they're doing, they're not targeting the masses,' she finished. 'Oh, and Father John …'

'That's all good stuff, Petra, but please don't bother me with it right at this moment. I have to go through the file you copied off Tony's computer. If I can select three or four wedding guests who'll be flying back to London,

Frankfurt, and Paris or Geneva, Hubert will have someone examine their luggage. It'll take some serious string-pulling to arrange but we're both convinced it'll be worthwhile.'

'What about your uncle? Aren't you concerned that he's involved in all this?'

'If he's mixed up in something illegal, he'll take what's coming to him. Family ties only go so far.'

'Right answer!'

'I'm glad you approve of some of my morals.'

'With emphasis on the "some", Mercutio. Go and do your computer work. I want to phone A.K.'

'It's Easter Sunday.'

'Holidays and weekends don't mean anything to him. That's why he always calls me when I'm away. Right now it's late morning in Ontario.'

'My advice is to get all your ducks in a row before you call him. Ciao.'

Carlo picked up the hotel notepad and pen and slipped out of the room.

Petra ran through what she wanted to say to A.K. It was almost a week since she had spoken to him. The time had gone so quickly and they had covered hundreds of kilometres. She hoped he would understand that she'd been travelling in areas with no phone signal and in any case didn't have anything definitive to report. Perhaps it would have helped if he had told her why Vicky was so important.

After a few minutes' reflection, she took a deep breath and dialled his number from memory. The line when he answered was fuzzy but serviceable.

'I've been expecting you to call. How's Vicky Dunlin?'

'I don't know, Sir.'

'Why not? You've had a week to find her.'

Not quite, Petra thought, but A.K. didn't worry about niceties. He was obviously displeased.

'I did my best and I think I know where she is.'

'You think? Where?' His tone was brittle.

'On a farm about a hundred and thirty kilometres north of Cape Town.'

'What's she doing there?'

'Working with pregnant women. She posted about the Collective's outreach programmes and her prenatal massage skills on her Facebook page.'

'Oh boy!'

For the first time since she had known him, Petra detected emotion in A.K.'s voice.

'Who is Vicky Dunlin? Why is she so important? Is she some celebrity who needs protection? I'm on leave you know.' Petra was practically shouting into the phone.

'Vicky Dunlin is my niece. She has a rare blood disorder that requires constant monitoring. If something goes out of kilter, she could need urgent treatment.' A.K. cleared his throat. 'Her father tried to stop her going to South Africa but she was adamant. She wanted to help others less fortunate than herself. She has to be in a major centre where she can get help fast.'

Petra suddenly felt afraid. The community village or farm, whatever it was, was way off the beaten track. The cleaner at the church in the little town where they had shopped for supplies had intimated that the women and their babies were not well cared for. If Vicky was there, she was risking her health and quite possibly her life. And if she wasn't there, she could be in an even more remote village run by the Tabernacle Youth Collective or Higher Ground Interchange.

A.K.'s next words were so quietly spoken Petra could hardly hear him. 'Where are you?'

'Touring in Namibia, and going on safari.'

'I see.'

Petra waited for what would come next. The dull edge to A.K.'s voice tore at her heart. He was human and hurting. She knew he didn't have any children. Vicky must hold a special place in his affections.

At the same time she felt a rising anger. What was her decision to be if A.K. asked her to go and find Vicky straightaway? This was a holiday to die for. She had agreed to his previous requests because he was her boss and that was the way it should be; how could she refuse now? And if she did go to look for Vicky, how would she persuade her to go back to Cape Town?

'It's a three-day drive back to where I think Vicky might be. And I'm spending the next three days game-viewing in Etosha National Park.'

There was a short pause.

'Can you change your plans?'

Petra ignored the sick feeling in her gut. 'It's not just me. This affects a lot of other people too. And I can't guarantee Vicky is where I suspect she is.'

Petra felt as despicable as if she were walking away from a burning homestead torched by savages. But what right did A.K. have to lay this on her? She was a super-conscientious cop, worked her ass off in the name of justice, exposed herself to danger time after time … and once again he wanted his pound of flesh. Maybe it was time to leave the Force and work to her own schedule.

A.K. was waiting for an answer.

What would Carlo say if she capitulated? What would

he do? And what about Megan and Hilary? They were all so close now, nearly in Etosha.

'It's not easy,' she whispered, on the verge of tears.

'Nothing that's right is easy.'

'I'll call you back.'

54

Petra looked up as Carlo entered the room. He was carrying a bottle of French champagne that he waved in the air.

'Not Veuve Clicquot rosé, I'm afraid, but the best I could do.'

A tear rolled out of the corner of Petra's eye. She wiped it away with the back of her hand.

'What's the matter, *tesoro mio*? Have you been fired for not keeping your ducks in a row?'

Petra screwed up her eyes, not knowing whether to laugh or cry. 'I think I just shot myself in the foot.' In a leaden voice, she began to explain.

'This is – what do the Americans say? – bullshit! It's got nothing to do with your job. You're not responsible for A.K.'s family.'

'I can't let him down, Carlo.'

'What about letting me down? That's all right, is it? We're just getting to the high point of our trip, Petra!'

'Carlo, don't! Can't we work something out?'

'Like what? Cancel the rest of our vacation, lose our deposits, drive like maniacs for nearly two thousand kilometres on bad roads … for what?'

'You know for what. To help someone who could be in serious trouble.'

'I thought you were keen to get to Etosha to catch up with your young friends because you were afraid they were in trouble.'

Petra felt the fight go out of her. It was replaced by a drained feeling that turned her face into a white mask. 'What's the right thing to do, Carlo?'

He studied her for a long moment.

'First, you need a hug.' He put the bottle of champagne on the dresser and walked towards her. 'We'll get to that later. Come here.'

He held her tightly for what seemed like minutes and kissed her hair before releasing her. 'Better?'

'Yes,' she said in a small voice. 'Thank you.' She sniffed loudly and walked into the bathroom to fetch a tissue.

'Let's sit on the balcony,' Carlo said. 'Maybe if we look far enough out, it'll give us some perspective. Driving all that way doesn't make sense, especially given the uncertain outcome. That guy in the Higher Ground van already warned us off. You can bet he wouldn't be pleased to see us again.'

'We could go there in something other than Lucy.'

'Which would mean more distance, more delay and more expense to rent a different vehicle.'

'What about flying?'

'We're supposed to fly back to Cape Town from Windhoek on Friday night.'

'We could change that and maybe charter a small plane to go to Langebaan?'

'On our pittances? You're crazy, Petra.'

'A.K. might help.'

278

'I'd be very surprised. He's a master manipulator. He's wagering you'll do his bidding as you always have in the past.'

'OK, so if we fly back as planned,' Petra said, thinking aloud, 'I could get a car and drive up to Langebaan while you go to Stellenbosch to take photos at that wedding.'

'Now you're talking!'

Petra blew out air. 'I'm sorry, Carlo. I haven't forgotten what you need to do. It's just that I don't want to disappoint A.K. and I'm seriously worried about Vicky. But maybe a few days won't matter, and at least I'll have a chance to make sure Megan and Hilary are fine.'

'You can't take everyone under your wing, Petra,' Carlo said gently. 'These girls have to take responsibility for themselves. If they make wrong choices, they'll learn from their mistakes.'

'Isn't that rather a callous thing to say?'

'No, it's life.'

Petra sat silently thinking. 'The problem is, even if I do go to the farm and find Vicky there, how am I going to persuade her to return to Cape Town with me? I can just see it: I turn up out of the blue, she has no idea who I am, I try to drag her away from something she feels she's been called to do – her destiny, as she insisted in her letter to Mrs. Pinderally …'

'You could …'

'That's it!'

'What?'

'Mrs. Pinderally!'

'I don't see …'

'I'll send Ali an email, a letter to give to Mrs. P. Once she understands what has to be done, she'll do it I'm sure.

She loves Miss Vicky and her massages and is willing to give her a permanent home.'

'You really think she'll be able to convince her?'

'Mrs. Pinderally will find a way.' Petra clapped a hand to her head. 'But how am I going to give her directions to the farm? She'll never find it!'

'Oh yes she will. I have the coordinates right here.' Carlo pressed a button on his innocuous-looking watch.

'Bingo! Sometimes I love you, Mercutio.'

The pimply youth in shorts was sitting at the hotel's computer playing a game. Petra stood in the doorway and folded her arms. He didn't react but knew she was there. 'Fuck!' he said, ending his game and firing up another screen.

'Time to vacate, buddy!'

'You screwed up my game. I can't play when someone's watching.'

'Too bad.'

'Says who?'

'Says me. RCMP.' Petra pulled out her ID. 'I'm on a secret mission and if I don't send an urgent email, this hotel will be crawling with terrorists, so off you go.'

His eyes were as big as satellite dishes. Petra smiled grimly. She didn't like to throw her weight about but it did produce results.

She logged into her boatgirl email, typed in Ali's email address and began to compose. First the message, which she marked high priority:

Dear Ali,
Please deliver the following letter urgently to Mrs.
Pinderally. Miss Vicky's life may depend on it.

Thank you for your prompt attention.
Sincerely,
Petra Minx

Setting the right tone for the letter to Mrs. Pinderally was difficult. After several false starts she wrote:

Dear Mrs. Pinderally,
I have asked Ali to bring you this letter in the hope that you can lend a hand in a very pressing matter. But first, Carlo and I would like to thank you again for your magnificent hospitality and all your teachings. I can tell you in confidence that we are setting traps for the diamond smugglers.
The matter to which I refer concerns Miss Vicky. Carlo and I have discovered that she is in a perilous situation: her life may be threatened if she cannot be brought back to Cape Town very quickly. You are the only person we can trust who has the talents and resources to accomplish this.
We believe she is on a farm near Langebaan where that sleaze ball Father John is keeping dozens of girls who have fallen into pregnancy. The GPS coordinates are approximately 33.1772°S, 18.2452°E. If you can save her, she will surely repay you with complete loyalty and infinite massages.

Petra read over what she had written and grimaced. Was it too melodramatic? Too flowery? Too obscure? Was adding Carlo to the mix a good idea? What else could she do to induce Mrs. Pinderally to get involved? Perhaps if she saw herself as the hero of the hour …

Petra continued:

Mrs. Pinderally, the circumstances call for heroic measures. If you can rescue Miss Vicky, the ending will be happy.

If not, I fear the worst. We cannot go to her aid ourselves because we are in Namibia, closing in on the villains. Once we have them, we will return to Cape Town.

Time is of the essence. We are counting on your support.

Petra and Carlo

Petra read the letter again. Was it too long? Would it galvanize Mrs. Pinderally into action? Or would Mrs. P. think she was pulling her leg? Her finger hovered over the send button.

The pimply youth took a tentative step through the archway.

Petra turned. 'I'll let you know when I've finished. Go away and let me think!'

She'd be able to assess the letter more objectively if she did something else for a few minutes then came back to it. Something mindless, like writing reviews of the campsite at Sesriem and Sossusvlei.

She logged in to Trip Advisor where she occasionally posted reviews and typed quickly:

Friendly staff, excellent individual pitches, clean toilets and showers, and easy access to the park. What better introduction to the spectacular dunes at Sossusvlei!

Petra heard a noise behind her. The pimply youth was back, accompanied by a portly middle-aged man.

'You being rude to my son? You've no right to monopolize the computer.'

'Government anti-terrorism measures, Sir,' Petra said, pulling out her ID again.

'Baloney!'

'I assure you, I'm not joking, Sir. Terrorism is everywhere. Depending on your definition,' she added under her breath.

'What?'

'Give me five more minutes.'

Petra reread her letter to Mrs. Pinderally, tweaked a sentence here and there and sent the message. However much time she spent trying to second-guess Mrs. P.'s reaction, she knew she wouldn't succeed. She doubted even Mr. Pinderally could have done it.

Carlo had procured two wineglasses, a dish of olives, and a wine bucket in which the bottle of champagne was sitting. As soon as Petra opened the door, he threw her guidebook onto the bed and jumped up.

'How did it go?'

'It's gone, high priority email. I don't know whether it'll do the trick. With luck, I'll have a response one way or the other before we leave tomorrow. I'll check after breakfast.'

'I'm sure Mrs. P. will rise to the challenge. She needs something to occupy that sharp mind of hers. Now let's celebrate.' He picked up the bottle and began to ease the wire off the bulbous cork.

'Don't we normally do this at the end of a mission when everything has been resolved?'

'Yes, and we will. But I reckon we're on the home straight. Hubert's pulling strings like there's no tomorrow and is over the moon at the prospect of killing two birds with one stone.'

'You must have been taking lessons from Mrs. Pinderally to talk like that, Mercutio!'

'Isn't English wonderful!'

'My sister would say clichés are infra dig.'

'Not *infra dignitatem?*'

'Just open the bottle.'

CHAPTER

55

Henny walked back into the chalet without knocking. The six girls had finished the first bottle of wine and were opening the second.

'Time for the daily lecture, is it?' Hilary asked.

'Why don't you go and buy us some more wine instead?' Megan threw out.

'Good idea,' chorused the remaining four.

'I have news,' Henny said, putting down the bag he was carrying.

'What news?' Megan demanded.

'The itinerary's been changed.'

'You can't do that,' Hilary barked.

'The Higher Ground Tours brochure states quite clearly that the itinerary can be changed at any time if the circumstances warrant.'

Hilary shot a glance at Megan. 'And who decides that?'

'The organizers in conjunction with the tour leader.'

'So it's your fault!' Megan trilled. 'Trying to get us off your back so that I won't lodge a complaint, are you?'

'I thought you and Hilary had decided not to continue the tour,' Henny said with a smirk.

'The others have rights even if we leave. You can't gyp them out of what they've paid for.'

'You might be pleased to hear what's on offer.'

'If it involves you I doubt it.'

Fucking bitches. God, he'd be glad to hand them over to the Master.

'Conditions at Cape Cross make it impossible for us to go there. Instead we'll go straight to Etosha and spend an extra few days there.'

'What conditions at Cape Cross?' Megan asked. 'I don't believe you.'

'The campsite has been closed due to contaminated water,' Henny said, making up lies as he went.

'We can take extra water with us.'

'Not enough for showers or washing.'

Then he played his trump card.

'I have a special video message for you from the tour organizers. They are doing their best to make good and will refund a percentage of the tour price if you are not satisfied with the alternate arrangements.' He saw scepticism on their faces then curiosity.

Out of his bag he took a video camera. The left side of the machine opened up into a decent-sized rectangular screen. He inserted a tape and looked from one to the other.

The hand holding the camera was sweating profusely. He changed hands and wiped off the moisture on his khaki pants. He gestured for the girls on the sofa to move over.

'You'll all be able to see and hear if I sit in the middle and you gather round.'

'No way, creep. I'll hold it. OK, girls. Let's see who these organizers are.'

The four girls crowded round Megan and Hilary.

Henny leaned back against the wall next to the kitchen and folded his arms. He had watched the video and waited to see their reactions.

The opening shot showed the Etosha pan in the early morning – a vast expanse of flat silvery sand that shimmered like the open sea. A column of springbok and a few zebra were heading for a hillock that floated like an island, on their way to lick the salt.

Next, the camera focussed on a waterhole where a lone bull elephant was quenching his thirst. He stopped drinking as a formidable opponent hove into view: a hulking white rhino built like a tank. The two animals faced off, edging closer. Then both decided that avoiding dehydration was more important than establishing supremacy.

The camera switched to a different view. The girls watched intently as two enormous male lions got up from under a tree and moved off through the short grass. Their paws were as big as dinner plates and their muscles rippled with latent energy as they walked.

For the first time on the tour, there was no talking, just a few oohs and aahs. The lions disappeared behind a bush and a family of giraffes took their place. The gawky baby reached for the lower leaves while Mum munched higher up and Dad surveyed the scene from above.

When the camera zoomed in on a shaggy dog-like animal occupying the centre of a waterhole, Hilary gestured to Henny. 'What's that?'

'A brown hyena. Trying to get relief from the heat.' He was back in the guiding seat.

The waterhole in the next frame teemed with game, sharing the space and the water.

If that's what the girls were expecting, Henny knew

they'd be disappointed. At this time of year, after the rains, the vegetation would be lusher and the great Etosha pan would hold some water. The animals would be more dispersed, but there would be plenty of babies.

Once again Henny took his hat off to the Master. He was a wizard at setting things up, truly a mastermind. The girls had already fallen under Etosha's spell. They had forgotten all about the Cape Cross seals and Damaraland. And as soon as they saw the next part of the video, they would be well and truly hooked. The only thing left to do would be to reel 'em in. He chuckled to himself.

The next shot showed a long straight gravel road running across a plain where antelope grazed. Whoever was filming from the vehicle was doing a good job of keeping the camera steady. At a crossroads, the vehicle turned left and soon came to a sign for Halali. The girls watched avidly as the vehicle drove through the camp into a secluded area. It came to a stop next to a Higher Ground camper van like the one in which they were travelling.

Someone was unloading equipment, facing away from the camera. Lithe, dressed in tight black jeans and a black stretch T-shirt with a rock band logo on the back. A guy with blonde hair almost down to his shoulders.

Hilary nudged Megan. 'He's hot. I could use a bit of that.'

'I concur. A lot sexier than our group leader,' she said throwing a glance at Henny.

The guy's movements filled the screen. He lifted a large box out of the van and put it on the ground. Then he straightened up and spun round like a dancer. The camera zoomed in on his face.

Megan and Hilary's jaws dropped. The other four girls pushed in closer for a better look.

'Oh my God, look at those lashes!'

'What a waste on a guy!'

'I don't agree,' Megan countered. 'They're brill. And those eyes.'

'Like the Mona Lisa. They follow you everywhere.'

'I hope he's going to be our new guide.'

'Me too.'

'And me.'

'I'll vote for him.'

'I'll screw him,' Hilary proclaimed.

'Me first,' Megan said.

The Master hadn't said a single word and the six girls were falling over themselves to get a piece of him. His effect on women, young and old, was astounding. He didn't have to do anything, Henny thought with a flash of anger. Just turn his big blue eyes on them and gaze at them through those incredible eyelashes. Regular guys didn't stand a chance.

The Master's face filled the screen. He was beginning his spiel. Henny moved to one side of the sofa so that he could see it.

'Welcome to Higher Ground.'

Four simple words and you could hear a pin drop. The Master's limpid gaze encompassed each and every one of the watchers.

'During the first part of your tour, you will have experienced some of the magnificent sights and sounds of Africa. You will have learned to live in harmony with nature and as a group.'

Henny held his breath but there were no raucous comments from the girls.

The Master smiled fleetingly. 'Now you will join my

team and begin the next phase of your journey of discovery. The essence of Africa lies in its wildlife, its wilderness, and its unchanging nature. I will work with each of you individually and show you how you can make your contribution.'

The six girls were nodding in unison, ripe for the plucking.

The camera zoomed in so that the insignia on the Master's shirt came into focus: the words "White Tribe" in stylized large print followed by the words "live in concert" above the image of a blonde rocker facing a sea of white female faces.

The camera returned to the Master's face. 'Our spiritual advisor, Father Joe, will help you if you have questions or special needs. He has stood by my side since the inception of Higher Ground. He is the rock on which this organization is built. Listen to him.'

The Master's face faded out. Father Joe strode into view. A commanding figure in his black robe and leather sandals, plus the shaggy mane of hair and the leonine eyes. His aura was not as strong as the Master's, yet the audience hung on his words.

'Our mission at Higher Ground is to ensure a brighter future for this land. Through your willingness to volunteer and your commitment to the community, we will succeed. Come with us to find enlightenment and fulfill your destiny.'

The camera panned across a rocky plain towards a fenced kraal. The high fence was made of tree branches and rough stakes set close together so that there was no view of what was behind.

The Master's face reappeared, superimposed on the

fence. His eyes roved over the audience, caressing each member in turn. As his face faded to nothing, four words stayed on the screen: 'Higher Ground needs you.'

Henny wiped perspiration from his brow.

After a few seconds' silence, Hilary spoke. 'That Father Joe's a bit of all right too.'

Megan shrugged. 'If you like older men …'

'I wonder what he's got under that robe …'

A burst of coarse laughter erupted from the group.

'OK, so where do we meet these guys?' Megan asked Henny.

'In Etosha.'

'How long will it take us to get there?'

'If we leave really early, we can be there by tomorrow night.'

'What do you say, girls, shall we do it?'

There was no doubt about the answer.

56

Petra rushed to the hotel computer as soon as she had had breakfast. She was delighted to find a note from Ali.

Dear Miss Petra,

Mrs. Pinderally begs me to tell you that she will immediately initiate hush-hush measures to rescue Miss Vicky and nab the wrongdoers.

Do not fear. All will be well.

Your dutiful servant,

Ali

Laughing at the vocabulary, she fired off a thank-you note. Just as she finished, another email came in. Astonished, she saw that it was from Higher Ground Interchange. She opened it with a degree of apprehension. It read:

Dear Miss Minx,

You wrote recently expressing your interest in our Outreach Programmes. At that time, we had no openings for volunteers or counsellors. However, circumstances have changed and we now have positions available in several of our villages.

Since you indicated that you were travelling, I presume you are no longer in the Saldanha Bay area. If you will let us know where you are, I will find you a suitable position.

I look forward to hearing from you by return.
Sincerely,
Marcus Zen
Outreach Programme Coordinator

Petra's brain flooded with questions. Why were positions suddenly available? Was one of them in Langebaan? Could something have happened to Vicky Dunlin? What should she say to Marcus Zen? She kept her hands poised over the keyboard as her mind raced to work out the best response.

A rude noise caused her to turn round. The pimply youth was standing in the doorway.

'Government business, I suppose?' he sneered.

'Yes. Get lost!'

The stupid kid had interrupted her train of thought. Now she was out of time. Carlo had gone to put their bags in the van and would be coming to check out. It was a long way to Etosha and he was anxious to get started. Perhaps she should just ignore the email … but if she did, she'd always wonder what Zen might have done next. She had nothing to lose by replying even if the wording wasn't perfect. She typed as fast as she could:

Dear Mr. Zen,
Thank you for your email. I am still interested in your organization but at the moment I am in Namibia and going to Etosha on safari.
I will be returning to Cape Town at the end of the week and would prefer to volunteer somewhere not too far away: Langebaan or Stellenbosch would be perfect.
Please send me details of what positions are available.
Sincerely,
Alice

Petra pressed the send button and hoped she hadn't said too much or too little. She was about to sign out when a notification from Trip Advisor arrived in her inbox. 'Recent reviews of Sesriem' it said. Something caused her to open it despite the time pressure she was under.

First, the usual thanks for her review. Then a link to reviews posted shortly before hers. Petra clicked on the link. She scrolled past a review in German and one in broken English and stopped at the third.

If you camp in Sesriem, be careful when walking around at night. The campsite is good but predators (human) can easily hide and attack you. Watch out for some of the guides and whatever you do, don't travel with Higher Ground Tours. They take your phones away, make you do all the work, and our guide Henny is a real prick. We're leaving the tour in Swakopmund and going to Etosha under our own steam.

The review was signed by The Chalet Girls. Petra read it for the second time. There couldn't be that many chalet girls in Southern Africa travelling with Higher Ground Tours. It must be from Megan and Hilary. She stared at the screen as if she could find proof between the lines.

It sounded as though there'd been some kind of incident at the campsite, probably involving one of the guides. Petra had asked the burly ranger there about Florian and Father John, but not about the guy with the Mohawk hair and the limp. If she phoned the camp office, she might be able to determine whether "Mohawk" was Megan and Hilary's tour guide Henny.

Petra pushed back the chair. She had forgotten about its wobble and nearly tipped herself onto the floor.

'Finished at last?' asked the pimply youth who had reappeared.

'It's all yours. Out of my way!'

Petra rushed into the reception area. Carlo was thanking the young lady at the desk for a wonderful stay and exceptional service. 'There you are,' he said. 'I was just coming to find you. We've got to get on the road.'

'Carlo, I need to make two phone calls.'

'I've already checked out and returned the room keys.'

'I have to call A.K., to let him know that I've made arrangements for someone to fetch Vicky and to tell him that I'll follow up myself as soon as we get back to Cape Town.'

'It's the middle of the night in Canada.'

'If he doesn't answer, I'll leave him a message. Then I have to call the campsite at Sesriem.'

'Whatever for?'

Petra explained the essentials to Carlo.

'Even if there was an incident there, what are you going to gain?'

'Confirmation about the incident and confirmation that this Henny is Megan and Hilary's tour guide.'

'Was, not is. They said they were leaving.'

'OK, was. I can still keep an eye out for him and …'

'And what?'

'If we see him in Etosha with other girls, we can warn them.'

'About what? To be careful when they're walking around at night? Isn't that something all young women are aware of?'

'They should be, but sometimes they forget.'

'As I said before, Petra, you can't take everyone under

your wing. Africa is a big wild place; people have to fend for themselves. I blame A.K. for asking you to look out for Vicky Dunlin. That's what started all this.'

'You're wrong, Carlo. It was that scene outside the restaurant in Cape Town when Megan and Hilary's phones were stolen that started all this. I've had misgivings ever since. Then there was the wedding.'

'What about the wedding?'

'The bride wasn't happy and there were all kinds of odd things going on.'

'So now we're back to Julia.'

'Yes, and Florian.'

'All right, but make it quick. In six hours' time, we'll be well on our way to Etosha.'

CHAPTER

57

In the back of the van, the six girls were singing at the tops of their voices. For fifteen minutes it'd been Frère Jacques in a round – round and round and round, driving Henny mad. Now they'd started on She'll be Coming Round the Mountain. After the second refrain, Hilary changed the words.

'She'll be wearing silk pyjamas when she comes' they sang.

Henny snorted. He could supply verses that would beat anything they could come up with. He knew better than to suggest them. If he did, the sneaky bitches'd never stop singing.

An open truck carrying farm workers braked suddenly in front of him and veered left onto the grass verge. Henny cursed and pulled out to avoid a collision. The car coming towards him blasted its horn. The singers didn't miss a note.

He had managed to coax all six into the van by 7 a.m., an hour later than he would have liked. The main road from Swakopmund would be heavy with traffic as far as Karibib. Once he turned left onto the C33 to Otjiwarongo, he would lose the Windhoek-bound vehicles, but the road was more challenging. Even with reasonably well-paved surfaces, it would be mid-afternoon before they reached the Etosha park gate at Okaukuejo. Then it would be another two hours through the park to get to Halali by sundown.

By lunchtime no one was in the mood for singing. Henny's leg was so stiff he could barely straighten it when they stopped for a ten-minute break.

'If you're tired of travelling, we could stop tonight near Otji and carry on tomorrow morning. Then we'd have plenty of time to look for animals on the way to the camp. As it is, we'll be lucky to get there by closing time even if we go full tilt.'

Megan and Hilary looked at each other and then at Henny.

'What are you trying to say? That you won't do what you said you'd do and take us to meet our leader today?'

'I'll take you there, but don't blame me if something goes wrong.'

Ten hours later, Henny checked them into the camp.

'You just made it, man,' observed the ranger. 'Fifteen minutes more and the gate would have been closed. Your tour leader's here with his group, but I can't put you in the same zone. It's a busy weekend. All the pitches are taken.'

'No matter. I want to get my lot settled before they join the others for dinner. A dozen women fighting over one guy ain't easy to manage.'

'You won't get no sympathy from me, man. Just give me the opportunity to try!'

Henny drove his brood to their assigned pitch and looked at his watch. 'We have two hours to set up and get ready for dinner.' He smiled sardonically. 'That's when you'll meet our esteemed leader. Not before, OK?'

Megan glanced around the campsite. 'Right, girls, let's get to it. Then we can clean up and dress for dinner. Leave us alone, prick. You can pitch your own tent.'

Henny listened to them chattering incessantly about clothes, make-up, and men as they worked. But they had learned something during the trip, he thought with satisfaction. The Master couldn't fault him on that.

When they went off to have showers, he made for the other end of the campsite. The Master's vehicle was a larger version of his own, capable of seating twelve plus the driver and his mate. A bronzed bearded guy with hairy arms and legs was sitting in a folding chair under the side awning. On the camping table in front of him stood a beer, the sight of which made Henny's mouth water.

'Higher Ground Tours. I just arrived with my party. Can I join you?'

'Sure. Help yourself from the cooler.'

'Thanks, mate. The name's Henny.'

'Diego.'

'Henny!'

With an inward groan, Henny swung round.

'Over here!' The Master's imperious tone left no room for vacillation.

When Henny reached him, the Master laid a hand on his shoulder. 'I'm pleased to see you made it. Come with me.' He began to walk him away from the campsite. The hand weighed on Henny's right shoulder like an iron shackle, forcing him to exacerbate his limp. After several minutes that felt like hours, they came to an unpopulated area behind a storeroom labelled "Staff only".

The sounds of talking and laughter from the main camp had faded to nothing. In the far distance, a lion roared. Henny felt his guts knot. The Master pointed to a stone bench.

'Sit!'

Henny sat and tentatively stretched out his leg.

The Master folded his arms and stood facing him. 'I'm sorry you had a tough group, Henny. Was it really bad?'

'Ja, man! One of the worst I've ever had.'

'They looked like a fine bunch in the pictures you sent from Cape Town.'

'In that department they're all OK. Megan and Hilary are the best. In fact, Megan's a cute little thing but her voice drives me crazy.'

The Master rocked back and forth on his feet, as limber as a prize fighter. 'There are ways, aren't there, Henny, of keeping them quiet? You should know. You're an old hand at this.'

Henny chuckled. 'I can think of a few. Trouble is I didn't get a chance to work them through.'

The Master raised his eyebrows. 'You're my most trusted scout, Henny. Your methods are of interest to me. Do you want to tell me what happened?'

Henny opened his mouth to speak then caught sight of the expression on the Master's face. He suddenly realized he had made a terrible mistake. There was no camaraderie, he wasn't part of the inner circle, he was a means to an end, a tool just like the women.

The Master kicked Henny's foot savagely aside. His voice was like a whiplash. 'Don't ever mess with the participants, Henny. I've seen the review. Try anything ever again and you'll find yourself missing a very important part of your anatomy, and I don't mean your leg. Go round them up. I'll meet you in the restaurant.'

On the far side of the restaurant, at the edge of the terrace, a table was set for twelve plus one at the end. Thirteen in all. A sign in the centre proclaimed "Reserved for Higher Ground Tours".

Following a few steps behind Henny, Megan and Hilary led their party to the table. All six had put on make-up and their lowest cut tops and skinniest jeans. Their hair had been washed and brushed until it shone so that it mirrored the smiles on their faces.

Megan and Hilary seized the two seats nearest the single chair at the end of the table. The other girls arranged themselves next to them. Henny waited for Diego to arrive and introduce the four girls in his group: Ana and Raquel from Spain, Pam and Joanna from England.

Bottles of cheap South African wine were already on the table.

'Help yourselves, ladies,' Henny said. 'There's plenty more.'

'Where did you get those Ts?' Megan shouted down the table. Every member of Diego's party was wearing a stretch T-shirt identical to the one in the video they had seen in Swakopmund.

Ana pointed past Megan's head.

'From me,' said a honeyed voice. 'I am Florian, your leader. You are now members of White Tribe. Tomorrow you will ride with me. We will leave at sunrise on the final leg of your journey of discovery.'

CHAPTER

58

Carlo waited in Lucy while Petra borrowed the hotel phone and made her calls. A.K.'s phone rang three times then went straight to voicemail, which she knew he didn't like. Neither did she. It was better to speak directly to someone, although in this instance she was glad that he couldn't put more pressure on her. She would have found it hard to resist.

The phone at the campsite rang more than a dozen times before someone whose voice Petra didn't recognize finally answered. At the end of a difficult conversation on a bad line, she was closer to identifying "Mohawk" as Henny but had no evidence that would withstand scrutiny.

Grumpily, she got into the van.

'I gather from the storm clouds on your face that you weren't successful,' Carlo said.

'I left a voicemail for A.K., and I think the guy at Sesriem told me Henny had a limp just to get rid of me.'

'Tell me about Mrs. Pinderally's response. You said it was positive.'

Petra quoted Ali's email verbatim and had to laugh. Then she remembered the letter from Marcus Zen.

'We won't be able to get email again until we get to Windhoek or Cape Town,' Carlo reminded her.

301

'I know,' Petra said. 'Which is why I indicated that I'd like to volunteer in Langebaan or Stellenbosch.'

'Is there any point getting further involved if Mrs. P. has extracted Vicky by the time we get back?'

'It isn't just about Vicky. I want to know what this Higher Ground operation is really about.'

Petra fell quiet then suddenly tapped her forehead.

'I am so stupid!'

'Not usually, *cara*. Why today?'

'In their review, the Chalet Girls said "they take your phones away". I could have added a comment to say I'd found Megan's phone.'

'What good would that do?'

'They might see it and …'

'Those malaria tablets are definitely affecting you, Petra.'

'I've only been taking them for two days.'

'Yes, but you're not thinking clearly. Forget about the Chalet Girls and Vicky Dunlin. Just enjoy the ride.'

'When will we get to Etosha?'

Carlo answered after a moment's pause. 'Tomorrow.'

'What? You told me we'd get there today.'

'I told you that in six hours we'd be well on our way. That's not the same thing.'

'What are you playing at, Carlo? I let A.K. down because we're going on safari.'

'I phoned Tony Broselli this morning to find out if he'd be in Stellenbosch this weekend. I said I'd like to see him again before I leave. He asked about you and said we'd both be welcome.'

'Will there be room given the big wedding?'

'He offered us Julia's room in the manor house then he passed me over to Sandrine.'

'What did she want?'

'To know exactly where we were. When I told her, she insisted that we go to a place near Otjiwarongo and stay overnight. She donates a lot of money to the Save-a-Cat Foundation and has the use of a private bungalow there. She gave me instructions, and that's where we're going.'

'Why, Carlo? We don't want to waste our time on cats! And you keep telling me we have reservations to keep.'

'These are BIG cats – leopards and cheetahs. They're the most difficult animals to see in the wild, particularly leopards. The Foundation specializes in rehabilitation and puts radio collars on some of the animals so fatthey can be tracked. That's what we'll be doing this afternoon.'

Petra shook her head. 'I don't know what to say. I was hoping we'd see one in Etosha.'

'Extremely unlikely, especially now after the rainy season. Sandrine's invitation virtually guarantees us a sighting.'

'But isn't it odd that she didn't make us this offer before? Why wait until this point in our trip?'

'It's curious, I agree, but my step-aunt is a bizarre person.'

'A control freak, you mean. When she calls, you jump!'

Petra pored over the animal sightings logbook she had bought at the Foundation's shop just before leaving that morning.

'I didn't realize we'd seen so many different animals,' she said, busily ticking boxes. 'Oryx, kudu, impala, duiker, springbok, zebra, warthog. And, thanks to Sandrine, giraffe and leopard!'

'To see three leopards on one outing was terrific. Did you hear what that German tour operator said at breakfast?'

'The guy who had camera lenses even bigger than yours?'

'Right. He's been to Etosha over forty times and has seen a leopard there only twice. Sandrine did us proud!'

There was a hint of something in Carlo's voice that made Petra say: 'That doesn't excuse her illegal diamond smuggling activities.'

'Of course not, but it makes me feel better disposed towards her.'

'Beware of difficult ground, Carlo.'

Petra sensed that he didn't want to pursue the issue and returned to her book. 'We've spotted one out of the Big Five,' she said with satisfaction. 'Only four to go!'

'You won't see them all.'

'Why not? Don't tell me there's another change of plan.'

'Etosha doesn't have buffalo. Most of the year there's not enough water. But it has two types of rhino, black and white.'

'Are they both in the Big Five?'

'No, only black rhino. We're more likely to see white rhino. They're placid grazers, bigger than their bad-tempered cousins though much the same colour.'

They sped along the well-tarred road and it was barely half an hour before Carlo announced: 'We're coming into Outjo. We'll stop and get fuel and a few provisions. For the next three days, it's back to camping. No more luxurious lodges.'

'I'd rather camp when we're on safari. It seems to go better with the whole idea of viewing animals in the wild.'

'As long as there's a sturdy fence round the campsite!'

'I agree with you there. Oh, I forgot to tick black-backed jackal. We've seen several.'

Carlo put his indicator on to turn into the Engen service station. After filling up, he checked the tires and the spare wheel and pronounced himself satisfied. 'All the roads in Etosha are gravel and some are pretty rough and rocky, according to Uncle Tony.'

'I guess everyone is going the same way as we are now.'

'At least until we get into the park. There are some waterholes and drives and a couple of newer camps in the western end, but most people stay in one of the three main camps: Okaukuejo, Halali, and Namutoni.'

'This is a real dream come true, Mercutio.'

'I know, *cara*, for me too. I'm glad you didn't go to Spain with Betty Graceby and that friend of yours, Martin,' he added lightly, glancing in Petra's direction.

'Hmm, it would have been wonderful,' Petra said, returning his glance. 'But this is more fun.'

'You mean that?'

'Mercutio, you're jealous! I don't know why. Martin and I are just good friends. He's like a brother. In the same way you and I are good friends, very good friends.'

'True, *cara*.' Carlo lapsed back into silence.

An hour later, they pulled up at the park gate and picked up an entry permit.

'Now I can begin spotting,' Petra exclaimed.

'We might not see much on this stretch of road. It's another twenty k to Okaukuejo. Uncle Tony said to stop there and buy a map of the park. We can take a look at the waterhole and I'll get my camera organized. After that, we'll take it slow and stop whenever we see something interesting. As long as we get to Halali before the gate closes around 5 p.m., we'll be OK.'

'Carlo, what do you call those white vans? Not camper vans; these are taller and have a panel in the roof that opens up to give more space.'

'Kombis, you mean?'

'Yes, that's it. I think there's one following us.'

'I'm sure there are lots of vehicles following us, all trying to spot the same things we are.'

'I'm serious, Carlo. I noticed this one when we turned into the gas station. It pulled into the forecourt and parked over to one side. Nobody got out, and as soon as we left, it did too.'

'Maybe the driver wanted to use his phone.'

'It's a South African registration.'

'Like ours.'

'When we went to the supermarket, the same thing happened. The kombi turned into the parking lot, I didn't see anybody get out, and it left shortly after we did. What do you make of that?'

'Maybe they love our paintwork, or whoever's in the vehicle is on holiday like us.'

'Following exactly in our footsteps? That kombi was in Okaukuejo and at the next waterhole too. I even caught a glimpse of it when you missed that turning and had to reverse. It pulled off the road the minute it saw you stop. Then it followed us down to Olifantsbad, keeping well back, behind a couple of other cars.'

'You see! Tons of people are going the same way. I wondered why you were watching the mirrors and turning to look behind us.'

'I have a funny feeling about it. Can we test my theory? Make a few turns in rapid succession?'

'I don't think there's anywhere to do that in the park, this isn't a town with multiple options.'

'Well, we could drive a short way down one of the side roads, make a U turn and see if they do the same.'

'They'll just think we saw an animal on the other side of the road and want to get close too.'

'How about sitting at the next waterhole for a long time? See if they do that as well.'

'Only one problem with that, *cara*. It's getting late and we have to reach Halali. Look, if you see the same kombi following us tomorrow, we'll make a plan.'

CHAPTER

59

Halali camp was buzzing with people. Because they arrived late in the afternoon, the pitch they were assigned was a small one in the middle. Petra and Carlo stood looking at it.

'I don't like this,' Carlo said. 'Too many noisy neighbours.'

'Me neither. Cops and Canadians prefer open spaces.'

Carlo gestured towards a group of four young men. 'They're already well into the beer. I doubt we'll get much sleep, and tomorrow we need to start as soon as the gate opens to see the sun come up over the pan. Wait here, Petra; I'm going to walk back to reception and see what I can do.'

'Try talking to that female ranger who looks like Queen Nefertiti!'

'Just what I had in mind.'

'I want to have a look round.'

'Fine. I'll see you in a while.' He locked the van and pocketed the keys.

Petra set off to explore and, as Carlo had probably guessed, to look for the vehicle that had been following them. The sun was setting and she knew night would fall quickly. She walked up and down the rows of tents and

308

camper vans. There were several white kombis but none with the registration number she had memorized.

She came to a bunch of signposts with animal names on them, pointing to areas where various chalets were located. They were much more spread out than the camping pitches. If she tried to cover them all, Carlo would be kept waiting and might start to worry.

She began to head towards the campground. A lot of people were walking away from it, all going in the same direction towards the perimeter. When she arrived back, Carlo was setting out their folding table and chairs.

'No success, I see.'

'Not for tonight, although I was making good progress. Queenie gets off work at eight o'clock.'

'Mercutio!'

'Oops, when you call me that in that tone I know you're not happy. We have a solution for tomorrow night. She's booked us in at Namutoni – a nice pitch with a braai, guaranteed. We'll be able to explore the east side of the park easily from there.'

'I'm overjoyed to hear our schedule isn't as inflexible as Sandrine's.'

'It's actually a better plan than mine was. Getting to Windhoek on Friday to catch our flight should be faster. How did you do?'

'No luck around the campsite. I didn't check out all the chalet areas.' Petra pointed to the stream of people walking away from the camp. 'Where's everyone going?'

'To the waterhole, to see who comes to drink at sundown.'

'Of course! Let's go. We might miss the black rhino.'

A steep stony path led to an overlook where dozens

of avid game viewers sat perched on dusty benches or on huge boulders beneath a wooden canopy. Petra and Carlo stood silently at the back until a bench became available. A line of springbok trooped away from the water. An elephant finished his evening drink, trumpeted and went on his way. There was no sign of the rhino.

As the temperature dropped, people began to leave. Petra put on her sweatshirt. Carlo nudged her elbow and made a beckoning motion. She shook her head.

'Be patient,' she whispered. 'It's just like a stake-out.'

'I hate stake-outs.'

A head turned. 'Sssh.'

At the waterhole and under the canopy nothing moved. Darkness fell alleviated only by a few subtle lights. Carlo's eyes began to close.

'There he is!' Petra's finger shook as she pointed towards a lumbering barrel shape with two horns emerging from the trees.

Carlo grabbed his camera.

'Bonzer!' an Aussie drawled.

The rhino approached along a well-worn path. He drank then paused to listen, drank again, listened again and so on until he departed, his thirst slaked.

Carlo nudged Petra's elbow again. 'Time for dinner.'

They half slid down the dimly lit path. Back on the flat, Carlo asked: 'What do you fancy – apart from Florian – pork 'n beans out of a can, or whatever's on offer at the restaurant?'

'I'll take the latter, and for the record, I don't fancy Florian.'

'But he fancies you. I'm sure he's dying to see you again before we leave.'

Petra felt her face flush. 'Do you know something I don't, Mercutio? Is Florian going to be in Stellenbosch at the weekend?'

'I know lots of things you don't, but not that. Neither Uncle Tony nor Sandrine mentioned goldilocks.'

Carlo looked at the blackboard outside the restaurant. 'It's ostrich steak with rice and peas, followed by peach ice cream.'

'Not bad. Ostrich meat is good for you: it's cholesterol and fat free …'

'And can be as tough as old boots.'

'Bonzer camper, mate,' said the Aussie they had seen at the waterhole as they stood in line for the ostrich.

'Isn't Lucy wicked? Lucy in the Sky with Diamonds,' Petra explained.

'Gottcha! Can't miss ya in that! Which way ya headin' tomorra?'

'Up at sparras, mate, to see the sun over the pan …' Carlo answered.

'Then we'll play it by ear,' Petra cut in. 'No fixed itinerary, that's us.' She tugged at the back of Carlo's shirt as he picked up his tray and started to carry it outside.

'Let's stay in here.' She pointed to a table at the back of the room.

'Fine, but why are you so jumpy all of a sudden?'

'I don't like personal questions. And the ranger at Sesriem said Father Joe, a.k.a. John, was supposed to be here today. I don't want to see him or him to see us.'

'Why not?'

'Because I want to make sure Vicky Dunlin is safe first.'

'That's illogical.'

'Not to me.'

Carlo poked at his ostrich. 'This might be OK.'

'Here's your friend.'

The regal ranger with braided hair sashayed up to their table, nodded to Petra, and bestowed a lingering look on Carlo. Who responded by batting his eyelashes exactly as Petra anticipated.

She kicked him under the table. 'You look like Florian,' she muttered.

The ranger broke into laughter. 'Master Florian: you know him?'

'Yes. Is he here?' Petra asked, trying to sound casual.

'He was. Left yesterday with a busload of women.'

'Do you know where they've gone?'

The ranger shrugged. 'I'm given orders, not information.'

Like me, Petra thought. 'Was Mohawk with them, the guy with the limp?'

'Henny? He left on his own early this morning. He gets his R & R in Port Nolloth.'

'What about Father Joe – black robe, wild hair?'

'Joe, John, Jono – he wows the ladies too. Haven't seen him in a while.'

'I thought he was due here today.'

The ranger put her hands on her hips. 'You sweet on these guys? Want to join their bus tours? They'd give you a ride any time, I bet.'

She gave Carlo a wide white-toothed smile. 'Let me tell you the best places to see tomorrow morning. Quickest route to the pan is left out of the gate, then right when you get to the main road. The lookout is clearly signposted. On the way back here for breakfast, you can take in three waterholes: Nuamses, Goas and Noniams.'

'Breakfast? I didn't plan on that,' Carlo said.

'You'll be famished by nine o'clock. A hot breakfast'll set you up for the rest of the day. I have a couple of vouchers for you.'

'That sounds good, Carlo.'

'You see, someone has sense! Come back through Helio Hills. After breakfast, take Rhino Drive and Eland Drive to Springbokfontein and Batia. There've been great sightings of a lioness with two cubs this week, about halfway along Eland Drive.'

'We haven't seen any lions yet,' Petra said.

'Do as I say and you will.'

60

The road to the lookout ran for three kilometres straight out into the pan. According to Carlo, the rains had not been particularly plentiful so the flamingos had not come to nest. The sun gained height swiftly, bathing the silvery sea of sand in rosy hues. Cloven hoof tracks in single file showed where antelopes had come and gone.

The first waterhole was very deep. Carlo took a few pictures of the perimeter and the tall reeds in the centre. Petra didn't bother. The only wildlife was a pair of Egyptian geese.

They backtracked for several kilometres and turned left at the signpost for Goas and Noniams. There was no sign of the kombi. The Goas waterhole was large, flat and open. A herd of elephants with several calves was drinking, much to Petra's delight. She was also able to add hartebeest to her list of antelopes once she had properly identified the red-brown creature with the sloping back. Carlo drove to the other side of the waterhole to photograph a long-legged kori bustard stalking through the grass.

Noniams returned a zero, but they stopped again at Goas. The elephants had disappeared.

'They come and go so quickly,' Petra said.

'I learned a long time ago that you have to be really lucky to get good sightings. Patient too. Not my strong suit, but we can wait a few minutes if you like.'

A white Toyota drove up, slowed, and continued on down the road. Next came a high clearance 4 x 4 driven by the Aussie who liked Lucy. He pulled over and gave them a thumbs-up. After a short time, he too left.

Carlo switched on the engine. 'Let's go. There's nothing happening,'

'You're wrong, Mercutio.' Petra pointed to a family of three giraffes which appeared from behind a clump of mopane trees. They picked their way to the water.

'See how they splay their legs and bends their knees to get low enough to drink! This is heaven, Carlo.'

'Aren't you hungry yet?'

'No.'

'Well I am. Let's go.'

By the time they had passed through the hills and stopped several times for Carlo to photograph the view, Petra had to admit that she was famished. Game viewing was almost as strenuous in its own way as being out in a boat on the water.

Carlo's exotic ranger came to their table on the terrace as soon as they sat down.

'Order eggs how you like. Bacon, sausage and pastries are on the buffet. I'll make sure you get fresh juice and plenty of coffee.'

'What did I do to deserve such special treatment?' Carlo asked her.

'Not enough. Maybe next time.'

Carlo watched as she sashayed away.

Petra scowled.

After the first few kilometres they were in new territory. The Rhino Drive was the southernmost road in the park and the farthest from the pan. The terrain was rougher and the trees stunted.

'Not many vehicles going this way,' Petra commented.

'Right, and nobody following us. Once it gets hot, the animals tend to seek shade so a lot of people take a break and go out again after lunch.'

'After that breakfast, we should be able to make it through to Namutoni,' Petra said, patting her stomach. 'I didn't digest the information your ranger gave us until now, but I'm so mad that we missed Megan and Hilary, and Henny, their guide. Do you think Florian has taken them on his bus to Namutoni?'

'How the hell would I know? And actually I don't care. Look, there a wildebeest.'

'A what?'

'A gnu, and four zebras.'

The road became even more difficult to navigate and began to zigzag through desolate country. Carlo struggled with the steering wheel and put the van into low gear, muttering something about a 4 x 4.

'Thirty-three kilometres of this,' Petra remarked. 'Is this where lions like to hang out?'

'They usually hang out not too far from their next meal.'

Half a dozen baboons scampered across the road in front of them.

'There it is,' she said.

'They don't like baboons, but if there's nothing else they'll eat them.'

They jolted on through the barren landscape. At every

turn, Petra was filled with new hope, but they didn't see anyone or anything.

'This wasn't such a good idea, Carlo. I wish you hadn't listened to that ranger.'

'Me?'

'Well, we. Sorry …' She let out a great sigh.

'Is something the matter?'

'I've got a headache and my stomach's not feeling good.'

'That's the last thing we need. What happened to the iron cop?'

'I think I'm going to be sick.'

Carlo groaned. 'Brilliant! We can't get out of the car under any circumstances. It's too dangerous.'

'We haven't seen any animals for ages.'

'You don't know what might be lurking. If you want to set yourself up as bait, go ahead. But I suggest that you just open the door and lean out if necessary, and be prepared to close it real fast.'

'I'll try and hang on. The map shows a picnic spot with toilets near Springbokfontein.'

'Let me look.' Carlo pulled the map onto the steering wheel. 'OK, we'll make for that. Close your eyes and take deep breaths.'

'Yes, doctor.'

It was impossible to go any faster along the still winding and rocky track. Finally they rounded a corner and Carlo was pleased to see a grassy plain in the distance. Petra's eyes were closed and her hands were crossed over her stomach. Her face was ashen. He turned right at a T-junction. A little farther on, he spotted a sign to the picnic site.

As he slowed to make the turn, he saw movement out of the corner of his left eye. Two enormous male lions were threading their way through an area of boulders and scrub. The compass on the dashboard of the van showed that they were heading north, in the direction of the pan.

'There are your lions, Petra! Wow, they're huge, and in fantastic shape.'

The only response was a deep moan.

'I'll take you into the picnic site then I'll go and get some pictures and come back for you. You don't mind, do you?'

Petra shook her head, keeping her eyes closed. 'Fine. Just get me to the bathroom.'

Carlo drew up in front of an electrified gate hung with high voltage warning signs. It must have been five metres high. A large notice announced that the gate was activated by pressing the red button on the right. The park accepted no liability for visitors to the site. To reach the red button, the driver of the vehicle had to get out. Carlo looked right, left and behind him.

As quickly as he could, he pressed the button and jumped back into the van. The gate opened noisily and began to close as soon as he had driven through. He drove past the picnic tables, all of which were empty, and stopped right in front of the female toilets next to the only other vehicle, a white Toyota camper.

Carlo leaped out and went to help Petra. 'I'll look after your bag.'

'No, there are some things I might need in it.'

He helped her up the steps and risked a peek through the doorway into the bathroom. 'Two stalls, the one on the left is occupied, the other's free. Are you sure you don't want me to stay with you?'

'Quite sure. I'm not as bad as I was. I'll wait outside for you.'

When he got back to the road, Carlo couldn't see the lions anywhere. He paused at the next T-junction as two cars went by, heading to the right, and decided to follow them. He slowed as he neared the Springbokfontein waterhole, hoping to pick up his quarry. The shallow depression held nothing more than a few ducks swimming in and out of the reeds. He banged his fist on the steering wheel.

Petra's map of the park fell to the floor. Carlo picked it up and smoothed out the centre pages. She was a great navigator, and it took him a minute to orient himself. There was another waterhole just two kilometres away.

He turned onto the spur road. Keeping his eyes peeled, he rattled along. A mongoose flashed across the road in front of him. He braked hard as he saw a bunch of vehicles parked haphazardly on both sides of the road.

The two lions had covered a lot of ground and were advancing steadily. Carlo squeezed the van in between two others, eliciting angry gestures from the occupants. He reached for his camera and lenses and began taking shots.

Petra walked unsteadily across the bathroom and into the open stall. She pushed the door closed and looked for the hook to put into the eye to lock it. No hook. Never mind, she was beyond caring. She sat down and put her bag against the door even though the floor was dirty.

She put her head in her hands and passed out.

CHAPTER

61

The two lions had positioned themselves behind a rock a hundred and fifty metres from the waterhole. Carlo noticed the tracks and the churned mud around the edge that indicated that game had come and gone. For the time being, he could see only a family of warthogs scratching in the dirt on their knees. Mother suddenly stood up and smelled the air, followed by baby. Father paused and got to his feet. The three, baby in the middle, trotted off in single file into the bush, tails held high. Carlo captured the whole scene and waited to see what would happen next.

The lions were as static as the rock that shielded them from view. Carlo laid his camera carefully on the seat beside him. The cars next to him pulled away. He knew he should go back to the picnic site for Petra, but something kept him glued to his seat.

Overhead the sky was a brilliant cloudless blue. The air-conditioning struggled to keep the interior of the van cool. Carlo's eyelids began to droop.

When he opened them, the first thing he saw was a cheetah sidling towards the waterhole. The lions must have gone. He grabbed his camera and took shot after shot.

Then he caught sight of the lions again. They got up, shook their manes and left.

Over an hour had gone by before Carlo arrived back at the picnic site. Several of the picnic tables were occupied and he scanned them for Petra. If she was feeling better, she would be mad at the long wait but surely delighted with the footage.

He parked the van and checked the tables again. No sign of her. If she was still in the bathroom, that wouldn't be good news. He strode across to the toilet block and asked an older woman who was just coming out of the ladies if there was a young woman with long black hair inside. The woman gave a big shrug and shook her head.

It seemed as though she hadn't understood what he was saying, so he put his head round the door and looked in. Both toilet stalls were open and there was nobody at the single metal sink. He checked out the gents and drew a blank.

Flummoxed, he began to walk around the site. He stopped at each of the occupied tables and asked if anyone had seen a tall, slim girl with long black hair and a pale complexion, wearing beige shorts and a khaki T-shirt. No one had.

He climbed into the van and turned on the engine. The afternoon sun was relentless. A couple more cars came through the gate. There had been only one vehicle in the compound when he left Petra, and he hadn't paid much attention to it. It was a white Toyota camper, that's all he remembered. He leaned back in his seat and let the air-conditioning play over his face.

A few minutes later, he sat up and reached for his camera bag. It was on the floor, where Petra's feet should have been. That morning he had taken a full-length picture of her on the edge of the pan, proudly wearing her new khaki T-shirt stamped with African animals in black, white and gold. He scrolled back, found the picture and got out of the van.

He canvassed all the picnickers, showing them the photo and asking again if anyone had seen her. Still no luck. He waited until the ladies' bathroom was empty, went in and checked it thoroughly. He checked the gents, as well as a small white hut marked "Staff only" that was firmly padlocked. He banged on the door then walked round the back and stood on tiptoe to look through a barred window. The hut contained cleaning supplies and a plastic chair but was otherwise empty.

He walked once more round the whole compound until he was certain he had spoken to everyone and covered every inch of ground. There had been no sightings of Petra either at the site, leaving the site or outside the site. And she had left no note, message or other clue as to where she had gone or what had happened in his absence. She had literally vanished into the dry thin air of Etosha.

He got back into the luridly painted camper Petra called Lucy, drawing some pitying looks and a few shouted Good lucks. He unfolded Petra's map and stared at it for a long time as if it could answer his unspoken questions. Why had she left? How had she left? What should he do? Which way should he go? The picnic site was almost exactly halfway between Halali and Namutoni camps. Halali was isolated in the middle of the park, Namutoni close to the east gate and to several private lodges. In the developed world, if someone went missing on his watch, he made an urgent call and issued an alert. Here in the wilderness he had no phone signal, no radio, no back-up and no idea what to do for the best.

Carlo made up his mind. He left the site, turned right, and right again onto the main road. Petra knew they were due to spend the night at Namutoni. He hoped she was already there getting medical help. If not, the camp would have resources that would facilitate his search. He drove as fast as he dared. He ignored vehicles and animals on the side of the road and roared past waterholes. From time to time, he wiped the sweat off his palms on his grey shorts. When he reached Namutoni, it was four o'clock in the afternoon.

He drove through the gates of the old fort around which the camp was built, stopped in front of reception, and ran in. The wooden chairs around the walls were empty. Carlo went straight to the counter where the ranger in charge was dealing with a middle-aged couple. They reacted angrily when he interrupted, brandishing the photo. Quickly he explained what had happened. They studied the photo and the ranger showed it to his colleagues in the back office.

'Nice-looking girl. She definitely hasn't checked in. Try the museum and the shop.' His expression was sympathetic but Carlo suspected that he didn't believe his story. 'Afternoon is always busy,' the ranger added. 'I can't help you now. Come back later.'

For half an hour, Carlo prowled the fort and its facilities searching for Petra. No one had seen her. When he returned to reception, he was nearly frantic. He learned that the police had no local presence: the nearest station was in Tsumeb, over a hundred kilometres away. Ditto the hospital. The phone in the back office that they allowed him to use was a disaster. When he did get through to the police station, they refused to issue any kind of alert. Clearly they thought he was a nutter.

From time to time, Carlo had to remind himself that it was true – he was crazy. Petra had fallen sick. He had left her. And she had disappeared. It was his fault. He should never have left her to photograph the damned lions. If he couldn't find her, how was he going to explain his conduct to the people who would need to be informed?

But it was no good wallowing in guilt. Action was what was needed. He tried using the phone again. This time he got a line and it was picked up by someone at Halali after six rings. He asked for the tall regal ranger who knew Petra. She had finished work at lunchtime and wouldn't be back until the following week.

He dialled the number for the hospital in Tsumeb but couldn't get a connection. There was no internet either. Finally, one of the rangers suggested he get a room at the Bush Hotel outside the park. It had a business centre and Wi-Fi.

Carlo made it to the gate just before it closed. First, he had to present all his receipts for the overnight stay at Halali and the park entrance fees to the gatekeeper. Then he told him his story and showed him the photo of Petra. The gatekeeper shook his head.

'Can you give me a list of the vehicles that have exited the park since noon?'

'No boss, not possible.'

After a rather heated discussion, Carlo decided that the records were probably incomplete and the gatekeeper didn't want to get into trouble. Also the sun was setting rapidly.

In his frustration, Carlo nearly missed the turning to the

hotel. The receptionist insisted that she hadn't seen Petra and after a short battle, found him a twin room. He sat down on one of the beds and picked up the phone. On the third try, he got through to the hospital in Tsumeb. No one called Petra Minx had been treated that afternoon.

He said he would call again later and opened the can of Castle beer he had brought up from the camper. It was over five hours since he had left Petra at the picnic site and he was making no progress with his enquiries. There must be something he had missed.

He took a couple of swigs from the can, looked at his watch and decided to call Hubert in Paris. He would have to tell him there was a real possibility that he wouldn't be flying back to Cape Town on Friday or Saturday with Petra, and definitely not without her.

Hubert's voice was matter of fact as he ran through various scenarios with Carlo. 'At this stage, you can't discount anything. She felt sick so she could have had a fall, even a stroke, and passed out; if someone tried to help her, they wouldn't have known who she was travelling with …'

'I've thought of all that and contacted the police and the hospital. No joy.'

'What about violent crime? It's possible if unlikely.'

'There was no evidence of that at the picnic site.'

'How about abduction?'

'Again unlikely. Petra wasn't wealthy or well-known like my step-aunt Sandrine or a friend of ours, Mrs. Pinderally. She was a cop who had worked undercover and knew how to defend herself. And who would attempt an abduction in a public place in broad daylight?'

'Was she pissed off with you?'

'Probably, but she wouldn't have gone farther than Namutoni without leaving me a message, I'm sure of that.'

'What about friends? Missing teenagers are often found among their peers.'

'It would be a coincidence if she ran into friends in the middle of Etosha National Park.' Carlo sat up straight. 'But she was trying to find a couple of English girls she met in Cape Town.'

'There you are! Were they driving in Namibia?'

'They were on a tour, a company called Higher Ground. Actually, my step-aunt's son Florian acts as a guide for some of those tours.'

'OK, so it's friends and family. Chase that down and I bet you'll find her. By the way, everything's set for the sting.'

CHAPTER

62

Everything was hazy and obscure and muffled. Her eyes were locked shut. It was as if the muscles had atrophied so that they would never open again. She tried to see through the fog inside her eyes and her brain. She strained to move some part of her body, any part. But she couldn't feel. A huge distance separated her from herself. She mewled like a kitten.

A far-off voice said: 'I think she's coming out of it.'

'Give her some more then.'

Something brushed Petra's arm. She tried to shake it off. The needle sank in and she gave a convulsive twitch.

'That'll keep her quiet.'

Through the cotton-wool in her ears and head, Petra heard a faint rushing sound. Like wind in the trees or air through a tunnel. She felt hot and sweaty. She wanted to sit up and throw off whatever it was that was weighing her down. But she couldn't. She had no strength and no willpower.

The rushing sound was still there, like wind in the trees or air through a tunnel. And now there was vibration. For the first time in who knew how long, she sensed that she was lying down. Flat on her back on a hard surface. Her nose was stuffy, her eyes gritty beneath the heavy lids. If she lifted her hand, she could rub them. Then they might open. The information from her brain failed to reach her hand. Her head began to spin. The next minute she was flying.

A voice echoed in the darkness surrounding her. 'We have to stop for petrol.'

'I'll give her another shot.'

'Has she moved?'

'Not even her eyelids.'

'Then there's no need. He doesn't want her out cold when we get there.'

'I'll watch her.'

The rushing noise had abated but the vibration had increased. Gradually Petra realized that she was in a vehicle. One that was now travelling more slowly over rutted ground. The jarring didn't help as she tried to piece together what was happening.

She couldn't remember how she got where she appeared to be: in a car or van with two other people, a man and a woman. Every time she tried to bring a shadowy recollection into focus, it eluded her. The effort caused her to sigh.

Petra felt the vehicle come to a stop. Her normally sharp hearing was fuzzy, but a scraping noise suggested a gate being dragged open. A dull thud followed by a sliding noise warned her that they were coming for her. It wasn't difficult to keep her eyes closed and her leaden limbs motionless.

She felt herself being lifted, on the same hard surface.

Panic gripped her as the surface tilted. Her world revolved about her ears.

'Watch what you're doing.'

'She's strapped. She can't fall off.'

She felt as though she was falling down a long rabbit-hole, like Alice in Wonderland. Then she was lowered and everything stabilized. She was flat on her back again with something lumpy under her head.

Another voice, distorted yet familiar.

'Welcome to the fold, my lovely. Let me wake you with a kiss.'

CHAPTER

63

Petra felt something land on her face and tried to swat it away. Now it was on her lips, brushing them gently. Then it began to press harder. She squirmed uncomfortably. Whatever it was, it was a nuisance. Something she wanted to get rid of but couldn't. Her body was tingling as it might if she had come into contact with an electric fence. She had no strength with which to resist so she surrendered herself to the touch that was setting her nerves on fire. When it stopped, she moaned softly and slept.

Several times she awoke to the sensation of someone standing over her, watching her, studying her. Once she felt a weight on top of her and in the beginning struggled to push it off. But it was so smooth and smelled so good and was so like a protective mantle that she clasped it to her and inhaled deeply before falling into oblivion.

At last she opened her eyes.

Florian was standing at the foot of the bed, holding a lock of black hair. Her hair. 'Welcome again, my lovely.'

She closed her eyes and the vision was gone.

When she woke later, Petra found that she was lying on a cot, naked under a rough blanket that was scratching her skin. Images flooded her brain. Rage engulfed her, then fear. Her body felt violated yet whole.

Had Florian really been standing at her feet? She had no recollection of undressing herself. Surely he hadn't done it? Where was she? What had happened after she and Carlo had seen the lions? She wished she could remember but she had felt so deathly sick and her memory was a black hole.

She heard a rustling sound and looked up. Above her, a thatched roof rose to a peak. Where the thatch joined the wooden walls, vents had been created to let in air and light. And a large lizard was clinging to the thatch. If it fell off, it would fall on top of her.

Petra flexed her fingers and when they responded reasonably, she threw back the blanket and swung her feet over the edge of the bed. Keeping an eye on the ceiling, she sat for a few seconds wiggling her toes. The floor was made of bare concrete. She stood up and looked around the room for her clothes. Realizing they had gone, she wrapped the blanket round her middle like a sarong.

She began to take stock of her situation. The hut was built of rough planks. It had a door (locked from the outside, as she suspected) but no window. Light came from the air vents. An unlit oil lamp and a dish containing a couple of matches stood on a square table against the wall. Also on the table were a basin and a pitcher of water, and on the shelf underneath a small towel. A bucket with a lid stood in one corner.

Moving right along: she had no clothes and no shoes. She was hungry and thirsty. She was locked up and had no idea where she was. On the plus side, her mind was working, she appeared outwardly uninjured, she had a blanket, a bed and a lumpy pillow, and water to wash in even if she didn't want to drink it. Oh, and the bucket.

She lifted the lid off the bucket which was more like an old-fashioned milkmaid's pail. To her great astonishment, her fringed leather shoulder bag was stuffed inside. She pulled it out, shook it and emptied the contents onto the bed. Out fell her wallet, her keys, her camera, passport, a packet of tissues, a comb, a double roll of Polo mints Tom Gilmore had given her in London, a small bottle of drinking water (half full), a high energy health food bar, and a sealed pack of disposable panties.

Petra sat on the bed next to the pile of loot and took a few sips of water. She ate the health food bar and sipped more water, taking care to leave some for later. Then she picked up the bag and felt deep down inside. Before leaving Canada, she had created a special pocket in the stiffened base. It was invisible unless you turned the bag inside out.

This she did. She opened the pocket, extracted her cross and hung it round her neck. The blanket round her waist had come untied. She let it fall to the floor and began to open the pack of disposable panties. They were made of the same sort of blue and white material as kitchen cloths. Her RCMP colleagues, roaring with laughter, had presented her with them as soon as they heard she was going on safari. Petra blessed them now. With Florian around, anything to cover her nakedness was better than nothing.

She had one foot in a pair of the panties when she heard the door open and shut behind her. She whirled round. Florian, wearing black jeans and a rock band T-shirt, stood with arms crossed and a mocking smile on his face.

Petra turned away from him and pulled up the paper

panties. She grabbed her cross and waited, trying to calm her breathing and gather her strength. Tom Gilmore had taught her a few down and dirty tricks that she hoped would work.

'The back is even more desirable than the front. Of course, I've already seen the front and the unknown is always attractive.'

Petra couldn't do anything to prevent the rush of blood through her body as Florian cooed his greeting. She knew what she wanted to do – or at least what she had to do – but her body was not cooperating. And she had forgotten how like a cat he was: silent and stealthy until the time came to pounce.

Before she was able to take hold of her emotions, he seized her from behind and began kissing her neck. She arched her back as he moved lower with his mouth and tongue, all the while keeping an iron grip on her shoulders. He pressed against her so that she could feel him like a rock in her back.

Fury stoked by desire left Petra temporarily incapable of movement. Florian laughed and began again at the base of her neck. Her hand fell away from her cross.

Suddenly he spun her round to face him and grabbed the tip of the cross, pulling the chain taut.

'Father John wants this. As his reward for saving you. You could have died if he and Gina hadn't rescued you. I knew you'd find it among the little treasures in your portmanteau. I told him I'd get it for him.'

While Florian talked, Petra took an imperceptible step forward to relieve the tension on the chain which she knew would not break without a great deal of force. At the same time, she reviewed her limited options and prayed that her assessment of Florian was correct.

'Never,' she said, steeling herself for what she had decided to do next. 'At least, not yet.'

She lifted her chin, gazed adoringly into Florian's oh-so-blue eyes, put one hand round the back of his head and drew him towards her. His initial surprise turned to merriment then to annoyance as she covered the cross with her other hand and lunged for his groin with her knee. He was fast enough on his feet to retreat before the blow could connect.

Petra put as much space between them as she could. She crossed her hands over her chest, hiding her necklace as well as her bare breasts. She watched him like a hawk and held her breath. Would he accept the blow to his male pride or turn violent? For what seemed like an eternity, her safety hung in the balance. Then he regarded her coolly.

'It'll be fun taming you. And believe me, I will. But there's no rush. I have plenty of girls to cater to my needs while I wait for you. Father John will marry us tomorrow.'

'Father John is a phony.'

Florian laughed. 'Does it matter? All my girls are married to me, and to him, and to our philosophy. I'll send him over to claim his due. He'll be pleased to know that you have his measure.'

Petra kept quiet.

'You can stare silently at me all you want,' Florian said, a touch of irritation in his voice, 'but by tomorrow afternoon you'll be mine. Get your beauty sleep.' He opened the door and picked up a bundle that he had left outside.

'I know you're crying out for it. You caught the bouquet, remember? Now catch this!'

CHAPTER

64

'Leave me alone, girl! The cucumber is not correct. You have no training.' Mrs. Pinderally lifted the cucumber slices off her eyes and glared at the masseuse who backed hurriedly towards the door. 'How can I meditate with these limp discs? Fetch your manager!' Mrs. Pinderally threw the cucumber slices onto the floor and closed her eyes.

A tap on the door roused her some time later.

'What is taking you so long?'

'I came quickly, Madam, when I heard the news.' Ali picked up the cucumber slices and placed them on the masseuse's trolley.

'This is not your job, Ali, but maybe you can get fresh from the restaurant.'

'I think, Madam, there is something more urgent that demands your attention. Miss Vicky is in trouble. That is why I have come.'

'Miss Vicky is indeed in trouble. To reject my offer of employment out of hand and out of sight is …'

Ali coughed politely.

'There is a message, Madam.'

Mrs. Pinderally opened her eyes. 'Goody! Is Miss Vicky coming back? Read me the news, Ali.'

Ali inclined his head. 'Sorry, not possible, Madam. No paper. But I have it in memory.'

'Very well. Tell me when Miss Vicky wishes to return.'

'Madam, it is not Miss Vicky but Miss Petra who sends the message, Miss Petra and Mr. Carlo. They are busy setting traps for diamond smugglers in Namibia, meanwhile Miss Vicky is in a perilous situation. Heroic measures are needed.'

Mrs. Pinderally pulled herself up into a sitting position. 'Recite, Ali, from the beginning to the end.'

Ali stood up straight and puffed out his chest.

"Dear Mrs. Pinderally,

I have asked Ali to bring you this letter in the hope that you can lend a hand in a very pressing matter. But first, Carlo and I would like to thank you again for your magnificent hospitality and all your teachings …"

'Hurry, Ali! The gritty nitty!'

'Yes, Madam. It is coming.' He rewound to *"But first"* then carried on until he got to *"Time is of the essence. We are counting on your support"*.

Mrs. Pinderally clapped her hands. 'Just so. The coordinates, Ali, recite the coordinates again.'

'33.1772ºS, 18.2452ºE.'

'Perfect. We must mobilize at once. Ali, help me up.'

An hour later, dressed in a purple beaded trouser suit with a mandarin collar, Mrs. Pinderally convened a planning meeting in *Scheherazade*'s main salon. The captain, his two deckhands, Ali, his two lackeys, and the chauffeur sat around the dining table on which three plates of biscuits shared the space with a large map.

'We will rescue Miss Vicky from the clutches of that sleazy ball, Father John, who hides many girls on a farm near Langebaan,' Mrs. Pinderally announced. 'If we had known this before returning to Cape Town, it would be easy. Now we must go back quickly.'

The captain pinpointed the coordinates on the map and the chauffeur scrutinized it carefully.

'In one hour and a half we are at the crossroads, here,' he said. 'Then we must locate the farm. If it is off the beaten track, as I fear, the limousine will not be happy. A 4 x 4 would be preferable.'

Mrs. Pinderally helped herself to a fig roll while she thought. 'Ali, call Mr. Pinderally Junior.'

'Madam, he is in Mumbai. It is sleeping time.'

'No matter. Ask him to borrow his Hummer and his helicopter.'

'No need, Madam. He left keys and all necessary information with me. In case.'

'In case what?'

'In case you have need of a magic carpet.'

Mrs. Pinderally nodded with a cheerful smile on her face. 'Just like his father, God rest his soul. Call the necessary people, Ali. We need magic carpets now.'

The driver of the Tabernacle Youth Collective van rumbled over the cattle grid and closed the electric gate behind him. He drove as fast as he could down the rutted track, throwing up dust as he went. A mile farther on, he slowed to assess a vehicle that was coming towards him at a ferocious pace, creating a veritable sandstorm. He honked his horn. There was no room for two on the track.

The oncoming vehicle took no notice. He leaned on the horn and at the last moment veered to the left. But not far enough. It was a bloody armour-plated Hummer with wicked wheels that were going to clip the side of his van and run him off the road.

Which was exactly what Mr. Pinderally Junior's bodyguard-cum-driver did. The van careened down a slope and rolled over.

A few minutes later, a pink and very dusty limousine hove into view. Mrs. Pinderally leaned out of the window when she came alongside the scene of the accident. Ali was standing over the form of a young man clad in a black T-shirt and jeans, holding a heavy pistol.

'Goody, goody. One man down. Is he dead, Ali?'

'No Madam. Battered only.'

'Tie his hands and put him in the Hummer. He can lead us to Miss Vicky.'

The bodyguard pulled a set of handcuffs from the pocket of his camouflage jacket. He cuffed the youth, who was spitting and snarling, patted him down and extracted the key to the gate.

'Onward, Ali! I hear the helicopter. All must arrive at once. It is the element of surprise. But first ask that silly young man who is at the farm. Be sure to get details.'

Ali asked the question and waved the pistol menacingly. When the youth refused to answer, he let off a shot that glanced off a rock near the youth's feet.

'Thirty girls, some pregnant, some with new babies, some with small children.'

'What about men? Guards?'

The youth remained silent until Ali let off another shot that echoed around the countryside.

'Six men counting me to cater to the women. No guards.'

338

'Goody, goody. And the masseuse, Ali? Miss Vicky?'

Another shot from the pistol elicited the information, accompanied by a lot of spitting and snarling, that there was another young woman, a recent recruit, who was caring for the girls.

'And who is the big boss man of this, how do you say, stud farm? Ask him, Ali!'

This time the youth answered quickly. 'Our pastor, Father Joe. You can talk to him.'

'Father Joe-John has no respect for womankind. We must make haste!'

At the electric gate, the convoy stopped and waited until the pink helicopter was overhead. Ali dumped the youth onto the cattle grid then opened the gate and left it open behind them. 'To make the getaway,' he said.

'Good thinking, Ali. Now give me the walkie-talkie.' Mrs. Pinderally fiddled with the knobs on the radio. 'Come in, Magic Carpet 2, Magic Carpet 2, come in. Can you hear me? Over.'

'Magic Carpet 2. Go ahead.'

'You go ahead and tell me what you see.'

The helicopter flew across fields of crops towards clusters of white buildings inside a high wall.

'Magic Carpet 1, come in.'

'Magic Carpet 1 coming in. What see you?'

'Ladies, Madam, lots of ladies in blue dresses. Children too. They are waving.'

'Roger waving. Wave back and land. Defend your airship but do nothing until we are here. Repeat, do nothing until we are here. Over and out.'

By the time the limousine reached the courtyard, the helicopter was surrounded by young women and children who were fascinated by the visitors. Mrs. Pinderally's captain and the helicopter pilot were defending their doors from a posse of youngsters who were trying to board.

'Throw the sweets, Ali!'

Ali opened the door of the limousine and carpeted the ground between the car and the helicopter in sweets and chocolates. 'Candy time!' he yelled as the children rushed to pick them up. He clicked his fingers and his two lackeys got out and began to throw more candies to distract the children.

One of the blue-robed women walked over to the limousine. Mrs. Pinderally leaned out of her window. 'Fetch me your Father Joe. I have to pick a bone with him.'

'To pick a bone?'

'Indeed. Fetch him now.'

'Father Joe is not here.'

The wind went out of Mrs. Pinderally's sails. 'How so not here?'

'He's gone away for a few days.'

'Goody, goody. Then fetch me Miss Vicky. I am taking her home.'

CHAPTER

65

Carlo took another few swigs from his can of beer and called the manor house in Stellenbosch. After what seemed like an inordinately long time, the phone was answered by Wellington.

'Miz' Broselli and Mr. Tony are not at home, Sir.'

'It's Carlo, Wellington. Will they be back tonight?'

'Not until very late, Mr. Carlo. How is your trip? How is Miss Petra? I understand you will be here for the wedding this weekend. When will you be arriving?'

Carlo swallowed. 'We have a small problem … I need my uncle's help.'

'If there is anything I can do …'

'Wellington, after Julia's wedding, Florian took a group to Namibia. Do you know where he is now? Do you know how I can get in touch with him?'

'I'm sorry I don't. Miz' Broselli would be the only one who might have that information.'

'What about Julia? She's on her honeymoon in Europe. Have my aunt and uncle heard from her? Do they know her itinerary?' Carlo pulled himself up short. 'Of course they know her itinerary. Sandrine arranged it all. What time did you say they'll be back?'

Wellington coughed. 'Mr. Carlo, Miss Julia's not in Europe.'

'Not in Europe? What do you mean?'

'She changed the arrangements.'

'How do you know, Wellington?'

Wellington coughed again. 'I lent my assistance, Sir.'

'Where is she then?'

'Miss Julia and Mr. Max were going to Victoria Falls and Botswana. You could try the Chobe Game Lodge where Elizabeth Taylor and Richard Burton remarried.'

'Thank you, Wellington. You are a tower of strength. I won't need to speak to my aunt and uncle. With luck, Miss Petra and I will see you this weekend.'

'Thank you, Sir. I hope so, Sir. Good night, Sir.'

Carlo sat for a few minutes while he digested the unexpected information. Then he drained his beer and went to the business centre to find the phone number he needed. It took a few attempts before the call went through.

'Max, it's Carlo. Can I speak to Julia?'

'Who?'

'Max, I know it's you. This is an emergency. Please let me speak to her.'

Julia came to the phone.

'Has something happened to my father?'

'No, he's fine. It's Petra. I think Florian's got her.'

Carlo related the events of the day.

Julia sighed. 'That sounds like Florian. He never gives up. It doesn't matter how many women he has, if someone takes his fancy or he wants revenge … Where are you?'

'At a hotel outside Namutoni. Where would Florian have taken her?'

'To one of his communes, his African villages as he calls them.'

'There's more than one?'

'He has two in Damaraland, but the main one is in the Zambezi Region, between Rundu and Katima Mulilo.'

'How long will it take me to get there?'

'You won't be able to find it on your own. You'll need our help. Wait a minute.'

Carlo sat chewing his fingernail until Julia came back on the line.

'Max and I will charter a plane in Kasane and meet you in Rundu. If you leave at dawn, you'll be there in four hours. Say we meet at nine? Do you have a 4 x 4?'

Carlo groaned. 'Not exactly.' He described Lucy then said: 'I can leave now. I don't mind driving at night. We need to get Petra out of there.'

'Carlo, Florian isn't going to hurt her.'

'How do you know?'

'Because that isn't his style. He has supreme confidence in his ability to seduce, to conquer. He's a narcissist not a rapist. He'll play with Petra for however long it takes, until she capitulates. Then he'll enjoy her and discard her.'

'You sound so sure.'

'I am. He did it with me. Which is why I'm carrying his child.'

Carlo couldn't prevent a sharp intake of breath.

'Relax, Max knows. I told him on our wedding night. I won't go to Europe until we've avenged ourselves on Florian. This will be the beginning of the process. By the way, how did you find us?'

Carlo explained.

'Don't worry, Carlo. Get some rest. We'll see you in the morning.'

CHAPTER

66

Petra sat down on the edge of the bed, clutching the blue bundle Florian had thrown to her. Despite all her years in law enforcement, many of them working undercover with a host of unsavoury characters, she was scared. Scared of being forced into something that was so far from what she wanted to do that it didn't bear thinking about. She had never before met anyone quite like Florian. He was so cocksure, so confident of his ability to get whatever and whomever he wanted and so bloody attractive with those eyes that pierced your soul. And the way he could kiss …

Forget that, she told herself firmly. She should never be even remotely attracted to a man like that, and she wasn't. Florian was a dangerous predator who had to be stopped. To foil his plans for the morning, she would have to think outside the box.

She didn't have much in the way of weapons, except for the one her Italian priest ancestors had concealed in the cross. But the five centimetre stiletto wouldn't help her unless she could find a way to ambush Florian and disable him quickly. Even if she could, was violence the right solution? So far, he had not used force against her, nor to her knowledge against any of the women. If he decided to, she might find herself in a much worse position.

And what about Father John, whom Florian had threatened to send to claim his due? He was a big man, strong, and driven by the same philosophy as Florian, a philosophy she was beginning to comprehend even if she didn't yet fully understand it. She would have to stay alert. If they returned to the hut together, she would have little chance of preventing them from doing whatever they wanted with her.

In a difficult situation, focus on the positives. Her RCMP instructor had half-jokingly carried on to say: *There's always something you can do until you're dead.*

'Well I'm not dead and not planning on it,' Petra said, loudly enough for anyone who might be hanging around outside the hut to hear. Florian was ruining her holiday. It was a holiday of a lifetime, but not one to die for! She would make a plan and be ready for one or both of them if they came for her. Florian might consider himself omnipotent, yet she had succeeded in hanging onto her cross and rattling his cage. He had also brought her a bundle of something and left her with the contents of her shoulder bag, which she had been careful to keep out of sight.

The bundle was tied with a belt made of the same blue material and contained something heavy. She opened it up. It was a blue robe like the one the girls at the "farm" near Langebaan had been wearing. Wrapped up inside were two small bottles of water, some slices of bread and dry sausage. So Florian didn't want her to die of dehydration or starvation and he didn't want her to stay naked. Progress of a sort. She put on the blue robe, ate a small amount and washed it down with water.

Then she turned her attention to her necklace. There was an ingenious way of detaching the stiletto from inside the cross. She pressed the top two stones to open the cross, carefully extracted the stiletto and put the cross back together. If Father John took it from her and suspected that it was more than just a crucifix, he would find nothing inside. She hid the stiletto in the pocket in the base of her shoulder bag. Now she was dressed and armed and ready for the next phase. The lack of footwear didn't bother her – bare feet made no noise.

Petra realized that the light outside had faded. She could scarcely see to light the oil lamp. It must have been close to twilight when Florian came to see her. He had talked about having plenty of girls to cater to his needs while he waited for her. Hopefully they would keep him well occupied during the coming night. He had also mentioned Gina. If she was here, there was a good chance that she would keep Father John busy. And Florian had taken Ana, Raquel, Pam and Joanna as well as Diego with him on his guided tour of Namibia. Were they here too? There was only one way to find out.

Petra climbed onto the wooden cot that served as a bed and peered through the vent at the top of the back wall of the hut. It was too narrow and too high up for her to see anything. The table, though, was taller than the cot and quite sturdy. She used the lidded bucket to climb onto it. Still she could see nothing but a strip of darkness.

Taking care not to make a noise, she moved the table to another wall. Again, no joy. It was essential that she get an idea of where the hut was in relation to the rest of the camp, otherwise she might force the door open and find herself right in the middle of things. Through the vent on the third wall she detected a glimmer of light in the sky. That must be the west. And there seemed to be noise – voices perhaps – coming from the same direction, some distance away.

Petra moved the bucket and table again and climbed up to look through one of the vents next to the door. This time she was sure she could see flickering lights and the dark shapes of other buildings ... and movement. It was the same when she looked through the vent on the other side of the door. People seemed to be moving towards the west. Was that where Florian planned to spend the evening, staging a somewhat unorthodox stag party?

Leaving the table where it was, Petra decided to wait for the festivities to get underway. Then she would use the stiletto or a card out of her wallet to slip the door catch. She had heard Florian come into the hut and listened as he went out. The door did not sound as if it had a strong latch. In fact, why would it? Florian was used to young women doing his bidding, not trying to avoid him or escape.

Petra lay back on the cot, thinking and planning. She had an innate sense of time and over years of stake-outs had developed the ability to catnap while her partner kept watch and wake up the instant she was needed, or to stay wide awake when most people would be sleeping. She ought to wait a couple of hours before venturing out. A nap would refresh her for the task ahead. First, though, she placed the table in front of the door. If anyone tried to come in, it should slow them down a bit. She set her mental timer and settled down.

A hundred and ten minutes later, she sat up and blinked to focus her eyes in the dim light of the oil lamp. Then she listened with fierce concentration to separate sounds that were close by from those that were farther away. In the immediate vicinity of the hut all was quiet, but in the distance to the north she heard an animal cry and to the west, drumbeats and bells. She checked the view through the vents once more and made up her mind.

The stiletto took care of the door lock in a few seconds. Keeping it in one hand, she slowly opened the door until she could see out. No guards, no women, nobody. She stood on the threshold in the darkness studying her surroundings. It was a dark night with a mere sliver of a moon. In front of her was an open area then several clusters of thatched huts. On each side of her hut were similar square huts. The noise of celebration was coming from the west, to her right. On the east side of the compound, to her left, there appeared to be a number of other structures. Once she had absorbed as much information as she could from what she could see, she closed the door silently behind her, slung her bag across her chest and began to reconnoitre.

First she checked the perimeter of her hut. Behind it there were a few metres of hard sand then a four-metre-high fence made of heavy planks topped with sharp points. Petra leaned against the fence to test its strength. It didn't budge or flex in the slightest. The fence ran uninterrupted along the back of the compound behind three other square huts which were locked and felt deserted.

Staying away from the west side of the compound, she snaked her way through the silent rondavels towards the east side where her intuition told her she might find something she could use to get herself out of there. She found an outdoor kitchen with a dying fire, a few dirty pots, and the lingering smell of meat stew, adjacent to a collection of long tables and rough benches. She carried out a rapid search for knives or a hatchet, but those had been tidied or taken away. Nearby were a variety of solidly built structures that would take time to penetrate and examine. She discounted the two closest to the kitchen: they probably housed food and supplies. The question was which of the others to target.

She froze and raised her head to listen as another animal cried out. But it was way off in the wilderness. Overhead the sky was bright with stars, uncontaminated by city lights. She stared upwards, racking her brains. So far she had seen no mod cons like electricity or running water on this remote site and had accomplished nothing by leaving the hut. But Florian and his gang had to have a way of getting there, short of his mother's helicopter. Somewhere there must be vehicles.

Petra found them a few minutes later, under a thatched canopy beyond the structures she had yet to explore. One Higher Ground camper van and a smaller white Toyota van with no markings. She had a feeling she had seen the Toyota before but didn't recognize the number plate. Working swiftly, she tried all the doors and windows – locked as expected. Florian might be complacent about his women but he wasn't about to let them out easily. The main gate to the compound would be on the south side and firmly barred.

Once again, she heard her instructor's voice. *A cardinal rule of reconnoitring. Don't waste your energy. Calculate your best bet and go for it. And if you don't want to get caught, don't be too long about it.*

Vehicles needed fuel. If she could find it, maybe she could start a fire … then what? Burn down a few huts and bring the wrath of Florian and God's phony representative

Father John down on her head? No sense in that. What about trying to burn her way out through the fence? Then she'd be in the middle of nowhere in the company of wild animals … No. Best to try the locked buildings.

Three looked promising. Then she noticed what looked like an antenna strapped to a pole on the top of the middle structure.

'Bingo!'

The door lock was much more substantial. The seconds ticked by as Petra worked it with the stiletto in the beam from the penlight on her key ring. Just as she was about to give up, she heard a final tiny click. She opened the door and slipped inside. On the opposite wall stood a piece of equipment that looked as if it might be an old-fashioned radio transceiver. She sat down on the wooden stool in front of the machine and studied the switches and dials.

If she had been out on her boat on Lake Huron or sailing off the east coast of Canada with a friend, she would have known exactly what to do to use the VHF radio for local transmissions or the Single Sideband for long distance calls. This African dinosaur had a primitive microphone as well as what appeared to be a straight key for sending signals in Morse code.

Tentatively she flipped a switch above a paper label on which a call sign was written in faded ink. A green light came on and the needles on several gauges swung wildly before settling down.

'Bob's your uncle,' she whispered. 'Now let's see if I can make contact with an earthling.'

CHAPTER

67

The cacophony of drums, cow bells and rattles was sweet music to Florian's ears. He drank deeply from the gourd that contained the sour fermented mash that gave him strength to carry on his crusade. This was the second batch of four novices to be initiated since Etosha. The first group was already infused with the true spirit of Higher Ground. He could see why Henny had had trouble with Megan and Hilary. A guy who was imperfect had no place in his organization. Only the Master could exert supreme control. Diego, though, was a happy addition to the team. His massages kept the girls in the right frame of mind to receive Florian's gifts. They were vying now for the opportunity to be first.

He drained the liquor and felt it reach his loins. Tossing the gourd to one side, he turned to Father John who was reclining next to him on a mattress of straw.

'Bring me those two Tudor roses. I'll take them together, here.'

'You've learned your lessons well, my boy.'

'As you should too. Tell your new handmaiden to fetch beer and *dagga*, then get the incense and go prepare my bride for the morning. You'll marry us at noon.'

'She will do her penance and I'll claim my reward.'

'After me, old cock, after me. The first group is yours to minister to tonight.'

The radio appeared to be battery-powered. Petra hoped there would be enough charge in it to get a message out. Carlo must be going out of his mind. She twiddled some more dials and switched on the microphone. It was covered in dust and looked as if it hadn't been used for eons. Since she had no idea of amateur radio protocol, the best she could do would be to issue an all stations alert and pray that someone heard it. She rattled off the call sign, sensing that she was running out of time.

'Victor Five One Foxtrot Alpha Zulu calling all stations. This is Petra Minx requesting immediate assistance. I am being held against my will.' There was a slight whirring noise but no audible response. She repeated the message and listened hard. A burst of static then nothing.

There was one other thing she could try, but should she? Was her situation dire enough to warrant sending an SOS in Morse Code? She hesitated, her hand above the key. Suddenly, she sneezed and the back of her neck began to prickle. Something was happening. Someone was coming.

Petra switched off the radio and her penlight, grabbed the stiletto out of her bag, and took up position behind the door. She tensed as a key turned in the lock and forced herself to wait until the visitor was well inside before slamming the door and locking one arm round the visitor's throat. She raised her other hand, the one holding the stiletto, to the visitor's cheek. It was a girl, a fraction taller and broader than herself.

'Don't make a sound, unless you want to get hurt.'

Gina felt a pinprick on her cheek and tried to cough.

'Are you alone?' Petra relaxed the pressure on the girl's throat but kept her arm round her neck and the stiletto close to her cheek.

'Yes.'

'OK. I'm sorry, Gina, but I have to do this. I have to know what's going on. Where are Florian and Father John?'

'In our recreation area.'

'On the far side of the compound?'

'Yes.'

'Who's with them?'

'All the girls, and Diego.'

'How many girls?'

'A couple of dozen.'

Incredible. 'What are you doing?'

'Father John sent me to fetch beer and *dagga*, and the incense which is kept in here. He's going to come to your hut. How did you get out?'

'It's too long a story for now. Can I rely on you, Gina? Will you work with me?'

'I'll do my best if you tell me what to do.'

'Right then. Here's what we're going to do. You need to get back to the party, and I'll go back to my hut and lock myself inside. Make sure you come with Father John when he comes to see me. As long as you do that, I think I can handle the rest.'

'Jojo wants your cross. And he wants you,' Gina added sadly.

'I might let him have my cross for the time being, but he'll never get me. Neither will Florian. I'll cripple them first.'

353

CHAPTER

68

Max steered the white 4 x 4 he had rented at the airport along the rutted sand and gravel track. Julia sat beside him, giving directions and holding on tight as they bounced along. Carlo had climbed in the back and was leaning over Julia's shoulders, watching where they were going.

They had passed numerous fenced kraals on their way from Rundu. In some cases, the fencing was made of trimmed planks, well put together and maintained, that successfully blocked the view of what lay inside. In other cases, the fences were built of branches roughly cobbled together, leaving glimpses of the villages that lay behind.

The terrain got steadily worse as the villages became few and far between. Eventually, Julia pointed to a track leading off to the right. 'It's about a kilometre from here, past those hills. We all know how we're going to play this, don't we?'

'I'm going to stay out of sight initially,' Carlo replied. 'You and Max will go in and find Florian, Father John too if he's there. Max will make a scene and say he's brought you back, he doesn't want you any more. While all that's going on, I'll look for Petra.' He looked across at Max and saw the pain in his face. 'Can you handle that, Max? I know it's difficult.'

Max gripped the steering wheel until his knuckles went white. 'If it means those bastards get what they deserve, I'll do it. And I swear to you Julia, the child you're carrying will never be brought up as a bastard. He or she is ours.'

The Higher Ground kraal, as described by Julia, was a square enclosure containing over a dozen round thatched huts – living quarters for the women – and several rectangular huts, two of which were used by Florian and Father John. There was an outdoor kitchen and dining space under a wooden canopy, a food store and a few ancillary structures, plus a recreation area on the far side. The fencing around the kraal was more solid and higher than anything Carlo had seen en route. He noted the single gate in the middle of the front fence.

'Get down, Carlo. Drive right up to the gate, Max. It opens inwards,' Julia said. 'And blow the horn – three long blasts followed by two short.'

Max leaned on the horn and they waited. Nothing happened. He repeated the procedure. This time, after a few seconds' delay, the gate opened and Max drove into the centre of the kraal. Carlo kept his head down. 'Good luck,' he whispered.

Max got out of the 4 x 4 and opened Julia's door. He seized her arm and shouted 'Out!' She shook him off and he made a pretence of pushing her towards the women's huts. Young women clad in pale blue shifts were beginning to emerge. Julia's red dress stood out in stark contrast.

Max leaned into the 4 x 4 and sounded the horn again. More young women emerged. Then Father John came striding out of one of the rectangular huts followed by Florian wearing a white jacket and black trousers. Max began to shout and gesticulate. He pointed at Julia then at Father John and Florian.

'I don't want to see her again,' he yelled. 'Take her!'

'I already have.' Florian smiled his supercilious mocking smile. 'I knew you'd come to your senses, Julia. Welcome back.' He picked up her hand and kissed it. 'You're just in time to be a witness at my wedding. You too, brother.'

Max lost it completely. He abandoned his performance and went ballistic. He put his head down and charged at Florian like an enraged bull. He grabbed him round the thigh, wrestled him to the ground and stomped on first one knee then the other. Then he looked for Father John.

The phony priest was halfway across the compound, running in his long white robe and black scarf, to where a Higher Ground vehicle and a white van were parked. Carlo scrambled out of the 4 x 4 and took him down with a flying tackle. He kicked him repeatedly in the ribs and left him writhing on the ground.

Max steered Julia away from the other women, some of whom were bending over Florian, others looking shocked and unsure what to do. 'Get in the van, you'll be safe there.'

'I'm OK, my love. You've taken care of Florian. Everything will be fine now.'

Carlo sprinted to the back of the compound. The door of the centre hut opened. Petra stood framed in the doorway, in a white lace dress. She came forward to meet him.

'Nice job. What took you so long?'

Carlo spread his hands. 'Is that all the thanks I get? You could have joined in.'

'You were doing fine without me. But there are a couple of little things I have to do.'

Petra walked over to Father John who was curled up in the fetal position, cradling his ribs. She forced him onto his back and retrieved her cross from around his neck. 'Asshole!'

She left him whimpering like a baby and went to find Florian.

'How the mighty have fallen,' she said as she gazed into his blue eyes, searching for just a hint of regret or remorse, seeing only arrogance and madness.

'We will rise again.'

'This one won't for a while!'

Carlo flinched and Julia and Max watched in awe as Petra gave Florian a savage kick in the groin. There was a murderous look on her face. Florian's eyelashes fluttered and his eyes closed.

'Leave him, Petra. Whatever he might have done, he's broken now.'

'No punishment will ever be enough,' she said. Briefly, she wondered what Sandrine would do when she saw her golden boy.

Behind her, Max and Julia were talking to the girls and organizing transport for Ana, Raquel, Pam and Joanna, along with Megan and Hilary and as many others as they could fit into the 4 x 4 and the Higher Ground camper van. Gina and Diego seemed in no hurry to leave.

'Thanks for what you did to help me, Gina,' Petra said. 'What are you going to do now?'

'We'll stay and clean up the mess.'

CHAPTER

69

Three days later, Petra said goodbye to Megan and Hilary. They were leaving the Waterside Hotel and joining a bus tour that would take them along the Garden Route to Port Elizabeth. Once there, they would decide what they were going to do next.

'No more volunteering, girls,' Petra said, 'unless you're absolutely sure what you're getting into. And watch out for beautiful boys with long eyelashes,' she added.

'We know,' they chorused as they snapped photos of Petra and each other with their phones.

Petra watched them go with a sinking feeling in her stomach. Had they really learned anything from their experiences?

She looked at her watch and hurried down the steps. Mrs. Pinderally would berate her for her tardiness if she was a minute late.

'Madam begs you to make haste,' Ali said when she arrived at the foot of *Scheherazade*'s boarding ladder. 'She is going swimmingly.'

Petra ran up the wide low-rise steps that led from the aft deck to the flybridge of the yacht. Mrs. Pinderally was thrashing around like a large brown whale in the middle of a seething whirlpool. A sturdy young woman was kneeling by the side of the pool.

'Come on, Mrs. Pinderally, you can do it! On your stomach! That's it! Imagine you're a dog paddling to the shore.'

Mrs. Pinderally rolled over with a splash and began to flap her hands up and down, in and out of the water.

'Feet off the bottom, please! It's not far!'

Vicky Dunlin shouted encouragement as her pupil flailed her way to the steps at the end of the pool. Then she reached in to help Mrs. Pinderally onto the deck. Quickly Petra averted her eyes: Mrs. P. was stark naked except for her white bathing cap. Equally quickly, Vicky encased her pupil in a white towelling robe and led her to a padded sunbed. She settled her on a mound of pillows, replaced the bathing cap with a towel turban and instructed her to close her eyes and relax.

'First we observe proper etiquette: Miss Vicky meet Miss Petra. Now call Ali. I must take refreshment after my exertions.'

Petra and Vicky exchanged smiles and handshakes.

'I'm so glad to meet you at last. A.K. was desperately worried about you.'

'I'm sorry I caused so much trouble, I had no idea. Thank you for what you did.'

'Don't thank me, thank Mrs. Pinderally. She's the one who sent in the cavalry to fetch you.'

'Cavalry? Not so. You are the horsy woman. We use magic carpets.'

'Magic carpets! Just the ticket, Mrs. P.! I knew you'd come through.' Carlo bounced onto the deck carrying a blue and white striped carrier bag. 'I brought you a little thank-you present.'

Mrs. Pinderally peered into the bag. 'Goody, goody, sugared almonds. No diamonds, I hope.'

'I don't think so. I checked the colour of the stones on the lid, but go easy just the same.' He twinkled at Mrs. Pinderally who patted his hand.

'Charmer!'

'The operation is going well,' he said in an aside to Petra. 'It looks as though we'll get all the proof we need to nab the villains.'

'Does Sandrine have any idea what's going on?'

'None at this stage, but she'll be furious when she finds out. Hubert's photographer got some good footage of Sandrine distributing tins, some with red and blue stones in the middle, along with instructions to the wedding guests to put them in their luggage. Talking of which, we must go. We don't want to miss our flight to Geneva.'

Mrs. Pinderally sat up and removed the white turban from her head. 'It is impossible for Miss Petra to leave without a Rolling Sands massage. She is full of tension and turmoil.'

'There's no time, Mrs. Pinderally. Thank you anyway,' Petra said.

'I have another rabbit up my sleeve. Ali is bringing messages. Then he will explain the devious means by which we were able to rescue Miss Vicky and play you the video.'

'Messages?'

'Indeed. Here he is.'

Ali appeared carrying a silver tray on which were an envelope and a gaily wrapped package. He bowed to Petra and handed her the envelope.

'An email from Mr. Zen, offering position on a farm near Langebaan, and an email from a new man, Mr. Martin Johnson. He wants to tell you all about his visit to Spain with Betty Graceby.'

Petra grinned. 'Thank you, Ali.'

'Mr. Zen is too late,' Mrs. Pinderally said. 'And who is this new man? Is he handsome? Do you lust for him?'

'Martin is an old friend, nothing more,' Petra said, trying not to smile at the glower on Carlo's face.

Mrs. Pinderally looked from Petra to Carlo and rubbed her hands. 'Ah! Romance is so exciting! Leaving now would be a shame. Miss Vicky has a message.'

Vicky stepped forward with a sheet of paper on which were printed the words "One week's vacation extension all expenses paid. With our heartfelt thanks for saving the day, from Arnold Dunlin and Uncle A.K.".

'My Magic Carpet Number One pink limousine is at your disposal. See to it, Ali. Now the package!'

Petra took the package and cocked her head at Mrs. Pinderally. 'For me?'

'From Mr. Pinderally, God rest his soul, and myself in remembrance of your momentous visit.'

Petra unwrapped the package and opened the box. Inside was one of Mrs. Pinderally's jewellery trees holding the most magnificent diamond ring she had ever seen.

'I can't accept this, Mrs. Pinderally!'

'Why not? That is my favourite lady and the ring is a Petra Diamond. Miss Vicky says I should sell some of my ladies to pay for a school and home for those poor babies, and that is what I will do. But this one I give to you.'

Petra slipped the ring onto the fourth finger of her right hand. It fitted perfectly.

Mrs. Pinderally heaved a huge sigh of satisfaction. 'Now Miss Vicky will give you your Rolling Sands massage. For that you must take off your clothes.'

'All of them?'

'Indeed.'

'Promise I won't look, *cara*.'

Petra shrugged. They were high above the level of the other boats, Florian and Father John were incapacitated and miles away, and Carlo would be out of taunting range while he returned Lucy to the airport.

That evening, after everyone else had gone to bed, Petra and Carlo sat on *Scheherazade*'s aft deck and shared a bottle of Veuve Clicquot.

Carlo raised his glass to Petra. 'Another job well done, *tesoro mio*! I salute you! And Interpol salutes you and has extended my vacation for as long as it takes to clear up the Broselli/Delapore smuggling ring.'

'I'm glad, Carlo. I couldn't leave yet. It's been such a crazy three weeks that I need time to come to terms with it all – the beauty, the fraud, the doublespeak. I can understand why Sandrine and Tony did what they did, but Florian?'

'To understand Florian, you have to understand Africa, how it can breed someone like him, an animal, a beautiful animal, someone who believes he's king of the jungle.'

'What do you think will happen to him now?'

'I don't know. But he won't want to be in a cage.'

GLOSSARY

Afrikaans	a language of southern Africa derived from Dutch
Afrikaner	Afrikaans-speaking white person
Amarula Cream	liqueur made from the fruit of the marula tree which elephants love
bateaux mouches	flat-topped cruise boats on the Seine River in Paris
bobotie	South African dish of curried minced meat with a savoury custard
bontebok	small antelope with a chestnut back, white face, belly and rump

braai	South African word for barbecue, from Afrikaans
cara	Italian for 'dear'
carissima	Italian for 'dearest'
dagga	South African word for cannabis or marijuana
dragées	sugared almonds
eland	the largest African antelope, with spiral horns and a dewlap
fynbos	distinctive type of vegetation found on the southern tip of Africa
ha-de-da	greyish-brown ibis with a distinctive call: ha-ha, ha-ha, de-da
hartebeest	red-brown antelope with a sloping back and small horns
ja	Afrikaans for 'yes'

klipspringer	small antelope with a bristly grey-yellow coat found in rocky areas
kopje (also koppie)	small rocky hill in a generally flat area
kraal	traditional African village of huts, usually fenced
kudu	large grey-brown antelope, the male with corkscrew horns
mopane	tree with butterfly-wing leaves found in arid regions of southern Africa
nee	Afrikaans for 'no'
omumbiri	resin used by Himba women of Namibia to perfume their skin
oryx	ash-grey antelope with long straight horns and bold black facial marks
pan	hollow in the earth containing water or salt if the water has evaporated

rand	currency of South Africa
Sperrgebiet	forbidden zone, formerly reserved for the diamond mining industry
stoep	verandah in front of a house
tabarnak	French-Canadian swear word, from tabernacle
tesoro mio	Italian for 'sweetheart'
veldt (also veld)	open country or grassland in southern Africa
wildebeest (gnu)	ungainly antelope with dark coat and mane

ACKNOWLEDGEMENTS
AND AUTHOR'S NOTE

As always, I owe a huge debt of gratitude to my husband who suffers from neglect when I am in the thick of writing or re-writing a novel. He is the sounding board for my ideas, my technical advisor, my driver and guide in Southern Africa, and my anchor in the sea of life. Sincere thanks, too, to my beta readers who gave me useful feedback on earlier versions of this novel.

During the creation of *A Holiday to Die For*, my desk was piled high with travel brochures, books and maps, but one publication deserves a special mention: *The Bradt Travel Guide to Namibia* by Chris McIntyre. This superb book was indispensable when I travelled in Namibia and became my "bible" when I was checking facts and spellings for Petra's third adventure. Any errors are my responsibility alone.

Talking of spelling, Petra Minx is Canadian. As a result, I use Canadian spelling in my novels which is essentially a cross between English and American. If this seems confusing or there are lapses, I apologize.

Colloquial English has absorbed many foreign words. To lend colour and authenticity to my story, I have used a number of South African, Afrikaans, and Italian words. In general the meaning is clear from the context, and to make reading easier I have chosen not to italicize most of them. For interest I have included a short glossary.

A Holiday to Die For is the product of my (like Petra's) overactive imagination. The characters and plot are pure fiction and all organizations, places and settings in the novel are used completely fictitiously. I hope you enjoy it.

I hope too that you will have the opportunity to visit South Africa and Namibia, two wonderful countries that have successfully made the transition to majority rule. My thanks go to all their peoples for inspiring me to write *A Holiday to Die For*.

Marion Leigh

BY THE SAME AUTHOR

THE POLITICIAN'S DAUGHTER
by
Marion Leigh

Introducing Marine Unit Sergeant Petra Minx of the Royal Canadian Mounted Police in a fast-paced adventure with lots of local colour and subtle undertones

When Emily Mortlake, daughter of a high-flying Toronto politician, goes missing after taking a summer job aboard megayacht *Titania*, RCMP Marine Unit Sergeant Petra Minx is recalled from vacation to investigate.

Despite the misgivings of her mentor Tom Gilmore, Petra poses as a student and joins the crew of the same yacht. Surprisingly, no one denies Emily was aboard, but the stories surrounding the reasons for her departure are various.

As Petra follows Emily's trail from Monte Carlo to Spain and then Morocco, she is drawn into the glamorous world of *Titania*'s owner, the ruthless and charismatic Don León. With conflicting emotions, she continues her relentless quest to uncover the truth before it is too late …

DEAD MAN'S LEGACY
by
Marion Leigh

*An exciting new adventure in the Petra Minx series with
all the ingredients for a gripping holiday read*

Sergeant Petra Minx of the Royal Canadian Mounted
Police is ecstatic when her quirky boss, A.K., orders her
to Nassau to meet the legendary Betty Graceby, a retired
Canadian singer and ex-Vegas dancer. The complaints
Betty has been filing against her obnoxious grandson Ken
have finally caught the attention of the authorities. But
why the sudden interest?

Martin, a journalist with a great nose for a story, has
heard rumours of a new arts centre to be financed by an
anonymous benefactor … and Betty's fortune has tripled
since the death of her husband, Joe LePinto, who was
killed in a car driven by her smooth-talking son Cliff. So
is money the key and how far will the Graceby 'boys' go to
secure their future?

As the action moves from the Bahamas to Las Vegas and
on to the Great Lakes, Petra develops a deep affection for
Betty, and her fact-finding mission becomes much more
personal. She uncovers a viper's nest of hatred, greed,
treachery and lust and realizes that LePinto's influence is as
pervasive in death as it was in life.

The dead man's legacy is a weighty one …